THE KISS WAS JUST ~~~~~~~~~~~~~~~~~~~~~~~~~~~ finally surrendered to the urge, he wanted to draw the pleasure out. He explored her lips, learning the shape of them, their softness. They were delightfully full and blissfully moist. The taste of her was as fascinating as the stars that had burned across the sky. Fascinating and strangely familiar.

He felt like he had kissed her before, which was crazy. Hope Montgomery wasn't anything like the women he usually pursued. Not a model or beauty queen or, as he'd liked in his younger days, a sorority girl. She was a homespun schoolteacher, and not just a schoolteacher, but a *kindergarten* teacher. The flavor of her mouth—not sophisticated French champagne, but hot chocolate chip cookies fresh from the oven on a cold winter's day—stirred his blood.

And she felt like heaven in his arms.

By Emily March

Angel's Rest
Hummingbird Lake
Heartache Falls
Lover's Leap
Nightingale Way
Reflection Point
Miracle Road

Miracle Road

An
Eternity Springs
Novel

EMILY MARCH

WITHDRAWN

BALLANTINE BOOKS • NEW YORK

A Ballantine Books Mass Market Original

Copyright © 2013 by Geralyn Dawson Williams

Excerpt from *Dreamweaver Trail* by Emily March copyright © 2013 by Geralyn Dawson Williams

Published in the United States by Ballantine Books, an imprint of The Random House Publishing Group, a division of Random House LLC, a Penguin Random House Company, New York.

BALLANTINE and the HOUSE colophon are registered trademarks of Random House LLC.

This book contains an excerpt from the forthcoming novel *Dreamweaver Trail* by Emily March. This excerpt has been set for this edition only and may not reflect the final content of the forthcoming edition.

ISBN: 978-0-345-54228-1
eBook ISBN: 978-0-345-54229-8

Cover design: Lynn Andreozzi
Cover illustration: Robert Steele

Printed in the United States of America

www.ballantinebooks.com

9 8 7 6 5 4 3 2 1

Ballantine Books mass market edition: November 2013

In deep, dear, loving memory of my mother,
Pauline S. Dawson, who made every Christmas
a miracle for our family.
Miss you, Mom.

Miracle Road

ONE

❦

March Madness.

Lucca Romano stood at the window of his office on the campus of Landry University and gazed out at green grass and purple bearded irises without actually seeing them. In his mind's eye he focused on another place, another time, when a white ten-passenger van traveled a ribbon of dark asphalt highway bisecting a barren winter plain.

Despite the warm sunshine beaming through the window glass, cold permeated Lucca's bones, and he shuddered as the memory washed over him. *Pings and whooshes as text messages arrive and depart from a half-dozen different cellphones. The rhythmic beat of rap. Young men's laughter as a yapping chocolate brown puppy claws his way over the front passenger seat.*

Everyone's spirits are high after a win, especially after the first win of the season. Sure, it was just an exhibition game, but it proved that the Midwest State University Ravens are tough competitors.

"Keep the dog in the back," Lucca says, reaching for the little pup. Why had he allowed Seth Seidel to bring

that dog home, anyway? The kid lives in a dorm. He has nowhere to keep a dog.

He'd done it because the people selling the puppies out of the back of their truck had been puppy mill people. Lucca's own heart had gone as soft as Seth's upon seeing the "display." Lucca had even loaned the kid some cash to buy the dog.

"Sucker," he mutters, passing the pup now christened "Sparky" to the backseat.

Five minutes later, Sparky is back. Lucca sighs and stretches for the puppy. Sparky wiggles out of his hand and falls, his sharp little claws reaching for purchase and finding the driver's arm. The driver startles and stomps the brake, and in an instant, Lucca's world changes forever.

The wheels lock. Tires skid on black ice. The van slides . . . slides . . . slides in slow motion.

Standing in his sun-drenched office, seventeen months and a thousand miles away from the horror, Lucca swayed and reached out to brace himself against the inevitable crash.

Tires skid off the road, and the van tilts, then rolls, again and again and again. People and possessions fly. The boys scream. Lucca's body jerks against the seat belt. His head hits something hard, and the world goes black.

He regains consciousness with a pounding head; cold, icy air; and panicked voices. "Alan? Oh, God. Alan! Coach! Somebody! Help me! Coach!"

He opens his eyes and sees splatters of blood on the dashboard.

"Coach?"

Jerked back to the present, Lucca glanced over his shoulder to see his graduate assistant in his office doorway, a puzzled expression on his face. How long had he been standing there?

Lucca cleared his throat. "Yes?"

"It's ten after four."

Lucca's gaze shifted to the clock on his wall. He had called a team meeting for four o'clock, so he was late. He was never late. No wonder his assistant looked confused. "I'll be right there."

The young man nodded and left. Lucca wiped away the perspiration beaded on his brow and sucked in a pair of deep breaths, seeking the calm for which he was known at courtside. Unfortunately, calm proved elusive.

When his wall clock chimed the quarter hour, Lucca shook his head. He wiped the beaded perspiration from his brow, then slipped on his suit coat. As he exited his office, he attempted to gather his thoughts. He had a list of instructions to give his team prior to the event that Landry University's athletic department had planned to celebrate the Bobcats' success in the NCAA tournament.

When Lucca took the head-coaching job a year before, he had inherited a group of players who had the raw talent to win. Once he convinced them to buy into his system, he'd been confident they would play well enough to win their conference and make the tournament. When he'd made his traditional preseason bet with his brother Tony, the new head coach at Colorado, he'd predicted a tourney berth and first game win. Making it all the way to the Sweet Sixteen had been a thrill.

A thrill that hadn't lasted beyond the dream he'd had during the flight back to Texas following the tournament loss.

He'd awakened with a jolt somewhere over Alabama, the repressed memories fresh, the terror real. He'd spent the balance of the flight trying to lock them away again, but as the hours passed, it was as if the nightmare had plowed the field of his psyche and kicked up a cloud of pain and misery that had churned into a tempest worthy of a 1930s-era dust storm.

He pushed open the door of the men's locker room and got a whiff of that familiar sweaty scent that had been part of his life for as long as he could remember. Not even the high-dollar NBA venues had been able to get rid of the acrid, musty locker room smell entirely. Today when the stench hit his nostrils, his stomach took a nauseated roll. A storm was brewing inside him.

March Madness.

He walked past a locker whose door hung open. Without a conscious thought, he jabbed it with his elbow, and the metal door clanged shut. Someone had left a pair of athletic shoes on a bench, and one of them had fallen onto the floor into Lucca's path. He swung a hard kick at the sneaker and sent it crashing against the far row of lockers. Then he picked up the other shoe and threw it hard after the first. A janitor mopping the shower floor glanced up ready to complain, but his growl transformed to a gawk when he saw who had made the noise.

Lucca understood the man's surprise. Coach Romano didn't slam things. He didn't kick things. He certainly didn't throw things. He'd patterned his professional behavior after legendary coach Phil Jackson's philosophy of mindful basketball, which included teaching his players to be aggressive without anger or violence and stressing the value of focus and calm in the midst of chaos.

Today, Coach Romano seemed to have lost his Zen.

He exited the locker room and walked out onto the hardwood floor of Bill Litty Arena.

His assistant coaches and players stood with their attention focused on the Jumbotron hanging at center court. A quick glance upward showed Lucca that it was video of their Sweet Sixteen loss, specifically the final two minutes of the game during which his Landry University Bobcats had scored eight unanswered points and came within a whisker of making the biggest upset of the tournament. They'd been a twelve seed playing number one, and they'd held their own against one of the best teams in the country. He'd been so proud of his team.

Why he could barely manage looking at them now, he couldn't figure. On the whole, this was a good group of kids. His point guard had a legitimate shot at making it in the NBA, and what the rest of the team lacked in talent, they made up for with hard work. They'd slipped their size-thirteen feet into Cinderella's slippers and danced their way to the Sweet Sixteen. Even before their final game, Lucca had fielded a call from a representative of a prominent "basketball school" who had wanted to congratulate him on his team's season. Rumor had it that the school's icon of a coach planned to retire after one more season, so Lucca believed it had been a courting call.

His sister Gabi's words whispered in his mind. *"You're a star now, bro."*

Shame washed over him, and he set his teeth against it.

His players groaned as the replay showed the missed jumper that had broken their streak. "You should have passed it back to me," the power forward said. "I'd have made it."

"I should have kept it myself," the point guard fired back.

"Don't let Coach hear you say that," the center said. "Surrender the 'me' . . ."

"For the 'we,'" the others finished, quoting one of Lucca's favorite sayings with some laughter.

"Lame," the point guard said, giving a dismissive snort.

At the sound, Lucca halted midstep. His team was mocking him.

His temper flashed. *Don't they know how lucky they are? Don't they have a clue? They are healthy and whole*

*and playing a game. An effing game! On scholarship!
They're not broken, confined to a wheelchair.*

They're not dead.

Fury coursed through Lucca's veins. He imagined
himself giving his star player a swift boot in the ass. Instead, he barked out a command, "Everybody to the
baseline. We're running ladders."

His players turned to stare at him, their expressions
ranging from incredulous to smirking. His voice deadly
calm, Lucca asked, "You think I'm kidding?"

No one spoke. Lucca focused on the point guard.
"Norris?"

The young man hesitated, then grinned. "Yeah, I do,
Coach. Season's over."

Lucca folded his arms and put all of his angry disgust
into his glare.

After a moment, Norris's cocky smile died. Lucca
jerked his head in a "get going" motion. His team shared
a shocked look, then started running.

For the next half hour, Lucca drilled them hard, his
voice harsh, his manner cold, which wasn't at all his
customary way of coaching. More than once he caught
a player darting him a "WTF?" look. Twice his assistant
coach approached him to inform him of the time, but
Lucca stopped him with a flick of a hand. Only when
people began filing into the arena for the celebration did
he send his team to the showers, giving them fifteen minutes to clean up and return to the court. He heard the
grumbling and saw the scowls, but his players weren't
stupid. They knew not to cross him today.

Too bad he had a boss to deal with, he acknowledged
as he spied the athletic director's sixty-something secretary approaching him with a scolding frown on her face.

"For heaven's sake, Lucca," Mrs. Richie said. "Mr.
Hopkins is not at all happy. He has a group of donors
waiting to meet you and Jamal Norris. The AV people

wanted access to the arena floor an hour ago so they could set up their microphones. I have parents who expected family time with their students before tonight's event knocking on the door of my office. Why in the world did you hold a practice this afternoon?"

Lucca closed his eyes. He didn't care about the AV folks, and helicopter parents made him crazy. But schmoozing with the alumni and soliciting donations was a big part his job. He could be good at it when he wanted. Today, he simply didn't have it in him to make nice. "My team needed it."

"Well, you are wanted in the director's office ASAP. This practice completely disrupted our schedule."

Mrs. Richie reminded him enough of his late, beloved grandmother that he swallowed his caustic response. "I'll go right up."

She nodded, then checked her watch. "And Jamal?"

Lucca had no intention of singling out his point guard that way. The press did enough of it as it was. While it was true that Norris had turned in a stellar performance in the tournament, all the attention had overinflated the young man's opinion of himself to an extent that Lucca believed was detrimental to both Jamal and the team. He searched for a compromise.

"You can let AD Hopkins know that I'll invite our visitors into the locker room at the end of the night. That should make everybody happy."

Surprise widened Mrs. Richie's eyes. Lucca never allowed visitors into the locker room. "I'll call him and tell him you are on your way."

Due to the mood he was in, Lucca considered the ten minutes he spent glad-handing the donors to be excruciating. He found the congratulations and back slaps annoying. When one of the donors asked him if he'd like new televisions for the team's rec room, he almost told the man to send his money to the girls' swim team. Those young women had heart and rode to their meets in a six-year-old van that made Lucca cringe every time he saw it parked in the lot.

He breathed a sigh of relief when the athletic director announced that the time had come to adjourn to the arena. As the men filed out of the office, an investment banker from New York stepped in front of Lucca and put a hand against his chest. "If I can have just a moment, Coach?"

Lucca sucked in a breath as the urge to slap the man's hand away rolled over him like a tidal wave. Damn, he was on edge. He'd better get himself together or he just might do his career irreparable harm. *Would that be so terrible?*

The donor didn't seem to notice Lucca's bad attitude. He was too busy slipping something into Lucca's jacket pocket. "Some friends and I want to make sure you know how pleased we are to have you here at Landry. You're a great coach. You proved it last year when you motivated that ragtag group of kids at Midwest State all the way to an NCAA berth and—"

"Those kids played their hearts out," Lucca interrupted, nausea churning in his stomach.

"Sure they did. Sure they did. But you knew how to motivate them, didn't you? Dedicating their season to their dead teammates. That was a brilliant bit of coaching."

Brilliant coaching, my ass. "That was the team's idea," Lucca said carefully. "It was a difficult time for—"

The donor talked over him. "What you did with this team this season . . . what can I say? Jamal Norris had no intention of attending Landry until we managed to steal you away from Midwest State, and Norris is the reason we played in Atlanta this year. If you can manage to keep him out of the NBA's clutches for another year . . . a national championship is within our grasp. You're a special coach, Lucca Romano. You've got a great future ahead of you, and we want to do everything in our power to make sure that future is here at Landry."

He gave Lucca's pocket a little pat, then stepped back. "We want you to remember our gratitude when the Dukes and Kentuckys of the world come calling. And don't you worry, we'll see that you get regular reminders, too. Now, we'd better hurry to catch up with the others. Don't want the festivities to start without us, do we, Coach?"

Don't call me Coach, Lucca wanted to say.

The donor motioned for Lucca to precede him from the office. Lucca shook his head. "You go ahead. I have to take a leak."

The donor gave him a knowing grin, dropped his gaze to Lucca's pocket, then winked. He obviously thought Lucca couldn't wait to check out the "gratitude" in his pocket. The man couldn't have been more wrong.

Lucca was battling the need to puke.

Ragtag players. Knew how to motivate.

The van sliding, rolling. The screams. Dear Lord, the screams.

"*My son,*" Mrs. Seidel said at the funeral, her eyes stricken, her tone broken. "*Did he suffer?*"

"*Coach. Help me. Please, Coach.*"

Bile rose in Lucca's throat, and he headed for the lavatory connected to the athletic director's office. He made it to the commode just in time.

Once the spasms ended, he went to the sink, turned on the water, rinsed his mouth, and then splashed his face. When he glanced at his reflection in the mirror, he wanted to vomit all over again.

Instead, he exited the bathroom and his boss's office. Rather than following the pulse of music that now rose from the arena, he turned toward his own office, went inside, and locked the door behind him.

Then, Lucca lost it.

Breathing hard, seeing little beyond the haze of rage and heartache and guilt roaring through him, he swept his arm across his desktop, sending everything crashing to the floor. Next he eyed the trophies on the wall shelf. *Crash*. He picked up his notebook computer and threw it onto the floor, hard, then kicked it for good measure.

Within minutes, he'd trashed his entire office. With nothing whole left to destroy, he turned on himself, balling up his fist and punching the wall.

He was pretty sure he broke some bones. The pain felt good. It felt deserved.

Using his bloody, damaged hand, Lucca removed the folded check from his pocket and looked at it. Fifty thousand dollars. Because he'd felt sorry for a dog, killed two kids, and paralyzed another? He tossed the bloodstained check away. It floated toward the floor and landed atop shards of a shattered crystal trophy.

Lucca quit the room and the campus. Within days he'd departed the state, and by the end of the month, he'd fled the country. Lucca Ryan Romano couldn't live with himself. He was done.

March Madness.

T W O

❦

Hope Montgomery flipped through the curriculum planner with the scheduled events for the upcoming school year. When her gaze settled on a particular date, she sucked in a sudden breath. March 15. The most horrible day of her life. The day her world changed forever.

She closed her eyes and absorbed the hurt. This was the way it happened now, five years later. Rather than being her constant companion, the pain would slither up and strike when she wasn't prepared or braced for it.

" 'Beware the Ides of March,' " she softly quoted.

She shut her planner and set it aside, then reached for her coffee. Her hand trembled as she raised the china cup to her mouth, but she concentrated on savoring both the smell and the taste of the aromatic, full-bodied brew. Using her senses helped anchor her to the present, and besides, the coffee at Angel's Rest Healing Center and Spa was truly sublime.

Nevertheless, she teetered on the brink of tears until Celeste Blessing swept into the old Victorian mansion's parlor saying, "I'm so sorry I'm running late, Hope. It's been one thing after another today. First we had a plumbing problem in the showers beside the hot springs pools, then one of our guests suffered a death in the family, the poor dear, and I helped arrange emergency transportation home. Finally, my sister phoned, and I'm afraid I lost track of time."

Hope stood and smiled at the vital, active, older woman whom she'd come to view as the matriarch of Eternity Springs. The owner of Angel's Rest, Celeste wore black slacks, a gold cotton blouse, and a harried smile.

"Celeste, I love your new haircut," Hope said.

"Thank you. I do, too." Celeste lifted a hand to fluff the short, sassy style, her blue eyes twinkling. "One of my male guests told me I look just like Judi Dench. He's an old flirt and I think he was hoping for a discount on his bill, but I'll accept the compliment."

"As well you should," Hope agreed. "He's right."

"Thank you, dear. I'm going to tell my sister you said that." Celeste wrinkled her nose as she added, "She told me I was too old for this style."

Hope couldn't help but smile. She had met Celeste and her sister when they'd rented the South Carolina beach house next door to Hope's vacation rental the spring before last. The sisters had caught Hope crying on the beach one March morning, and they'd offered comfort to a stranger and changed the path of Hope's life. Like most sisters, they'd bickered, but the love they shared had been obvious. Hope could picture Desdemona making the hairstyle remark to Celeste. "How is Desi doing these days?"

"She's well. Busy, but then, aren't we all? She tells me she's let her hair grow and dyed it bright red."

Mentally picturing the tall, flamboyant woman, Hope grinned. "Is she still traveling quite a bit?"

"Constantly. As a result we don't have the opportunity to see each other as often as we'd like. I'm trying to convince her to visit Eternity Springs sometime soon.

She asked me to tell you hello and to blame her for my tardiness, but we're both to blame. It was downright rude of me to ask for a ride to the baby shower and then not be ready on time. Please forgive me."

"Don't be silly, Celeste. We have plenty of time." Besides, no matter how happy Hope was for the expectant parents, baby showers were always a little tough for her. She thought that being with Celeste might make the day easier. "Your front desk worker gave me a cup of spectacular coffee, and I used the time to my benefit, looking over some of the paperwork Principal Geary gave me this morning. It's hard to believe that school starts in just three weeks."

Hope picked up her purse and slipped the strap over her shoulder. "Can I help you carry anything?"

"Thank you. I have a few gifts in the kitchen."

Celeste led Hope down the hallway toward the kitchen. Upon entering the cheery room, Hope stopped and laughed. The kitchen table was covered in gaily wrapped and ribboned packages and bags, all in nursery themes in shades of a beautiful baby blue. "A few bags?"

"It's the latent grandmother in me, I fear. I just love buying for little ones."

Hope's smile softened to bittersweet as she recalled stacks of pink onesies and a closet full of ruffles. "I do, too."

They loaded the gifts into Hope's crossover SUV, chatting about the presents they'd chosen. This would be Hope's first visit to Jack and Cat Davenport's mountain estate, Eagle's Way, and she looked forward to seeing it. She'd heard it was fabulous.

They picked up two more passengers for the drive, Maggie Romano and her daughter, Gabi. An attractive widow in her early fifties, Maggie was the newest full-time resident of Eternity Springs, having relocated at the beginning of the summer to be nearer to two of her adult

children. Gabi was the town's deputy sheriff, though
with her long legs and high cheekbones and her mother's
beautiful blue eyes, she could have been a model if she'd
wanted. Hope was in the early stages of friendship with
the Romano women. She liked them both very much,
but considering her history, she was cautious about letting anyone get too close. Experience had taught her
that people invariably got too nosy, or they failed to be
a friend when she needed one the most.

Celeste Blessing had been the lone exception. Being
around Celeste was like slipping into Angel's Rest's inviting hot springs pools—sans the sulfur smell—on a
cold winter's night. She simply made Hope feel better.
She'd planted the seed about moving to Eternity Springs
during those beach house days, then nurtured the notion
with phone calls. Once Hope expressed real interest in
making the change, Celeste had championed her with
the principal and school board. One job offer later,
Hope packed her bags for a fresh start in a place that
called to her, instead of in a place she'd run to, like the
last move she'd made.

The four women made small talk as their trip com-
menced. Gabi relayed a story about the sheriff's office
dispatcher's unfortunate experience with online dating,
and with the laughter the story elicited, the melancholy
that had lingered within Hope after the unfortunate lesson planner incident began to dissolve. She turned onto
the road that climbed out of the valley, and her spirits
rose along with it.

They were halfway up the ridge when Maggie observed, "I've not been up this road before. What a spectacular view!"

"Isn't it lovely?" In the front passenger seat, Celeste
twisted around to speak with Maggie directly. "This is
one of my favorite Gold Wing rides. There's a scenic over-
view before the turnoff to Jack and Cat's place where you

can look down on Eternity Springs. It just makes me feel good to be there. And when I travel on up to the highest point of the road, I sometimes feel like I can reach into the sky and touch heaven."

"Maybe I'll have to get a motorcycle," Maggie mused. "We could form a gang, Celeste."

Gabi let out a groan and buried her head in her hands as Celeste laughed out loud.

It was a beautiful summer afternoon. Temperatures hovered in the mid-seventies. Snow-capped peaks climbed into a sapphire sky dotted with puffy white clouds. The road wound around a mountainside to reveal an alpine meadow carpeted with wildflowers. "Oh, how gorgeous," Hope observed. "What are those purple-blue flowers called?"

"Gentians. They're one of my favorites," Celeste said. "Up near Heartache Falls they . . . oh dear."

Hope braked to a stop as they came upon a small herd of bighorn sheep congregated on the road in front of them. Celeste clucked her tongue. "These animals are becoming my nemesis. This is the third time they've delayed me this month. Sarah Murphy will have my guts for garters if we're late to the shower."

"We have plenty of time," Hope assured her.

"Yes, but Sarah is not her usual cheery self these days. I need a distraction. What's the latest on your project, Maggie?"

Gabi rolled her big blue eyes and groaned a second time. Her mother sniffed with disdain, then beamed at Celeste. "Actually, I have exciting news. Jim Sutton has accepted my offer for his great-grandmother's Victorian on Aspen Street. With a little renovation, it will make a perfect B&B."

"That is exciting news," Celeste said.

"Congratulations." Hope's brows knit as she tried to

place the house. "On Aspen, you say? Which house is it?"

"The yellow one between Fifth and Sixth."

Hope realized Maggie must be referring to the dilapidated three-story whose faded, flecking paint sometimes floated on the air like dandruff. She pictured an overgrown yard, broken shutters, rotted gingerbread trim, and plywood-covered windows.

"It needs a little work," Maggie added, as if reading Hope's mind.

"And Murphy Mountain is a little hill," Gabi drawled.

"Now, honey . . ."

Gabi slipped on a pair of designer sunglasses. "Zach is quaking in his hiking boots. I heard him tell Savannah to be quick and hide his tool belt."

"I promised I wouldn't ask your brother to help," her mother protested. "He's the sheriff, for heaven's sake. He doesn't have time to be my handyman."

"I'm the sheriff's deputy," Gabi whined. "Why am I instructed to report for cleaning duty first thing Saturday morning?"

"Zach gets newlywed dispensation. Besides, he and Savannah won't be home from their trip to South Carolina to visit her nephew until late Friday night. I won't try to drag him out of bed early Saturday morning."

"He's *so* your favorite."

"Right now, yes."

The exchange surprised Hope. In her experience, mothers denied the existence of a favored child even if the charge was true. Taking her attention off the bleating roadblock that was finally beginning to move, she glanced into the rearview mirror to observe the Romano women.

Gabi caught her look and flashed a grin. "It's okay, Hope. Zach is due a turn at being favorite."

She wanted to ask why, but she wasn't that nosy. Celeste

obviously didn't share her concerns. "Hope moved to Eternity Springs in January, so she wasn't here for all the excitement last August. She probably doesn't know your family history. Tell her about Zach, Maggie. She loves happy endings as much as I do."

"It *is* a happy ending, isn't it?" Maggie sighed with pleasure, then explained. "I'll share the short version, Hope. Our family is dealing with a rather unique situation. I got pregnant with Zach when I was fifteen and I gave him up for adoption. Gabi and her brothers tracked him down and we were reunited last year, so I have a lot of pent-up love to shower upon him."

Oh. A lost child, found. Hope's throat grew tight.

"Mom has always been a big proponent of sibling equality when it comes to parental favoritism, so my sibs and I understand it's Zach's turn," Gabi added. "That doesn't mean the rest of us won't complain about it. Especially under current circumstances. I can't be your handyman, either, Mom. It's too big a job. You need a contractor—shoot, you need a miracle worker— if you're going to turn that broken-down behemoth into a bed and breakfast."

"I know, Gabriella. I actually have something different in mind. Someone different. I know a man who is good with his hands who desperately needs a project. He's a hard worker who needs a miracle."

"A miracle? Who do you know who needs . . . oh. Lucca."

"He's one of your twins, isn't he?" Celeste asked Maggie. "The one who coaches for Colorado?"

"No. That's Anthony. Lucca took the Landry University Bobcats to the Sweet Sixteen last March. Then he . . . well . . ."

"He wigged out," Gabi said, a bite of temper in her voice. "He quit his job and took off, didn't tell the family where he'd gone. He invested his NBA contract money wisely, so he has the means to do that sort of thing, but running off without any word like he did . . . he acted like a total jerk and it hurt us. I'm warning you, Mom. It's going to take some time for me to forgive him. And what makes you think he'll come here anyway? According to Max and Anthony and Zach, he's perfectly happy lounging in his Mexican beach chair and getting drunk on tequila and tugging the ties on bikinis. He has absolutely no intentions of ever coming back."

Maggie squared her shoulders. "He's my son. I have not begun to utilize all the weapons in my arsenal. He will come."

Hope followed college sports, so she'd made the connection between her new friends and the well-known collegiate basketball coaches. She'd been aware that Lucca Romano had publicly crashed and burned and alienated the power brokers in his professional field, and soon after meeting Maggie and Gabi, she'd yielded to temptation and Googled him for more detail on the incident.

Hope recognized that the man had suffered a tragedy, and she sympathized with his pain. She did not, however, respect the way he'd chosen to deal with it. Quit everything, quit on everyone, and run off to become a drunken beach bum? It demonstrated a distinct lack of character as far as she was concerned. His mother must be so disappointed in him.

"I hope you're right, Mom," Gabi said. "I'm not so optimistic. I'm afraid you're going to be hurt."

"He'll come," Maggie replied, her blue eyes gleaming with confidence. "Now, look at that beautiful iron sculpture up on our right. It's an eagle in flight. How graceful."

Celeste nodded. "That's our Sage's work, a gift to Jack."

"So this is Eagle's Way?" Hope asked. "We're here?"

"Yes." Celeste checked her watch, then beamed. "With three minutes to spare, thank the dear Lord."

They drove through an open gate and along a road that wound through a meadow painted with wildflowers. The large, sprawling house was built in the traditional mountain-log-home style, with windows facing what had to be one of the best views in Colorado. "Wow," Hope said.

"Wait until you see the inside," Celeste said. "And the patio and pool area. Gabe Callahan is a landscape architect, and what he designed is perfect for such a heavenly spot."

Jack Davenport stood on the front steps, and he waved at Hope to pull her car onto a circular driveway where Cam Murphy, Gabe Callahan, and Colt Rafferty stood acting as valets. "Hello, dears," Celeste said, climbing from the car. "I'm surprised to see you here. I thought the girls decided they wanted a traditional females-only baby shower."

"We're just here to provide muscle," Jack said. "As soon as everyone arrives and all the loot is hauled inside, we have a date with fishing rods and the creek."

"You have a lovely home," Hope told him.

"Thanks. We do love it up here."

Just then the front door opened and Nic Callahan called, "Thank goodness you are here. Sarah and Cat are ready to get this party started."

"Are we the last to arrive?"

"Rose is running late, but she had a patient. She's asked us to start without her."

Hope stepped into the great room, and her gaze was torn between three gorgeous sites: snowcapped mountains displayed like a fine-art painting through the wall of windows; a glowing Cat Davenport holding her sleeping four-month-old son, Johnny, in her arms; and Sarah Murphy, sprawled in an overstuffed easy chair, her feet propped up on an ottoman, a grumpy scowl on her face, and a baby belly so big that Hope wondered if she might be having a litter rather than a single baby boy.

"Sarah, you look beautiful," Hope told her.

"You are a liar, Hope Montgomery, but I appreciate the effort."

"How do you feel, darling?" Celeste asked.

"Fat. Grouchy. Ugly. Fat. My back hurts. I haven't seen my feet in weeks. My so-called friend and neonatologist tells me I could go another week, curse her black heart."

The physician in question, Sage Rafferty, rolled her eyes. "I'm not your doctor, Sarah. I gave you my personal opinion, not my professional one."

Sarah pouted, then turned to Nic. "Sage is right. I should have asked you instead of her. You're a vet. I'm a cow. When should I head for the barn and lie down on the straw? Or would I stand up? Do cows have their babies lying down or standing up?"

"Mother," Lori Murphy chastised, her expression long-suffering. "Just stop it. The baby is healthy and you are healthy and you look lovely."

"Your father called me a whale!"

As one, the women in the room gasped.

"No, he didn't." Lori explained to the others, "He called her a great white because she'd just bitten his head off for accidentally sloshing coffee onto the kitchen floor."

"It was clean. I want a clean house when I go into labor. But I shouldn't have snapped at him, and he spoke the truth. Big fish, big bovine . . . what's the difference? I'm fat! I wanted this baby very much, but why couldn't I have a little bump like Cat had? I'm bigger than Nic was and she had twins! I'm a blimp and I'm ugly and I'm too old to be doing this. What woman has her first and second children more than twenty years apart? I can't do this!"

Hope blinked. Was the normally confident, composed Sarah Murphy sliding toward the edge?

"Sure, you can." Nic Callahan crossed the room to sit on the arm of Sarah's chair. "And I thought this was supposed to be a baby shower, not a pity party."

Sarah's lips quirked. "Can't it be both? I'm a hundred and twelve months pregnant."

"I'll bet you didn't sleep last night, did you?"

"Not much. Between the heartburn and his constant kicking and the fact he has his butt right on top of my bladder . . . and his father snores!"

"You've never done well when you're short on sleep."

"Newborns don't sleep. I'm going to be a terrible mother."

"You're a wonderful mother," Lori protested. "The best. And this time, Cam will be around to help."

Sarah sniffed. "I love you, Lori. And I love your father and my friends. I love our baby. I have a wonderful life. I don't know why I'm being such a witch."

"It's the late-pregnancy hormones," Sage said.

"I hope it is hormones and not the new me. But my emotions are a mess. I'm happy and excited, but I'm also anxious and nervous and worried. At sixteen I was too young and stupid to know what the deal was. Now, I know what it means to parent and I'm scared to death."

"Of course you are," Nic said. "That's normal."

"She's right," Ali Timberlake chimed in. "Every mother-to-be is a little bit afraid."

You should be afraid, Hope thought, though she wouldn't dream of speaking the warning aloud.

"Don't be so hard on yourself, Sarah." Cat took a seat in a wooden rocking chair, then shifted her infant son to lie against her shoulder. "What you have to remember is that the risk and worry are worth it because the reward is so great."

"Excellent advice," Sage Rafferty said. "On that note,

I say we get down to business." She made a flourishing gesture toward a table piled high with gifts. "Presents!"

Sarah's eyes went misty. "There's a mountain of them. You guys went crazy."

"A little," Celeste admitted. "But it's so much fun to buy for babies."

"At the rate we're reproducing, someone should open a children's store in town," Nic observed.

"Is that an announcement?" Gabi asked.

"Bite your tongue," Nic responded as Ali handed Sarah the first gift to open.

Hope enjoyed the afternoon. She liked these women and she appreciated the way they welcomed newcomers into their circle of friendship with such genuine pleasure. She didn't know if it was a small-town thing or particular to Eternity Springs, but either way, she felt as if she had found the people who were meant to be in her life and the home she was meant to have.

She'd found a new life, a good life, to replace the one that had been stolen away from her.

And when she watched Sarah Murphy ooh and ahh over three-month-sized overalls and took her turn cuddling little Johnny Davenport, she reminded herself to be thankful for what she had. Positive thinking took work, but Hope knew that it was work worth doing. Negative thoughts could be dangerous and destructive and lead a person to consider dangerous, destructive acts. She knew that firsthand.

The memory of one particular bleak afternoon floated through her mind, and as always, she gave thanks for the ember of hope within her that continued to burn even today.

Because sometimes, dreams come true. Sometimes an infertile couple had their little Johnny, she thought as she gazed down into the precious face of the cooing baby in her arms. When Sarah opened a hand-knitted baby blanket and burst into tears, it proved that sometimes long-lost lovers returned to create the family that had been meant to be.

So, why couldn't it happen to her, too? She couldn't live her life in a constant state of waiting amid misery and depression, floating in the numbness of prescription pain killers. But if she kept her thoughts positive, continued to put one foot in front of the other, and move forward on this road of life, well, then, who was to say she couldn't have her own miracle some day?

Jack and Cat Davenport had their new son. Cam and Sarah Murphy were married and awaiting their second child. Maybe someday she would get her miracle, too. Maybe someday, Holly would come home to her.

Sometimes, kidnapped children were found. Sometimes, miracles did happen.

THREE

❦

"If he was like this in Mexico, it's a miracle he's still alive," Zach Turner said.

At the sound of the sheriff's familiar voice, Lucca scowled and pulled the pillow over his head. Apparently his bedroom door wasn't shut, because the pillow didn't muffle nearly enough.

"I wonder if that's the problem, Zach," his sister stated, a grim note to her voice.

Shut up, Gabi.

She continued, "Right now, however, his problems have become our problem. We can get by without arresting him once, but if he does this again, we won't be able to avoid it."

Arrest? What the . . .

Lucca tugged the pillow away from his face and pried open his eyes. Whoa, the room was bright. He snapped his eyelids shut, and it took a few seconds for the image of what he'd seen to sink into his brain. Bars. And not the wooden kind with beer taps and cardboard coasters, either. Cell bars. Jail bars. He wasn't in his bedroom. He'd woken up in jail. Again.

He heard keys jangle, a lock release, and hinges creak. A familiar female voice said, "Lucca Ryan Romano, you smell like a goat. Wake up."

Oh, crap. Mom. What a great start to his day. He delayed, taking a moment to remember waking up to a view of the crystalline water off the Yucatán Peninsula. How had he gone from thirty to thirteen in less than a week?

"Son, do you hear me?"

A deaf man could hear Maggie Romano when she spoke in her "mother" tone. His mouth was as dry as good vermouth and his tongue felt hairy, so his answer came out as a croak. "Yes, ma'am."

He sat up, stifling a groan. He tried to recall how he'd ended up here, but the pounding in his head made it difficult to think.

"I truly thought I was done bailing my children out of jail when Max graduated from college."

"You're not bailing him out, Mom," Gabi corrected. "We didn't actually arrest him."

"A technicality." Maggie waved a dismissive hand. "You know that a mother shouldn't have to see her son like this. I'm disappointed in you, Lucca. This is a disgrace. I raised you better than this."

Just shoot me now. He loved his mother more than anyone else in the world. Disappointing her was the worst.

Lucca dragged a hand down his bristled jaw. Memory of the events of the previous night returned as he climbed to his feet from the uncomfortable cot. He felt like hell. He needed to take a shower. He wanted to get away from the disapproving stares of his brother, sister, and mother.

Then you shouldn't have sat your ass in the local pub until almost closing time and snagged a six-pack at the gas station afterward.

He gratefully accepted the bottle of water Zach handed him and made a stab at self-defense by saying,

"I entered this office voluntarily last night, and I did nothing that would warrant an arrest."

Zach shrugged. "Could have hit you with public intoxication."

"I was sitting on a bench beside the creek, not making any noise, minding my own business."

"At three o'clock in the morning with four empty beer bottles at your feet!" Gabi snapped.

"So what, you saying the night shift deputy hauled me in for littering?"

She braced her hands on her hips. "I'm saying that you were too drunk to find your way back to your house."

"What sort of an example does that set, son?" his mother asked.

Annoyance slithered through him. He was no longer in the business where setting examples mattered. Of course, Maggie Romano wouldn't care to hear that he didn't give a crap about what people thought of him. From the day her children were born, the woman had high expectations at all times for the way they behaved. Yet, this was her home, and Zach and Gabi's home. He should respect that.

Respect didn't keep the chill from his voice as he offered a sincere apology. "I didn't make a public spectacle, but I'm sorry if I embarrassed you. This town is now your home, and I need to remember that. So, have I forgotten a family meeting or something this morning? If not, I'd like to head home and grab a shower."

His mother shared an uncertain look with Zach and Gabi. Zach raised his hands, palms out, and stepped away saying, "I need to get started on my workday."

In other words, his oldest brother was washing his hands of the situation. Zach was still new at the sibling business. He still had a lot to learn.

Gabi said, "No meeting. Mom and I met for breakfast, and she walked back with me to bring Zach a blue-berry muffin. We didn't expect to find you sleeping off a drunken binge."

Mother, apparently, decided the time had arrived to offer a truce. With a tentative smile, she offered, "I have an extra muffin. Would you like one?"

"Thanks, but I'll take a rain check." Lucca picked up the blanket from the cot and folded it. He handed it and the pillow to Gabi, saying, "I appreciate the sheriff's department's hospitality. Now, if you ladies will excuse me?"

He leaned down and kissed his mother's cheek, but before he could leave the cell, she grabbed his hand. "Lucca, can I have just a moment?"

He wanted to say no, but not even the worst hangover in history would cause him to be blatantly disrespectful of his mother. His father would rise from his grave and whip his ass if he did. Lucca waited, unconsciously squaring his shoulders and stiffening his spine.

Maggie didn't speak until Gabi left them alone. "Honey, I want you to know how thrilled I am that you agreed to make an extended visit to Eternity Springs, and I meant it when I said I wouldn't be a bossy, buttin-ski mother once you arrived."

She paused, her teeth tugging at her lower lip. He waited for the "but."

She gave it to him. "But, I'm worried about you, Lucca. I'm really, really worried about you."

I'm sorry. "I'm okay, mom."

The look in her eyes said *No, you're not.* "Tony advised me to give you space, and I learned thirty years ago that no one knows you better than your twin, so I am determined to listen to him. That said, I want you to know that you have people here who are ready and will-ing to help you. We love you, Lucca."

Why that caused his heart to twist and his throat to

tighten, he didn't know. But then, he didn't know much about anything these days, did he?

Leaning down, he kissed his mother on her cheek. "I love you, too, Mom. That's why I agreed to come to Eternity Springs."

"Is there anything we can do for you, Lucca?"

He looked away from the sudden pool of tears in her eyes. "I appreciate the patience, Mom. I'm just trying to get things figured out. It's nothing to fret over, I promise."

Following a long pause, she nodded. "You'll come over to the house later? I bought a new sledgehammer and there's a non-load-bearing wall with your name on it."

His mouth lifted in a wry grin. "Well, what red-blooded man could resist an offer like that? I have something to do this morning, but I'll be by this afternoon. Okay?"

"Excellent." She smiled brightly, if rather falsely. "I'll see you later, then."

Lucca gave finger salutes to his sister and brother as he sauntered out of the sheriff's office into the sunlight—the bright, brilliant sunlight that stabbed into his eyes like a fiery sword. Confidently, he turned north, although in all honesty, even stone cold sober, he wasn't exactly sure how to find the house his family had rented for him. Since Gabi and Zach had dragged him here three . . . no, make it four . . . days ago, he'd done little exploring. He'd been too busy sleeping.

Jet lag, he told himself. Or exhaustion. He'd gone at it hard and fast those first months he'd been gone. In Rio, Buenos Aries, Cancún, and places in between, he'd lost himself in sun and sea and sex. About a month ago, he'd run out of steam in a little beach town in Quintana Roo, Mexico, and that's when he'd quit shaving and eating regularly and started drinking more and sleeping a lot.

Reaching an intersection, he noticed a carousel of sunglasses inside a convenience store. He checked his pocket to see if he'd managed to keep his wallet the night before, and then looked inside it to see if he had any cash. "Excellent," he murmured, finding three twenties, four tens, and three ones. He bought the first pair he tried on, a big bottle of water, and a small bottle of ibuprofen. Hydrated, medicated, and shielded, he stepped back out into the sunlight and tried to find his way back home, figuring he'd get there eventually. The town wasn't that big.

The fresh air and the exercise proved to be helpful medicine, too, and once he spied the bank on the corner of Spruce and Fourth, he knew which way to go. Fifteen minutes later, he stood in a steaming shower and remained there until the water ran cold. He toweled dry, brushed his teeth, then crawled naked into his bed knowing another couple hours of shut-eye would finish off the hangover. He yawned into his pillow and prepared to drift off to sleep.

That's when he heard the noise. Shrill, keening sounds. Mewling. Lucca's eyes flew open. What the hell?

Rats. This house must have rats. Great.

Thinking to scare them away, he reached for the book on his nightstand and threw it hard against the closet door from where the noise appeared to be originating. *That'll scatter 'em.* He'd see about a more permanent solution to the problem after his nap. He closed his eyes, wished the ibuprofen would kick in soon, and . . . *meee meee meee.*

"Grrrr . . ." Sighing heavily and mentally flipping his family the bird for putting him into a rat-infested dwelling, he rolled to his feet, grabbed the iron poker from the tool set beside the fireplace, then approached the closet's half-open door. "I warned you. You should have run when you had the chance."

He lifted the poker with his left hand, yanked the door wide open with his right, and prepared to bash rat heads.

Lucca froze. Not rats. They looked like rats, but those weren't rats. "Puppies?"

He set down the poker and squatted to get a better look. Yes, puppies. Three of them. Unless that bump was . . .

Lucca reached into the closet to push aside a pile of his clothes. He absently noted a sound behind him, but his hangover-dulled wits didn't process it. Pain, however, processed immediately, so when the fangs sank into his ass, he knew instantly what had occurred. "Ya-eeh!" he yelled, jerking and shoving to separate the mother dog from his butt.

"Yarrrrgh," the mutt growled back, letting loose of Lucca and planting herself between him and the closet, keeping her teeth bared.

Sprawled on his naked, aching ass, Lucca snarled back at the dog. He recognized her. She was little and fluffy and brown. Probably a terrier mix of some sort. She belonged to the sexy redhead who lived next door. "So why the hell did you whelp in my house, in my closet, on top of my favorite jeans?"

He went to stand and she lunged at him again. Crap. He shifted backward, giving her the stink eye as he climbed to his feet. He rubbed the bite and saw blood on his hands. Sonofabitch. The dog wasn't wearing a collar. Wasn't wearing tags. The lady next door damned well better have made sure the mutt had had her shots.

Lucca's ass ached, his head pounded, his temper surged. He backed away from the dog, strode into the bathroom, and washed the bite with soap and water. He rummaged through the supplies his mother had added to the house but didn't find any antiseptic. "Figures," he muttered. Who planned for a dog bite? "Well, then, guess I'll just have to borrow some from the neighbor."

He paused long enough to grab a pair of gym shorts from the duffel lying on his bedroom floor and slip them on. He marched out his front door and arrived on her porch thirty seconds later. His gaze fell upon her doorbell, but that didn't do it for him at the moment. He made a fist and pounded the door. Hard. Then he braced his hands on his hips, his legs spread in an aggressive stance, and waited for her to answer.

He waited. And waited. Pounded again. Waited. Waited. Yelled, "Hello?"

Hell. She wasn't home.

He rubbed the burning bite and turned to leave, then stopped abruptly. Just like her damned dog, she'd sneaked up on him.

She had earbuds in her ears and a garden hose in her hand, and despite his general pissed-off frame of mind, Lucca couldn't help but appreciate the view. Curls and curves, he thought. His favorite combination. He noted the burnished wisps that escaped the thick knot of red hair piled atop her head to frame big brown eyes. Faint freckles dusted a thin, straight nose above full cherry lips. She wore an oversized white tank top over a black sports bra and pleasingly short running shorts. Full breasts, shapely legs. Cute little bubble butt. Nice. Very, very nice.

But a hot body didn't make up for poor dog-owner practices, he told himself when he shifted his weight and again felt the burn of the bite. He should call the cops and have her ticketed. He might do it, too, if the mutt's shots weren't up to date. He had connections, after all. Might as well make use of them.

Yeah, right. Like he'd ever want his brother and sister know he'd let a ten-pound mutt take a chunk out of his ass. The throb seemed to intensify as he started toward her. "Hey, lady."

Not having seen him, she'd turned away and now stood at the side of her house watering a group of herb pots set upon a whimsical castle-shaped iron planter. While she watered, she swung her shoulders and hips in such a way that made him think a rock tune belted through her earbuds.

He stepped closer, raised his voice, and repeated, "Hey, lady!"

She startled, jerked around.

The ice cold water from the hose soaked his shorts.

He yelped and jumped sideways, away from the stream.

Hope squealed and dropped the hose. She yanked off her earphones and got her first good look at the man in her yard. *Oh, no. I shot the sheriff.*

Almost immediately, she realized otherwise. He wasn't Zach Turner. The eyes blazing out at her weren't Zach's striking blue eyes. These were emerald green shards of ice.

Not Zach. The brother. Lucca. My, oh my . . .

Hope gave him a closer look. He was tall, more than a foot taller than her own five feet five inches. He had the look of an athlete, with broad, muscular shoulders and flat abs and . . . her gaze lingered on the wet gym shorts plastered against him. All parts of him. Oh, wow. The man was big all over.

Hope felt heat sting her cheeks as she forced her stare back to his face. Unnerved, she went on the offensive, though the voice that emerged pitched higher than normal. "Excuse me, this is private property and you're trespassing."

"Your damned dog bit me."

"What?" She glanced toward the fenced section of the backyard where Roxy should be. Had she dug out or found a hole? She'd been back there drinking from her water bowl not too long ago. "Where?"

"I'm halfway tempted to show you. On my butt, that's where."

His butt? Hope's mouth twisted in disbelief. If Roxy was a Great Dane, maybe.

"I meant where were you when you were attacked?"

"In my bedroom."

"Then you must be mistaken, mister . . ."

"Romano. Lucca Romano. And I'm not mistaken. Your dog bit me."

"Actually, I don't have a dog."

"Oh, yeah? You say you don't have a little fluffy brown yappy mutt? Then what are those?" He pointed at the two dog bowls sitting on her kitchen stoop.

"What I mean is that I'm not her real owner. I'm taking care of a neighbor's dog until they get settled in their new home."

"Not very well, apparently. You lost her."

You lost her. Hope closed her eyes. Her knees went a little weak. Of all the things he could have said . . .

"You let her invade my house and my privacy."

His tone held that same accusatory note that her ex-husband had used with her, and it sparked Hope's own temper to life. The jerk. The jock. Athletes often think they're God's gift to the world. Mark, her ex, had played college baseball and sometimes he'd been exactly the same way. She put the frost of a Rocky Mountain winter in her voice as she said, "I beg your pardon?"

"Yes, you should."

"You have some nerve." Hope braced her hands on her hips and lifted her chin. "Listen, mister, if Roxy found her way inside your house then you invited her in by leaving it open. Roxy is a sweet dog. If she bit you, then you must have done something to provoke her."

His gaze had slipped to her chest. It remained there. Pig. She crossed her arms. "What did you do to her?"

"Nothing. I didn't do a damned thing to that dog. All I did was look to see what was making the noise in my closet and she bit me on the ass."

"Closet? I don't understand. Are you saying Roxy was in your closet?"

"Yes. That dog is a pain in my ass in more ways than one. She had puppies in my closet on top of my clothes."

Hope froze. "How did she get inside your . . . whoa . . . did you say . . . puppies?"

"Yes, puppies! Three of them. Maybe four."

"When did she have puppies?"

"Sometime last night, I imagine. Maybe earlier this morning. Haven't you seen her? Some sort of dog-sitter you are. I heard them a little while ago. I was trying to get a closer look when she came out of nowhere and sank her fangs into me."

"Where?"

"I told you." He hooked a thumb toward his rear, his expression peeved.

Hope pursed her lips to squelch the smile. She didn't think now was the right time for it. "Not the little nip. The pups. I don't know where you live."

"It wasn't a little nip. Think alligator mouth. The little bitch drew blood. And I live next door."

"That makes sense," Hope replied, thinking aloud. "Her former owners lived next door. Isn't there a doggie door in the back? That must be how she got in. It's her home, so maybe that's why she went there to have her babies."

Lucca nodded toward Hope's house. "Well, that's her home now so let's get a box or a basket and get them moved."

Hope frowned. "I don't know . . . is it safe to move them? They were just born. I don't have any experience with puppies. I didn't even realize she was pregnant. I thought she was getting fat because she liked the brand of dog food I gave her."

Shoeless, shirtless, and whisker-stubbled, Lucca Romano stood in Hope's front yard oozing sex appeal. However, his eyes shot green fire as he braced his hands on his hips and declared. "Those dogs are not staying in my closet."

Hope contemplated turning the water hose on herself. Instead, she walked over to the faucet and twisted the spigot, cutting off the flow of water. Her thoughts spun. Puppies. She'd had two female dogs in the past. Both had been rescue dogs whom she'd adopted and had come to her spayed. She'd wanted a puppy before Holly was born, but Mark had vetoed the idea. She knew puppies were a lot of work, but honestly, she couldn't help but be a little excited.

"I'll call Nic Callahan. She's our town vet and she'll tell us what to do."

"You. She'll tell you. I'm not dealing with puppies."

And Hope wasn't moving them unless Nic gave her the okay to do so, but that argument could wait. "I need to look up Nic's number. I'll be right back."

She left him standing in the yard like a grumpy Roman god as she entered her house and walked through the mud room to her kitchen where she kept her iPad. She accessed the Internet, searched for the Eternity Springs Veterinary Clinic website, then added the number to her telephone's address book. She could have done it from her phone, of course, but she'd wanted a little space from the man.

How had someone as nice and friendly as Maggie Romano raised such an ill-tempered son?

Hearing a noise, she glanced up to see Lucca Romano standing on her stoop, glaring at her. "What? I had to get the number."

"I thought you might be trying to dodge me."

Rather than dignify that nonsense with a response, she moved toward him. As she walked past her washer and dryer in the mud room, she scooped up an oversized rose-colored bath towel. When she opened the screen door, he stepped aside to let her pass, and she tossed him the bath sheet. "You're all wet, Mr. Romano."

He caught the towel and smirked. "You're funny, Ms. . . . what did you say your name was?"

"I didn't." And she wouldn't. Not even a Roman god physique could overcome the disposition of a badger.

He dragged the towel across that expanse of male chest and waited. She decided to let him wait longer. She thumbed the number of Nic's veterinary clinic, and after three rings the answering machine clicked on. Feeling petty, Hope managed to leave a message without mentioning her name.

As she prepared to disconnect the call, Lucca interrupted. "Ask her if she gave that dog a rabies shot."

Hope slipped her phone into the pocket of her shorts. "Roxy's shots aren't due until January."

"Good. Glad to know that . . . Gertrude."

She returned the smirk. She didn't know why she was being stubborn about telling him her name. It was stupid, really, but something about this man brought out the ornery in her.

He wrapped the towel around his hips, eyeing her speculatively. "Ready to go get the puppies?"

"I do want to see them."

He made a sweeping gesture and bowed his head. "After you, Ethel."

This time instead of smirking, she snorted, then started across her lawn toward his house. He trailed after her, oblivious to the curious looks he attracted from a car with Kansas plates. "If you won't tell me your name, of course I have to guess."

As they crossed her front walk, Hope took the conversation in a different direction. "I really like your mother, sister, and brother."

"You know them?"

"Of course."

"Right. Of course. They're pillars of the community."

Hope's eyes widened at the bitterness in his tone. He might have heard it himself, because a moment later he added, "They are good people. I have a great family and I love them very much."

Okay, maybe he wasn't one hundred percent jerk. Ninety-five, maybe. No lower than ninety-three. "I know your mother was thrilled that you agreed to help her with her B&B."

"I don't know how much help I'm going to be. My remodeling talents are limited." He shrugged and changed the subject. "I think there's an empty box in my garage that you can use for moving the puppies. The clothes she used for her nest will need to be tossed, but I'll donate a couple towels to the cause."

"How generous."

By now he'd overtaken her with his long-legged strides. He glanced back over his shoulder and flashed her a smile with plenty of teeth and masculine challenge. "Oh, Esmeralda, you don't have a clue as to just how generous I can be."

Hope almost stumbled as sexual awareness rose up like a trip wire. Holy guacamole. The man wielded that smile like a weapon, and it wasn't even a very nice smile. Imagine what he could do with a real one—a smile that reached his eyes.

His brother Zach had a nice smile, something she'd noticed at a baseball game the week before when she'd watched him flirt with his wife, Savannah. If Lucca Romano had any of his brother's charm in him, he'd be lethal.

Not that he'd ever turn any charm he might have on her. She wasn't the type of woman who attracted the attention of a man like this. He was a professional athlete and coach, a Ferrari who lived his life in the fast lane. She was a girl-next-door kind of girl, closer to a golf cart than a sports car.

This truth didn't improve her frame of mind one bit.

Grumpily, she asked, "Are you always this big of a jerk?"

"Maybe, but it doesn't help that the painkillers haven't kicked in."

She frowned. "Is the bite really that sore?"

"If I said yes would you kiss it and make it better?"

She halted abruptly. Her jaw dropped. She couldn't believe he'd said that. They had just met, and he didn't even know her name, and he went and spouted something like that. Unreal. "You are a pig."

"Goes without saying," he fired back, shrugging. "I'm a guy. The bite feels better, thanks for asking, Beulah. So does my head."

"You had something wrong with your head? Why am I not surprised?"

Again, he showed her that smile. "Hangover."

"I repeat: Why am I not surprised?" And his mother was such a nice person. Poor woman. Imagine this horror sitting at the dinner table on Sunday.

As they approached his house, he increased his pace so that he reached the front porch well ahead of her. The hinges on the screen door creaked as he yanked it open, then motioned for her to precede him.

Hope knew what to expect inside the house. She'd visited many times after she first moved to Eternity Springs. Her neighbor Louise Morrison had been a widow in her seventies who had befriended Hope and taught her things that had helped her adjust to life in a small Rocky Mountain town. When Louise died in her sleep the previous March, Hope had been devastated. Louise had left both her house and the care of her beloved Roxy to her nephew.

It hadn't been a good match. The nephew's family hadn't liked small-town living, so as soon as they could manage, they'd moved back to Colorado Springs, leaving Roxy behind but promising to send for her as soon as they could find a new apartment that allowed pets.

She wasn't holding her breath for that phone call.

A wave of sorrow washed over Hope as she walked inside. She missed Louise.

"It's that way," Lucca said, pointing toward his bedroom. "Go on in. I'll get the box."

Hope didn't bother to tell him that he could get all the boxes he wanted, but she wasn't going to relocate those puppies until Nic Callahan gave the okay.

Entering Lucca's bedroom, she only vaguely noted the unmade queen-sized bed and the open duffel bag on the floor. Her attention was focused on the closet, a long, narrow opening with bifold doors that stood completely open. She saw Roxy stretched out on a pile of clothing on the floor.

Hope went down on her knees just outside the closet opening. In a soft, gentle tone, she said, "Hey there, Roxy. Hey there, girl. Look at you, little mama."

The dog lifted her head, and Hope got her first good look at the nursing puppies. Her heart melted. "Aww . . ."

They were tiny, no bigger than the palm of her hand. Two tan and one dappled, tan and white. Roxy lay her head down once again and Hope rolled back on her heels. Puppies. They stayed with their mother what, six weeks? Eight? Then they were taken away? Ripped out of their mother's life?

Tears stung her eyes. "Oh, Roxy. Roxy."

Who decided that was okay? Who decided that animals didn't grieve for their offspring?

"I'm in trouble," she murmured. She knew that Louise's nephew would never actually send for Roxy. It had been three weeks since they left town, and she'd not heard one word from the man. So in reality, these four dogs were now her responsibility. Was she supposed to start looking for homes for them? Four separate homes? She couldn't do that. But then that would mean . . .

"I can't keep four dogs." What was she going to do?

Her cellphone rang and she reached for it like a lifeline. Checking the number, she breathed a sigh of relief and answered. "Hello, Nic. Thank you so much for returning my call. I'm afraid I have a bit of a situation, and I don't know what to do about it."

She explained what had happened and asked for Nic's guidance. Nic asked a few questions, gave Hope some instructions, then offered to stop by to check on Roxy and her litter that afternoon. Surprised, Hope asked, "You make house calls?"

"Just looking out for my own interests," Nic replied. "With two girls headed for kindergarten soon, I figure it's never too soon to suck up to the teacher."

Hope laughed. "Thanks, Nic. I'll see you later."

She ended the call and rolled to her feet. Turning around, she saw Lucca standing just inside the door, a cardboard box in his hand. She stepped past him, saying, "I'll be back."

He reached out. "Hold on there. You're forgetting something."

His big hand wrapped completely around her upper arm. He didn't squeeze; it wasn't painful. He simply prevented her from moving beyond the threshold of his bedroom door.

He stood close, smelling of soap, a fragrance she recognized as one of the men's soaps his sister-in-law's shop sold. He stood so near to her that she could feel the heat of his body. When was the last time she'd stood this close to a man in a bedroom?

"You're taking the pups."

"Yes, but later."

"How much later?"

Hope's mind was spinning with a list of supplies. "I need to prepare a place for them to stay. The vet told me what to do and how to do it. Once it's ready, I'll come back and get the dogs."

He gave her a dubious look. "How long is this preparation going to take?"

"Not that long."

He narrowed his eyes and studied her. "Why don't I help you? We'll get things done twice as fast."

"Thank you, but what I have to do is really a one-person job. I'll be back in an hour. Two at the most."

After a moment's pause, he nodded, and his hand dropped to his side. "I'm going to trust you'll make this fast. I might not know your name, but I do know where you live. I can move the mutts myself if I have to."

"Please don't. I'll be back for them. I promise. I really am sorry about this—sorry about the bite. I know it's disruptive to have puppies in your closet. I'll be two hours, tops, Mr. Romano."

Again, he flashed a smile, only this time the darn thing seemed resigned. Almost genuine. It lit up the emeralds of his eyes, and her mouth went a little dry at the sight. *Oh, my, he's really gorgeous.*

He led her across to the front door, then he held it open for her. As she stepped out onto his porch, he repeated, "Two hours, tops. See you soon, Bertha."

The screen door banged shut behind her, and despite herself, Hope grinned.

An hour and forty minutes later, she was back. She'd moved some furniture out of the room she used as a home office and set up the whelping pen on loan from

Nic that she'd picked up at the vet clinic. She'd lined it with layers of newspaper and fabric and ordered absorbent puppy pads online that should arrive the following day. After talking to Nic, she was both nervous about what she'd committed to do and excited for the new experience.

Carrying a laundry basket filled with towels and a blanket, she knocked on Lucca Romano's front door. Minutes passed. She knocked again. She heard no sound at all from inside the house. Knock. Knock. Knock. "Mr. Romano? Lucca?"

Nothing.

"Well, hurry up and wait," she muttered. It figured that he'd be the type to demand punctuality in others but consider himself above the common courtesy in return. She didn't have time to waste. She wanted to get Roxy and the puppies all settled by the time Nic arrived to check on them so that she could advise her if she'd done something wrong. Knock. Knock. Knock. "Lucca?"

She listened. Nothing. She tried the doorknob. It wasn't locked. *He did tell me to come get the dogs. That's a tacit invitation inside, I'd think.*

Hope stepped into the house and moved confidently toward the bedroom. As she passed the hall bathroom, she noted that he'd left the wet gym shorts he'd been wearing lying in a heap on the floor. Such a slob. Bet Maggie would just love to see that.

At the door to his bedroom, Hope stopped cold.

Lucca Romano lay sprawled on his stomach across the top of the bed, a white sheet tangled around his hips. She heard a slight snore rumbling from beneath the pillow he had pulled over his head. She took a minute to appreciate the view. Italian skin deeply tanned from a summer spent south of the border, muscles developed by years of athletic training filling out his long, tall frame: he was a gorgeous specimen of masculinity. She could easily imagine him in a charcoal Armani suit, white dress shirt, and a tie with green stripes to subtly complement the color of his eyes. Definitely GQ qualified.

She could just as easily imagine him without the sheet covering his hips, with his buttocks bare and firm and . . . *Oh, for heaven's sake. Get the dogs before you begin to drool or he wakes up and catches you gawking.*

She turned away and set about her work. She lured Roxy outside the closet with a dog treat and instructions to go outside to potty. Then she gently gathered up the puppies and placed them into her laundry basket. Picking up her burden of cuteness, she turned around and halted.

Lucca stood beside the bed facing her, his back arched, his torso twisted, his arms outstretched and muscles flexed as he stretched and yawned. She wondered if one of his Italian ancestors had modeled for Michelangelo's *David*.

"You're wearing *Sesame Street* boxer shorts," she observed stupidly.

"Elmo." He gave a lazy smile and arched a challenging brow. "Like 'em, Brunhilda?"

"I'd have pegged you more as Oscar the Grouch."

"That's what my mom said when she gave them to me. I have a whole *Sesame Street* set."

"Your mother gives you boxer shorts."

"And socks. Every Christmas and birthday."

"And you wear them."

"Why not?"

He dragged his hand down his bristled jaw and yawned once more. The sound shook Hope from her stupor. "I'd better get these little guys settled."

"Need any help carrying them?"

"I'm good. Thanks." Hope continued toward the door, awkwardly searching for something to say before settling on a simple "Welcome to Eternity Springs, Coach Romano."

In an instant, he went from looking like a Roman god to an angry Mafia don. "Call me Lucca. Just plain Lucca."

She sucked in a breath. There was anger, and yet there was such pain in this man, too. She understood pain. She sympathized with it.

Gentling her tone, she said, "I'm Hope, just plain Lucca. You can call me Hope."

FOUR

As early morning sunlight sparkled like diamonds on the surface of Hummingbird Lake, Zach Turner saw his wife and mother off on a two-day shopping trip to Denver with a hug and kiss and a caution to drive carefully. He waited until they'd turned off Reflection Point Road and disappeared from sight to make a fist pump in the air. Today was his day off and no one had claims upon his time. He loved Savannah to distraction, and he considered married life pure bliss. Getting to know his birth mother and siblings and having them as part of his daily life enriched his world. But his bachelor and sans-family days hadn't ended all that long ago, and while he'd never admit it aloud, sometimes he missed the freedom that came with being alone.

Whistling beneath his breath, he walked toward his garage—dubbed his "toy closet" by Savannah—and opened the door. Standing in the threshold, he debated his choices. What did he want to do today? Ride his bike? Take a cruise on his motorcycle? Grab his fishing tackle and head up to the Taylor River? Maybe he should load up his climbing gear and give Storm Mountain a go. The possibilities were endless and invigorating . . . until the sound of an approaching vehicle made him tense.

He recognized the peculiar ping in the engine of one of his department's Range Rovers. Why would Gabi drive out to Reflection Point today? Had there been an emergency, the office would have called. Anything short of an emergency, well, days off were sacrosanct.

He walked out to meet the truck, wondering if her visit was deputy related or sister related or both.

Gabi parked her Range Rover and approached him wearing a tired smile. The dark circles beneath her eyes made him frown. "What's up?"

"I know it's your day off and this won't take long, but once I made the decision, I knew I needed to go ahead and tell you."

Zach didn't like the sound of that. "What decision?"

Gabi sucked in a deep breath, then let it out slowly. "I'm giving my two-weeks' notice. I'm leaving the department."

He searched her eyes, so similar to his own, and spied the worry. She was fearful of his reaction, he realized. He wasn't entirely surprised. He'd suspected for some time that she hadn't been happy. While this was definitely a sheriff's-deputy moment, the brother spoke to his sister and said, "Well, that sucks for me. Is it my coffee? You've finally had all you can stand?"

Her smile wobbled and a frown creased her brow. "Admitting this makes me feel like such a loser, but Zach, I don't want to carry a gun anymore."

She swallowed hard and blinked back tears, and Zach opened his arms to her. "C'mere."

"No. I can't." She held up her hands, palms out, and took a step backward. "If I let you hug me, then I'll cry, and that will be the cherry on top."

"Cherries are good for you," Zach responded, ignoring her protest as he pulled her into his arms. "They're fruit and you are the farthest thing from a loser out there, Gabriella. You gave me my life."

When old enemies attempted to murder Savannah the previous summer, Gabi had shot and killed a woman seconds after that woman had shot and damn near killed Zach. His sister's first aid and clear thinking had saved him from bleeding out on the floor.

Now she sputtered a little as she tried not to sob against his shoulder. "That's the problem. I'm so thankful I was there to back you up, and I'm proud that I saved you, but the thought of having to draw my gun again . . . to use it . . . gives me the creeps. I could do it if I had to—I know that—but the fact is that I walk around with a little ball of dread in my gut all the time, even here in Eternity Springs where the crime rate is next to nothing. I don't want to live this way, Zach."

"Then you shouldn't."

"That's what my counselor said, but this is my career. I wanted to be a cop, and the bottom line is that I can't cut it. That makes me feel lousy."

"That's bull," Zach fired back. "The bottom line is that you did your job when it counted most."

"But that's before the little ball of dread. I can't be counted on to be there the next time. I don't trust myself."

Zach let out a snort of derision. He'd taken a life in the line of duty before, so he could relate to what she was feeling, but he also knew his sister. He stepped back and held her upper arms, waiting until she met his gaze to say, "Well, that's just silly. I understand leaving if you're not happy. That's no way to go through life. But don't do it because you don't believe in yourself, Gabi. There's not a doubt in my mind that you wouldn't perform under fire or in any sort of emergency. Frankly, if I had any doubt at all, I wouldn't have put you back on the job."

She let out a long sigh. "I wish I could be as certain. But even if I were, I don't think I'd want to stay. Something has changed in me since the shooting, Zach. It makes me sad, but the uniform doesn't suit me."

"Tell that to all the male tourists who get whiplash watching you stroll around town."

"I said it didn't suit me, not that it didn't look good on me." She sniffed pridefully, then grinned for an instant before becoming serious once more. "I feel like I'm at a crossroads. It's time for me to turn in a different direction."

A thought occurred to Zach, and his heart gave a little lurch. "Will you stay in Eternity Springs?"

"Definitely. I'm going to ask Mom if I can work with her at the B&B. She's going to need help whether she'll admit it or not."

"True." Zach wondered, though, if having Gabi as Maggie's helper was a good idea. He'd never forget the argument they'd had over how to scramble eggs when he was convalescing. Those were two hardheaded women.

"So, you and I are okay? You don't think I'm a coward?"

Zach grinned. "You and I are just fine, and I think it takes an exceedingly brave person to want to work with our mother."

Ruefully, Gabi shrugged. "Maybe I'm just crazy."

"Maybe."

They discussed resignation-related procedures for a few minutes, then Gabi departed. Watching her go, Zach experienced a vague sense of unease. He knew the woman well as a deputy and a friend. He knew her less well as a sister. Was the idea of working with their mother a good thing for Gabi and Maggie, or a bad thing for them both? Adult children working with parents faced a peculiar set of challenges. For that matter, parents working with adult children did, too. And Maggie was still trying to figure out widowhood.

Yikes. Maybe he should try to talk to them, caution them. Better yet, get Savannah to do it. She was tight with both Gabi and Maggie.

No, he'd better stay out of it. When did an attempt to mediate with two women ever work out for a man?

Nevertheless, in the wake of Gabi's announcement, he felt the need to share his concern with someone who had a better grasp on the effect of this development on his newfound family. Since this was still his day off, he figured he could multitask.

Twenty minutes later, he pulled his pickup into the drive at the house that would be his mother's bed and breakfast and called to the man on a ladder scraping paint from the north-facing wall. "Hey, Lucca. Want to go fishing?"

Lucca descended the ladder and rolled his shoulders to ease the stiffness in his muscles. He stuck his paint scraper into the back pocket of his jeans and met his brother halfway to his truck. "I guess today is your day off?"

"Yes. And it's all about me. Savannah went with Maggie to Denver. Thought I'd go fishing above Heartache Falls. Why don't you come with me?"

Lucca looked at the partially completed job. "I hate scraping paint."

"I have extra gear in my truck. We can be there in half an hour."

Lucca's smile was wry. "I'd love to, but I told Mom I'd finish paint prep while she's gone. She wouldn't be happy with me if she came home and found the job half done."

Zach's eyes gleamed with wicked amusement. "I can help you out with that. I have that "favorite kid" thing going on right now. I'll tell her I begged you to come with me and she'll be delighted."

"You have a point there." Lucca looked from his brother to the house and back to his brother again. "Let me lock up."

The road Zach took up beyond Heartache Falls was

little more than a tire-rutted path. The scenery was a feast for the eyes with snowcapped mountains, wildflower-dotted meadows, and a heavenly blue sky. The first part of the drive passed in comfortable silence between the brothers, but as they climbed up toward the timberline, Lucca picked up on the fact that Zach had something on his mind.

He braced himself, expecting some sort of probe about his emotional well-being. Instead, Zach surprised him. "Gabi resigned from the sheriff's department today."

"What?" That came right out of the blue. "I thought she really liked her job."

"She gave me her two weeks'. She says she's going to help run the B&B."

"What?" Lucca's mouth gaped. Gabi work with Mom? That was borderline lunacy. "But it won't be ready to open for months."

"I know. She says she doesn't want to carry a gun anymore." Zach summarized the conversation he'd had with Gabi that morning, then added, "I know how to handle this as her boss. I don't know how to deal with her as a brother. Any advice?"

Lucca rubbed the back of his neck. "I'm not sure I have any to give you. As often as not, the women in our family confound me."

"As often as not, *women* confound me, period."

"I hear you, brother." Lucca gave him a sidelong look. "Trouble in paradise?"

"With Savannah?" Zach gave a slow, satisfied grin. "No. None at all. But that doesn't mean I always understand her. This is the first time I've ever lived with a woman. I had no sisters growing up and my mother wasn't much on drama. Me and Savannah, we have some issues, we have drama."

"Leaving law enforcement will mean lots of drama with Gabi."

"That's what I thought. What about Maggie? How will she take it?"

Every time Lucca heard Zach refer to their mother as Maggie, he felt a little sad for her. He respected the fact that Zach still considered his adoptive mother his mom, but he knew Maggie Romano well enough to know that part of her craved to hear Zach refer to her using that term. "Honestly, I'm not sure. Mom has changed since Dad died. In some ways she seems stronger to me, but in others . . . I don't know. I still sense a fragility inside her." He paused a moment, then added, "A lot has happened to the Romanos in the past couple of years. Now we're a bunch of head cases."

Zach gave him a peculiar look and Lucca winced. "That didn't sound right. I don't mean you, Zach. You've been the best thing that's happened to our family since we lost Dad."

Zach opened his mouth but obviously had second thoughts about what he'd been about to say. Lucca arched a questioning brow and Zach shrugged. "Tell me about him."

"Dad?"

"Yes. Since I never got to meet him, I'm curious. What was he like?"

"Well, as you've probably guessed because he passed the trait along to the rest of us, he was tall and athletic. He was the son of Italian immigrants. Came from a large Catholic family. Between Mom's family and his we have so many cousins I've lost count."

"I've heard those types of details. I'm curious what he was like as a father."

"He was a great dad. We all looked up to him. He was smart as a whip and very charismatic. He could have sold a snowball to an Eskimo. Everybody loved him."

"Sounds like Gabi."

Lucca nodded. "I always thought she was more like Dad than any of his sons are. He treated her differently, not only because she was the only girl, but because I think he saw himself in her. Not that he let her get away with stuff. He was strict with all of us, but he left the disciplining up to Mom. He was the threat she used to keep us in line. 'Don't make me tell your father.' We didn't want that, either, believe me. The very worst thing in the world was disappointing Marcello Romano."

"So you were all a bunch of angels?" Zach asked.

"Not hardly." Lucca grinned at the idea. "Max, Tony, and I got into our share of trouble, but Dad's 'boys will be boys' category was pretty big. He didn't give us grief about sneaking out of the house or underage drinking or sleeping around—as long as we got out of the house and back into it without Mom finding out, didn't mix drinking and driving, and swore we wore condoms."

"Did he have that same attitude where Gabi was concerned?"

"Oh, no. Dad was old-fashioned. Mom was a stay-at-home mom, and Dad wouldn't have had it any other way. If Gabi hadn't earned a basketball scholarship, I'm not sure he'd have sent her to college—unless it was nursing school or beauty school."

"What did he think about her becoming a cop?"

Lucca smiled at the memory. "It was World War Three. Mom stood up for Gabi, though, so he couldn't do much more than grumble and bluster. Mom didn't take positions against him often, and when she did, she usually got her way."

"I know that feeling," Zach said. "Savannah is like that. Most of the time, she's pretty easygoing, but when something really matters to her, she's implacable. There is no changing her mind."

"Speaking of implacable women, what can you tell me about my next-door neighbor?"

Zach glanced his way. "I assume you don't mean Mrs. Winsted?"

"Is her first name Hope?"

"Catherine."

Mrs. Winsted must be the elderly woman who lived in the house to his south. "I'm talking about the redhead with the dog and the big Bambi eyes."

"Ah, Hope Montgomery. I didn't know she had a dog."

"An annoying, yappy little terrier mix. With puppies."

Chuckling, Zach asked, "You don't like little dogs, Lucca?"

"I don't like dogs, period," Lucca fired back.

Zach looked taken aback by that. "Really? I'm surprised. Gabi has told me about the antics of the Labradors you and Tony got for one of your birthdays. I thought you were a dog lover, too."

Lucca had never told anyone about the puppy that Seth Seidel had brought onto the Ravens' team bus or the part it had played in the accident. "No, not particularly. Back to Hope . . . Montgomery, was it? She's always coming and going from her house. What does she do for a living?"

"Easier question might be what she doesn't do. I heard Celeste say just last week that from now on when she's going to use the cliché 'busy as a beaver' she'll say instead 'busy as Hope Montgomery.' She teaches at our school. Kindergarten and high school English, I think. Or maybe math. This summer she's been working at the tourist office, conducting tours for the historical society, helping out up at the Davenports' camp, and once a week she leads an alpine mountain bike tour. I think she's become fairly good friends with Maggie and Gabi, actually. So, are you interested?"

"If she's friends with Mom and Gabi, not anymore."

Zach smirked. "That's probably smart. You'd be letting yourself in for all kinds of interference."

"I already have more than my share of that." Then, feeling the need to change the subject, he asked, "So, I understand you're an avid fisherman. Want to hear about the barracuda I caught off Cozumel?"

Talk turned to fish stories until they arrived at Zach's destination where they set about turning talk into action. When he caught his first trout forty minutes later, Lucca realized he was enjoying the morning more than any in recent memory.

He had always loved being outdoors. Spending so much of his time in a gym had given him a real appreciation of fresh air and blue sky. Fishing for trout in a burbling mountain stream on a sunny day was about as good as it got. He was glad he had accepted Zach's invitation.

But just as he drew back his rod to send the line sailing, a trio of ugly truths slithered through his brain. *Seth Seidel doesn't get to go trout fishing. Alan Palmer doesn't get to enjoy a summer afternoon. Brandon Gates might, but he does it from a wheelchair.*

In that moment, his enjoyment of the day evaporated like mist. He set down his fly rod, shoved his hands into his pockets, and walked away from the creek headed toward the road, trying to outpace his demons. He walked downhill—for how long he couldn't say. He was lost in his thoughts and the misery of his memories.

Eventually, Zach's truck pulled up beside him and the passenger side window rolled down. "Want a lift?" Zach asked.

Shaken from his reverie, Lucca hesitated. "Hey man, I'm sorry. I just . . . I needed to walk."

"No problem. Let it go, Lucca. The whole purpose of

coming up here was to do what we felt like doing. Hell, sometimes I'll come up here to go fishing, and I never touch a fly to water."

Lucca nodded, grateful for the unstated understanding, and climbed into the truck. "Thanks for bringing me along, Zach. It's a peaceful place."

"Lots of places around Eternity Springs are peaceful. You'll be surprised what you'll find and where you'll find it. All you have to do is open your eyes to the possibilities."

Hope was physically tired and emotionally exhausted when she arrived home following the end of a session up at the Davenports' summer camp, the Rocking L Ranch. While volunteering in the craft studio the past week, she'd befriended a little girl from Louisiana whose personal story about losing both her mother and brother to cancer had ripped Hope's heart out.

She wanted to soak in a hot bathtub, read a book, sip a glass of wine, and unwind. Unfortunately, she discovered that her water heater had picked that day to go out, so she not only had to spend an extra half hour on the phone making arrangements to have it replaced, but the bath she'd looked forward to wasn't going to happen.

Instead, after tending to the puppies, she pulled on a sweater, poured her wine, and stepped out into the backyard, Roxy at her side. The temperature had dropped with the setting of the sun, making it the chilliest evening in recent weeks and heralding the advent of autumn, which was just around the corner.

Hope took a seat on the lounge chair that sat next to the fountain she'd installed earlier that summer, and Roxy hopped up into her lap. Hope stroked the dog's coat and smiled. She loved the sound of flowing water, and since she couldn't afford a home on Angel Creek, she'd decided this was the next best thing. Against the backdrop of a burbling fountain, she gazed up at the star-filled night sky, drew a deep breath, then exhaled the stress of the day. Picking out the Big Dipper, she thought about her daughter. Was Holly out there somewhere looking up at the same stars, too? She'd like to think so.

Roxy lifted her head from Hope's lap and let out a low-throated growl. "Well, now," Hope chided. "What's that for?"

A voice floated from out of the darkness. "I trust you'll keep hold of old scissor-teeth there. I'm not in the mood to nurse another dog bite."

Startled, Hope stared in the direction of Lucca Romano's voice and after a moment, made out the shadowed figured of the man lying on the ground. "Are you drunk, Mr. Romano?"

"Why would you ask me that?"

Because she'd heard through the grapevine that he'd taken to spending most evenings at Murphy's Pub. "You are lying on the ground in the dark. Seems to me like something a drunk would do."

"You and your dog are a lot alike, aren't you? You're both suspicious and mean."

"Roxy isn't mean; she's sweet. She was protecting her babies when she bit you. And I'm not mean, either." Suspicious, however, was another thing entirely. What was the man doing out here in the dark?

"Sure you are. You haven't even asked if I'm okay. What if I tripped on something and fell and broke my leg and I can't get up?"

"Is that what happened?"

"No."

"Then I'm not mean for ignoring your broken leg, am I?"

"That's a technicality. You still shouldn't have thrown drunkenness as your first pitch."

Hope sipped her wine and considered it. "All right. I concede the point. So what are you really doing lying in your backyard in the dark?"

"Stargazing. It's a hobby of mine. I took astronomy in college because it was supposed to be an easy A class. It wasn't easy, though. I worked hard for my A. Never expected to fall in love with the night sky, but I did."

Now she was intrigued. "I can find the Big and Little Dipper, but beyond that, I've never been able to pick out the constellations. My mind doesn't see the lines between them."

After a moment's hesitation, he asked, "Do you have a good grip on that dog?"

"She's not going to hurt you," Hope replied, rolling her eyes.

She heard a rustling and watched the shadow rise. He strode into her backyard, his features still hidden on this moonless night. "There's too much light here. Why don't you take the mutt inside and turn off your house lights. I'll show you the stars."

Hope's pulse sped up. Her sense of self-preservation told her to take Roxy inside and stay there. Maybe it was her fatigue or the wine or the fact that she hadn't enjoyed any male companionship in longer than she cared to remember, but she didn't want to listen to any voices of reason whispering inside her. Without responding, she rolled to her feet, deposited Roxie with her pups, switched off the lights, and returned to the backyard.

Lucca had pulled a second lounge chair beside the one she'd been sitting in and he'd lowered the headrests of both chairs flat. He lay on one of the chairs, his head pillowed in his hands. Hope hesitated, then stretched out beside him.

"It's a good night for stargazing," he said. "Cloudless sky, and since we're on the edge of town, limited ambient light."

"I have binoculars in the house."

"Don't need them. Constellations and large comets and meteors are best observed with unaided vision. If you develop your skills this way you'll have better success once you move on to binoculars and telescopes. Tonight, I'll be your star chart. Let your gaze wander around the sky and choose something you are curious about."

"I want to see a constellation. Really see it."

"Any one in particular?"

"No."

"Well, then, since you already said you can find the Big Dipper, why don't we start with the Great Bear."

"Ursa Major," she said.

"That's right. You already know it?"

"Only the little I picked up from shows on PBS."

"How scientific do you want me to be?"

He was close enough that she could feel the warmth of his body. She wished she could see his eyes—see his expression. She felt a tension in the air that she couldn't quite interpret without reading him visually. "What do you mean by 'scientific'?"

"Reality or mythology?"

"Honestly, I like the mythology best."

"All right, then. Find the Big Dipper."

"Got it."

"The handle of the dipper is the Great Bear's tail. The dipper's cup is the bear's flank. Now, Ursa Major is a large constellation, so keep your field of vision wide. You're looking for the bear's head now."

He removed his hands from behind his head and pointed toward the sky. "The bright star at the top of the Big Dipper's bowl is Dubhe. If it's the center of a clock, you're going to draw a line at about one o'clock to the next brightest star. That's part of the bear's head. Got it?"

"It's too dark to see where you are pointing."

He rolled over onto his side facing her and took hold of her right hand with his. Lacing their fingers, he extended their arms toward the night sky. "Put your index finger against mine."

His hand was so big. His skin so warm. He leaned forward until their faces almost touched. Hope's pulse began to race. His voice was low and gravelly against her ear as he moved her hand. "Big Dipper. Dubhe. One o'clock. Bright star. You with me?"

Breathlessly, she murmured, "Yes."

"We take that line this way to the next brightest star. That's the tip of the old guy's snout. See it?"

"I do." Hope fought the instinct to snuggle against the heat of him.

"Now we're going to come back and down toward the bottom star in the Big Dipper's bowl, but first, we stop here. Got to give the old guy his front legs."

Hope's attention wandered. He must have showered shortly before he went outside because the scent of the sandalwood soap his sister-in-law sold in her shop clung to his skin. She'd managed not to snuggle, but she couldn't help but lean forward and sniff.

"We are about halfway between the snout and the lower star in the bowl of the dipper. Okay?" She nodded, and he continued, "Take your line down curving here to what looks like a double star, his knee joint."

"Are they called knees in bears?"

Lucca seemed to bury his nose in her hair, and goose bumps skimmed up her neck. In a low, intimate voice, he asked, "What else would you call them?"

She couldn't think of anything, and she forced her attention back to the night sky. "Is the star down from there at five o'clock the foot?"

"Very good."

She felt his breath on her neck. She shuddered and

closed her eyes, and yearned. If she turned her face toward him, would he kiss her? It had been so long and she'd been so alone. What would it hurt? Just to feel connected with someone for a short time would be so . . . welcome. "Lucca, I . . ."

He stilled for a beat, then subtly moved away without releasing her hand. Rather than intimate, his tone now sounded instructive. "Now, see if you can find the bear's hind legs. Start from the bottom of the Big Dipper."

It took Hope a moment to drag her attention back to the sky, and upon doing so, she discovered she really didn't care about the bear's hind legs. She also couldn't see the stars very well because her vision had blurred.

Watery eyes from the chill in the air, she told herself. Not tears. Tears would be stupid. He was her grumpy next-door neighbor with whom she had nothing in common except an affinity for his mother and sister and an appreciation for starry nights.

How pathetic. Really, a little male kindness and she's suddenly desperate enough, lonely enough, to melt all over the lawn. *Where's your pride?*

She picked out a star and with a hand that slightly trembled, drew a line.

"Nope," Lucca said. "The line goes to one star here"—he moved her hand—"then it branches. Here and here and that's it. The Great Bear, Ursa Major."

He released her hand and moved back onto his own lounger. "So, can you find it now?"

Hope stared up into the heavens. She found the Big Dipper, then retraced the paths he'd pointed out moments before, and a slow smile spread over her face. "I can. I see it."

And really, now that she thought about it, wasn't this gift better than something as fleeting as a kiss? "You explained it very well. You are a good teacher. Thank you, Lucca."

He didn't respond, and Hope wondered if she'd inadvertently wandered back into the same no-man's-land that she had landed in when she'd called him "Coach." The moment stretched, and the silence grew awkward and uncomfortable. She was still searching for something to say to interrupt the quiet when he finally spoke.

"You know, I liked it. Teaching, I mean. I never taught academic subjects, but I always believed that sports offer students valuable lessons that they'll use the rest of their lives. It's so much more than winning and losing."

"I agree with that. Knowing how to work as part of a team is invaluable."

"True. Sports teach the value of discipline, of sacrifice. They teach the value of goal setting and how to deal with failure. Sure, the so-called money sports have that entertainment factor as part of the package, but really, what's wrong with that? Some people like to be entertained by reading a novel. Others prefer to watch professional baseball. To each his own, I say."

Hope's mouth gaped slightly. Why, who knew Lucca Romano had that many words in him? Positive words at that?

"I've never believed that sports figures should be considered heroes—that term should be reserved for people like my brother Zach, who has put his life on the line for others more than once—but then I don't think that about Hollywood stars or politicians or other people our society decides are celebrities, either. But these star athletes, they started out just like everybody else in Pee Wee football or on school teams. People aren't born knowing how to throw a ninety-two-mile-an-hour fastball or hit a twenty-foot jumper. They learn it through hard work and practice and paying attention to what coaches are trying to teach them. That's something a kid at home who watches and dreams can pick up on and learn from."

This had the tone of being an old argument. Hope wondered where his defensiveness came from. "I agree with that, too," she told him, honestly. "I think sports teach a lot of good life lessons."

Her comment seemed to stop him. After another long moment of silence, he said quietly, "And, some not-so-good life lessons, too."

With that, he swung his legs off the lounge chair and stood. "I need to go. Sorry about the soapbox."

It happened so fast that he was halfway to his house before Hope found her voice. "Lucca? Thanks for teaching me the stars."

"No problem."

She heard his footsteps on his back porch and the creak of the screen door. Then, out of the darkness, he said, "The easy A factor wasn't the only reason why I took that college astronomy class. Back in middle school, I had a teacher who taught a unit on Native American folklore, and many of the stories she taught were based on the constellations. I never forgot them. The tale about Ursa Major is about hunters who chased the Great Bear into the sky and wounded him. In the autumn, the bear's blood spills from the stars onto the earth, turning the trees red."

"Well, that's a gruesome picture."

"Lots of those tales were violent. I loved them. The point I want to make is . . . well . . . teachers can be heroes, too."

"I'm a teacher."

"I know that. Good night, Ms. Montgomery."

The shadows were so deep that she couldn't see his expression. Why, then, did she picture a smile on his face? The screen door banged shut. Inside her house, Roxie let out a *yip yip yip*.

Hope looked up at the starry sky and smiled.

FIVE

"Lasagna," Lucca said, accepting the pan from his sister and pasting a smile on his face while his stomach sank with dread. Gabi had to be the world's worst cook. "My favorite."

"I hope you like it. I know Mom's recipe is hard to beat, but I thought I'd try something a little different."

Oh, joy. In the two weeks since he'd arrived in Eternity Springs, he'd endured a number of his sister's culinary experiments. Why was it that such a smart woman couldn't manage to follow a recipe? "Great. Do you want to come in?"

"I just have a few minutes," she said, stepping into the house and following him back toward his kitchen. "Zach hired a replacement for me and he starts the job tonight. I'll be working the evening shift with him, showing him the ropes. I had just enough time to run this by and, well, I wanted to ask you a question."

Lucca set the pan of lasagna on the counter and tried to recall if he'd done something worth getting an ass-chewing over since he'd last seen his sister. He didn't think so. Warily, he asked, "About what?"

"Mom. You've been working at the house for over a week now. How do you like it?"

The house? Lucca knew his sister well enough to understand that she wasn't truly asking about his experience. "Are you having second thoughts about leaving your job?"

"No. Not really. I know leaving is the right decision. It's the 'where I go next' that's making me insecure."

Lucca didn't like the uncertain look on his sister's face, so he snorted. "Oh, come on, Gabi. You are the most confident woman I've ever known. You don't have an insecure atom in your body. What is this really about?"

She offered him a tender smile. "You can be a sweetheart when you want, Lucca Romano. Now, give me the scoop. What is it like at Aspenglow Place?"

Lucca opened the oven door and slid the pan of lasagna inside. He set the temperature at two hundred degrees. "I have the siding scraped and sanded and ready to prime."

"I mean being with Mom all day."

"I'm not with her all day, Gabs. I'm working outside and she's usually indoors. But having her boss me around isn't really anything different than what's she's been doing all my life."

Glumly, Gabi asked, "So she still treats you like you're ten years old? And I'm thinking about working with her full-time? Great. Just great."

"Honey." Lucca folded his arms. "If you're having this much doubt and you haven't even spent a day with Mom, I think you should take a long, hard look at what you are doing."

"You are supposed to make me feel better."

"Darlin', that is not my job."

"Sure it is. You've been doing that all our lives. You've always been my go-to brother when I needed to feel better."

"Well, babycakes, times have changed. I have my hands full on that front as it is."

Gabi cocked her head and studied him. "How is that going? Is Eternity Springs working its magic on you?"

Lucca aimed a deliberate look toward the wall clock. "Don't you need to get to work?"

"Seriously, Lucca. How are you doing?"

"I hear your boss is a hard-ass. You'd better get going."

"It's one little question. Answer it." He didn't respond, and after a moment, Gabi said, "Well, I think it's a good sign that you haven't ended up in the sheriff's office drunk tank again."

"Eternity Springs has a drunk tank?"

"Not really, no. But people do gossip. I wish you'd talk to me, brother."

He scowled at her. "Nice weather we're having."

"I see you obviously haven't been here long enough."

"Good-bye, Gabriella."

She flashed a grin, then walked over to press a kiss to his cheek. "Good-bye, Lucca. I love you, Lucca. Enjoy your lasagna, Lucca."

He reflected on her question as he sat at his kitchen table a few minutes later and cautiously speared a bite of her lasagna with his fork. Was he glad he'd come to Colorado?

His thoughts drifted back to the previous evening and the time spent with the sexy schoolteacher. He had enjoyed her company. Hell, he'd come close to enjoying it too much. A couple of times there he'd been a breath away from kissing her.

Something about her stoked him. It wasn't only her looks, though that glorious hair and curvy ass absolutely did do it for him. But she had this, well, glow about her that drew him. She was light and bright and that appealed to him. He was tired of being dark.

Kissing her, however, would have been a colossal mistake. He had a tough enough job as it was keeping a healthy balance of family involvement in his everyday life; no way did he want them involved in his love life.

"Not that I have a love life," he grumbled and stuck the bite of pasta into his mouth. The moment the food hit his taste buds, he grimaced. Way too much salt. How could she screw up lasagna so badly? *If she does end up working at the B&B, Mom better keep her far, far away from the kitchen.*

With a silent apology to his sister, he dumped the lasagna in the garbage and made a ham sandwich. He sat down in front of the television to watch the Rockies game, but by the fourth inning, the walls were closing in. He could head over to Murphy's Pub, order a beer, and sit out on the patio for a while. He would limit himself to one beer, maybe two. He wouldn't stay until closing time. Just long enough so that he could come back and fall asleep without feeling claustrophobic.

But instead of grabbing his wallet and heading for Murphy's, he opened a bottle of Cabernet. Next he grabbed two wineglasses from the cabinet, exited his back door, and walked across his backyard to Hope's where he stretched out in the same lounge chair he'd occupied the night before. He poured a glass and waited, his face tilted toward the sky.

Ten minutes later, Hope opened her back door. "Lucca, is that you?"

"You expecting somebody else?"

"I'm not expecting anyone. I thought an animal had gotten into the yard. Roxy has been pawing at the back door and barking."

He started to make a comment about his own animalistic desires, but thought better of it. "Come on out, Hope. It's another beautiful evening and I want to show you Cassiopeia."

She joined him and they passed another enjoyable two hours talking about stars and kindergarten and autumn activities in Eternity Springs. As he poured her a third glass of wine—her last, she insisted—she asked, "What's it like to be an identical twin?"

He considered it, then took the question to the stars. "Gemini, the Twins. The best time to see that constellation is in December. To see it now, we'd have to look for it shortly before dawn. Gemini has always been my favorite, and I'll never forget the first time we found it, Tony and I. We were ten, I think. Maybe eleven. We snuck out of the house in December and climbed onto the roof at the high school. We had our star charts and a flashlight pointer. When we knew we'd found it, we looked at each other and that connection between us got a little stronger. After we researched all the different myths, Tony and I argued for weeks about which of us was which. In Babylonian astronomy, the main stars were known as the Great Twins and regarded as minor gods."

"I'll bet you just loved that."

"Oh, yeah." He grinned at the memory. "It was the Greek mythology that brought us to blows, though."

"Why is that?"

"The Greeks made one twin a god, and the other a mortal. Castor and Pollux were the children of Leda and they were Argonauts. But Pollux was the son of the god Zeus and Castor was the son of the king of Sparta, a mortal. Of course, Tony and I both wanted to be Pollux. We ended up compromising by switching who got to be who every other month."

"So did Pollux have the better role in the mythology?"

"Not really. Both brothers were Argonauts and they were two parts of a whole so when Castor died, Pollux begged his father, Zeus, to give Castor immortality, and he did, by uniting them together in the heavens."

"Are you and Tony two parts of a whole?"

Lucca considered the question, picturing his brother

the last time he'd seen him. Lucca had been sleeping off a wild night in a Caribbean beach cabana when Tony tracked him down. It was the first time in a long time he'd seen the same disgust on his brother's face that he'd seen on his own when he looked into the mirror. "At times in our lives, yes. Other times, not so much. These days, we are in one of those not-so-much cycles."

"Why is that?"

He went silent, not at all willing to answer her question. "Let's change the subject. When do you start school?"

When she didn't respond right away, he thought she might press the issue. He didn't relax until she said, "I start Wednesday. The first day for students is next Tuesday."

"And you said you teach something in addition to kindergarten?"

"Last year I taught history, but I'm changing classes this year. With a small school like ours, most teachers wear a lot of different hats. Our phys ed teacher resigned yesterday, so I'll be taking on that job. I'll be recruiting coaches for our school teams. Want to help?"

"No," he said flatly, firmly, hoping she wouldn't press him, because if she did he'd get up and leave, and he wasn't ready to leave yet.

Luckily, she let it go. "My principal called this morning and asked me to make the change, so the timing of our conversation last night was perfect. I might have made a push to keep my history classes, but what you said about the influence that sports can have on a student's life made a real impression on me. I'm looking forward to the challenge."

Her scent distracted him. Some of his sister-in-law's soap, he decided. The almond-vanilla scent Savannah called Autumn Rain. "I bet you are good at tackling challenges."

Now it was her turn to hesitate before responding.

"Not always. Some challenges have knocked me on my rear. Others, I'm managing, but just barely."

"Tell me about one of them."

"I'm divorced. My ex contacts me every so often out of the blue, and that unfailingly threatens to throw me into a tailspin."

"How does he contact you? Phone? Email?"

"Both. It varies."

"Why don't you block him?"

"I can't. The why is a long story I'm not prepared to tell tonight. Now it's my turn to ask that we change the subject. So, what did you do today?"

Lucca was intrigued. He wanted to press her, but since she'd respected his wishes, he could do no less for her. "More paint prep. Found a few boards that needed to be replaced, so I had to make a run to the lumberyard. Since that's just down the street from the bakery, I stopped in for a cinnamon roll. Those things are sinful. Anyway, I walked into the middle of a sitcom. The owner was in labor and her husband was tearing the place up looking for car keys. Then there was this weird-looking dog running around with some sort of half-chewed hose in his mouth and two college-age kids shouting at each other because somebody'd dropped a cellphone and broken the screen."

Hope laughed. "The dog's name is Mortimer, but Cam usually calls him the Terminator. He's a Boston terrier. And yes, the Murphys are having their baby. Celeste called me a little while ago to tell me they've gone to the hospital. Finally. Sarah's more than a week overdue."

"Cam Murphy. He's a friend of Zach's, isn't he? Runs the sporting goods store."

"Yes." Hope gave him a brief background of the Murphy family, and finished by saying, "They are very nice people. It's such an exciting time for them."

He started to ask her if she had any children, but since

she'd put the brakes on any discussion about her ex, he figured he was better off staying away from that subject. "I never did get my cinnamon roll."

"Your arteries thank you. Now, I'd better go inside. I have an early meeting at school tomorrow morning that I need to prepare for. Feel free to stay and watch the sky for as long as you want. Thanks for the lesson and the wine."

"You're welcome." He waited until she'd almost reached her back door, a question hovering on his tongue. Did he really want to do this? He couldn't forget that she was friends with his mother and sister. Did he really want to get any more involved with her and potentially complicate his life that way? His life was already complicated. Why add the redhead to the mix?

Because she intrigues you?

Hell. His indecision decided it for him. He said simply, "Good night."

He remained in her backyard, on her lounge chair, staring up at the crystal-clear sky for another twenty minutes. When he spied the streak of a falling star, he thought about today's date. Mid-August. It was a beautiful night, perfect conditions.

Rising, he picked up the wine bottle and empty glasses and made his way home, where he set his alarm and crawled into bed. Some things in life a man simply shouldn't miss.

When he awoke to the *brrrr* of his alarm at three thirty-five A.M., he rolled out of bed and spoke into the darkness. "Or, a woman, either."

In her bedroom, Hope lay dreaming.

I sit in the wooden rocking chair nursing three-month-old Holly, and I'm overwhelmed by pure, unadulterated love. The baby makes cooing sounds as her little fist

*beats against my bare breast. Softly, I sing, "You are my
sunshine, my only sunshine."*

I glance up as Mark sweeps into the kitchen still tying
his tie. He's wearing the blue one that his mother gave
him for Christmas, and he looks so handsome that my
heart, already warm and tender with love as I nourish
our child, melts. Remembering the wildness of his lovemaking the night before, I smile almost shyly. "Good
morning."

He offers me a distracted smile. "Have you seen the
thumb drive I left on our dresser?"

"You put a silver one in your briefcase last night before you came to bed."

"Oh. That's right. Do I smell bacon?"

"Holly's been awake awhile. I thought you might like
a big breakfast for a change. Your plate is keeping warm
in the oven."

"I have a breakfast meeting. You should have asked
me before cooking, Hope."

He approaches me and reaches down for Holly. The
baby is clamped down hard on my nipple and when
Mark yanks her away, I gasp in physical and emotional
pain. Holly cries and I rise from my rocker, reaching for
my baby, but Mark places Holly into his briefcase and
walks briskly toward the door.

"Mark. No. Don't. My baby! Bring me back my
baby."

"You lost her. You made breakfast. You made a stupid
decision. You gave her away. You lost her. You lost her."
The door slams shut. A woman cackles with laughter.
"She's mine now. All mine."

"No!" Quicksand sucks at my feet as I fight my way
to the kitchen door. It won't open. I pound on the window. Pound. Pound. Glass rattles. "No! Holly! Bring
her back! Holly!"

Pound. Glass rattles. A dog barks.

Her heart racing, breaking, Hope opened her eyes to darkness, blinked twice, and realized she'd been lost in a dream. A nightmare.

Pound. Pound. Pound. Rattle. Roxy barked. What in the world?

Her window. Someone was knocking on her window. Fear washed through her, and for a moment, she sat frozen. What should she do?

Call 911. But as she reached for the telephone beside her bed, she heard the voice. "Wake up. Hey, Hope. Wake up!"

Her thoughts came a mile a minute. Zach? Maybe her house was on fire! She grabbed the robe lying at the foot of her bed even as another possibility occurred to her: Lucca. She glanced toward her alarm clock. Red numerals glowed three forty-eight.

Pound. Pound. Rattle. "Hope!"

Not Zach. Lucca. At three forty-eight. *He must be drunk.*

She moved to the window and wrenched it open. "What in the world are you doing?"

"Finally. You sleep like the dead, woman. Hurry, get dressed. Something warm. I'll be outside."

"Um, no. I'll be in my bed under my covers. Go away, Romano."

"The next few hours will be the best of the year to see the Perseids. The waxing crescent moon has set. We have dark, clear skies. I know there is a spot up on Sinner's Prayer Pass that's perfect for viewing. I wouldn't want to drive that road in bad weather, but tonight it's fine. Come with me, Hope."

Perseids. "A meteor shower."

"Yes."

Her gaze trailed back to her clock. She had an early meeting at school and she didn't function well on too little sleep. She could tell him no—and go back to her bed and to her nightmares. "Give me five minutes."

Hope dressed in jeans and a sweatshirt and hiking boots, then grabbed a jacket on her way out of the door. Excitement hummed in her blood, and she told herself that it was the prospect of seeing a meteor shower that thrilled her rather than the man.

He had the truck running with the heater on and a steaming cup of coffee waiting for her in the cup holder. "Bless you," she said, taking a sip. "You make good coffee."

"It's from K-Cups. I'm almost as helpless with a regular coffeepot as Gabi is with a frying pan."

They made the trip up to Sinner's Prayer Pass in companionable silence. He pulled off the road at a scenic overlook, then grabbed a quilt and a duffel from the backseat of the extended cab. "It's a five-minute hike to our spot. We want to be away from the road so that our night vision won't be compromised by any oncoming headlights."

"I don't imagine there will be many cars on this road at this time of the morning," she observed, trailing after him. "Can I help you carry anything?"

"Grab our coffee cups. I have a thermos in my bag." He pulled out a flashlight equipped with a red filter. "Stay close to me and watch your step."

After a short hike, they reached the observation spot he had chosen. Lucca spread the quilt on the ground, then said, "After you, Ms. Montgomery."

"Which direction do I look?"

"Doesn't matter. The Perseids radiate from a point in the constellation Perseus, the Hero, but you don't need to watch it because the meteors appear in all parts of the sky. Just fill your field of vision with the stars and sky and you'll see them."

"I'm excited," she said, as she lay on her back and pillowed her head in her hands. "What time are they supposed to . . . oh! I see one."

The bright ball with a vivid train streaked across the sky, and Hope felt a rush of delight. "It's been a long time since I've seen a shooting star."

"Keep watching. The Perseids strengthen in number as the night goes on. It's possible we could see as many as fifty an hour."

"That would be so cool!"

And it was. It was a magical night, like the Fourth of July, only directed by the hand of God. She oohed and aahed and felt silly because of it. She didn't want to blink for fear of missing something spectacular.

Time ticked by while a truly heavenly show burst across the sky. The night air chilled her, and she hugged herself, running her hands up and down her arms. Lucca must have noticed because he sat up and pulled a wool blanket from the duffel. He spread it over them both, and as the growing warmth chased away the chill, Hope gradually became aware of a different sort of warmth rising within her.

She'd never been on a date with a man as hot as Lucca Romano. Not that this was a date. But it was a . . . well . . . she didn't know what to call it, but whatever it was, lying on a quilt beneath a shooting-star sky with him created an air of intimacy and anticipation. On her side, anyway. Lucca showed no signs of reciprocation. He might as well have been lying next to Roxy as to her. And he never touched her dog if he could avoid it.

For a man who played professional basketball, he'd certainly not demonstrated any ability to throw a pass.

He's not interested. So what? Let it go.

The man was a head case, and she had enough of that in her life just dealing with herself. He'd been nice to include her tonight; she needed to leave it at that.

"Still cold?" he asked her.

"A little. I'm glad to have the blanket."

Matter-of-factly, he put his arm around her and tugged her against him. Startled, Hope stiffened for just a moment, then allowed herself to relax against him, absorb his body heat, and wallow in the masculine scent of him.

"Do you know the story of Perseus?" he asked her.

"Actually, I do. Greek mythology intrigued me as a teen. I kinda had a thing for him."

"Like the Greek god type, hmm?"

She almost asked if he was fishing because heaven knows, he qualified. But that would cross the line to flirtatious, and despite the fact that she was lying beside him, she didn't think she should go there. "He saved the princess. Gotta love a man who saves the woman in jeopardy."

"You're not one of those modern women who expects the princess to save herself?"

"I'm all for gender-neutral heroism. But if I'm a princess about to be eaten by a monster and a hot hero offers his sword, I'm not going to turn down his assistance."

"That's reasonable."

Was he aware that his thumb had begun to stroke up and down her arm?

"When we talked about heroes once before, you mentioned your brother Zach. Who else are your heroes? Your father, maybe?"

"My dad was my superhero. Gabi probably occupies that spot for me and the rest of my family now. You know she saved Zach's life last year."

"Yes. She's amazing."

"She is. So is . . . whoa . . . did you see that?"

"I did! I counted six."

"Eight. There were two more at ten o'clock."

"Incredible!"

"Yeah." After a moment of quiet, he picked up the thread of conversation. "I have a friend who is a firefighter. He lost his sight in an explosion. Still managed to save a little kid's life. He's definitely one of my heroes. What about you? Who are your heroes?"

Daniel Garrett came to mind immediately. She never talked about him or shared how important he was to her. Yet, here on this crisp, dark morning as she lay watching the heavens where with no warning, her hopeful anticipation was spectacularly rewarded again and again, it felt proper to mention him. "I have a friend who has quietly devoted his life to helping families who are in the midst of a crisis. Doing so takes him into some dangerous places, and more often than not leads to heartbreak. But he puts himself out there, puts himself through that, because he's . . . well . . . a hero."

"Sounds like a good guy. What sort of crises?"

Hope had skated as close to her own problems as she intended.

"He looks for missing people," she replied, knowing he would interpret that as searching for runaways. Ready to lighten things up, she added, "Then, of course, there is Amanda Reed. She's a real hero of mine."

"Why is she a hero?"

"Bags. She designs the most spectacular handbags."

"Through talking about serious stuff, are you?"

"Pretty much, yes. Lucca, why does that one star seem to twinkle more than the others? It's almost like it's winking at me."

"Scintillation."

"Excuse me?"

He rolled over onto his side and went up on his elbow. Though his form was cloaked in darkness, his gaze upon her was tangible. Hope went still and watchful. Anticipation welled within her.

"Stars appear to twinkle because we see them through the thick layers of moving air that make up the Earth's atmosphere. Their light beams are refracted many times in random directions as they hit different densities of air. That random refraction results in the star appearing to wink out or twinkle. The scientific name is 'stellar scintillation.'"

"I see," Hope breathed.

"Or astronomical scintillation." He lifted his hand and trailed a finger down her cheek.

Hope shivered, but this time, she wasn't cold. "Ah."

He leaned forward, his warm breath whispering across her face. "Irresistible scintillation."

Then, just as the first rays of dawn stretched into the eastern sky, Lucca Romano touched his lips to hers.

SIX

The kiss was just a whisper. Now that he'd finally surrendered to the urge, he wanted to draw the pleasure out. He explored her lips, learning the shape of them, their softness. They were delightfully full and blissfully moist. The taste of her was as fascinating as the stars that had burned across the sky. Fascinating and strangely familiar.

He felt like he had kissed her before, which was crazy. Hope Montgomery wasn't anything like the women he usually pursued. Not a model or beauty queen or, as he'd liked in his younger days, a sorority girl. She was a homespun schoolteacher, and not just a schoolteacher, but a *kindergarten* teacher. The flavor of her mouth—not sophisticated French champagne, but hot chocolate chip cookies fresh from the oven on a cold winter's day—stirred his blood.

And she felt like heaven in his arms.

He stopped thinking then and deepened the kiss, losing himself to sensation. His tongue slid into her soft, wet mouth. His hand trailed over the satin of her cheek, and his fingers threaded through the silk of her hair. At the sound of her throaty moan, Lucca's passion blazed.

He wanted her. He wanted to strip away the barrier of their clothes and feel those full breasts of hers flattened against his bare chest. He wanted to explore her with his hands, to trace the taut stretch of her muscles, the feminine curve of her hip. He wanted to taste her. He wanted to see her. Badly.

Badly enough that he knew he'd better apply the brakes. But, in a minute.

He needed just one more minute. One more endless minute to lose himself in the erotic pleasure of her kiss.

Because now her arms had lifted and twined around his neck, and her fingers played along the sensitive skin just above his collar. She was hot and trembling and when she purred, the sound vibrated through him. *Now, Romano. End it now, before it's too late.*

He lifted his head and eased away, opening his eyes. The hazy light of dawn cast a golden glow across flushed cheeks and lips red and swollen. Her chest lifted and fell in quick pants. When her lids fluttered open and she stared up at him with soft, arousal-drugged eyes, it took all his willpower not to lower his head again.

He fought for something to say and came up with a stupid "Good morning."

"Oh. Wow."

It pleased Lucca to know that he wasn't the only one suffering from stupid. "That's a nice way to begin a day."

"Yes. Yes, it is. Was. Nice. I enjoyed it." Her chest rose, then fell with one big breath. "Not just the kiss. The entire night was special."

With another woman, Lucca would have fired a comeback filled with sexual innuendo, but something about Hope caused him to simply say, "Yes, it was. I'm glad you shared it with me."

And with that, their evening with the Perseids came to an end.

They hiked back to the truck in silence, Lucca lighting their way with the flashlight. On the way down the mountain to Eternity Springs, the mood between them felt awkward. He asked if she had a busy day ahead, which she did and had already told him about. She asked him what paint colors Maggie had chosen for Aspenglow's interior walls. As if he'd paid a bit of attention because he did all his work around the place outdoors.

Lucca sensed that the kiss had changed something. She was pulling back from him. Just as he was pulling back from her.

He pulled his truck into the driveway between their two houses. They both climbed down from the truck and Lucca hesitated. Ordinarily, he'd walk a woman he'd just spent half the night with to her front door. But if he did that since he'd kissed her earlier, he'd have to kiss her again, wouldn't he?

Have to, Romano? What a hardship you're considering there.

Hope glanced at him. "Thanks again for including me, Lucca. The meteor shower was a spectacular show."

What about the kiss? Maybe the fact she hadn't mentioned it meant she wouldn't go inside and call his sister and spill the beans. He'd dated one of Gabi's friends in the past. He knew how all that worked. Once Hope told Gabi that he'd kissed her, he'd be dealing not just with Hope, but with Gabi and Mom, too. Madness. *You need to take a big step back.*

He cleared his throat. "It's a good way to put a period on the summer. I'm headed to Boulder to visit my brother and by the time I get back, school will have started. You'll be busy. I guess stargazing late at night won't work for your schedule. I probably won't see you much."

She offered up a fake smile that made Lucca feel like a heel. "You're right. I have no leisure time once school starts. If I were to try to fit something else into my schedule now, well, I would need to want it badly. I'm afraid stargazing will have to wait until the situation suits my desires. Have a nice trip to Boulder."

Well, then. She'd put him in his place, hadn't she? He shot back a smile just as false as hers. "Thanks. I intend to."

She started toward her house, giving him a backward wave. "Bye. Today is trash pickup. Don't forget to carry your can to the curb."

Lucca stood watching her until she disappeared inside her house. "Carry my can to the curb?" he muttered. "Was that some sort of crack?"

He wasn't certain, and it made him a little grumpy. Everything since the kiss had made him a little grumpy. As he grabbed his duffel and the quilt from the back of the truck and carried them into his house, he muttered, "Sleep deprivation. That's what this is. It's all it is."

He'd take a little nap before heading out to see Tony.

But when he sprawled across his bed and buried his head in his pillow, thoughts of Hope Montgomery drifted across his mind like wispy clouds. Better for them both that they stopped before they ever really got started. He wasn't looking for a relationship. Hell, he wasn't even looking for sex. Go figure. Since that self-destructive stretch during his Latin American sabbatical when he went around nailing anyone who was interested, he'd lost interest in meaningless sex. But he wasn't ready for sex to mean something, either.

Kissing Hope Montgomery had stirred him. Tempted him.

The memory of it plagued him when he tried to fall asleep.

After tossing and turning for twenty minutes, he gave up. He showered, dressed, threw a few things into a bag, and headed for Boulder.

He phoned his brother when he was twenty minutes

out. Tony wasn't through with work for the day. "I have another hour to an hour and a half here, and I didn't have time for lunch. I'm going to want food the minute I'm free. Want to play tourist for a while, then pick me up and we can go to dinner?"

Lucca considered a moment, then said, "Weather is nice. How about I stop at the grocery store for steaks and fire up the grill at your house? I can have it ready when you get home."

"Sounds great. Key is in the usual spot."

When Tony had been an assistant coach in Boulder, he'd lived in an apartment near campus. After he'd won the head-coaching job, he'd bought a house up in the Flagstaff area that had a great backyard and an awesome view.

Lucca stopped at a grocery and purchased everything he would need for supper, knowing the chances that his twin had a stocked refrigerator hovered between slim and none. He arrived at Tony's house, found the house key hidden on a rafter on the back porch, and let himself inside. By the time Tony drove up, Lucca had a salad made, baked potatoes ready, and two huge rib eyes ready for the outdoor kitchen grill.

Tony changed into shorts and a T-shirt and walked out barefoot carrying a bottle of Cabernet. He inhaled the aroma and exhaled with worshipful appreciation. With his gaze locked on the sizzling steaks, he said, "As of this moment, you are officially off the hook for the hundred you owe me."

"I don't owe you a hundred."

"Yeah, you do. American League won the All-Star game."

"Oh." The brothers had a standing baseball bet. "I didn't notice. Think I was taking in the sights on a nude beach in Brazil when that game was played."

"Asshole. I take it back. You still owe me." Tony decanted the wine and poured two glasses.

"Nope. Take-backs not allowed on bet settlements. Sit down and fill your face with rabbit food. Steaks will be ready in five."

Both men were hungry, and they didn't waste much time talking as they plowed through their meal. Afterward, they cleaned up, then Tony dished up two bowls of Rocky Road ice cream—their favorite—and carried them outside. Tony had a great backyard spot to watch the sunset.

Tony opened the conversation with a challenge. "I had hoped you might come by campus," he said. "You haven't seen the new practice facility. I'd like to show you around."

Lucca understood that his twin's offer involved more than a tour of a new basketball headquarters. He hadn't gone near a basketball court since the day of his meltdown, and Tony was asking if Lucca had his head on straight yet. The answer was no. "Maybe next time."

Tony set down his ice cream. "I'm thirsty. You want a bottle of water?"

"I'm good."

His twin snorted as he stood and took a water from his outdoor kitchen fridge. He lifted the remote and switched on the television mounted above the bar area. He thumbed to a basketball game then defiantly sauntered back toward Lucca, who shifted his chair toward the sunset—and away from the TV.

Tony muttered an expletive, then asked, "So, what brings you to Boulder so soon? You've been in Eternity Springs, what, two weeks? Is small-town life proving too boring already?"

"Actually, Eternity Springs isn't too bad. Mom wanted me to go to Denver to pick up some things she's ordered, and I'm not going to come that close and not visit you. Besides, I need to talk some family things over."

Tony stretched out, took another bite of ice cream, then asked, "You having trouble with Zach?"

"No. Not at all. I really like him."

Once the facts about their mother's adult "secret baby" had come to light, Lucca and Tony hadn't been as certain as Gabi and their brother Max that Zach would end up being a welcome addition to their family. The way it turned out, he'd been just what Mom had needed to jerk her out of her depression after their father died.

"It's Mom and Gabi," Lucca explained. "Both of them are acting weird, and I want a second opinion on how to deal with the situation."

Tony lifted his spoon in salute. "The doctor is in. What's the trouble?"

"I'll start with Mom. It's kind of hard to explain, but if you had to describe Mom, using three words, what would they be?"

"Loving. Witty. Loyal."

"True, but that's not what I'm looking for. Think business-related words."

"Mom was a stay-at-home mother. I don't think of her in business-related terms."

"Think PTO mom."

"Oh. Okay, then. Organized. Decisive. And worka-holic."

Lucca nodded. "I'd agree with those. So let me explain three things about the work being done at Aspenglow Place. Indoors, the first thing she did was have the up-stairs bathrooms painted."

"I thought they were all going to be renovated."

"They are."

"That's stupid. Why did she do that?"

Lucca ignored the question. "It gets better. She has purchased six colors of paint for the outside—not samples, mind you—but enough paint to paint the exterior six different times in six different colors. What's craziest of all, three times I've walked into that house in the middle of the workday to find her sitting in a rocking chair reading a book or watching TV. Watching soaps!"

Tony sat up straight. "Soaps? Mom? Our mom?"

"Yep."

"She doesn't watch daytime TV."

"She does now. And she's hooked. She got all teary yesterday when she told me about one of the characters coming back from the dead. Pregnant. With amnesia."

"That's bizarre."

"Gabi doesn't know what she's getting into. You've heard that she's quit the sheriff's office?"

"Yes. I understand she wants to help Mom run the inn."

"I'm not taking bets on how long that idea lasts. Gabi put together a renovation plan—a good one, mind you—but the changing paint palette is driving her crazy. Yesterday she told me she's beginning to wonder if working together might be harmful to their mother-daughter relationship."

Tony pointed his remote at the TV and started channel surfing. "I could have told her that."

"Yeah, well. I thought they needed to try it to figure it out for themselves. If you or I tell Gabi it's a bad idea, she'll dig in her heels and stay longer just to prove us wrong."

"You have a point."

"And I could be all wrong. Gabi and Mom could be the perfect working couple. At least Gabi's not afraid to say no to Mom, which is more than I can manage."

"Man, I've never been able to do that, either."

"I'm counting on Gabi to convince Mom she needs to hire a contractor."

"I thought that was your job," Tony observed.

"I can handle a little painting and repair and doing yard work outside, but I don't know a damn thing about plumbing or electrical work or carpentry. I don't know the subs in the area. If she wants Aspenglow to be a commercial success, the work needs to be done right."

Tony's cellphone buzzed, and he picked it up and sighed. His thumbs flew across the touch screen. "If somebody had told me five years ago that my job would soon entail tweeting, I'd have called BS."

He tossed the phone onto the chair beside him and glanced at Lucca. "Daytime TV, huh?"

"And laundry."

"Laundry?"

"She doesn't do laundry on a schedule anymore. I've seen her let dirty towels pile up for over a week. And there were breakfast dishes in the sink at dinnertime."

"Definitely bizarre." Tony took a thoughtful sip from his bottle of water. "You know, Lucca, considering everything, I hesitate to bring up the D word. . . ."

Lucca flattened his mouth. Damn, he didn't want to talk about this. Not even with his twin brother. "I know I was depressed. I did get some help when I was away. It's better. Now we are talking about Mom, not me."

Tony took a moment to absorb the news and Lucca could see questions lighting his eyes. His brother knew him well enough to understand that now was not the time to pursue the topic. He asked, "Do you think we need to be worried about Mom?"

"I don't know, but I don't think so. I think she's just . . . changing. Everything is different with Dad gone."

"It was easier when Dad was alive. Everything was his call. Now we're the ones with the responsibility."

"That's the problem right there. Mom would say that she's responsible for herself. And honestly, she's right."

"But she's our *mother*. Our *widowed* mother. We're her sons."

"Which makes us responsible," Lucca agreed.

Tony rubbed the back of his neck and thought the problem through. "All right. Here's my take. I saw her and Savannah during their Denver trip recently. Mom seemed happy as a clam to me. Maybe once she brings a contractor on board, the weirdness will work itself out. Could be she has too much to organize and it's overwhelming her. I say we do that, then wait and see."

"That's what I was thinking. Glad we're thinking along the same lines."

"We usually do." Tony rolled to his feet and carried the empty ice cream bowls to the outdoor kitchen's sink. "So, want to bet on how long Gabi lasts at Aspenglow?"

"I won't bet that she actually begins there." Lucca paused a moment, then said, "My next-door neighbor told me the school's PE teacher just quit and they haven't found a replacement. I thought maybe Gabi could . . ."

Tony was shaking his head before Lucca completed the thought. "Bad idea."

"She's an athlete. She knows basketball."

"She played basketball. She can't coach basketball. She's a terrible teacher. You know that. She has no patience. For the sake of the students, I'd let that one go."

Lucca sighed. "All right. You're right. I knew that. I needed someone else to say it out loud. Between her and Mom . . . I'm just worried."

"Good. You caused them both enough worry, disappearing the way you did. A little payback doesn't hurt a damned thing."

"I'm an ass. I know that."

"I'm glad we can agree, brother."

Lucca shot his twin the bird, and Tony laughed. "Look, I'm not worried about Gabi. She'll find something that's right for her. It may take her awhile, and she's bound to bounce around a bit, but she'll land on her feet. As far as Mom is concerned . . . well . . . I don't like the dishes-in-the-sink thing. Still, she's better than she was a year ago. That's a good thing. Deep wounds take time to heal. You know that, right?"

Lucca understood that here, his twin wasn't talking about their mother.

He nodded curtly, wishing he could explain the cloud that had descended on his spirit to his brother, but since he couldn't explain it to himself, that wasn't going to happen.

Tony gave him a long look, then lightened his tone. "So, before I turn my the-doctor-is-in-the-house sign over to read he's-outta-here and take this conversation in a more serious direction—namely, the dismal state of the Rockies bullpen—do you have any other women troubles we need to discuss?"

An image of Hope Montgomery lying in the golden light of dawn, her cheeks flushed, her lips pink and swollen from his kiss, shimmered like a dream in his mind. "Nope. No women troubles here."

"All right then. Did you catch the ninth inning last night? What the hell is wrong with our closer?"

The brothers talked baseball, fishing, a little politics, even the latest book in a fantasy series they both read. Twice Tony tried to bring up basketball, but Lucca shut the subject down fast. They closed the evening off with a swim, a best-two-out-of-three race, in that way of un-ending competition that had been part of Lucca's life for as long as he could remember.

He went to bed in Tony's guest room, pleasantly fatigued and comfortably relaxed.

As he sank toward sleep, his thoughts wandered back over the events of the day to the predawn celestial event. In his mind's eye, he saw sparkling meteors streaking across a black sky. He saw starlight and passion reflected in Hope Montgomery's eyes.

Lost in heavenly bodies, he drifted into sleep and into

dreams of stars and moons and meteors, starships and captains, and Lieutenant Hope Montgomery standing at a computer console dressed in a Starfleet uniform— a tight, bright red minidress and black boots.

Star Trek women had always been hot.

For Hope, the school year began with the *chug chug chug* of diesel as she started the school bus at a quarter after six in the morning and headed out on her rural route. She picked up seventeen students over the course of the next hour and delivered them to school in plenty of time for her to make it to her classroom to greet her students—the largest kindergarten class in some time in Eternity Springs.

The first day of class was always hard. It took all of her strength to meet her class on the first day without breaking into tears. What did Holly look like on her first day of school? She'd be starting fourth grade this year. Did she still wear her wavy red hair long? Did she have more than a dusting of freckles now? What books did she like to read?

Hope allowed herself a limited time to wallow in such thoughts, then she did what she always did—she soldiered on. She turned her focus toward getting to know her students as individuals, not as children the same age as Holly was when she disappeared, and by the end of the first week of school, her students loved her and she adored them in return.

Such was the joy of kindergarten.

During those first weeks of September, she kept busy and saw nothing of her prickly next-door neighbor. She told herself she was glad.

Even if she had relived that kiss more than once in her dreams.

Kindergarten was a half-day program in Eternity Springs, so in the afternoon, Hope taught one section of fifth grade social studies and three classes of PE. Between the two of them, she and Principal Geary had managed to coerce a couple of fathers in town to take charge of the football team. Hope had a target—three targets, actually—in mind to help with the basketball team, and she was waiting for the right moment to make her pitch.

In the meantime, she'd agreed to fill in. She'd played on her high school basketball team, and she could coach the middle school team. For the high schoolers, well, she had pinned her hopes on her targets: the Romanos. Gabi had played college ball. She probably would be happy to help once she finished transitioning from cop to B&B manager. Zach would help when he had time, Hope was certain. Lucca, everyone knew, was a long shot.

But practice wouldn't start for another couple of weeks, and Hope had bigger worries on her plate at the moment. As in the school carnival, Fun Night, in particular. It was the largest fund-raiser of the year for the school, and thus very important. She was committee chairman, and the final planning meeting started . . . she glanced at her watch. "I'm late!"

Hope grabbed her notebook and hurried from the classroom.

The carnival was organized by the Eternity Springs Community School's Parent-Teacher Organization and the chamber of commerce. Ordinarily, they'd hold the meeting in the school cafeteria, but today, Sarah Murphy had asked if they'd all come to her bakery, Fresh. "It's a win-win," Sarah had said when she'd called Hope to make the change and engage the phone tree to inform all committee members. "I'll provide the refreshments for the meeting, and I don't have to get the baby up from his afternoon nap."

Fall was in the air as Hope walked up Spruce then turned west on Second Street toward the bakery. Autumn set the mountains surrounding Eternity Springs aglow with a riot of reds, oranges, and yellows. The afternoon air had a bite to it, and people on the streets walked a little faster than they had even the previous week. Hope expected the first snowfall of the season wouldn't be long in coming.

Ignoring the CLOSED sign in the window at Fresh, Hope opened the door and stepped inside to the clang of a bell. She followed the sound of voices through the shop into the attached living space that was Cam, Sarah, and little Michael Murphy's home.

"Here she is," Sarah said as Hope breezed into the Murphy living room. "You're late."

"I know. I'm sorry. I had to do a locker search and even this early in the school year, it was a pretty disgusting activity. Took me longer than I anticipated, but I found the contraband."

"Cigarettes?" Gabi Romano asked.

"Chewing gum. I outlawed it after I stepped on some for the third time in a week." She glanced hopefully toward the nursery. "Is our boy still snoozing?"

"Yes." Sarah glanced at the clock. "If all is right with the world, we should have half an hour without interruption."

"Then let's get our business done so that we're free to play when he wakes up."

Planning committee members consisted of herself and her fellow teacher, Jim Brand; Sarah and Maggie Romano, representing the chamber; and PTO members Christy Hartford and Erin Ward.

"How have the nights been going with the puppies?" Hope asked Christy.

"Better," Christy replied. "They're not waking me up, though I suspect the kids are sneaking them into their beds. I admit I want a good night's sleep enough that I haven't bothered to check."

The Hartfords had adopted two of Roxy's puppies, while their next-door neighbors, the Wests, had taken the third. Hope had struggled with the decision to give up the puppies, but she couldn't find anyone to take Roxy and all of her babies, and six weeks of puppy care had convinced her that four dogs were too many for one person to care for properly. The West and Hartford kids had fallen hard for the pups, and Christy's suggestion that Roxy visit her offspring often had alleviated Hope's guilt.

"You'll have to bring Roxy over soon," Christy continued. "My girls have a gift for her—a Halloween costume."

"Really?" Hope responded, delighted.

Christy grinned. "They're hoping you'll let them take Roxy trick-or-treating with the puppies."

"Tell your girls it's a date." Hope turned her smile toward Gabi next. "Are you here in your mother's place today?"

"Yes." Gabi rolled her eyes. "She's in the middle of an argument with Lucca, and I needed to be away from there." She paused, then added softly. "Permanently."

Oh, dear.

Gabi pasted on a smile. "So, what's on the agenda today?"

Hope passed out the final room assignments for each of the carnival games. Erin reported on volunteers, and Gabi gave a recap of the prizes pledged by businesses in town. "Wow," Sarah said. "We're going to make a mint. Those are some awesome prizes."

Looking over the list, Hope nodded in agreement. When her gaze fell upon her own classroom and its assignment to be the cakewalk headquarters, she frowned. "Sarah, are you sure about this? Fifteen cakes?"

"It's what I donated last year."

"You didn't have a two-month-old baby last year."

"It is a lot of work," Jim said. "Why don't you cut back? We can invite some of the teachers and parents to provide cakes."

"I'll . . ." Gabi began, then stopped and scowled. "Oh, stop it. You all look like you're sucking on lemons. Fine. I won't bake."

"You're better at other things, honey," Sarah said gently.

Hope thought it best to move on. "I have an idea. What if you made one cake, Sarah? It could be the grand prize and we could sell special tickets to participate in that round. Higher-priced tickets."

"Make your Sarah's Special," Jim suggested. "I know folks in this town who would crawl through broken glass to get your . . . what's it called?"

"Chocolate Almond Joconde Imprime with Golden Raspberry Filling," Sarah said. "That's an idea."

"A great idea," Gabi said. "It's to die for and since you only make it around the holidays, there's a lot of pent-up demand in town for it."

"Isn't that a lot of work?" Hope asked.

"Yes, it takes me three days. But, it's still not as much work as making fifteen cakes."

At that point a little mewling noise emerged from the baby monitor. "Sounds like someone is waking up," Christy Hartford observed.

"Early, too," Sarah said with a sigh. "I could have used another ten minutes off my feet."

The mewling rose to a cry, and Hope bounced to her feet. "I'll pick him up."

"He'll need changing."

"Doesn't scare me away."

"Then be my guest."

Hope made her way to Michael's nursery, which was decorated in a koala bear theme in recognition of Cam's years in Australia. Their artist friend Sage Rafferty had painted a glorious mural on the room's far wall that made Hope smile whenever she saw it. Plus, it was far enough away from Piglet and Pooh that Hope's déjà vu didn't kick in every time she stepped into the room.

The infant lay on his back, his arms and legs flailing, his little round face red as he worked up a cry. "Shush, now, sweet boy," Hope said, slipping her hands beneath the baby's head and bottom and lifting him to rest against her shoulder. Immediately, her heart swelled with bittersweet joy, and her eyes went damp with tears. Holding a baby brought comfort, albeit temporary, to that hollow place inside her. The weight of an infant, the powdery scent, and the way plump little cheeks begged for kisses soothed her.

Her friend Daniel Garrett, whom she met six months after Holly had been taken, couldn't understand her. The parent of a kidnapped child himself, he had the biggest heart of any man she'd ever known, but he found it difficult to be in the company of little ones. Hope didn't know why the company of children eased her heartache, but "why" didn't really matter, did it?

"Let's get you changed, little man," she said softly, carefully laying Michael Cameron Murphy onto his changing table. He cried when she put him down, so she briskly and efficiently changed his diaper.

He nuzzled at her breast as she carried him to his mother, and longing filled her. She had wanted a sister or brother for Holly, and when their firstborn turned three, she and Mark stopped using birth control. A month later, he'd been assigned to a death penalty case, and their opportunities to conceive dropped significantly. It had been difficult for her to get pregnant when he all but lived at the office.

She carried Michael into the living room, where the committee members stood waiting to see him. He put up with the cooers and kissers for a moment but soon announced his hunger in no uncertain terms. Hope handed the crying infant to his mother, then helped Gabi carry dishes to the kitchen. By the time they returned to the living room, the other committee members had departed. Sarah sat in a wooden rocker, her baby at her breast.

"Sit down and talk to me," she told them. "Now that we have business out of the way, I want gossip."

Hope sat in a floral-accent chair. Gabi plopped down onto the sofa and said, "I'm game. First, though, I've been meaning to ask. How is your mom doing, Sarah?"

Sarah's mother was an Alzheimer's patient living in a memory care facility in Gunnison. "Physically, she's fine. Mentally, not so good." Sarah gave a brief update of her mother's condition, then added, "I took Michael to see her. That proved to be just about the toughest thing I've ever done. I lived at home when Lori was born, and Mom helped raise her. She loved Lori so much—was such a big part of her life. Knowing Michael won't have that . . . it's so hard, losing someone you love this way, but at the same time, not losing them."

"Absolutely," Hope said, a little more heartfelt than necessary, judging by the curious looks she received from Gabi and Sarah.

"Do you have experience with Alzheimer's?" Sarah asked.

"Not personal experience, no. My parents both died young—a plane crash when I was in college." Loneliness washed over Hope. "Sometimes, girls just need their mommies."

"That's true," Gabi said. "I'm so sorry for you both. It's never easy to lose a parent."

Sarah moved the baby to her shoulder to burp him, and asked, "How is your mother doing, Gabi? Maggie always seems to have a positive outlook, but do I remember that she mentioned an unhappy anniversary coming up soon? She was so sad. Is it the anniversary of your father's death?"

"No." Gabi shook her head. "Dad died in the spring. The anniversary we have coming up is Lucca's bus wreck."

"That's right." Sarah's eyes widened then rolled as little Michael gave out a surprisingly loud belch. "You're all worried about him."

"We are. He's definitely more his old self these days, but every so often he has a day where he's dark and gloomy and will hardly speak a word."

"Depression is a hard one to handle, too," Sarah said. "I think it's difficult to admit when simply being down becomes something more—especially for men."

"It's difficult to watch people you love go through it. With Lucca . . . he was always the cheeriest of us. Now he's a grumpy old cuss more often than not."

A grumpy, blows-hot-and-cold cuss whom Hope couldn't imagine describing as "cheery" under any circumstances.

She shifted in her seat, crossing her legs. The conversation made her uncomfortable since it didn't seem right to gossip about a man she'd kissed. Not with his sister, anyway. Yet, she wanted to find out as much as she could about him, so she ignored her unease and attempted to hide her interest by casually observing, "I'm not home a lot myself these days, but I don't see much sign of him next door."

"He's spending most of his time at Aspenglow trying to get the majority of the outdoor work finished before winter. We have a new contractor starting work next week, though, so I expect Lucca will have more free time. Whether that will be a good thing or a bad thing, I'm not sure. He might revert to doing his Oscar the Grouch imitation if he doesn't have plenty to keep him busy." She sighed heavily and added, "But then, I'm not sure of much of anything these days—other than the fact that my mother is driving me crazy."

"I worked with my mother for years," Sarah said. "It certainly has its challenges."

Gabi sighed. "Mom and I have always been good friends, and I thought this would be a good thing for us both. When I first broached the idea, she was all for it. Even now she's all for me helping, but . . . she's gone bonkers, and I can't stand it."

"Bonkers?" Hope asked. She'd visited with Maggie just yesterday, and she'd seemed perfectly normal.

"The electrician was scheduled to work today. When he showed up at eight A.M. ready to go to work, she told him to go home. She said she'd pay him for the day, but that she wanted a pajama day all by herself. She told Lucca to stay away, too."

"What's wrong with that?" Sarah asked. "Pajama days are heaven."

"Yeah, but they're not Mom. It's just very weird and I—"

The women paused when Michael let out a happy gurgle. Sarah lowered the baby onto her lap and made faces at him. Gabi finished her sentence by changing the subject. "He is such a doll, Sarah."

"I am head over heels in love."

"As well you should be," Hope said, trying to suppress the envy. "Enjoy every minute of it."

"I do. It's amazing, so different from last time, thank goodness. Looking back, I don't know how I ever raised Lori without Cam there to help."

"If Michael's through nursing, can I hold him?" Gabi asked. In a sly, purposeful tone she added, "I need auntie practice."

Sarah's gaze zeroed in on her, her eyes bright with delight. "And why is that?"

Gabi grinned and stared at her manicured fingertips. "I'm not saying a word."

She didn't have to say a word, Hope thought. Her expression said it for her. Handing her son over to Gabi, Sarah demanded, "Savannah's pregnant? Oh, Maggie is going to be over the moon. Every single time she sees Michael she goes into rapture at the idea of being a grandmother."

"No, Savannah's not pregnant. Not yet." Gabi made faces at Michael. "She told me they're about ready to start trying, though."

"I'm sure Zach's ready to work hard at the effort," Sarah said with a grin. "Cam certainly was dedicated."

"This onesie is too cute, Sarah." Gabi tickled the terry-cloth monkey stretched over the baby's tummy. "You know, maybe I should take Nic's idea about opening a children's shop in Eternity Springs more seriously."

"Do you think you'd like to be a shopkeeper?" Sarah asked.

"More than I'd like working for my mother at her B&B," Gabi replied. "I think that's part of the problem. Aspenglow is her idea, her dream. I think I'd like to have my own."

"You should work retail around here first and see if you like it. I'm sure Savannah would love the help at Heavenscents."

"See, that's the thing. Heavenscents is her baby, just like the B&B is Mom's. Fresh was your dream, Sarah. Vistas is Sage's. Ali has the Yellow Kitchen. How will I know if anything is really right until I dive in and do it? How did you decide that you wanted to be a kindergarten teacher, Hope?"

She took a moment to formulate her response. "I worked in advertising out of college, but after my divorce, I was drifting. I needed a career change and the idea of working with children pulled at me. I was able to get my teaching certification without much trouble, and as for kindergarten, well, I love the little guys."

"So you knew what you wanted," Gabi said. "That's my problem. I'm still looking."

"Keep looking," Hope replied, her tone insisting. "We have to keep looking and never give up believing that someday, we will find . . . what we seek. Keep looking, Gabi. Don't settle. Don't accept. Believe."

"Wow," Sarah said. "I'm hearing a lot of passion."

"You must really love being a kindergarten teacher," Gabi added.

"I love children. I really, really love kids. And you've had Michael long enough. Hand him over, Gabi. It's my turn. I get to hold him."

Keep him safe.

Oh, Holly, I'm so sorry.

SEVEN

Lucca walked into the Eternity Springs Community School on Saturday night with his mother and sister under protest. *Somebody really should have considered the college football schedule when they lined up this event.* There were three games on that he wanted to follow. He hoped his phone picked up the Internet in the school okay because he'd need to check scores from time to time, and he'd discovered that Internet access could be hit-or-miss in this remote little burg.

The guy who ran the local grocery store handed him a piece of paper listing volunteer assignments. Lucca read it over and frowned. "Why does Zach get to work the fishing booth and I have to work the art pavilion?"

"Because—" Maggie broke off as she abruptly stopped and slapped her palm against her forehead. "The cake. I forgot the cake. Lucca, would you go out to the car and get it? It needs to go to the kindergarten classroom. That's down this hall"—she pointed toward the right—"third door on the left."

The kindergarten classroom. Lucca's mind immediately went to the kindergarten teacher. He'd been right the morning after the meteor shower when he'd said they wouldn't see much of each other. Except for the instance when he'd run into her in the grocery store one evening and they'd exchanged small talk for a few moments, in the past month he'd seen her only in passing. He told himself that was a good thing. He almost believed it.

His mother continued, "I can't believe I forgot it after all the trouble I went to in order to make it. Your grandmother's cake is too much work to make in an ill-equipped kitchen. It'll be so nice when Richard gets my new kitchen finished."

Richard was the new contractor working at Aspenglow; Lucca's grandmother's cake was the best cake in the history of the world, Italian crème. The mention of it stopped Lucca dead in his tracks. "You made Nana's cake?"

"Yes. For the cakewalk."

That didn't compute. No way. "You made Nana's cake and you're giving it away?"

"Well, yes. Sarah Murphy can't do all the work."

Maggie turned at the sound of her name, then crossed the hallway to visit with a couple Lucca didn't know. He looked at his sister. "She made Nana's cake."

Gabi grinned widely. "Yep. And I'm going to win it."

At the sight of his sister's smile, something familiar stirred inside of Lucca. Competitiveness. He answered her grin with a sly smile of his own. "Don't bet on it."

He left the building and retrieved the cake. For a brief moment, he considered absconding with it—mainly to mess with Gabi—but his sense of fair play wouldn't let him do it. Besides, his mother would kill him. On the way into the building, he saw Zach and his wife, Savannah, approaching, so he waited for them to catch up. "Hey, beautiful," he said to Savannah. "Why don't you ditch the lawman and run away with the better-looking brother?"

She lifted her brows innocently. "Oh, is Max in town?"

"Savannah!" Zach protested, scowling at her. He turned his attention toward the Tupperware cake carrier in Lucca's hands and smirked. "Have you taken up baking in your spare time?"

"It's Italian crème cake," Lucca said. "Mom made it."

Zach's smirk died. "Seriously?"

"Seriously. She's donating it to the cakewalk. I'm going to win it."

"The hell you say. That's the cake Maggie made for our wedding reception, isn't it?"

"Yep." His mother had been thrilled when Zach and Savannah accepted her offer to make the traditional Romano family fare when the two married almost a year ago. "You made a pig of yourself on it, as I recall."

"It was the best thing I'd ever tasted." Zach eyed the cake holder in Lucca's hands and gave a determined nod. I'm going to win this one."

Lucca shot his brother a smile full of challenge. "Don't bet on it."

Five minutes later, he sauntered into the kindergarten classroom carrying the cake holder with appropriate reverence and spoke his first words to Hope Montgomery in weeks. "Hello, Hope. Great sweater you're wearing. At what point will this cake be the prize?"

She wore black slacks and a fire-engine red sweater that hugged her curves and looked as soft as down. She stared at him as if he were a bug she didn't recognize. "Excuse me?"

"You look great in red, and I want to win this cake. How do I play?"

"The cakewalk begins in twenty minutes. It'll be two tickets and you can buy them at the tables set up in the front of the school."

"Excellent." Lucca glanced around the room that had been cleared of furniture except for two long tables laden with baked goods lining the walls. On the tile floor, hot pink tape formed numbered squares placed in an oval. "So, what is the game? How do you play?"

"It's like musical chairs without chairs. Participants walk around in a circle as the music plays. When it stops, they center on a number. The volunteer running the game will draw a number out of my basket, and the person who is standing on that number gets to choose a cake."

Lucca frowned. "So it's all chance? No skill required?"

"Nope."

"Well, that's no good." He scowled at the eight-foot tables piled high with cakes and cupcakes, looking for a better solution. Maybe he could leave Nana's cake inside its carrier and stack some cupcakes on top of it. Hide it in plain sight so that no one would notice it. His gaze settled on the table's centerpiece. "That's fancy. It'll be the first to go."

"It's our grand prize cake. We're having a special round for it."

"How does that work?"

She explained how the Fun Night committee had sold special tickets for the round, scheduled to be the final one of the night. While she spoke, Lucca found himself becoming distracted. She really was pretty, and that sweater she wore, while appropriately kindergarten-teacher modest, did wonderful things for her figure.

She finished by saying, " . . . twenty-five dollars each. We sold out on the first day."

Lucca did the math. "Six hundred twenty-five dollars for one cake? Not bad. What if—"

He was interrupted by his sister, who sailed into the room and asked, "Hope? How do I go about winning my Nana's cake?"

Hope glanced from Gabi to Lucca and then to Zach, who had followed Gabi into the kindergarten room. Jack Davenport, Colt Rafferty, and Gabe Callahan trailed in after Zach.

Colt said, "You sold out of tickets for Sarah's cake before I could nab one, but rumor has it that Maggie made that same cake she made for Zach's wedding?"

Lucca scowled at his siblings. "Loudmouths."

Hope folded her arms and studied the others. "How many of you want in on this?"

They all raised their hands.

"I repeat," Lucca said. "Loudmouths."

Zach suggested, "Change the game for Maggie's cake, Hope. Make it musical chairs. Winner takes Italian crème."

Interest popped up on all their faces. "Contact sport," Gabe said. "I like it."

Hope drummed her fingers and considered it. "You people are ridiculous. Men will turn everything into competition, won't they?"

"Excuse me," Gabi protested. "I'm in on this. Don't lump me in with those knuckle-dragging Neanderthals. I don't have a manly bone in my body."

"She speaks the truth," Zach said. "Gabi's the biggest girly-girl in town."

Gabi looked down her nose and said, "I'll take that as a compliment."

"You shouldn't think of us as ridiculous, either," Gabe said. "We're doing our civic duty. In fact, I suggest you up the price of the buy-in."

Hope appeared shocked by the suggestion. "Higher than Sarah's, you mean? Wouldn't that hurt her feelings?"

"Nah," Zach, Gabe, and Colt said simultaneously. Zach added, "The goal here is to raise money for the school. That's all Sarah will care about."

"If you're sure," Hope said. "What do you suggest? We double the price? Fifty dollars?"

"Make it a hundred," Lucca suggested. "It's a good cause."

Hope gaped at him. "A hundred dollars? You'd pay that?"

"Sure. How about the rest of you? Any cheapskates here?"

"I'm in," Gabe added. "I know it's in my best interest to contribute to the school. My girls will be starting here before I know it."

"Never too early to suck up to the kindergarten teacher, right, Callahan?" Colt observed.

Gabe grinned without apology. "Absolutely."

"Nic said that very same thing to me not too long ago," Hope said with a laugh. She folded her arms and considered the idea, then said, "All right. Since you guys are ready to put your money where your mouths are, so to speak, we might as well take advantage of it. So, tickets will cost one hundred dollars, plus a pledge of ten volunteer hours at the school. I suspect this might get rowdy, so I don't think it's a good idea to do it in front of the children. Italian crème musical chairs at eight P.M. Okay?"

Gabi elbowed Lucca hard. "I am so going to win."

"In your dreams, baby sister. In your dreams."

The school bell rang, signaling the official start of the event, and the volunteers dispersed to man their booths. Lucca served his time in the arts and crafts room, and while he wouldn't admit it aloud, he didn't mind painting little kids' faces, though he wondered if little boys had always been so enamored of fangs. Once his shift ended, he wandered around the building. When he spied a science classroom filled with dozens of mounted animals, he started to enter the room to investigate when a familiar sound attracted his attention.

Thump. Thump. Thump. Clang.

He'd found his way to the gym. Wouldn't you know it?

For a long moment, he hesitated. He really should go into the science lab and take a close-up look at that stuffed bear. Instead, like a puppet on a string, he was pulled by the sound down the hallway toward the open double doors.

Thump. Thump. Thump. Clang.

He stopped just outside the gym doors, his heart pounding and a cold sweat trickling down his back. A tall, lanky teenage boy was playing half-court one-on-one with Lucca's sister, and he appeared to be holding his own.

Watching Gabi, Lucca's thoughts drifted back to his childhood and all the times he and his siblings had played ball in the backyard. Their dad had been an athlete and a hoops fan, and once he saw that his growing sons would have his height, he'd had a concrete court poured in their backyard. Lucca couldn't guess how many nets they'd worn out over the years. Dad used to order them in bulk.

Gabi's voice snagged his attention when she bounced the ball to the boy and called, "Check. Next basket wins."

The boy threw the rock back to her and said, "Okay, show me what you got."

She stood at the top of the key, her gaze focused on the boy. Lucca knew by her stance and by his knowledge of her game what she'd do next.

Sure enough, she faked a jump shot, and when the boy went for it, she drove to the bucket for a layup. Damned if the boy didn't block the shot. Immediately, he took the ball outside the arc to the left of the basket and put up a jumper.

Nothing but net. The boy gleefully crowed "Game!"

Gabi groaned and said, "Two out of three."

"No way. I'll play ya PIG."

Gabi laughed maniacally—PIG was her game—and the sound pierced Lucca's heart as sure as an arrow. If he wasn't a chicken, he would stride right into that gym and show his baby sister just who owned PIG.

But Lucca couldn't make himself step on the gymnasium's polished wood floor.

"That's Wade Mitchell."

Lucca glanced over his shoulder to see Hope standing behind him. He stepped to one side, and she moved forward.

"His father owns Storm Mountain Ranch. They're an old Eternity Springs family, having owned that property for a hundred years."

"The kid has game."

"He only started playing recently. He didn't get his growth spurt until his sophomore year. He's a junior this year."

Lucca's gaze measured the boy. He had to be six foot two, and if he'd started growing late, he probably wasn't done. "Looks like he spends time in the weight room."

"We don't have a weight room. Storm Mountain is a working ranch, and Wade has helped his dad all his life. Wade is the best player on our team."

Lucca turned, putting his back toward the gym. He was done with the subject of basketball. "My mom told me you are in charge of this Fun Night event. How is it going? Are you going to meet your fund-raising goals?"

Her eyes went bright and caused Lucca to think about starshine. "We're going to exceed them by a significant amount. Depending how many of you show up for musical chairs, it could be our best Fun Night ever."

"Congratulations. Say, since you're here, I'm curious about something. What's with all the critters in the science classroom?"

"Critters? What . . . oh. Our mounted menagerie."

Lucca blinked. "That sounds sorta kinky, Ms. Montgomery."

"As far as I'm concerned, it's downright creepy. But I will say, the kids love it."

She explained how the collection had been donated to

the school by a local taxidermist named Bear. "I never met him. He moved away before I moved to Eternity Springs, but apparently he was quite a character, an old-fashioned mountain man. It's a lot of fun for me to witness the first look at the collection by our kindergartners. Their little eyes get so round and so big—pure wonder. We go to the science lab once a week, and they just love it. Of course, their favorites are the hockey mice. Have you seen them?"

"I didn't go inside the classroom."

"Follow me," she said. "You have to see this."

She led him into the science lab to a small desk in the back corner where a quartet of white mice decked out in full hockey gear stood upright on an ice rink model. "Okay, I get a hunter wanting to mount his ten-point elk so he can hang it on the wall of his man cave, and I admit I think mounted fish are cool," said Lucca. "If I ever was lucky enough to catch a marlin, I'd consider having him stuffed. But hockey mice? That is weird."

"The really weird stuff is in storage. He did some animal creation—wings of a hawk on the body of a rabbit. It's disturbing." Hope glanced up at the clock on the wall and said, "I need to finish my rounds if I'm going to get back in time for the big competition. Do you still plan to enter?"

"Oh, yes. I'll definitely be there."

"See you shortly, then."

Lucca watched her leave, admiring the way her black slacks hugged that spectacular ass of hers. He liked Hope Montgomery. Sure, he found her physically appealing, but it was more than that. Her attitude was attractive, too. She was friendly and confident. She made the day a little brighter for everyone around her. She wasn't indifferent to him, either.

Maybe he didn't need to be so guarded where she was concerned. So what if she was friends with Mom and

Gabi? She was a single adult. He was a single adult. If they wanted to explore the attraction between them, well, that was their business, wasn't it? He'd be honest up front and make it clear he wasn't looking for anything long-term. Maybe she'd shoot him down. Or, maybe that arrangement would suit her just fine.

He wouldn't know unless he asked.

Lucca shoved his hands into his pockets, shook his head one more time at the hockey-playing mice, and exited the science lab. His gaze drifted toward the gymnasium doorway and for a long moment, he hesitated. Then he blew out a heavy breath and muttered, "Screw it."

Dad would have kicked his ass if he'd been around to see Lucca afraid to step foot on the hardwood.

He strode toward the gym and straight through the open doors. His sister stood near the basket holding the ball tucked beneath her arm as she spoke to the boy. She casually glanced up and when she identified him, her eyes rounded in surprise.

Lucca grinned and slapped the ball loose, caught it on the bounce, then drove toward the basket and went up for a dunk.

When his heels hit the floor, he smiled, winked at his sister, then walked back out of the gym calling, "It's your day to lose, Gabriella."

He headed for the kindergarten class, his step lighter than it had been in months. Having scored a bucket on one of his demons, he was ready for a game of musical chairs.

During her first month of teaching in Eternity Springs, Hope had scored an ancient phonograph and collection of children's records at the Saint Stephen's church rummage sale. The songs were familiar, tinny recordings of such classic, beloved tunes as "Old MacDonald" and

"I've Been Working on the Railroad." Hope had installed the machine in her classroom and once a week, usually after science lab, the kindergartners had an old-fashioned sing-along.

Her students loved it. Ninety percent of the children who entered her classroom had never seen a record player or vinyl records. To them it was just as magical—maybe even more—than the electronic tablets they began learning on long before they were ready to read. From Big Chief tablets to iPads—education had certainly changed.

And yet, some things never changed. Kids liked to sing along with "Old MacDonald," whether the song came from a piano or a record player or an MP3 player.

And their parents, especially their dads, continued to cringe from repetitive renditions of "With an oink, oink here and an oink, oink there . . ."

She couldn't explain why, but the idea of having the big, tough men of Eternity Springs playing musical chairs to "Old MacDonald" made her want to giggle.

"Now that's a positively evil smile, Hope," Maggie Romano said as she sailed up beside her. "What are you thinking?"

"I'm thinking about this contest. I take it you've heard what's happening?"

"Yes." Amusement gleamed in her eyes and a satisfied smile stretched across her face. "Those children of mine. They're simply ridiculous sometimes. I admit the cake is good, but in my family it took on ridiculous significance—mainly because my mother-in-law made it that way. Care to guess how I finally got the recipe? She passed it along in her will."

"Really?"

"Oh, yes. My children loved their Nana, but I have to tell you, she was a pain in the patootie as far as mothers-in-law go. Rumor has it there might be as many as ten entrants. Can you believe that? A thousand dollars for one cake!"

"Not to mention a hundred volunteer hours for the school."

"The need to compete is hardwired into some people, isn't it? So, what can I do to help get things ready?"

"You've already done the important part," Hope said, nodding toward the prize tables, now empty but for the Tupperware carrier holding Maggie's cake. "There's not much else to do. Jack and Gabe are bringing adult-sized chairs from the cafeteria."

"Don't you think it would be much more fun to use kindergarten chairs?"

"I think this might be physical enough as it is," Hope replied ruefully. She walked to her desk and pulled a blue bank bag from a drawer. "Would you like to collect our entry fee from our participants?"

"I'd be delighted to do that. I get particular joy accepting money from my children, considering it's so often been the other way around." Maggie accepted the bank bag, then asked, "So, what music have you chosen for this battle to come? The theme from *Rocky*?"

"Closer to *Rocky and Bullwinkle*."

"Excuse me?"

"Rocky the Squirrel. Or maybe Alvin and the Chipmunks?"

Maggie clasped a hand to her chest. "Not the Chipmunks. Please, not that."

"What about 'It's a Small World'? 'The Barney Song'?"

The horror on Maggie's face coaxed another laugh out of Hope. "Don't worry. I haven't decided just how annoying I want to be. Considering it's a thousand bucks, perhaps I should be nice."

At that point, Gabe, Jack, and Colt arrived with chairs. The rest of the players soon followed, one of them a newcomer to town, Richard Steele. As Maggie introduced her contractor to Hope and the others whom he'd yet to meet, Hope heard Gabi tease, "Mom, you must be overpaying him if he's going to pop a hundred bucks to lose a cake."

He flashed Gabi a challenging grin and said, "I smelled this cake baking all day. I'm motivated. Prepare to lose, Gabriella."

Gabi sniffed with disdain, then handed over her ticket fee—an IOU since she never carried much cash—to her mother and took a place in front of a chair. Once the field was positioned, she remained the only woman.

Celeste Blessing, who had slipped into the room with some of the players' wives, observed, "Be still my heart. What a breathtaking collection of men."

"A lot of good it does me," Gabi said. "They're all either married or related to me."

"Richard isn't married," Maggie said.

Something in her tone caught Hope's ear, but she didn't have time to figure out what it was because after taking a look at the men who were busy ribbing and challenging one another, she decided to change her music selection. She handed a piece of paper to Celeste and asked, "Celeste, would you read the rules for us while I cue the music?"

"Rules?" Colt Rafferty asked. "There are rules? What fun is that?"

"This is a kindergarten class," Celeste responded. "Of course there are rules. I'll have you know that I competed in the Musical Chairs World Championship two years ago."

"The what?" Lucca asked.

"Shut up and listen," Zach shot back. "I want to win my cake and take it home. I'm hungry."

Celeste read the rules, which included such items as "There shall be no use of hands, arms or shoulders to forcefully obtain a chair, save a chair, or force another player out of a chair," and "Only one person per chair," and since this was, after all, a kindergarten class, "No biting."

Once Celeste finished, Hope said, "Is everybody ready?"

The contestants nodded.

Hope smiled, "Begin walking once the music starts to play. May the best man—or woman—win."

She clicked the Play button on her classroom sound system and the first measures of the Weather Girls' "It's Raining Men" blasted from the speakers.

As one, the men in the room groaned. The women laughed and cheered.

What followed was the closest thing to a brawl that Hope's classroom had ever seen, but even as the men pushed, jostled, elbowed, and shoved, they laughed— and told their women to stop the blasted singing. The Romano siblings fought a good fight. Gabi lasted several rounds, primarily because nonfamily members hesitated when it came to shoving her around, and she took advantage of it. Her brothers weren't that nice, and a hip shove from Zach put her out of the game.

Eventually, motivation, a little luck, and quick-as-a-minute reflexes produced a winner. To the victor, Richard Steele, went the Italian crème cake.

Afterward, Hope found Maggie Romano crying in the ladies' room. "Maggie? What's wrong?"

"Nothing's wrong. I just . . . oh my." Maggie tugged a paper towel from the dispenser and wiped her eyes. "Lucca laughed. Really laughed. Did you see that?"

"I did." Hope had been hard-pressed to drag her gaze away from him.

"It's been so long. I'm glad . . . so glad . . . that my family discovered Eternity Springs."

Hope considered Maggie's words as she exited the school a little while later to make the short but chilly walk home. Discovering Eternity Springs had been a blessing for her, too. This town had provided her refuge and given her friends. It brought laughter back into her life when she'd thought she'd lost that joy forever.

A form stepped from the shadows. Lucca asked, "Mind a little company on the walk home?"

Her heartbeat kicked up its pace. "That would be nice."

"Good. Because I have a bone to pick with you." He fell in beside her. "Disco? Really?"

A smile teased her lips, but she didn't respond.

"If someone had bet me six months ago that I'd be playing musical chairs with a bunch of grown men while my mother and sister sang along to a bad dance tune at the top of their lungs I'd have called him crazy. That had to be the weirdest thing I've seen since I spied the big orange lizard puffing up for the lady lizards on a tree branch in Honduras."

"I'm sorry you didn't win."

He snorted. "Which brings me to my bone. You got it wrong, Madam Judge. My cheek hit that seat ahead of the handyman's."

"I call 'em as I see 'em."

"You have a lot of experience watching men's butts?"

"It's a pastime I can appreciate."

"Pretty risqué statement for a kindergarten teacher."

"Hey, I'm not all apples and ABCs."

"Don't I know it," he drawled, and the sound of it sent little shivers racing up her spine.

Hope didn't know why after weeks of ignoring her he'd suddenly shown up and started flirting. She knew she probably shouldn't let him get by with it, but both his laughter and his mother's tears had gotten to her. That, and she empathized with him. Wounded souls needed time to heal.

Besides, he was hot, and she was lonely. Basking in his

attention for the length of a five-minute walk home didn't mean she had "doormat" tattooed across her forehead.

"So did you break your fund-raising record?" he asked.

"By a mile."

"Congratulations."

"Thank you."

The night's weather called for a brisk walk, but instead, the two of them strolled toward their homes. In the eastern sky, a near-full moon rose above the mountaintops and lit the street in a silvery glow. They walked half a block and were almost to her front walk when she asked, "Have you been doing any stargazing lately?"

"Not much. I've put in long workdays at Aspenglow prepping for winter. Now that the cake-stealing contractor is in town, I'll have more time. So, you want to go to dinner Friday night?"

Stepping up onto the curb, Hope tripped. Lucca's arm shot out to steady her. "Did you just ask me on a date?" she asked.

Hope felt herself blush. Had she just blurted out that question? How embarrassing.

"I did."

Apparently, her out-of-control mouth wasn't done because she stupidly continued, "But . . . why? You haven't spoken to me since . . . since . . ."

"Since we kissed. I know. I was being cautious."

"What changed?"

"I shot a basketball today. I haven't wanted to do that in a very long time."

And, you laughed, too. And I haven't had a date in sixteen months. "Yes, I would like to have dinner with you."

"Great. Shall I pick you up at seven?"

"Sure."

"Great," he repeated, smiled down at her, then bent

and brushed a quick, casual kiss against her lips. "See you then, teacher. Good night."

He walked on, his hands shoved into his pockets. Only then did she realize that they'd been standing at the foot of her front walk.

Hope all but floated into her house. Roxy came running to greet her, and Hope bent to pick the dog up just as her cellphone rang. Distracted by the dog and the man, she didn't check the caller's number before she thumbed the green button. "Hello?"

"Hope," a man's voice said, his words slurring as he continued. "You know, you really should change your name. Hopeless. No, careless. That's more appropriate, isn't it?"

She closed her eyes. "Hello, Mark. Is there news?"

"Yes, there's news."

Her heart lurched and climbed to her throat, and she held her breath. She knew better, *knew him*. Nevertheless, the ember of hope within her never died.

And Mark Montgomery reveled in periodically crushing it.

"My mother says the scrapbook she gave us for Holly's fourth Christmas is missing."

Breath escaped from her. Her mother-in-law had given Mark a car that Christmas. The scrapbook had been her gift. It was on the shelf of her bedroom closet.

"Good-bye, Mark." Hope ended the call.

Hope put Roxy back down onto the floor. She wasn't aware of the tears rolling down her cheeks. She didn't hear Roxy whining. She didn't recognize that her feet had begun to move, to carry her toward her closet. Toward her memories. Toward heartache.

Toward Holly.

EIGHT

❦

Lucca entered his house, his spirits lighter than they'd been in a long time. Who would have guessed that he would have had such a good time at a school carnival in a small mountain town? It was almost embarrassing. Musical chairs? What was next? Pin the Tail on the Donkey?

Spin the Bottle wouldn't be so bad.

He smirked and headed to his kitchen. He was hungry. He'd been thinking about that cake, dammit. Opening the door to the fridge, he peered inside. Nothing worth consuming had magically appeared while he'd been gone. He really needed to go to the grocery store tomorrow. His gaze lingered on the gallon of milk. What he really wanted was Italian crème cake. That handyman played dirty.

He grabbed a beer and microwaved a bag of popcorn.

He carried his snack into the living room and sat down in front of the television. He kicked off his shoes, propped his feet up on his ottoman, and picked up the remote. The screen flickered on to the most recent channel. News. He wasn't in the mood for news. Maybe he'd find a movie to watch. He pushed the channel button and began to surf.

Then, still buoyed by the evening's good feelings, he

made a stupid mistake. When he surfed to a classics sports channel and the 1985 Villanova versus Georgetown NCAA title game was showing, he took his finger off the channel button. Lucca began to watch. Soon, thoughts of musical chairs and his good mood were gone. Ten minutes into the game and lost in his memories, he went for the scotch.

March Madness.

How long he sat staring at the screen, he couldn't say. Long enough for the alcohol level in the bottle to sink by two fingers more than a couple of times. The basketball game ended and a replay of the last four holes of the final round of the 1986 Masters came on. Lucca didn't see Jack Nicklaus birdie the seventeenth hole. He was lost in his nightmare.

Damned ice. Damned dog. Damned preseason, meaningless game.

It had happened two years ago the following Wednesday.

At first he thought he imagined the ring of the doorbell, then the knock. Ignoring the noise, he took another sip of his drink. Then he heard her call his name. Through the fog, he heard pain. He heard the sound of heartbreak that echoed the hollowness inside of him.

Hope. Sounding hopeless.

Lucca went to his door and opened it. Cold air whooshed inside, little knives slicing through his shirt. She stood on his front porch, still wearing her red sweater and black slacks, but no coat. Something was obviously very wrong. "Hope, what happened? Are you okay?"

She stared up at him with swollen, tortured brown eyes, her cheeks tear streaked. "Lucca. I can't be alone."

Wordlessly, he opened the screen door. She stepped into his house, into his arms. She buried her face against his chest. She was so cold. *Like me. Just like me.*

"I can't be alone," she repeated. "Not now. Not tonight. Please . . ." She lifted her face to his. "Make me forget?"

Whatever her problem, he understood the feeling. He knew it very well. Right now, after the evening he'd spent, he wanted oblivion, too. Holding a woman in his arms was so much better than booze.

What else could he do? Lucca kissed her, and he tasted pain and heartache. He would have wondered why, had he not been numbed by alcohol and caught in the grip of his own pain and heartache.

She'd asked him to make her forget. *Make me forget, Hope. Make me forget what happened two years ago. Make me forget all the grief I've caused.*

He backed her up against the living room wall and kissed her, wanting, seeking, needing the escape. Their bodies melded together. She yanked and tugged and pulled at the buttons on his shirt until it hung open, and then her desperate hands streaked over his bare skin. Lucca sucked in a breath as her nails scraped across his nipples.

On the edge of sinking entirely into the moment, he was too responsible to ignore the faint chime of alarm bells, barely audible beneath the fog of alcohol and desire. He mumbled against her lips. "Hope? Are you sure about this?"

"Make me feel better, Lucca."

He picked her up in his arms and carried her to his bed.

What took place there during the next few hours in the muted golden light of a single lamp was raw and physical and mindless. It wasn't making love, but it was more than just sex.

Lucca immersed himself in his senses. He stripped her naked and feasted on the sight of those curves that had tantalized him since their very first meeting. He bent over her and inhaled her scent—feminine and fresh and hot with arousal. He stroked his calloused hands across her smooth, soft skin and learned her body, using his fingers to coax throaty moans and whispered gasps from lips swollen from the pressure of his mouth.

He tasted the salt of her tears and knew the echo of his own. They were kindred spirits, each running from something, trapped in the throes of a private, painful, anguished memory.

October Madness.

No. He shoved the intrusion of thought from his mind and concentrated on the woman beneath him. *See her flush, hear her whimper.* "You are beautiful, Hope."

He nibbled his way down her neck, across the hard ridge of her collarbone to the soft, generous swell of her breasts. Her hands never stopped stroking and exploring, even as he suckled her sweetness and lost himself in the pleasure of the here and now, not the then. Forget the then.

Make me forget.

Hope Montgomery was now. Here, now, with him. And she was wild—driving him wild. He took her and she took him and they took each other. She cried out her pleasure and her pain. He repeated her name over and over. A wish. A prayer. Hope. Hope. Hope.

How many times throughout the night, he had no clue. He'd lay spent, thinking it done, and then she would reach for him and it would begin anew. At some point, finally, emotionally spent and physically exhausted, they slept.

Lucca awoke as a golden dawn began to chase away the night's shadows, a pleasant weight and warmth sprawled across him. Following a moment of surprise, the events of the evening flooded back. Damn. He lay still, his head aching, attempting to process what had happened. *Make me forget? Oh, holy hell.*

Then he sensed the growing tension in the body lying entangled with his. *She's awake.* Before he could decide on the best way to handle this particular morning after, she quietly and cautiously inched away from him. For a minute, she paused, and he felt the weight of her gaze. Deciding he'd let her take the lead, he feigned sleep as she slipped from the bed. He watched through slitted eyelids as she gathered up her clothes, cast one fearful look in his direction, then exited the room.

He expected to hear the bathroom door close. Instead, a few moments later, he heard his front door open, then softly close.

What the hell? Lucca sat up, staring like a fool at the empty doorway. She left? She just up and left?

Damn. That was a first. No woman had ever done that to him before.

So, the kindergarten teacher comes over for a booty call, then sneaks out at first light? What is that all about?

Completely sober now, he replayed the scene from the previous night in his mind. He recalled her desperation, her pain. *Why couldn't she be alone last night? What did she want to forget?*

He thought about the sex. It had been . . . wild. Primal. She'd clawed at him, and he knew for certain that when he showered, he'd see the scratches to prove it. A sudden worry occurred. He hadn't hurt her, had he? Was that why she had sneaked away? Sure, he'd been lit, but he hadn't been falling-down drunk. He didn't hurt women in bed.

No, he hadn't hurt her. She'd acted as if he'd saved her. She'd acted as if he'd been her lifeline.

There's another first. He'd never been anyone's lifeline before. He didn't know how he felt about the idea. Talk about role reversal.

Why? What misery had driven Little Miss Sunshine

Kindergarten Teacher to such despair that she needed mindless sex to chase it away?

As he rose from his bed and padded toward his bathroom to take a shower, Lucca decided he wanted the answer. Now, how best to go about getting it?

Hope spent Sunday holed up in her house. She was embarrassed, mortified, and—honesty made her admit it—deliciously satisfied. She couldn't believe what she'd done Saturday night, but she couldn't entirely regret it, either.

What shamed her was the fact that she'd snuck out of his bed and house without having the courage to face him. Never in her life had she been so . . . what? Cowardly? Needy? Out of her mind? All of the above?

Was it shame that was making her feel warm as she remembered it? She'd never, ever tried to use sex to distract her from her pain. Why last night? Why with Lucca Romano?

Because he was damaged, too. Because whether he knew it or not, they had that in common.

And, frankly, because he did it for her. She'd hungered for him. She'd wanted the feel of his large hands on her, wanted his mouth, wanted to experience the sensation of having his body lying atop hers. Man, oh man, she'd gotten what she wanted. It had been the single most erotic experience of her life.

And she'd said thank you by sneaking out of his bed like a thief in the night.

That's what shamed Hope. Not that she had turned to him in her pain, but that she didn't have the guts to face him the morning after.

Lucca deserved an explanation. If she had any guts at all she would march over there and tell him why she'd acted the way she had. But she couldn't do it. She could share her body, but not the secret of her heart. Not yet, anyway. After Mark's call and her evening with the scrapbook, she needed a little more time before she could talk about Holly.

If she peeked out of her dining room window toward Lucca's house a time or twelve just to see if she could catch a glimpse of him, well . . . who could blame her?

Following a mostly unproductive day, she dreamed about him that night, tossing and turning, sleeping fitfully and waking up tired. She drove her bus route, and by the time she picked up her last student, she had made a decision. Running away and hiding wasn't right, nor was it working for her. After school, as soon as she was free, she'd track down Lucca and talk to him. She'd apologize for sneaking off Sunday morning and explain that she'd had an upsetting call from her ex and lost her . . . well . . . hmm. She couldn't say good sense. That sounded insulting.

Well, she had all day to figure something out.

Or so she thought, until a knock on her door at the end of third period prompted her to look up from her paperwork. Lucca Romano stood in her classroom doorway. He wore jeans, a Colorado Buffaloes T-shirt, and a leather jacket. She couldn't read the expression on his face as he said, "I'm here to serve one of my volunteer hours."

In what way? Her cheeks flushed with warmth as an image that had no business in a kindergarten classroom flashed through her mind. "I planned to go see you after school."

"Oh, yeah?" One corner of his mouth kicked up in a slow grin. He leaned against the doorjamb and folded his arms across his broad chest. "Maybe my volunteer efforts can wait another day."

She glanced at the clock. "I have a parent conference in five minutes, but my lunch period is after that. Do you like chicken salad?"

"I do."

"Want to share my sandwich?"

Challenge lit his green eyes. "Got any chips to go with it?"

"Carrot sticks."

"Oh. I'm afraid that's a deal breaker."

"I could probably scare up some potato chips."

"All right, then." He straightened. "It's a date."

A date. Hope blinked. She'd forgotten all about their Friday dinner date. Had he?

Well, no matter. Friday was still five days away. Lunch was in half an hour. "It's a nice day. There's a small courtyard off the teachers' lounge where I like to eat my lunch. I usually have it to myself. I could meet you there in thirty minutes."

He nodded. "Thirty minutes, then. In the meantime, I'll see if Principal Geary doesn't have something I can do to knock out half an hour of my volunteering sentence."

Hope rolled her eyes, but when she left her classroom for her meeting moments later, she was smiling.

She met Wade Mitchell's mother in the conference room. A trim woman in her late forties, Darla Mitchell wore jeans, a blue chambray shirt, and cowboy boots that befit her position as a rancher's wife. "Hello, Mrs. Mitchell."

"Ms. Montgomery. Thank you so much for seeing me."

"I'm always happy to speak to parents. I have to tell you, Wade is such a nice young man."

"Thank you."

"Is there a problem I'm not aware of?"

Darla gave a heavy sigh. "Not a problem, exactly. More of . . . well . . . it's complicated. Wade tells me the school hasn't hired a basketball coach? Practice starts soon, and you're filling in?"

Oh, now Hope understood the reason for the conference request. "Mr. Geary did hire someone, but he quit right before school started, and Mr. Geary couldn't find a replacement. I'm the only teacher here who played ball in high school."

"I see."

"So do I, Mrs. Mitchell. Wade is an excellent player and he deserves a better coach."

"Well, that sounds embarrassingly rude, but . . . yes. You see, he has a complicated situation at home. If I share the story with you, may I have your word that you will be discreet with the information?"

"Of course."

"Okay, then." She exhaled a heavy breath. "I am squarely in the middle here, and I feel like I'm betraying my husband by doing this, but . . . Wade wants to go to college. He and I believe that the only way to make it happen is for him to earn an athletic scholarship."

"Colleges offer financial aid, Mrs. Mitchell. I'm sure—"

"The money isn't the problem. Well, it's part of it, but Wade's biggest stumbling block is his father. He doesn't want Wade to go to college. He doesn't see the need for it. Frankly, the idea scares him half to death because of something that happened in the past."

She went on to explain that her husband was fighting for all he was worth to save the family ranch. "It's his legacy, it's Wade's legacy, and my husband thinks Wade can learn everything he needs to know by working the ranch."

"Wade doesn't want to be a rancher?"

"No, that's what is making this tricky. If he didn't want to be a rancher, he could defy his father and go off and pursue whatever dreams he has. But he loves the ranch and he wants a future in ranching. He just wants to go to college first. He wants that experience before coming home and settling down, but my husband is afraid to let him go. You see, my husband has been down that road before. His much younger brother—who was more of a son to him than a sibling—went off to college and never returned to Storm Mountain. He won't admit it, but that broke my husband's heart."

"I can understand that," Hope said, sympathy washing through her. "What I don't understand is why a basketball scholarship would be different from an academic scholarship to him."

"I won't claim that this whole thing makes sense because it's all based on emotions rather than logic. It's different to David if one is recruited rather than applying."

"All right, then. What assistance are you looking for from me?"

Again, Darla Mitchell inhaled a deep breath, then exhaled loudly. "I want to do what is best for both my son and my husband. As the team leader this year, you can be Wade's advocate. I'm not trying to be rude, but someone with my son's raw talent needs someone with the knowledge and experience to develop it. I can't hire or even request a private coach. It would cause too much dissension in the family. But, as this year's coach, you can bring someone on to help the team. I know that Gabi Romano played college ball. She shot baskets with Wade at the fund-raiser last week. Sheriff Turner played college basketball, too, so he could help if he could find time, though I know he has his hands full running the sheriff's department. Then, of course, there is Coach Romano."

She said it like "There is the Holy Grail."

This time Hope was the one releasing a sigh. "I'm with you, Mrs. Mitchell. Both Principal Geary and I have been thinking in that same direction. He told me just this morning that he spoke to Zach and Gabi over the weekend. They've agreed to help as their schedules allow. As far as Lucca Romano goes . . . that's tougher."

"Wade saw him dunk the ball Friday night. He hasn't stopped talking about it since."

Hope had watched the boys' basketball team play last year, and she knew that Wade was a talented player. "Lucca claims to be retired from coaching. I believe he is firm in that decision."

"Maybe if we couched it in terms other than coaching? Consulting, perhaps? If Zach and Gabi can help with Wade's fundamentals, and maybe get their brother Tony to visit for a private coaching clinic for Wade, then maybe Coach Lucca Romano could advise you on what Wade needs to do to catch the notice of scouts and recruiters?"

"Maybe." Hope thought it over. Wade's mother had a point. Who knew what Lucca would think of the proposal? Maybe it would be just the sort of thing he needed to ease back into that part of his life. "I certainly don't see what it would hurt to ask. Heaven knows, I can use all the help I can get."

"Thank you, Ms. Montgomery."

"Hope. Please, call me Hope."

"It's a fitting name. I'm sorry to put you in the middle of family business, but I justify it because it's part of a coach's job to advocate for her players. However, I'm not a helicopter parent. No matter what happens from this point on, I give you my word that this is the last you will hear from me on this topic."

"I will do my best to help Wade. I agree that it is part of my job. I'm glad you came to me, and, please, don't hesitate to contact me about any concerns you may have in the future."

Hope made small talk with Wade's mother as she escorted her to the school office where she signed out of the building. A glance at the wall clock told her she had just enough time to stop by her classroom to grab a jacket and her sack lunch, and then duck into the cafeteria and purchase a bag of chips for Lucca.

She arrived at the courtyard to find him already there. *He's washing windows?* His jacket lay draped over the picnic table. He had a squeegee in one hand, and a spray bottle of cleaner in the other. A white rag hung from the back pocket of his jeans. She watched his biceps bunch as he lifted his arms, and her mouth went dry.

Get your mind back where it belongs. Clearing her throat, she asked, "Washing the windows?"

"Just the top row. It'll save your janitor quite a bit of time. He needs a step stool to reach it." He gathered up his cleaning supplies, used a bottle of water to rinse his hands, then wiped them with the rag from his pocket while Hope set out their lunch.

"The weather is colder now than it was earlier," she observed as she set out the chips. "This courtyard is nice because it's sheltered from the wind. I heard we have a chance for snow later this afternoon."

"I don't know that I'm ready for snow," he said. "Are those Cheetos I see?"

"And Fritos and pretzels and potato chips. I wasn't sure of your junk food preference, so I bought some of each."

"Love 'em all." He lifted his long legs over the bench of the picnic table and sat. "Thanks. So, carrot sticks aside, you're not one of those food-police types?"

"Not at all. I scored brownies for both of us in the cafeteria. They're not as good as what Sarah bakes, but they're not bad, either."

"Excellent."

He took a bite of sandwich, nodded his approval, then observed, "This is a nice little spot. I'm surprised it's not overrun with students."

"Access is restricted to faculty and staff. It's our refuge, our little garden of tranquillity. I have a later lunch than the other teachers due to my half-day kindergarten, so I almost always have it to myself."

"I'm glad, because I figure this conversation is better done in privacy." He pinned her with a steady green-eyed stare. "So, tell me why you planned to visit me this afternoon."

Hope looked down at her sandwich and felt her cheeks warm with a blush. "What . . . no easing into this?"

"I don't know how much time you have for lunch."

She twisted her mouth ruefully and then popped a grape into it to give her a moment to collect her thoughts. Its sour taste made her pucker. "I wanted to apologize to you for sneaking out of your house Sunday morning. That wasn't well done of me."

"Apology accepted." He reached for one of her carrot sticks and bit into it with a crunch. While she frowned at him—hadn't he claimed carrots sticks to be a deal breaker?—he studied her. He came to some sort of decision, because he nodded once and said, "I owe you an apology too, Hope. You were obviously upset and if I'd been a gentleman, I would have put the brakes on things."

"I didn't go looking for a gentleman, Lucca. I went looking for escape."

"Escape from what?"

Hope sucked in a heavy breath. She had to go down this road. Part of the way, anyway. She owed him that much. "I had a phone call from my ex. It wasn't pleasant."

"Ah." He took a bite from his half sandwich and chewed thoughtfully. "Tell me about your ex."

"I'd rather not. It'd give me indigestion. Can we change the subject please? I'd like to tell you about the parent conference I mentioned."

He gave her a long considering look, and she could see

his inner debate. He wanted to press her. Hope lifted her chin. She had no intention of being pressed.

"All right, then," he conceded. "I'll keep my opinions about harassment to myself. Just tell me this. How long have you been divorced?"

Hope breathed a sigh of relief. "Four years. End of story. So, about my parent conference . . . we have a senior student named Wade Mitchell. His parents are local ranchers. He's a good student, but not an exceptional one. I expect him to graduate with a B+ average. He is, however, an exceptional athlete."

She didn't miss her lunch partner's subtle tensing. Nevertheless, she pressed on. "He's tall and strong from his ranch work. He has quick reflexes and he thinks on his feet. He plays basketball."

Lucca set down his sandwich. "Hope, if you're thinking what I think you are thinking, then save your breath."

"Just hear me out. Would you, please?"

"It won't matter."

"Our basketball coach quit just before school started. Our principal couldn't find a replacement. I'm filling in. Me. I haven't played basketball since high school. Wade has the raw talent to play for a college team, Lucca, but he needs to develop his skills and he needs . . . we need . . . to call him to the attention of the decision makers."

"No," he said flatly and wiped his mouth with a paper napkin.

Annoyed now, she wasn't going to let it go. It was time he stopped wallowing. "The first practice is this afternoon. Helping Wade could count for your volunteer pledge. Wouldn't it be easier to coach the young man a little than to go around the school washing the high windows? You could make a tremendous difference in that young man's life. Wade Mitchell needs you."

"I said no."

"Why?" Irritation sharpened her tone. "Lucca, you're not even thinking about it."

"I don't have to. No way, Hope. I saw the kid. You're right, he does have talent. But I'm not a mentor, a teacher, or a coach."

"What are you then? A paint scraper?"

"Presently, yes."

"Well, that's ambitious." She wanted to reach across the table and shake him. "What are you going to do beyond that? Continue to wallow?"

Irked, Lucca scowled at her. " 'Wallow'? Seems you didn't mind it the other night." He tossed down his napkin and stood up to leave. "I don't need this, Hope."

"I think you do. You need it more than you'll ever realize. You didn't die in that van wreck, Lucca. You are still here. And all you're doing is existing. You need to give something back and start living again."

Before he could retort, she went on. "There are people in this world who have lived through all nine circles of hell and are still putting one foot in front of the other. They give back. Do you know why? Because it helps. It makes you feel better. It reminds you that you're still alive even though you might wish you were dead."

His eyes angry, he fired his words like bullets. "Seems to me that I've already done my share of giving. I gave you all you could handle the other night, didn't I? You wanted escape, and I gave you a place to go. I didn't ask for explanations or strings, and I'm damn sure not asking for advice." He grabbed up his jacket. "So, thanks for the sandwich. And for the screw. Beyond that, we're done here."

Whoa. She sucked in a breath, wounded, and watched him walk away in stunned silence.

But as he reached for the door's handle, she found her voice and her backbone. "You ass."

She threw down her own napkin and rose. "How dare you? You sorry, selfish, poor-pitiful-me sonofabitch. I know you feel guilty because your players died."

He whirled to face her. "Do not dare to—"

She cut him off with a jab of her hand. "I understand that the success you had afterward didn't rest well on your shoulders. Probably made you feel guilty as all hell to win. I get that. It's hard to be the one left behind, Lucca. I understand that more than you probably realize. But do you know what? You just need to get over yourself and move forward, Coach. It's not all about you."

He stood frozen in place, as tall and stiff as the Ponderosa pine rising from the center of the courtyard. Hope was on a roll. She stepped away from the picnic table and approached him, her chin up, and her hands braced on her hips. "You have been given so much— talent and treasure and a face and body that make a woman swoon. You're a grand-prize winner in the genetics lottery. And what are you doing with those gifts? Nothing. It's a disgrace. You have no purpose. You could do so much good, but instead you are working as a second-rate handyman for your mother."

His jaw was set and as hard as the granite cliffs of Murphy Mountain, his eyes as cold as its summit in January. He was a full foot taller than she was; he loomed above her. Hope didn't give a damn. He needed that fine ass of his kicked.

She put her palm against his chest and shoved him. "You are not the only person in the world to suffer a tragedy, Lucca Romano. Other people suffer losses. But other people can't count on their big bank account or their large, loving family for support. Do you know what it's like to have no one? To be totally alone? No, you don't! You are a Romano."

"Dammit, Hope."

"Don't you curse at me! Other people have suffered

the worst that life can throw at them and they didn't quit. They climbed back up on their feet and they survived and they made a freaking difference. Well, guess what, mister. You could do that, too. You *should* do it, too. It's tragic that your van wrecked and your players died. It's horrible to be the one left behind who has to try to make sense of the incomprehensible. But it happens. Life happens, and life isn't all NCAA tournaments and roses. You need to knock off the pity party and get over yourself."

She reached past him, yanked open the door, and sailed through it, leaving him—and her lunch remains—behind. In a blind fury, she marched down the hall and around the corner until she reached the girls' locker room. Shoving open that door, she strode inside and kicked an open locker door shut as his words echoed through her mind. *Thanks for the sandwich. And the screw.*

"Thanks for nothing, lawn boy."

She took a deep, cleansing breath, then walked to her locker and changed into her athletic clothes. She had afternoon gym classes to oversee.

Not to mention the first basketball practice of the season.

NINE

With Hope's angry accusations ringing in his mind, Lucca exited the school, his shoulders hunched against the wind's chill. Brittle brown leaves skittered across the sidewalk as he walked beside the playground where squealing children ran for the shelter of the school.

He'd left his truck at Aspenglow, a five-minute walk from school. Halfway there, a flurry of fat snowflakes began to swirl around him. His leather coat didn't offer much protection from the elements. Soon he was as cold on the outside as he was inside.

His refusal to coach had definitely struck a nerve, and she'd fired back hard. Of all the lousy things she'd said, calling him a quitter rankled the most. For all his life, he'd been a competitor, never a quitter. The fact that he deserved the charge made him feel like crap. The truth really did hurt; it gave him one more reason to despise himself.

Knock off the pity party and get over yourself.

"Hell, Hope. I'm trying."

But was he, really? Had he tried to rise out of the funk he'd fallen into? He'd come to the mountains with his tail tucked between his legs and licking his wounds. He was playing handyman/gardener for his mother, scraping paint, trimming posies, and hiding from the world and from himself. Shameful.

Upon reaching his truck, he fired up the engine, pulled out onto Aspen Street, and started driving. He took the first turn that headed out of town, a little two-lane route that climbed up past the cemetery and into the mountains to the west. With no particular destination in mind, he drove, following the road wherever it led.

As the miles passed, Lucca slowly began to relax, to warm, to chip his way through the ice that had encased him since the moment Hope had asked him to coach.

Rounding a curve, he spied a scenic overlook ahead. He turned into the parking area, killed the ignition, and slipped into a jacket he'd left in the cab. He exited his truck and walked to the wooden railing at the overlook's edge.

The snow shower had blown over, leaving sunshine in its wake. Eternity Springs sat snuggled in the valley below, pretty as a Christmas card with a dusting of new snow. Lucca gripped the railing and stared down at the little town.

Get over yourself.

One corner of Lucca's mouth lifted in a cheerless smirk. In the past, he'd have heard that sentiment from his family, but they tiptoed around him these days. In fact, he couldn't remember the last time anyone had put him in his place that way. Leave it to a kindergarten teacher.

She really was something. Up at dawn to drive a bus. Teaching both five-year-olds and teens. And coaching, too?

Wade Mitchell needs you.

As Lucca gazed down at the town, he spied a vehicle ascending the road he'd just traveled. Chilly day to be riding a bike, he thought, before turning his focus inward. He recognized that he stood at a crossroads. He couldn't continue this way. He'd been playing four-corner offense for two years now. He needed to stop killing time and take his shot—or else call the game and go back to booze and beaches.

And forget all about kindergarten teachers.

His family deserved better from him. They'd been patient since he took up residence next door to Hope. Maybe too patient. They assumed that given enough time, Eternity Springs would work its magic on him and cure him of what ailed him. His brother Zach was one of the most solid, down-to-earth people he knew, and Zach honestly believed that the valley below possessed a special healing energy.

Maybe there was something to it. Despite a few curious incidents involving dirty dishes and pajama days, their mother certainly appeared to be as happy as a clam, a far cry from the sad, bereaved widow she'd been before she moved to Colorado. Gabi might not know what she wanted to do career-wise, but moving here helped her get over the lowlife she had dated in Denver.

And he . . . well . . . guess that's what he had to decide. Was he ready to get over himself?

It had been two years since the accident. He'd spent the first year and a half suppressing his memories and shutting down his emotions, and the last six months . . . wallowing. On the first anniversary of the wreck, he'd phoned the Seidels and the Palmers and Brandon Gates. Two of those calls had gone well. Seth Seidel's parents . . . Lucca closed his eyes. That one still ate at him.

They blamed him. They'd even threatened him with a lawsuit, though the notice he'd expected never arrived. He still heard the echoes of Seth's father's vitriolic accusations in his dreams. He didn't blame the man one bit.

But maybe, just maybe, he didn't blame himself quite

as much as he used to. Was it the Eternity Springs effect? Or was it Hope Montgomery?

Get over yourself.

From the corner of his eye he saw a bird—was it a hawk?—take wing from the top of a fir tree and sail out over the valley. He watched it for long minutes as it soared and circled against the blue sky. Majestic, he thought. Powerful and free.

It dove, swooped at ground level, and rose once more with what looked like a mouse wiggling in its talons.

"Okay, why do I feel like there's a message there for me?" he muttered. A reminder that life wasn't always pretty, perhaps? Or that death was a natural part of life?

He turned at the sound of an approaching motorcycle and recognized the bike and the rider who pulled into the overlook parking lot. Celeste Blessing killed her engine and swung her leg off her Honda Gold Wing. Removing her helmet, she tucked it into her arms and offered him a bright smile. "Well, hello, Lucca. It's a pleasant surprise to see you here. Did you come up to enjoy the first snowfall, too?"

"I was just out for a drive."

"It's a lovely day for it."

"It's bitter cold, Celeste."

"But there's a clear sky and the wind has died. It snowed just long enough to paint our town a heavenly white. I do adore changing seasons. That's one of the reasons I moved to Eternity Springs. We have four distinct and lovely seasons."

For Lucca, "changing seasons" had always meant football season into basketball season into baseball season. This was his first year for "changing seasons" to mean autumn leaves giving way to winter snowfall. Did he miss sports being the center of his life?

While he pondered that question, Celeste stood beside him and gazed down at Eternity Springs, sighing with utter contentment. "Isn't it beautiful? Eternity Springs is such a special place; the valley has such positive energy. Don't you feel it?"

"I'm too cold to feel much of anything."

She laughed and patted his hand. "Of course, it's the people who live here who make our home what it is. We're all so glad that the Romano family is becoming part of the fabric of life in our town."

She lifted her clear, winter blue eyes to study him. "Do you think you'll stay with us, Lucca?"

"That's what I'm trying to decide." He didn't know what it was, but something about Celeste invited confidences. "Someone told me today that I have no purpose. She's right. It's hard to know where I need to be if I don't know what I need to be doing."

"Well, you will figure it out. You do have a purpose, Lucca; it's just changing from what it once was. I don't want to tread where I'm not welcome, but if you'll allow me to give you one bit of advice?"

"Sure, why not?"

"Life is not meant to be an interstate highway. It's a winding mountain road with hills and dips, stop signs and school zones. Let friends and family be the data for your GPS satellite feed, and never forget that sometimes an unexpected detour leads to a hidden miracle."

Lucca gave her a sidelong look. "I think I understand what you are trying to say, but I'm just a jock. Maybe you could elaborate?"

"Just a jock," Celeste repeated, wrinkling her nose and sniffing with disdain. "And Albert Einstein was just a scientist. My point is that peace is a process, not a shot clock with seconds ticking away and a buzzer at the finish. It's the result of many decisions, not just one. Don't expect otherwise, and don't fail to recognize how far you've risen from the depths of your despair. An American poet, John Vance Cheney, wrote 'The soul would have no rainbow had the eyes no tears.' Your rainbow awaits, Lucca Romano. You can't rush the journey, but you can lift your foot from the brake and goose the gas a little. Slow and steady wins the race."

Lucca took a moment and allowed that to sink in. She'd said a lot in a few sentences. "You are quite a woman, Celeste."

"I've been around this world a long time. I'm experienced. And speaking of experience, this afternoon I get to babysit for Sarah while she gets a haircut, so I'd best be going. I'm afraid she'll put him down for a nap before I get there, and I'll miss cuddle time." She donned her helmet and fixed the chin strap. "What are your plans for the afternoon, dear?"

Lucca turned his attention back to the town nestled in the valley below and picked out the school. "I have some crow to eat. An apology to make."

Celeste smiled and gave his arm another pat. "Both are better with a sprinkle of sugar. I'm so glad our paths happened to cross today. Safe journey, Lucca."

"You, too, Celeste."

The air seemed to grow colder after she left, and when the sound of her motorcycle faded, the world around him was as quiet as Lucca could ever remember—quiet, but peaceful, too, and it allowed him the perfect opportunity to think his decision through.

He definitely owed Hope an apology. He'd been an ass at lunch, and he'd deserved the arrows she'd fired his way. Hadn't she been magnificent in her anger?

Of course, she'd been glorious in her misery, too.

What the hell had happened to Hope to put such pain and anguish in her tone? When she'd declared that other people had suffered tragedies and lived through all nine circles of hell, she hadn't come up with those points out of the blue. She'd spoken from experience. And what about her devastation Saturday night? What had her ex-husband said in his phone call that had destroyed her so thoroughly?

"What happened to you, Hope?" A tragedy, certainly. A hellish event. Something big and dark and ugly that no one in town knew about. Otherwise, he'd have heard about it. The small-town gossip network thrived in Eternity Springs.

Spying the hawk as it took to the air once more and flew out over the valley, Lucca found his purpose. He had given Hope Montgomery escape with sex, but escape was not what she needed. It wasn't what either of them needed. He knew that now as certain as he stood here. For the past two years, he had focused on his own heartache. Well, time to make a turn. Tragedy was no excuse for selfishness.

Get over yourself.

Well, you asked for it, teacher.

Of all the things she'd said to him at lunch, one sentiment stood out. *Do you know what it's like to have no one? To be totally alone? No, you don't!*

Unspoken were the words "I do."

So Lucca was going to give Hope Montgomery something more valuable than escape. He had a big, broad pair of shoulders. It was time he used them for something worthwhile. Hope had friends, but she didn't have a confidant. He could fill that role for her. He could offer her a meaningful friendship. He could offer to share her burden so that when desperate times occurred, she didn't have to escape into sex with a near stranger. She could come to him and say "I'm hurting" and he could reply "I understand. I can help."

Not that helping couldn't include sex if that's what she wanted. Hey, he had nothing against being a full-service friend. But the goal here, the purpose, would be to share her pain. To end her aloneness.

Family didn't fix that. Sure, they loved and supported,

and in doing so helped. But the whole "walk a mile in my shoes" thing had merit. No one who hasn't lived the despair can truly understand it.

Lucca had lived it. Now he would use that experience to help Hope find not escape, but healing. And in doing so, perhaps he'd find healing himself.

Grand plans, Romano. But how are you going to go about it? You really pissed the lady off.

Okay, then. The first step definitely needed to be the apology. As he returned to his truck and took the winding road back toward town, he considered how best to do it. He could send her flowers with a sincerely worded card. Or he could show up on her front porch with flowers and hat in hand and deliver the apology in person. That might work better.

Of course, the best way to do it would be to show up at the school and do it. At basketball practice.

His stomach took a roll. His foot tapped the brakes. Was he sure about this? Or had the cold frosted his brain?

He could just let this whole idea go. He'd gone along without purpose for a while now. He could continue down that road. He didn't need to know what her secret was. They'd had a one-night stand. He could chalk it up as a mistake and put it behind him. Then on the anniversary, he could wallow. He could be alone.

You don't want to wallow. You don't want to put it behind you. You want more than a one-night stand. You want to live with purpose again. You want to do something that matters. Basketball doesn't matter . . . but what you can do with basketball does.

Lucca drummed his fingers on the steering wheel. It was true, and he could do this. He wanted to do this. One corner of his mouth lifted in a crooked grin. Go figure.

She would think he was doing it for the boy, and in a

minor way, she'd be right. But Lucca had caught sight of a side road that interested him, and he'd decided to make a little detour.

Never forget that sometimes an unexpected detour leads to a hidden miracle, Celeste's voice echoed.

Lucca carefully, cautiously, gave the gas pedal a goose and headed toward Hope.

"I'm sorry to flake out on you, but I can't help with your basketball team today, after all," Gabi Romano told Hope when she called shortly before practice. "I had an unexpected trip come up. I'll be gone for two and a half weeks."

"Oh, really? Where are you going?"

Gabi told her about a wealthy couple from Tulsa who owned a vacation house in the mountains west of Eternity Springs. "They adore me because back before I left the sheriff's department, their beloved Precious escaped the vacation house and got lost in the woods and I found her. Now the Thurstons need someone to dog-sit while they travel with another couple. They gave me my choice of their beachfront villa in south Florida or the mountain mansion an hour out of Eternity Springs. It was a tough choice, but I chose white sand and a turquoise sea. And they're paying me more than I made at the sheriff's department."

"They don't have a second dog that needs sitting, do they? I wouldn't mind an hour commute from a mountain mansion."

"Sorry, Charlie. I do feel bad about leaving you in the lurch this way. But it's only a couple of weeks, and you'll still have Zach's help. He said he'd pitch in whenever he could manage, and this isn't usually a busy time of year for him." Gabi let out a sigh, then added, "I wish I could suggest you talk to Lucca, too, but I honestly think it would be a waste of breath."

Hope's only response to that was a flat "Hmmm."

The two women spoke a few more minutes, then Hope bade Gabi bon voyage and ended the call. She wished the timing had been better for her players, but she couldn't blame Gabi for taking advantage of such a great opportunity. A beach sounded lovely, too. Maybe during semester break, she could take a little beach vacation herself.

A glance at the clock showed her that she was five minutes late for practice. She grabbed her clipboard and exited the athletic office with a smile pasted on her lips. She was determined to convince her team that all was not lost simply because she was their coach.

She heard the multiple *thump thump thump*s of basketballs against the hardwood along with a number of *clang*s as balls hit the rim. Taking it as a good sign that the team had started without her, Hope's fake smile warmed to genuine. But when she stepped into the gym, she stopped abruptly.

Lucca Romano stood on the court directing her players in a drill. She couldn't have been more shocked if LeBron James had suddenly appeared in the school gym. Her players looked as if they'd died and gone to heaven. Lucca had a "tense, but holding on" look about him. Spying Hope, he nodded. "Hello, Coach Montgomery."

Questions spun through her mind. Why was he here? Was this a onetime thing? Or was he going to serve his volunteer pledge this way? Was there any chance at all that he'd take over the team completely?

Hope knew, however, that this was not the time for questions, so she swallowed hard, then cautiously said, "Coach Romano. Is there . . . ah . . . what can I do to help?"

He put her to work as his secretary, taking notes as he dictated. He spoke quietly so as not to be overheard as he evaluated the players' strengths and weaknesses. He kept his comments businesslike, and when he finished the evaluation, he suggested that she take a seat. "I know you've been working nonstop since before dawn. I can take it from here."

She studied him, unable to read his expression. She was tired—exhausted, to be honest—so she did as he suggested. As she watched him spend time with each boy individually, offering instructions and critiques, it occurred to her that he had avoided looking directly at her since she walked into the gym. She couldn't read him. What was he thinking? Why was he here? Had his brother or his sister called and chewed him out? Or had her own lecture pounded its way through his cranky skull?

That possibility made her smile.

Lucca worked with the team, as a team, until five minutes to five when he spoke to Hope for the first time in half an hour. "Are you scheduled to end at five?"

"Actually, it was four-thirty." Hope wondered if anyone else noticed the way he seemed to sag in relief just a little.

"Hit the showers, men."

With that, the cloud of awe that had surrounded the team dispersed, and the boys broke out in excited chatter. Soon, only Lucca and Hope remained in the gym. As she fumbled around for something to say to him, she had a memory flash of the school's former coach, Frank Gowdy, standing beneath the basket. He'd been a lovable, balding teddy bear with a beer belly and a constant smile. The contrast with Lucca Romano couldn't be bigger.

He looked handsome and hard and just a little bit angry. Gazing at him, her knees went weak.

He dribbled the basketball then passed it to her. "You have a mess on your hands with this team."

She bounced the ball twice, then threw it back. "They're enthusiastic."

"True." He turned and took a shot at the basket. Nothing but net. Hope jogged to retrieve it, then sent it back to Lucca. "The Mitchell kid. He's raw, but he has something to work with."

"Yes." Hope drew in a bracing breath, then cut to the heart of the matter. "Will you work with him? Will you help us, Lucca?"

Rather than respond, he took the ball up the court to the opposite basket and put up a jump shot. Hope's heart sank. After watching him with the boys, seeing how he'd related to them, she'd had her hopes up that this was more than a onetime deal.

Lucca took two more shots at the basket, then captured the ball and tucked it beneath his arm. When he met her gaze, his own was steady and sincere. "I need to grovel for a minute or two, Hope. I want to apologize for my remark at lunch. I felt cornered by your request, so I struck out at you. That's not an excuse, but an explanation. I'm very sorry I said what I did. It was crude, and I was an ass. Honestly, Saturday night was just about as nice a thing that's happened to me in ages."

Once again, Hope was flabbergasted. She did not, however, want to discuss Saturday night, so she simply said, "Apology accepted."

He nodded. "Thank you. So, do you have something else you need to do here, or are you done for tonight?"

"I'm done. Finally. It's been a long day."

"Seems to me like we're the last people in the building."

"I'm sure the janitor is still here," Hope replied, eyeing the trash can at the entrance to the gym. "He starts to work in the kindergarten wing, then works his way around here."

Lucca set the basketball in the ball rack. "I stuck a

six-pack in the fridge in the athletic office. Why don't you have one with me? We probably need to talk about this whole coaching thing going forward."

"A six-pack?" Hope repeated, pulling up short. "As in beer? You brought beer onto a school campus? You can't bring beer onto campus. You absolutely can't drink beer on campus."

"Sure I can. I don't do this very often, but today I'm pulling the Coach Romano card. I coached practice this afternoon. I get to have a beer. Besides, what's the worst that can happen to me? The powers that be can forbid me from ever coming back? Guess they could try to have me arrested, but the sheriff would simply sit down and have a brew with me."

Hope didn't know how to respond to that. He was right, but she wasn't going to admit it. She understood that he had faced down a demon today, but honestly. Some things just weren't done.

She followed him to the athletic office but shook her head when he pulled a beer from the dorm-sized fridge and held it up to her. "Tea?" he asked. "Water?"

"Water."

He handed over a bottle, then sprawled on the brown microfiber sofa that Coach Gowdy had left behind when he quit his job. Hope perched in the armchair beside the office door and sipped her water while Lucca took a long pull from his beer bottle. "Just promise me that if anyone walks in here, you'll hide that?" she asked. "Please?"

"Not much of a rule breaker, are you, teacher?" he asked, grinning.

She sniffed. *I slept with you, didn't I? You don't think that's breaking the rules?* "That depends on the rule."

He stretched his leg to kick a large cardboard box filled with T-shirts over in front of him to serve as an ottoman, then he propped up his legs on the box and crossed his feet at his ankles. He sighed heavily and dragged a hand down his face. "Am I glad that is over. I took a drive earlier this afternoon and ended up at a lookout above town. Celeste Blessing stopped while I was there. She's an interesting woman. Gave me the strangest advice—that somehow made a lot of sense to me. When I left the overlook, I knew I needed to make this practice today."

"Because of something Celeste told you?"

"That, and I figured a bouquet of flowers just wasn't a good enough apology considering the scope of my jerkhood at lunch today." He took another sip of beer, then rested his head back against the sofa and shut his eyes. "Celeste says that peace is a process, that finding it is the result of a bunch of little decisions rather than one big one. I think that maybe you are part of those decisions, Hope. I was lost in this funk when you knocked on my door Saturday night, and today at lunch your request sent me right back into the weeds. I know you know about the wreck that killed two of my players and put another in a wheelchair. I'd like to tell you the rest of it. Will you listen?"

Though she really, truly didn't want to discuss Saturday night, it sounded like he wanted to open up. Based on things that Gabi and Maggie had said, she knew he never opened up. The fact that he'd do it with her surprised her and, frankly, made her wary. She sensed that something more was going on here than what she understood. Nevertheless, she couldn't say no. "Yes, I'll listen."

"Good. You might have to be a little patient. I don't know how fast I'm going to be able to get this out."

Compassion filled her. This obviously wasn't going to be easy for him. "I have nowhere else I need to be."

He held his beer bottle with both hands propped on his belly. He stared down at the scuffed toes of his well-worn sneakers. "What I need to say . . . well . . . I've never said the words aloud. Admitting it makes me feel like a pansy-ass loser."

He exhaled a heavy breath and flatly admitted, "Last spring, I had a good old-fashioned mental breakdown."

Hope waited, watching him, feeling for him. He looked just miserable. "Oh, Lucca. I'm so sorry. You don't have to say any—"

"I do. Just let me get it out." He darted a quick glance her way, then refocused on his feet. "I've always been known for keeping a cool head. On the court. In life. But that day something . . . I don't know. Something inside of me just snapped. I can't explain why. I don't have a clue what triggered it. I just . . . went off. Went nuclear. It was ugly. I threw things. I broke things. I scared everyone around me. When I stormed out of the field house that day, I swore I'd never set foot in a gym again. Honestly, I didn't think I could. Just thinking about it made me break out in a sweat."

"It was because of the accident," Hope suggested. "A delayed reaction."

"Not only the accident, but what came afterward—the professional success. I felt like such a fraud. What sort of a man capitalizes on death? It disgusted me."

He unfolded from the sofa and stood and began to pace. "I couldn't deal with that, Hope. I tried to ignore it. I tried to deny it. I tried every mental exercise I could come up with. Eventually, it destroyed me. At least, that's what I believed last spring."

"But you don't believe it anymore?" she asked.

"Let's just say that ever since I let my siblings hitch me up to their tow truck and drag me to Eternity Springs, well . . . I've been learning to deal. Celeste talked to me about the GPS of life and stop signs and school zones and detours. I'm not certain I understand everything she tried to tell me, but I will say this. I sort of like this road

I've been on for the past couple of months. Sure, it's bumpy and potholed in places, but"—he shot her a quick little grin—"I especially enjoyed the picnic area."

Forget Celeste. Hope wasn't certain she understood Lucca. Was he, by chance, referring to Saturday night? Was he comparing her to a picnic?

What in the world had happened to him between lunch and after-school practice?

"So, that's basically my story. I hope it's helped you understand what's been making me tick. I don't claim to be healed or fixed or even better than I was this morning, but I'm going to try to get there. I am definitely on the road to recovery. As, I think, are you. I think if we share our company, it might make our journeys go quicker."

Suspiciously, she asked, "What do you mean?"

"When you knocked on my door on Saturday night, I had just finished watching the first basketball game I'd seen since last spring and drinking too much of a bottle of scotch, so I wasn't thinking as quickly or clearly. I am now. Today at lunch you said some things . . . about tragedy . . ."

Hope closed her eyes.

"And about moving on. It's obvious that you've had some experience. So tell me about it, honey. What tragic thing happened to you?"

TEN

Lucca watched Hope go stiff and maybe a little pale. He said no more, deciding to wait her out. He put the odds that she'd actually spill her beans today at less than fifty-fifty and that was okay. He had time.

He propped one hip on the corner of the desktop, snagged his beer off the top of the cardboard box where he'd left it, and took a sip, keeping his gaze on her.

Finally, she said sharply, "What is this? I showed you mine so you show me yours?"

"I care, Hope." He spoke the truth. He cared more about this woman than he'd cared about anyone in a very long time. "I can help."

Her eyes flashed with loathing. "Not a chance."

"Maybe I can't fix whatever it is and make it go away, but I can be your friend."

Still resisting, she lifted her chin. "I never said I'd suffered a tragedy."

He chided her with a look.

Hope closed her eyes and massaged her temples with her fingers. Her voice tight, she said, "I don't talk about it, Lucca. I don't talk about it to anyone, not even any of my friends in Eternity Springs. No one. I just . . . can't."

He studied her, noting the lines of stress on her brow and around her eyes. "In my experience, keeping the bad stuff bottled up inside can lead to trouble. That said, I don't want to cause you more pain. We don't have to drive the speed limit on this road. We can take our time. I'll be here to listen when you're ready to share." He polished off his beer and tossed it into the garbage can. "Ready to head home? Do you have your car or did you walk?"

She blinked. "I walked."

"Me, too. I hope you have a coat with you. It got cold this afternoon. Even snowed a little."

She stared up at him in wary surprise. "That's it? You're just going to drop it?"

"Don't you want me to?"

"Yes. But . . . I expected you to push harder."

He shook his head. "My family pushed. I didn't like it."

"I pushed you today."

"You did, but the timing was right for me, and you were the right person doing the pushing. Don't get me wrong, I still want to know what happened, but it needs to be when you're ready. I respect your privacy, Hope. I respect your wounds." He gestured for her to precede him from the athletic office. "Where's your stuff?"

"In the girls' locker room."

"I'll wait for you outside the locker room door and we can walk home together. If I have any luck at all, we might need to huddle together against the cold."

He grabbed his own coat from the bleachers where he'd tossed it upon his arrival, then took up position in the hall across from the locker room doors. He leaned against the wall, arms folded, and considered the afternoon.

It could have gone better, but it could have been much worse, too. Once he'd decided that he owed her not only a practice, but an explanation, too, he'd approached the school like a gallows.

But he'd managed. Gym stench hadn't made him puke, and his headache hadn't lasted past the first half hour of practice. When that short redheaded kid hit four out of five consecutive free throws and his face lit up like a scoreboard, Lucca had known a moment of joy reminiscent of what he'd felt when the Ravens punched their ticket to the Dance. Maybe Celeste knew what she was talking about. The GPS of life. *I'll be damned.*

He wished Hope had been able to open up, but he'd meant what he'd said. It would come in time. For the next few minutes, a Bible scripture played through his mind. *To everything there is a season.* Then, the Byrds began to sing. *Turn turn turn.* How many times had he heard that song while growing up? His mother had loved that CD.

From his memories of his mom dancing to 1960s music in her kitchen, his thoughts drifted to backyard hoops, and then to the rancher's son. Like the coach of old, Lucca spent a few minutes reassessing the young man's strengths and weaknesses. Wade Mitchell would need some real competition to hone his skills. *Wonder if they played any tournaments?* All the coaching and clinics in the world wouldn't substitute for game time. He'd have to ask Hope.

Hope. Where was she? He glanced at the hall clock. She'd had plenty of time to grab her coat. Hell, she'd had enough time to shower, dress, and dry her hair by now. Had she ditched him?

No. He didn't think so. Had something gone wrong? He knocked on the locker room door. "Hope?"

When he didn't hear anything, he cracked the door open and called her name again. Still nothing but the echo of his voice.

"Man in the locker room," he called out, stepping inside. He found her sitting on a bench past the third row of lockers, a single tear trailing slowly down her face. "Hope? Honey? What's wrong?"

"She's still missing, Lucca. My little girl. My Holly."

In my Fort Lauderdale condo, I hang up the telephone filled with despair. What am I going to do now? It's too late to find another babysitter. If I miss my cut-and-color appointment with Stephan again, he won't book me anymore. I don't trust anyone else with the task of turning my naturally red hair into the blonde that Mark loves.

I have roots. I saw Mark frowning at them yesterday. We have dinner with the law firm's partners and their wives on Friday. Leave it to my loving mother-in-law to cancel her promise to babysit at the last minute and make my life hell. Leave it to Millicent to do every possible passive-aggressive thing she can think of to interfere in my marriage.

I should have seen this coming. If Mark makes partner, there's a good chance we'll move to the West Coast office. Millicent won't have that. I should have suspected that she'd do something like this when she offered to babysit. Textbook Mommy Dearest. *She'll get her way no matter what. She always has.*

For a fleeting second, I consider taking Holly with me. Of course, that won't solve anything. Stephan doesn't allow children in his salon.

I glance at the clock. My stomach churns. If I don't leave in the next twenty minutes, I won't make it. I need this appointment. My marriage needs this appointment. I finally lost those seven pounds I put on over the winter and I bought a new dress and I want to wow Mark. I haven't wowed him in a very long time.

We haven't had sex in six weeks. We've had sex only once since Thanksgiving, and that was because it was the middle of the night and he'd been half asleep. When he's fully awake, he's always disapproving. Critical. Mean.

Is he having an affair?

No, it's the job. I have to remember that it's the job and not me. He's under stress. Major stress. Tears build in the back of my eyes and I blink them away. I have friends who have offered to babysit in the past, but with only a twenty-minute lead time? Maybe if I call Stephan, he will adjust his schedule?

And maybe the sun will rise in the west tomorrow morning, too.

But I decide to try. I'm that desperate. But as I reach for the phone, another thought occurs. Cynthia!

Bank executives Charles and Cynthia Larson live two flights up with their eight-month-old son, Hayden. "If you ever get in a bind for a sitter, don't hesitate to give our au pair a call," Cynthia had said. "I'd like Hayden to be around children a little more often. Babies learn from watching others. Holly's a sweet girl and so obviously smart. I think it might good for Hayden to have her around from time to time."

Mark likes the Larsons, too. He thinks that Cynthia is the kind of woman I should emulate.

Hope reaches for the phone, crossing the fingers of her free hand.

Five minutes later, she's standing at the Larsons' door holding Holly's hand and carrying a well-stocked backpack. Margarita opens the door with a wide, welcoming smile. She's a young woman with such a friendly face. I smile at her with relief.

Ready for her nap, Holly whines a little as I hand over the backpack and give Margarita instructions. "We will be just fine, Mrs. Montgomery," she says as she picks Holly up to comfort her. "Don't you worry about a thing."

I thank her profusely, kiss my daughter's soft cheek,

and inhale her sweet scent, then I dash for the elevator. Margarita stands in the doorway with my daughter and they both wave Holly's good-bye. My last sight of Holly is a tired, sullen smile.

At the salon, Stephan greets me with a smile that quickly turns to horror. How dare I neglect myself this way? I am ushered to his chair and spend the next two hours in "emergency repairs." I leave the salon feeling rested and renewed, confident in my appearance for the first time since my pants wouldn't button over my winter-depression belly. Delicious anticipation washes through me. I will wow Mark tonight.

I steal an extra half hour in the lingerie store two doors down from the salon and leave knowing that my husband doesn't stand a chance. Things will get better. They will.

I enter our apartment building, and thoughts of Mark fade. I have missed my sweet Holly. These three hours have been the longest I've been away from her in weeks. That will change when she starts kindergarten in the fall. She and I will both need to adjust. I tap my foot impatiently as the elevator ascends. I wonder if Holly will say something about my hair.

The door slides open. I swing my shopping bag joyfully as I step up to the Larsons' door and ring the bell. I hear Hayden crying inside. Poor little guy. I hope he hasn't felt neglected having to share his Margarita.

I wait, and when I don't hear footsteps, I ring the bell again. The crying escalates. I hear no other sounds from inside the condo. The first frisson of alarm skitters along my nerves. I try the knob. Locked. I use my fist to pound on the door. "Hello? Margarita? Answer the door please."

I put my ear against the door and hear only infant wails.

Alarm spikes to fear. I pound on the door. Bang bang

bang bang. *I thumb the bell.* Ring ring ring ring. *"Waaa waaa waaa."*

I drop my shopping bag and dig into my purse for my phone. I call the super. "It's Mrs. Montgomery from five. I'm at the Larsons' on seven. I need you to bring a key immediately. The baby is crying and Margarita isn't answering the door. My Holly is in there! Hurry!"

I keep my ear to the door, listening . . . praying to hear Holly. Calling out to her. Why isn't she answering? Is she asleep? Please, God, let Holly be asleep. I imagine Margarita lying dead of a heart attack on the floor, her hand clutched to her chest. Or maybe Holly had been playing with her toys in the kitchen and Margarita stepped on one and fell and hit her head on the black granite counter.

It's three minutes . . . or maybe three years before the elevator dings.

The super hurries out, a large ring of keys in hand. "He's calling for help. Hurry!"

The super bangs on the door as he slips the key into the lock and calls, "Hello?"

My heart pounds as the door swings open. Hayden's cries slice against my heart like shards of glass. Fear has turned my knees to butter. The super steps into the Larsons' apartment repeating, "Hello? Margarita? Mr. Larson? Mrs.—?"

I'm right behind him. The sight that meets my eyes stops me cold.

The baby sits in his car seat in the middle of the living room floor. Alone. Crying.

"Holly!" My head whips around. She's not in the living room. Panicked, I rush from room to room screaming my daughter's name.

But she's not here. Her backpack is not here. Margarita is not here.

"Where's Holly?" I demand as the super picks up Hayden. The baby can't answer me, of course—he's only eight months old. The super sends me a helpless look. I want to shake him. Instead, I dial 911. "I need you to issue an Amber Alert. My daughter is missing."

Five years later, in a girls' locker room in Eternity Springs, Colorado, Hope met Lucca Romano's sorrow-filled gaze. "Margarita Santana disappeared off the face of the earth."

"Oh, Hope." He grasped her hand and brought it to his mouth, pressing a gentle kiss against her palm. His mouth was warm, and she was so cold.

She didn't remember when he had taken a seat beside her on the bench. What exactly had she said to him, she wondered? Surely she hadn't talked to him about her sex life with Mark. That would be just too humiliating.

"At first we waited for a ransom call. It never came. Local police, FBI, private investigators . . . no one turned up anything. They disappeared into thin air. Mark blamed me, of course. His mother blamed me. How could I have left our child with a stranger! Never mind that Margarita had been with the Larsons since Hayden was born, and they'd done a thorough background check on her before they hired her. She'd taken excellent care of Hayden.

"I didn't care that they blamed me, of course. I blamed myself just as much. When Mark asked me for a divorce six months after Holly disappeared, I was relieved. By that time, he'd grown paranoid, convinced I'd planned the entire thing. They questioned me for hours. The same questions, over and over. My answers never changed. I told the truth. He still shows up on my door-step from time to time demanding to search my house for our daughter."

Anger flashed in Lucca's eyes. "That's sick. Damn, Hope. Why don't you get a restraining order on him?"

She smiled shakily and without amusement. "I have someone checking up on him, too."

"What?" he couldn't hide his shock.

"It got ugly between us, Lucca. And I honestly wouldn't have put anything past Mark at that point. My baby was missing and I knew in my heart that she was alive somewhere. My marriage was dead. I didn't mourn it."

She grew silent for few moments after that, torn between losing herself in her memories and the need to make a point. That's why she'd begun this whole sad story, right? Because she'd decided Lucca needed to hear it? *I'll see your nervous breakdown and raise you prescription drug abuse.*

"I almost killed myself, Lucca." As his eyes widened in shock, she hastened to say, "Not on purpose. At least, I don't think it was on purpose. I don't know . . . maybe it was. At this point, I can't remember much beyond being on autopilot. Staring at the phone, hoping for the ransom call. Praying for word that she'd been found. In those first weeks, I couldn't sleep. I couldn't bear the nights or the nightmares, so I stayed awake. I had horrible, horrible headaches, and one night when I went looking for aspirin, I spied a bottle of Vicodin left over from Mark's knee surgery. It took the edge off. Allowed me to sleep. Soon I was doctor shopping because it took more and more to dull my pain. It was frighteningly easy to do. A friend found me passed out on my living room floor one morning.

"I got help. Got off the drugs, but more important, I got on with living. That's what I wanted to say to you today, and it came out with a lot of anger and frustration. You see, I understand your pain. I understand your despair. I understand why you walked away from your family and your friends and your career. Because I do, I know what a big step you took today. I also have a caution for you—something I learned through bitter experience."

"What is that, sweetheart?"

She blinked back sudden tears and cleared her throat. "Emotional healing doesn't follow a straight line. It's often one step forward, two steps back."

"A curved mountain road with switchbacks and dips," he said, a faint smile playing on his lips.

"Exactly. I didn't know that, and when I descended into one of those dips, I grew terribly discouraged. I gave those setbacks more power than they needed to have. I was lucky because I had a friend who understood. He made me promise to call him day or night when I felt myself starting to slip. That saved me, Lucca. It continues to save me."

"Wait." Lucca shoved to his feet. "Wait just one minute. You already have someone? A guy? I thought you were alone. Who is this paragon?"

"Pardon me?"

"Your friend. The man who understands you."

"His name is Daniel Garrett."

"At risk of being blunt, where the hell was he Saturday night?"

Hope sat up straight and looked at Lucca in surprise. "I don't know," she said, wonder in her tone. "I didn't talk to him. I didn't call." Her brow furrowed and she added in amazement, "I didn't even think to call." *Instead, I came to you. I needed you.*

Lucca gave her a long look, then shoved his hands in his back pockets. "Does he live here?"

"In Eternity Springs? No, Boston. Daniel lives in Boston."

"Okay, then. That shouldn't change anything."

Hope didn't understand what Lucca was muttering

about or why he looked so cranky. She wasn't paying that close attention, either, though, because her mind had returned to Saturday night. The fact that she had walked next door to Lucca's rather than pick up the phone and call Daniel disconcerted her. It bothered her even more that she'd done it and never realized it.

In the past five years of their acquaintance, she'd called Daniel dozens of times when she'd been hurting. She'd visited him more than once while in the depths of despair.

She'd never had sex with him. That had never been part of their relationship. Yet, the first excuse she'd had, she'd gone to Lucca for sex. *What's up with that?*

Lucca dismissed the subject of Daniel by grabbing her hands and pulling her to her feet. Rather than release them, he clasped them tighter and waited until she lifted her gaze to meet his. "You are an amazing woman, Hope. Thank you for telling me about Holly. What happened to you . . . I cannot imagine. Has to be one of the worst stories I've ever heard. The fact that you not only are still walking upright, but thriving and doing wonderful things with your life . . . you shame me."

"I didn't tell you my story in order to shame you."

"I know that, and that's why it does. You were right to kick my ass today at lunch. I want to kick my own ass, now."

He had demons. She had demons. Different, true, but yet they could relate. Maybe that was why Lucca had come into her life. Maybe she was meant to help him. Maybe he was her purpose.

"Stop it, Lucca. Your pain is real, just as real as mine. That's the point. Grieving is individual and it's not right or fair for a person to say that my grief is worse than yours or that my tragedy is more tragic. That's stupid. I don't want to shame you, Lucca. I want to support you and celebrate with you. You faced one of your demons today. You conquered the beast."

"You helped me do it."

"Exactly. You've spent your time bearing your burden by yourself. Now it's time to rely on family and friends, time to reach out. Time to share the load."

"Great minds think alike." He gently brushed a stray curl away from her eyes. "You know, Ms. Montgomery, I get the sense that you are speaking to yourself as much as to me."

"You're right. I am." She released a long sigh. "I hate to be pitied, Lucca. It rubs me the wrong way."

"Note the lack of pity here. Sympathy, yes. But no pity. Even the hint of pity is curb-stomped by admiration."

"I'm glad." she smiled up at him. Lucca Romano could be a very nice man when he wanted. "Thank you."

"Yet another thank you. Aren't we just a mutual admiration society today?" Hope gave a little laugh at that. Lucca stepped closer and slipped his arm around her waist. "Since I'm speaking about admiration, Ms. Montgomery, allow me to mention how much I admire your mouth and how you use it. Use it on me now, would you?"

Lucca dipped his head and kissed her. She tasted of butterscotch and tears and . . . Hope. It began as a sweet kiss, a comforting kiss, but as their lips clung, fire kindled, and his hands began to roam. He backed her up against a locker and just as things got interesting, he heard a knock on the door. A man's voice called, "Janitor."

They didn't speak as they walked home, the mood between them comfortable. Lucca held her hand, and he kissed her thoroughly again at her front door, serenaded from inside by her barking dog. He wanted to ask her to invite him in, but he knew this wasn't the right time. "We still on for dinner Friday?"

Her teeth tugged uncertainly at her bottom lip. "You haven't changed your mind?"

"Not at all. I'm looking forward to it. I'll see you before then, of course. We have practice on Thursday."

"We do?"

"Yeah." He gave her one more quick kiss. "We do. I'm actually looking forward to it. G'night."

The bright smile she gave him warmed him the rest of the way home.

Later, after almost killing himself by attempting to eat the truly bad Mexican casserole Gabi had deposited in his fridge after cleaning out her own prior to her trip, Lucca settled into his living room recliner and called his twin. "Guess what I did today," he began.

"All right," Tony replied. "You tried to hang a picture for Mom at the B&B and she changed her mind seventeen times."

Lucca laughed. "No . . . only because we still have lots of work to do over there before we get to picture hanging. I helped coach at the local high school's hoops practice."

"Did you really?" Tony's voice echoed delight. "Well, hot damn. So, how's the team?"

Lucca started to reply "Pitiful," but changed his mind. "Full of heart, but shy on natural talent. Except for one kid. He could be a player."

"Oh, yeah? Tell me about him."

For the first time in longer than he could remember, Lucca and his twin talked hoops. It was something they'd done most all of their lives, and it was part of who they were as men, professionals, and brothers. "Damn, I've missed this," Tony said when the topic wound down. "I can't tell you how glad I am you called."

"Me, too."

His voice cautious, Lucca asked, "So, when do you think that you'll come back?"

"Back where?"

"To coaching."

"You mean collegiate coaching?"

"Yeah."

Lucca rose from the recliner and began to pace the room. It took him a few moments to figure out what to say, and then he only punted the question. "I don't know, Tony. I'm not sure that's what I want. I love the game, but even before the trouble I'd grown disenchanted with the big-business reality of college sports. That and the 'me' attitude of the players."

"Now you sound like an old fart: 'These young whippersnappers.'"

"I know." Lucca rubbed the back of his neck. "I'll tell you this much. I had more fun with these high school kids than I've had in a while. On a team like this, they do it out of love for the game, not because they're shooting for the NBA."

"But—"

"Let it go, bro."

After a beat, Tony asked, "So how is Mom?"

"She's not driving me *quite* so crazy. Having Richard around has helped in that respect. I think she's driving him crazy instead, poor guy. But I have to tell you, she's still not acting like herself. She's distracted and flighty and—are you ready for this? She colored her hair."

"That's not a big deal. Mom has colored her hair for some time now. You know how women are about gray hair."

"I'm not talking a touch-up. I'm telling you she's now a flaming redhead with highlights."

"What?"

"Gabi and I decided just yesterday that we have a role

reversal thing going on. It's like we are the parents and Mom's the teenager."

"That's scary."

"Tell me about it."

"Maybe it's menopause. You could ask her."

"You can kiss my ass. Better yet, why don't you ask her? And I'll be sure to pick you up off the floor when she's finished with you."

"She called me this morning about Thanksgiving. She wanted me to promise that I'd be there. I told her I had a tournament beginning Friday, but she got all teary on me."

"What did you do?"

His brother sighed. "I told her I'd show. I'll have to leave by four o'clock, though, and I reserve the right to change my plans if the weather looks chancy."

Thanksgiving. This would be the family's second holiday season without their father. He hoped like hell it would be easier than the previous year. Mom had cried through the whole meal.

His thoughts turned to Hope, and his heart did a little lurch. Bet she dreaded the holidays. He'd have to rope her into the Romano family orbit and help her get through them. *Unless she spends them with Daniel Garrett.*

That thought left a bitter taste in Lucca's mouth, and he frowned his way through the rest of his conversation with Tony, ending the call a few minutes later.

Next he turned on the TV and channel surfed for a few minutes, but nothing caught his interest. Finally, he rose and grabbed his coat, thinking he'd head to the pub for company and a beer. But as he reached for the front doorknob, he changed his mind. He went out into his backyard, stretched out on the chaise lounge, and gazed up at the star-filled night sky.

He found the constellation Pegasus and thought of winged horses and lightning bolts and a heavenly body.

Hope.

He wished he were a mythological creature who carried lightning bolts and could strike the ground with his hoof and locate Hope's Holly.

What a horrible thing. A little girl lost. Even if Holly turned up tomorrow, mother and daughter would still have lost five years. He'd thought it was bad what his mother had gone through when she gave up Zach for adoption, but it had been nothing compared to this. His mother had known where Zach lived and who he lived with, and that he was loved and treasured. Hope had only questions and what must be horrible imaginings.

Today he'd traveled a road that had changed him. Hearing her relive her tragedy and seeing the proof of her strength as evidenced by the life she'd created for herself in Eternity Springs had opened his eyes. She was well on her way along the rocky, winding road to recovery, but after facing a couple of his own demons today, he didn't think he was more than few car lengths behind her. So if she blew a tire or slipped a timing belt, he'd be there to help. And vice versa.

They were meant to share this road. He knew it in his bones. Because if her strength had opened his eyes, the kiss they'd shared in the locker room had opened his heart.

Hope Montgomery was special; she was medicine for what ailed him and balm to his wounded soul.

Maybe she should change her name from "Hope" to "Cure."

ELEVEN

After news got around that Lucca was helping with the basketball team, three more boys asked to join the Grizzlies. Technically where state high school sports rules were concerned, it wasn't too late to add players. The kids were athletes and would have improved the team, but Hope was inclined to refuse them. After all, they hadn't cared enough when the team didn't have a coach. Why should they come in to take a playing spot away from one of the boys who'd been willing to suffer through the season with her as their coach?

She took the question to Lucca, expecting him to make a case for the better players. To her surprise, he agreed with her. "Winning isn't everything. They had their chance. We will do just fine with the players we have."

"Really?" she asked, not believing it.

"Really. These guys are motivated by the right things—team and a simple love of the game. They have heart."

So, too, she recognized, did Lucca.

They had their date on Friday night. He took her to dinner at the Yellow Kitchen, and they kept the conversation light, talking about movies and books and music they liked. She was surprised to discover that they shared a joint interest in old horror movies. After dinner, she invited him back to her house to watch *Night of the Living Dead,* and they ate popcorn and recited dialogue along with the movie before he kissed her good night and departed. Hope floated to her bedroom where Roxy lay sleeping at the foot of her bed. She picked up the dog and cuddled her, saying, "It was fun, Roxy. He had a good time, too. I could tell. He was relaxed. He laughed. It was so good to see him enjoying himself. Lucca Romano could be a good friend. A girl can always use another friend, right?"

Over the weekend following the public date, she fielded all sorts of interested questions from his family and her friends and even casual acquaintances. "We're just friends," became her canned response, and while she did receive a few skeptical comebacks, most people seemed to accept her claim. Everyone knew he didn't intend to settle in Eternity Springs and besides, this time of year, she barely had time to eat, much less indulge in romance. Between bus driving duties, teaching, committee meetings, and volunteer commitments, by the end of the day, she was too worn out to do much more than play with Roxy and veg in front of the TV.

Which was why at eight forty-eight P.M. on Tuesday night when she heard a rap at her front door, she had to drag herself off the couch to answer it. She wasn't surprised to see Lucca standing on her front porch. She was aware of the significance of tomorrow's date—the anniversary of the wreck. "Come on in," she told him.

"I'd love to, but I can't. I'm on my way to Aspenglow. Mom called with a trumped-up reason why she needs me over there tonight. She's so transparent. She wants to make sure I'm not going to jump off Lover's Leap tomorrow."

"Does she have need to be concerned? I know what a beating anniversaries can be."

He waited a couple of seconds before he answered.

"I'm . . . fine. No jumping on the schedule. But I'd like to ask you for a favor, Hope. A big one. Could you take a personal day off from school tomorrow and spend the day with me?"

"Absolutely," she agreed without hesitation.

"Thank you. Be ready at nine, dress warmly in layers, and wear good boots. Bring an extra set of clothes in case you get wet. I'll bring all the other supplies. You're not claustrophobic, are you?"

"Claustrophobic? What are you planning?"

He flashed a grin. "Spelunking."

Hope gawked at him. She distinctly remembered Maggie saying not long ago that Lucca seemed to have developed an aversion to being indoors. "Caving? You want to go caving?"

"I do. I figure since chances are I'm going to be in a cold, dark place anyway, I might as well find one that's interesting. Zach told me about a cave not far from here that is easy and safe to explore. It's on private property— Cam Murphy's mountain."

"Umm . . . I don't climb ropes, Lucca."

"You won't have to. The most difficult thing we'll encounter is one little stint of belly crawling. I'm actually an experienced caver, Hope. It was a hobby of mine back before . . ." He shrugged, then added, "I know what I'm doing. You'll be safe with me."

"Okaaay," she said slowly. "Sure you wouldn't rather do a hike? I think the sun is supposed to shine tomorrow."

"Nope, I think I'd better do the cave. Is nine okay?"

"Nine is fine."

He leaned down and kissed her quickly. "See you tomorrow."

Hope shut the door and leaned against it, thinking. Anniversaries were big, bad, heart-wrenching things. They returned every year, and everyone reacted to them in their own way. How would Lucca handle tomorrow? Would he be a lion with a thorn in his paw? A grizzly bear waiting to roar? As his friend, how could she best help him get through the day? Should she attempt to distract him? She had intended to seek him out the next day at lunchtime and offer a horror movie marathon beginning after school. Caving was an option that wouldn't have occurred to her in a million years.

She'd have preferred the movie marathon. The thing about caves . . . you could expect bats. Bats terrified her. Too many horror flicks, she guessed.

She pushed away from the door and walked to her bedroom, where Roxy lay curled up on the bedside chair she'd adopted as her own. Hope sighed and spoke to her dog. "Well, I'm going to look on the bright side. Maybe this is just what I need. I do too much sitting this time of year, and I haven't been getting enough exercise. A day of caving might be just what I need to kick-start my energy level."

She called Principal Geary to arrange her day off and then phoned Christy Hartford to ask if Roxy could spend the day at her place. With preparations made, she called it an early night, went to bed, and dreamed she was a character in another old sci-fi horror film—*The Mole People*. She spent the night being chased by monsters through tunnels beneath the earth. She woke up tired and wondered if she could talk Lucca into another type of outing. But when she arrived home from her bus route and dropping Roxy off at the Hartfords, she found a note on her door. *I'm up early. Come on over when you're ready. L*

"If he's wearing a monster mask, I swear I'm not going into a cave with him."

When he answered the door, she took one look at him and forgot about her nightmare. Judging by his drawn face, his troubled eyes, and the lines of fatigue in his brow, he was dealing with one of his own. Then he gave her a relieved smile. "Hello, beautiful. Ready to go?"

"Well, that depends. Are you feeling okay?" She reached out and touched his arm. "Are you sure you want to do this?"

He covered her hand with his for a moment, silently accepting her unspoken comfort. "I didn't sleep well last night. Not a big surprise, considering what today is, but the weird dreams I had didn't help. Our talk about old horror movies stirred up my imagination. I had dreams about *The Mole People.*"

"You're kidding me."

"You know the movie?"

"I dreamed about it last night, too."

"Really? Why, Ms. Montgomery, I think we're a match made in heaven. So, before we go, let's make sure your gear fits okay." He picked up a bright yellow hard hat with an attached headlamp from a table and set it on her head. "Comfortable?"

"It's fine."

"Good." He handed her a backpack, asking, "Can you manage this?"

She tested its weight. Not bad at all. "Sure."

"Great." He picked up a backpack twice the size of hers. "Let's hit the road, then, shall we?"

Once they were in his truck and on their way, she peeked into the pack. A flashlight. A map of the cave. Energy bars. Glow sticks. A small first-aid kit. A large, folded black plastic garbage bag and smaller plastic bags. A roll of toilet paper. Oh, man. She hadn't even thought along those lines.

"There are water bottles in the back. Let's not forget to get them."

Her thoughts still on the toilet paper, she asked, "How long do you expect this exploration to take?"

"I don't have a timetable. Do you? Is there something you need to get back for?"

"No." She'd once managed to last a nine-hour plane trip without using the lavatory. She could avoid needing the toilet paper. "I'm all yours."

He shot her a grin. "I like the sound of that."

Hope settled back in her seat, a self-satisfied little smile on her face.

Twenty minutes later Lucca pulled his truck off the road and parked. "It's a ten-minute hike from here."

"Lead the way, Magellan."

She studied Lucca as he donned his pack and checked his map and his compass. He looked better already, she decided. He has purpose, something to do to occupy his body and mind on this most difficult of days. She understood how much that helped, and she was glad she'd decided to spend today with him.

They headed out. The ten-minute walk took them almost twenty, but Hope dawdled. It was a gorgeous day for a hike, the air crisp and clean, perfumed with pine and alive with birdsong. Patches of snow clung to shady spots and she spied animal tracks . . . deer? No, bigger than deer. Elk, most likely.

Which brought up a concern. "Um, Lucca? You know . . . we do have bears in Colorado. And mountain lions. They like to live in caves. I'll bet they don't like unexpected guests."

"Don't worry. I have this covered. I told you I'm experienced. Besides, Zach was out here just yesterday and he said everything checked out fine."

"Oh. Okay. Well, good." She went for an enthusiastic smile . . . but missed, judging by the amusement on his face.

"Don't worry, honey. You'll love this. I promise. Even though I haven't been there myself, my brother gave me a detailed description of what's inside. You don't need to be afraid. The worst thing that could happen is that when we get there, I fail my little personal test and can't make myself go inside. In that case, we'll find something else to do." He grabbed up her hand and brought it to his lips for a kiss. "Trust me."

Trust him. Well, she'd already done that once, hadn't she? She'd gotten naked with him. There's a level of trust. "Okay."

"Good, because we're here." He pointed toward a rock wall and a somewhat oval-shaped hole about waist high off the ground, some six feet wide and four feet high.

Warily, Hope eyed the opening. "You're going in first, right?"

"Of course. Now, strap on your hard hat and knee pads, and get your flashlight. You can lean forward and look inside before you step in. You might feel more comfortable then."

"Okay," Hope repeated. She could do this. All she needed to do was to remember that B-movie horror monsters never lived in Colorado. "What about you? Are you okay?"

"So far, so good."

He stepped through the opening, and she saw his flashlight flash around the walls. "No moles, humanoid or otherwise. There are bats down deep, but we're not going that far. It's safe for you to come in."

"Bats. Of course. Better than bears, I guess." Hope stepped up to the hole and studied the interior as he'd suggested. Well, it was a cave. Whoopee.

She slipped her backpack through the opening. "This is payback for my choice of music at Fun Night, isn't it?"

"That was torture. This is adventure." Lucca pulled on his pack and switched on his headlamp. Grinning, he held out his hand toward her. "According to Zach's map, we can walk upright for quite a bit. Ready?"

"Ready." Hope switched on her own headlamp and took his hand. Lucca led her into another world.

They descended a gentle slope into darkness that deepened as the trail twisted and turned until they moved beyond the daylight from the entrance into total darkness. She had expected bone-chilling cold, but instead, the air seemed warmer than that on the surface. Hope tugged the cave map from her pocket and held it in her headlamp's light. "We are about here?"

Lucca gave it a look. "Yes, just about. We're going here." He pointed to what looked like a lightbulb-shaped room another two inches away. "This little section here is the short, narrow passage. There are two spots before then with a bit of a drop-off, and these"—he pointed to three Xs on the map—"are where we might get a little wet."

"Drop-off?" she repeated. "Drop off to where? *Mole People* world?"

He snorted. "You know, teacher, fans of B horror movies don't usually believe they are true. It's a hop down for me and I'll help you. Now, come on."

He led her on a trek that sometimes sloped deeply, sometimes climbed steeply, but always remained dark as a tomb but for the beams of light from the headlamps and flashlights. As the passage narrowed, unease crept up Hope's spine. She'd never been claustrophobic before, but they'd come down so far. Into the mountain. Thinking about all the rock on top of them . . . she shuddered. And bats, to boot.

"Here's the first drop-off," Lucca said, his voice a hollow echo.

Hope held her breath as he sat, then scooted off into the darkness. She didn't breathe freely until she heard his feet hit the ground. The darkness was all but abso-

lute. From somewhere below him, she heard the sound
of running water. "You know, Lucca, I'm all for adventure, but I think it adds a lot to the experience to be able
to see it."

"Don't worry. Zach says Cam has left lanterns in the
dragon's lair. We can light up the entire room."

"The dragon's lair?"

"That's what Cam calls it. Says we'll understand why
once we see it. Sit down, honey, and let me help you."

"Dragon's lair. Great." Hope sat and let her legs dan-
gle. As she scooted toward the edge of the rock, Lucca
grabbed her around the waist and lifted her, lowering
her down slowly, her body pressed tightly against his.
When her feet finally touched the floor, still clasping her
body against his, Lucca spoke in a gravelly tone, "There.
That wasn't so bad, was it?"

She exhaled a shaky breath. "No fire-breathing mole
people yet."

"Gotta go deeper to run into moles. So, what was
your favorite *Twilight Zone* episode?"

"Excuse me? You're going to bring that up now?"

"I think you're too obsessed with moles. You probably should be worrying about Martians. Or nukes. Remember that *Planet of the Apes* plot? A nuke landed in
a cave but didn't explode and they worshiped it as a
god?"

"You are really weird, Lucca Romano."

Laughter rumbled deep inside him, and hearing it,
Hope felt warmth flowing through her. That she could
give him that on this day was a true gift.

They hiked for another ten minutes before his flashlight picked up a stake with a red plastic flag tied around
its top. "Here we go," Lucca said. "A short crawl, and
we'll be there. You have a set of elbow pads in your
pack."

Hope pointed her flashlight toward the hole in the

wall and her stomach fell. It wasn't much bigger than a
rabbit hole. "You're kidding. You can't fit in there. *I*
can't fit in there."

"Yes we can. Zach gets in and his shoulders are as
broad as mine. We have to angle in, then it widens out
immediately."

Dread closed in like the walls of rock around her as
she stared at the tunnel. "You'll get stuck and I'll have
to go for help and I'll get lost and end up a slave for
hairy, hunchbacked, one-eyed creatures mining ore with
a pickax."

"Wow. For such a brave woman, you are sure
chicken."

"Brave? You think I'm brave?"

"You are one of the bravest women I've ever met, and
you inspire me, Hope. You are the reason why I'm here
today and not in a bar drinking myself into oblivion."

His statement touched her, and while she could easily
have returned a flippant remark, she accepted the sentiment with the gravity it deserved. "Thank you. I'm glad
I'm able to help."

After a moment's pause, she added, "But if you get
stuck and I have to make the trip back to the surface
alone in order to get help, I'll make your life so miserable you'll wish the mole people got you."

"I understand."

Then, before she was quite ready for it, he slipped off
his pack, shoved it into the passage, and started crawling away from her. "Yikes."

With his light rapidly disappearing, the darkness
seemed to envelop her . . . as did the sense of being completely and totally alone. Hope swallowed hard, pulled
her elbow pads from her pack, and put them on. She
knelt at the entrance to the passage and peered inside. She
couldn't see a thing. Her voice squeaked, "Lucca?"

"The passage turns about eight feet in, Hope," his

voice echoed back to her. "I see the end of it about ten feet in front of me now. It's big enough that you don't need to push your pack. Come on in."

"No trolls? Spiders? Snakes? Bears? Bats?"

"Four out of five aren't bad odds."

"Aargh." Hope checked that her headlamp remained on tight and stretched out on her stomach. Taking a deep breath, she started crawling forward. "I am such a good friend," she muttered after making the curve, getting a mouthful of dust. When Lucca called, "I'm out," she took her first easy breath since his light had disappeared.

The effort seemed to take forever, but in reality, took only a few minutes. When she spied Lucca's hand reaching to help her out of the tunnel, she grasped it like a lifeline. "Do me a favor?" he asked as she found her feet.

Warily, she replied, "What?"

"Keep your face toward the wall while I light the lanterns. I want to see your expression when you first see the chamber."

That's easy enough. "Okay."

She heard him move clockwise, and slowly the wall behind her took on a golden glow. "Don't peek," Lucca said.

"I won't."

"Now, close your eyes." His fingers popped the clasp on her chin strap, and then he lifted the hard hat off her head and said, "Thank you for sharing this with me today, Hope. You've made the day bearable."

Then he leaned down and pressed a gentle kiss against her lips. "Now, open your eyes. Welcome to the dragon's lair."

She did and, immediately, her eyes rounded in wonder. "Oh! The walls sparkle. And they look like scales. And . . . oh . . . look at the ceiling! Stalactites."

"Definitely cool."

Hope turned around in a slow circle, her smile filled with delight. Glistening greens and vibrant blues, golds, and pinks. She gasped aloud when she saw the drawings. "Oh, wow. Lucca, look. Cave paintings. I wonder how old they are? Do people know about them?"

"Apparently, Cam explored this cave when he was a boy, but if people in town knew about it, they forgot it. He remembered it sometime last summer. He told Zach he's given permission to researchers from CU to begin a study next spring."

"This is the coolest thing I ever . . ." Hope's voice trailed off as she turned a little more and brought her gaze from the ceiling to the floor. "Oh."

"Pretty impressive, isn't it?" Lucca asked, his voice ripe with amusement.

"I . . . um . . . well." Hope pursed her lips, holding back a laugh as she studied the stalagmite rising from the cave floor. It was five feet tall and bore a startling resemblance to an erect penis. Then, because her mouth still tingled from his kiss and he looked so darned sexy standing there all dusty and outdoorsy, it seemed like the right thing to do. She turned a pointed stare to Lucca's crotch, licked her lips, and said, "I've seen better."

Lucca went to full arousal in seconds. He took a step toward her asking, "Do I take that as a compliment or a challenge or an invitation?"

She backed up a step. "We're in a cave, Lucca."

"Yeah. It's private. It's primitive. We wouldn't be the first people to be naked in here."

"Why do you say that? Is there cave-painting porn on the walls or something?"

"No, but there's a sleeping bag and a nice thick quilt. A bottle of champagne and a big box of condoms."

"What? I thought you said you haven't been here before."

"I haven't. It's private property, though. Cam and Sarah's private property. And, Zach might have mentioned bringing Savannah here."

Now she gaped at him. "So . . . this is what, the Eternity Springs version of Lover's Lane? Guys get together and talk about scoring next to the giant penis?"

"Actually, that talk is usually about scoring *with* the giant penis."

That made her laugh, so Lucca took another step closer. "And don't lay all the blame at the guys' feet. I think Zach might have said that the champagne was Savannah's idea."

"Zach 'might have said' quite a lot," she replied. "We've had one public date, Lucca. How have I acted to make them assume . . ."

"I'm family. It's not how you acted. It's how *I* acted." He caught her hand and brought it to his mouth, pressing a kiss into her palm. "You are different for me, Hope. You are special."

"You're trying to seduce me."

"Well, sure." He slid a hand around her waist and pulled her against him. "That doesn't mean I'm not speaking the truth."

She rested her hand against his chest, not stopping him, but not encouraging him, either. "Lucca, I came to you when I was desperate. I need to know . . . I know that today is . . . not that it's a problem. I just want to know . . . is that what this is? Escape?"

"No, Hope. It's not. Escape is the last thing on my mind, the last thing I want. I am exactly where I want to be, with whom I want to be with." He nuzzled her hair, inhaling the citrus scent of her shampoo, and nibbled at her ear. "I want you, Hope Montgomery. Tell me that you want me, too."

"Oh, I want you, Lucca Romano."

Despite the cool air of the cavern, the heat between them ratcheted up. Still playing with her hair, he whispered against her neck. "How about we take this movie script from PG to R?"

She laughed while wrapping her arms around him. "Somehow, I don't see you stopping at R. You're a triple X guy all the way."

When her hand slipped down to caress him beneath a layer of denim, he hissed in pleasure. "Cave porn. I like it."

Lucca knew that this time, she was giving herself to him. This time it would be without pain, without tears, without regret. This time she was inviting his touch, his body. Not demanding or needing it.

He reveled in the knowledge and in her expression: the glow in her eyes, the way her body moved toward his and melded into him as if created just for that space. Pulling her into his arms, he kissed her deeply, the action a trigger for them both.

The fire ignited, their clothes were shed, their bodies connected. Hope responded with an appetite that nearly drove Lucca to the edge at first thrust. Her smooth skin, her passion, her soulful eyes . . . she took his breath away.

As he made love to her, a rare feeling of possessiveness coursed through him. Hope made him feel things that he'd never felt in his entire life, and instinctively he knew it was more than he'd bargained for. As her voice echoed around them with the sound of his name, Lucca let himself follow her into the sweet bliss.

Clutching her close, he realized that whatever it was that had brought them together initially—empathy, sadness, shared tragic history—what they had right now was damned near perfect.

He kissed her tenderly and smiled at her tearful expression. She knew. Somehow, she knew it. Whatever this was between them, she clung to it, too.

Hope trusted him with her secrets, and he'd done the same. That had connected them, body and soul. Beyond that, Lucca didn't know.

Yet, lying on the cave floor with her sprawled and spent atop him, Lucca was certain of one thing: Hope Montgomery was light to his dark.

He couldn't stop touching her, stroking his hand up and down the silky skin of her back. He was exhausted. He'd slept fitfully the night before, and facing the cave had drained him more than he'd anticipated or admitted. But he'd done it. He'd actually enjoyed the experience once he'd gotten past those first couple of minutes and decided that he wasn't going to wig out. Having Hope with him had made all the difference. She hadn't been able to hide her lack of enthusiasm for caving, yet she'd never hesitated to face the challenge.

He learned so much from her. The woman was a teacher in ways she didn't begin to realize. How lucky he was to be spending this day with her. Last year . . . *No. Don't think about it.*

But by then he'd cracked open the door, and the memories came rushing back. The laughter, the music. The dog. The stupid dog.

Mewling. He hears mewling. The fog clears from Lucca's brain. The kids. Gotta get the kids. He reaches for his seat belt release. The van has come to rest on the driver's side, so he holds himself off the unconscious man. He looks behind him and sees . . . a nightmare.

Oh, God, he prayed. Help us.

He assesses. Directly behind him, Alan's head is crushed, his open eyes flat. Seth is bleeding profusely from a shard of something in his leg. In the next seat, Reed is sobbing and pulling on the handle to the van's sliding door.

Seth moves, reaching for the mewling dog, and blood spurts like a geyser.

"Lucca?"

Hope pressed a kiss against his chest and pulled him out of the nightmare. "You've gone tense."

She was right. His throat had gone tight. His teeth were clenched. His jaw had a thousand pounds of torque in it.

She ran her hand up and down his arm. He closed his eyes and willed his muscles to relax. He breathed deeply, inhaling her scent, and concentrated on the sensation of having her warm, naked body pressed against his. After a moment, he cleared his throat. "I'm okay. I was just thinking. About you."

She lifted her head and frowned at him. "And thinking about me made you tense?"

"Thinking about you makes me hard." He tugged her up so that his mouth could reach hers. He kissed her hard and quickly, then cradled her head against his chest. Against his heart. "Thinking about you fills me with awe. Your strength humbles me, Hope. I've been running from my monsters. You don't run. You face your biggest terrors head-on. If I were in your shoes, I couldn't have borne to be around children. What do you do? You surround yourself with them."

Light from the lamps flickered in her caring eyes. "Don't be so hard on yourself. Remember, I have three years more of recovery than you do. I didn't rush right into a kindergarten classroom the day that Holly was taken. You *are* conquering your fears. I'll bet that's what this trip has been about, hasn't it? It was a test of some sort. Like the gym. You're in a gym these days, coaching. It may have taken time, but you did it."

She had a point. Lucca also knew that if not for her, he'd still be hiding away.

"Have you been claustrophobic since the accident, Lucca?"

"At times, yeah." Enclosed places made him feel trapped and out of control. He couldn't shake the sense that disaster was about to occur any second.

Hope lifted her head again, and those big brown eyes of hers stared solemnly into his. "Want to talk about it?"

He stared up at the stalactites hanging from the roof of the cave. Wrapping one of her silky, burnished curls around his finger, he began to speak. "It doesn't always happen. I noticed it first when I flew to Mexico last summer. Longest plane ride of my life. That's the reason why I didn't come home for so long. I couldn't make myself get on a plane. Did all my traveling by car or boat."

He exhaled a heavy breath. "When the van rolled, the impact crushed the doors. We were trapped. I could smell gasoline and I thought we'd burst into flames any second."

"Oh, Lucca," Hope whispered.

"It was . . . awful. I'd let Seth bring a dog along. A puppy. During the accident the dog was thrown around. You could see that he'd been . . . broken . . . and Seth . . . Seth . . ." Lucca closed his eyes. "It was so random. He didn't have a scratch on him except for the shard of metal that had punctured his thigh. It nicked an artery. I tried to stop it, to clamp off the bleeding, but I knew it was futile. He bled out right in front of me and I couldn't . . . The whole time Seth held that crying puppy, crooning to him. They died within a minute of each other. The silence in the aftermath . . . it haunts me."

"That's why you reacted the way you did with Roxy's puppies," she said softly.

He shrugged. His thing with dogs was humiliating, and he didn't like to think about it. He'd loved dogs before the accident. "Thank God for cellphones. We were able to call for help. Still, it took two hours for them to get to us and get us out."

Two long, endless hours trapped with the dead, injured, and traumatized students for whom he was responsible while the fear of explosion hung over them.

He had to live with that memory for the rest of his life—live with the knowledge that his ego and pride had brought them to that point. "Guilt eats at me."

"It shouldn't." Hope rose up on her elbows. She gazed down at him, her eyes filled with tender sorrow. "I understand, believe me. It was a terrible, horrible thing, but it was an accident."

"I know, but that doesn't seem to matter."

"Then think about this. You kept your head when it mattered. I remember the news reports. I remember how steady and supportive you were for your team and their families. Those surviving boys loved you."

"And the dead ones . . . are dead."

"It was an accident. It's not your fault."

How could he make her understand? "For two hours that dog stared at me with flat, lifeless eyes. Accusing eyes. Now . . . hell." His voice cracked a little as he confessed. "I'm afraid of dogs, Hope."

"Oh, Lucca. No, you're not. You're wounded."

He whispered the words, "I can't forget."

"Of course not. You won't forget. You never forget. But you can heal. It takes time, but it does happen. It *is* happening. You're coaching. You brought me to a dragon's lair to face your fears, didn't you? That's such a lesson for me. You inspire me."

Her words made his heart swell and pressure build at the back of his eyes. He attempted to avoid the total humiliation of tears by clearing his throat and quipping, "I brought you here to get laid. Pretty smart, huh?"

Hope didn't let him get away with that. "Stop it. Listen to me. I want you to hear what I'm saying." She cupped her hand against his cheek and stared deeply into his watery eyes, her own eyes damp with tears. "You are a good man, Lucca Romano. Accept that. Believe it."

A single tear escaped his eye and trailed slowly down his temple. Hope leaned forward, kissed it away, and whispered in his ear. "I think I'll get you a dog."

TWELVE

On a Saturday morning ten days later, Hope awoke with a smile on her face and a naked man in her bed. Not just any man, she thought as she stretched slowly like a satisfied cat, but Lucca Romano, the oh-so-hot, been-on-the-cover-of-*GQ*-magazine former professional ballplayer who liked to show off his athleticism in bed. If a small-town kindergarten teacher was going to have a fling, she couldn't do much better.

Despite the fact that they'd shared each other's secrets, Hope had no expectations that this was anything more than a fling. Nothing had changed. Lucca was still a short timer in Eternity Springs, and she told herself that that suited her just fine—that she didn't want more than friendship and a fling. Honestly, after her disaster of a marriage, she couldn't imagine ever wanting to travel that road again.

"Good morning," rumbled the deep, sexy voice next to her ear.

"Good morning."

He cuddled her against him. "You know, my mother likes to wax poetic about how beautiful the sunrise is over the mountains. I have to say that when it comes to beautiful sights in the morning, sunrise in Eternity Springs takes a backseat to you."

She could have said the same thing. Instead, she offered to cook him breakfast, and interest lit his eyes.

"I'm starved. Breakfast would be great." But when Hope rose and reached for the robe lying draped across the iron footboard of her bed, he shot out a hand and grabbed her wrist. "How about an appetizer first?"

She grinned when he tugged her back into bed, and she tumbled on top of him. As he rolled her onto her back, a phone rang. His phone, she realized upon identifying the ringtone. She didn't have "Hell on Heels" on her cell. "Damn," he muttered. "That's Gabi. I'd better answer. She wouldn't be calling if it wasn't important."

Gabi was still away on her dog-sitting beach vacation and not due back until the middle of the following week. Lucca fished his phone from the pocket of the jeans he'd left lying on the floor, his expression tense. He answered saying, "Gabi? Are you okay?"

Hope watched him closely, and when he visibly relaxed, she did, too.

"No, I don't know what she's doing today," he spoke into the phone. "But I don't mind picking you up. What time, again?" He listened for a moment, then said, "Sure. See you then."

After disconnecting the call, he explained. "She's on a layover in Atlanta. The Thurstons cut their trip short, so she's coming home early. Mom said she couldn't pick her up at the airport, so I'm going to do it. How about Mexican food?"

"For breakfast?" Mentally, she reviewed the contents of her pantry and fridge. She'd been thinking bacon and eggs, but she could do huevos rancheros.

"A late lunch. Gabi's plane gets in at four. Zach has been singing the praises of a Mexican restaurant in Gunnison."

"Gloria's," Hope said. "I've been wanting to try it."

"Now's your chance. Or did you have plans for the day?"

Hope thought about her schedule. "I have some errands I planned to do this afternoon. If it's not too domestic for you, we could make a couple of stops in Gunnison and I could get it all done there."

"Perfect. Now . . ." He sank back down onto the bed. "Where were we?"

"Kiss me, caveman, and I'll show you."

By noon they were on the road to Gunnison. Almost before they'd reached the Eternity Springs city limits, Hope found her eyelids getting heavy. She stifled a yawn and gave her head a shake to keep from nodding off. Lucca noticed and asked, "Sleepy?"

"Yes. I guess I didn't get enough sleep last night."

"I'd apologize, but I'd be lying," he replied, an unrepentant look on his face. "Why don't you take a nap?"

"I think I will, if you won't mind. Just a short one."

He reached across the console and gave her thigh a pat. "Sleep as long as you want. I'll wake you when we get to the restaurant."

She drifted off almost immediately but awoke before they reached Gunnison when Lucca tapped his brakes too hard and muttered a curse. "Sorry. I didn't mean to wake you up. Some fool on a bike just had to pass me for the fourth time, and he cut in too close. If I wasn't paying attention, I'd have hit him and the woman he's got clinging to him like wallpaper. Idiot. Driving recklessly on these roads is asking for trouble."

"Why four times? Did you speed up to pass him back?"

"No. They're stopping at every scenic overlook so the chick on back can take photographs. They stay long enough for me to drive past them, and just when I think I'm done with them, here he comes again. Guy's driving a crotch rocket, too. Not even a big old Harley." He spared her an apologetic glance. "Sorry, honey. Go back to sleep. Hopefully, they're tired of stopping."

Hope checked her watch. She'd slept for over an hour, and she felt much better. Now she was curious about the motorcyclist who had given Lucca a slight case of . . . not road rage. More like road annoyance.

"I've slept long enough," she told him. She studied the area surrounding them. Having made this drive herself plenty of times, she knew they'd reach Gunnison in another half hour.

"There they are again," Lucca muttered as they approached a turnout with a historical marker sign.

Hope took in the bike. Sleek and powerful—so different from the big, bulky Harleys you saw in the mountains so often. The woman was standing on the ground, but she wasn't taking pictures this time. The man's back was to the road, shielding the woman from view, but his position didn't hide the helmets discarded at their feet or the fact that they were wrapped in a passionate kiss. Hope particularly noted the woman's boots. She loved them. Black leather with a fringe—sexy and strong, but feminine. Maybe she should let Celeste talk her into taking up biking to give her an excuse to buy boots like that.

"If they're going to act that way, they need to get a room. This is a public highway. Hell, they'd be about a button away from being arrested if Zach were to happen along."

"Oh, don't be such a grump," she teased him. "I'm told that riding a motorcycle can be a very arousing experience. All that vibration down where it counts."

His brow arched in surprise. "Is the kindergarten teacher hiding an adventurous spirit?"

"Maybe more than I previously realized. Something

about you makes me want to walk on the wild side, Coach."

"Really, now." He watched the road, a grin playing on his lips. "I think there is a cycle store in Gunnison. Maybe we'll add another destination to our shopping trip."

They kept their conversation casual the rest of the way into town. Lucca was hungry so he asked if she'd mind if they went to Gloria's first. The restaurant had changed hands in the past month, and the menu revisions had stirred quite a debate with her Eternity Springs friends. "Zach loves the changes the new owners have made," she told Lucca. "So do the Murphys, but Nic and Sage say they liked the old menu better."

"I judge Mexican food restaurants by chips and salsa and chiles rellenos."

"For me it's cheese enchiladas and guacamole."

They enjoyed a leisurely meal. Hope gave the new ownership high marks. Lucca declared his rellenos to be the best he'd had since his last trip to El Paso. "But you spent so much time in Mexico."

"We're talking Tex-Mex, here. Two different cuisines." He told her about some of the food he'd eaten during his summer down south, and when he took the conversation toward lizards, snakes, and bugs, just thinking about it made her queasy. Once queasy escalated to nauseated, she set down her napkin. "Excuse me. I'm a wuss. Thinking about eating bugs has turned my stomach, and I need some fresh air."

"I'm sorry. Go on outside. I'll pay the check and meet you in front."

The cool, fresh air helped, and by the time Lucca exited the restaurant a few minutes later, she felt better. "You still up to do errands?" he asked her.

"Absolutely."

"Walk or drive?"

"Let's walk. It's a lovely day, and I need some exercise."

"All right. Why don't you lead the way? I'm still learning where things are in this town."

"All right." Hope realized she could get used to the companionship of a man like him. Lucca was different from her ex. Mark had always needed to be in charge.

Hope led him north, then took a right at the next intersection. Her destination, the teaching supplies store, was halfway down the next block. When they passed a camera shop, Lucca's steps slowed. "Mind if we duck in here?"

"Not at all."

Ten minutes later she walked out of the shop a little shocked. The man had just dropped almost three thousand dollars on gifts for his family. She'd known he had money. Successful collegiate coaches made bank, and he'd been a professional athlete before that, but still. "Do you do that sort of thing often?"

"Spur-of-the-moment gift buying?" He shook his head. "It's an act of self-defense. I learned long ago that if I get an idea for Christmas or birthday gifts, I'd better jump right on it, because chances are Tony will come up with the exact same idea. I guess it's the twin thing. Anyway, our deal is that the first guy to buy it has dibs on giving the gift. I usually have all my Christmas shopping done before Thanksgiving."

"You certainly made that shopkeeper's day."

"I like to buy local, but since Eternity Springs doesn't have a camera shop, I figure this will do. Let me put this stuff in my trunk, and then we'll tackle your errands. Where are you needing to go?"

"The teaching supplies store," she replied as they retraced their steps to his vehicle. "They have a United

States map rug I'm considering ordering for my classroom, but I want make sure that it's well made enough to withstand kindergarten wear and tear. After that I need to pick up a few things at the drugstore, and if we still have time, I'd like to visit the yarn shop."

"Are you a knitter?" he asked, thumbing the door release button on his key fob.

"I crochet. My grandmother taught me when I was a little girl. I'm crocheting a christening gown for Michael Murphy, but I need one more skein of thread."

"That's cool," Lucca said. He piled his packages into his SUV, then shut the door. "My college roommate's mother crocheted, and she made me an afghan that is one of my prized possessions. I think . . . well now . . . look where our friend ended up."

Lucca hooked his thumb toward the motel across the street. The motorcycle sat parked in front of room 110. "Now we know why he was in such a hurry. What do you want to bet that the old Matterhorn Mountain Motel rents rooms by the hour?"

"Like I said," Hope observed, catching his hand in hers. "Good vibrations."

He snorted, and she hummed the old Beach Boys tune as she tugged him down the street toward the teaching supplies store. There, he played Santa Claus and purchased supplies not only for Hope's classroom, but for all the other Eternity Springs classrooms, too. By the time they returned to his SUV an hour and a half later, both his and her arms were full. The motorcycle remained parked in front of the Matterhorn Mountain Motel.

"Guess he's not always in a hurry," Lucca observed as he pulled away from the curb.

They arrived at the airport just as a tanned and happy Gabi Romano exited the terminal. Lucca got out of the truck to help her with her bag. Upon seeing her brother, she waved and smiled. When she spied Hope sitting in Lucca's vehicle, curiosity lit her eyes. "Well, well, well," she said when she reached the car. "This is a surprise."

"Gabi, you look gorgeous. Welcome home."

"So, you missed me so much you decided to tag along to see me two hours sooner?"

Hope didn't see any sense in being coy. Gabi had a bit of terrier in her personality and if she had questions, she wouldn't quit before she learned the answers. Besides, the thought of shocking her friend had some appeal. "I tagged along because I'm dating your brother and he invited me."

Gabi's surprised smile bloomed. "Really? Cool. Which one? Tony or Max?"

"Very funny," Lucca said.

Gabi slipped her arms around her brother's waist and gave him a quick, hard hug. "Good for you, bro. So you got through the anniversary okay?"

He met Hope's gaze. "I had a great day."

"I'm so glad." Gabi looked from Lucca to Hope appraisingly. Then she gave her brother another squeeze before stepping back and climbing into the rear passenger seat. "I can't wait to tell you about my trip. At the last minute the Thurstons decided to have their beach house painted so they flew me to . . . guess where. You'll never guess where."

"You're tan," Hope said. "Key West?"

"The French Riviera!"

"Seriously?"

"Seriously. They took me along on their trip as the official pet sitter. I flew first class and stayed in the same resort where they were." Gabi settled back against the car seat and released a satisfied smile. "I've decided what I want to be when I grow up."

Lucca's gaze flicked up to the rearview mirror. "Filthy rich?"

"You guessed it. But in the meantime, I'm starved. How about I buy you guys dinner? I've been dreaming about Mexican food all the way from Atlanta."

"Oh, Gabriella," Lucca whined. "We ate there for lunch. Not all that long ago."

"Fine. I'll buy you and Hope dinner at the Yellow Kitchen when we get home . . . but take me to Gloria's first. Please?"

"What do you think?" Lucca asked Hope.

"I have room for a sopaipilla."

As they drove back toward the center of town, Gabi chattered about her trip, though the looks she gave Hope told another story. She wanted answers. Hope suspected Gabi would be dragging her off to the ladies' room to dish as soon as they reached the restaurant.

Maybe she should try to avoid an encounter like that. She didn't know what she would tell her. Let her corner her brother, instead. *Maybe I'll learn what he thinks about us that way.*

The downtown area bustled on this Saturday night, and Lucca drove around a bit searching for a parking spot. "Don't worry about getting close on my account," Gabi told her brother. "I've been cooped up on airplanes for too long. A walk sounds really good."

"I'll make the block one more time," Lucca said. As they passed the Matterhorn, he pointed toward the empty parking spot in front of Room 110. "Looks like our biker friends have moved on. Finally."

"You are awfully interested in some stranger's sex life, Lucca."

"What?" Gabi leaned forward and propped her elbows up on the seat in front of her. "What did I miss? Whose sex life?"

"I'm not interested," Lucca replied to Hope, ignoring his sister's questions. "I'm just making an observation."

"Well, I observe a parking spot," Hope said. "Up ahead two blocks on the right. It's in front of the ice cream shop."

Lucca goosed the gas when the signal light turned yellow and made it safely through the intersection. He executed a skillful bit of parallel parking that disgusted Hope. "It would have taken me three tries to fit this truck in that spot. You made that look too darned easy."

"What can I say? I'm good."

She wasn't going to argue with that. She climbed out of the passenger seat and shut her door, then turned to Gabi. "So are you a fan of guaca . . ." Her voice trailed off. The color had drained from Gabi Romano's face and she stood frozen in place, staring in shock through the plate glass window of the ice cream shop.

The biker was there. So was the short woman with those boots Hope liked so well. He was sharing his ice cream cone with her, and she was licking it lasciviously. It wasn't until Hope heard Gabi make a strangled sound that she took a closer look at the biker, and then his babe.

"Is that . . . Mom?" Gabi croaked.

Having come around the back of the truck to join Hope and Gabi on the sidewalk, Lucca heard the question, spied his sister's wounded look, and froze. His gaze went from Gabi to the shop window. It took a few beats, but Hope recognized the instant that it clicked.

Shock, betrayal, hurt, then fury. Hot, fierce, murderous fury. His fists clenched at his sides and his jaw turned to granite. Hope reacted instinctively, threading her arm through his and holding on for dear life. She didn't care how she had to accomplish it, but she wouldn't let this escalate into a public brawl.

Then, as if Lucca's green eyes had shot magnetic laser beams across the distance separating him from his mother, Maggie Romano straightened on alert. She pulled her gaze away from the ice cream cone held by the biker—contractor Richard Steele, Hope now realized—and turned to gaze out the window.

She looked like a soldier on a battlefield who had caught a bullet, and staggered back. But Maggie Romano was apparently wearing Kevlar, because after that first devastating moment of stunned surprise, she squared her shoulders, lifted her chin, and silently told her adult children to go stuff themselves.

Richard Steele leaned down and licked a streak of ice cream away from the side of her mouth.

Lucca made a sound—a low, menacing growl—and Hope knew she needed to take action immediately. "Into the truck," she ordered, shoving Lucca toward the closest door. Ordinarily, it would have been like moving a mountain, but right now he was off balance. She grabbed the keys from his hand and released the locks, then yanked open the passenger door, and demanded, "Lucca, get in. Gabi, you, too."

She shoved him toward the opening, and blessedly, he went, taking a seat in eerie silence. Gabi remained rooted to her spot, her horrified gaze locked on her mother, so Hope repeated her action with the back passenger door and guided her friend inside.

Then, like a bat fleeing the dragon's lair cavern, Hope drove the Montgomery siblings away from the scene of their mother's crime.

For the first ten miles of the road back to Eternity Springs, nobody spoke. Lucca's head was spinning. He remembered how he'd felt that time he'd come home from college unexpectedly and walked in on his parents going at it. This felt similar, but worse.

When Hope braked at a road crew flagger's signal, Gabi emerged from her silent shock in the backseat to suggest, "Maybe it wasn't how it looked."

"It was exactly how it looked," Lucca fired back.

"We can't know that," she insisted, denial strong in her tone.

"We can damned sure infer." Lucca summarized the motorcycle incident for his sister.

Gabi's shaky voice said, "Maybe it was a different motorcycle. Mom wouldn't do that. She wouldn't. I can't believe this. The Matterhorn? Really?"

"Same boots."

"You noticed Mom's boots?"

"Yeah." He'd thought they were sexy. Knowing now that they'd been his mother's boots gave him the creeps.

"So you are saying our mother is having sex with her handyman."

"Contractor, Gabriella," he corrected. The other term was an invitation to tasteless jokes. "Tasteless" led him to recall the image of his mother's—his *mother's*—blatantly suggestive consumption of an ice cream cone. "I wonder how long this has been going on?"

"Puts a whole new perspective on the name 'Aspenglow,'" Gabi said glumly. "That's it. I'm through working at her B&B. I don't do threesomes."

Lucca grimaced and held his head between his palms. "Please, Gabi. It's bad enough as it is. I don't need you to put pictures in my head." He looked over at Hope. "Well, you haven't said a word. What do you think about all this?"

Hope cautiously said, "At the risk of annoying you both, I feel the need to stick up for my friend. Maggie is still young. She's vibrant. She's unattached. You and I are unattached. Why the double standard? So what if she's found someone she wants to be with?"

"Hope, it's not the same."

"Wait a minute," Gabi said. "Did I just hear what I think I heard? You're sleeping with Lucca? Jeez. A girl goes to the French Riviera for a few days and the world turns upside down. What's next? You're not going to tell me Tony has run off with a stripper, are you?"

"You didn't just call me a stripper, did you?" Hope asked.

"No!" Mumbling, she added, "I'm having trouble processing what I saw."

Lucca raked his fingers through his hair, ignoring his sister as he said, "You're right, Hope. It's a double standard, so sue me."

"Now, Lucca," she chastised.

"Dammit, she's my mother! I don't care how old you are, no child likes to think about his parent having sex."

"Yes, I'll give you that one. But that's *your* issue, Lucca. Not your mother's. It's not fair or right for you to expect her to quit living."

Yeah, well. Maybe so. It still sucks to see your mother doing . . . that. "I may never eat ice cream again."

"Who is Richard Steele, anyway?" Gabi asked. "Do you think he's after her money?"

Hope rolled her eyes. "Have you looked at your mother recently? She's gorgeous."

"Richard is not a bad guy. But he's not . . . Dad."

Gabi closed her eyes and massaged her temples. Her voice fluttered from the backseat like a little bird's. "I still miss him every day. They were married for decades. How can she be ready before I am?"

Lucca muttered a curse, and Gabi added, "What are we going to do, Lucca?"

He sighed heavily but had no answer. When Hope reached over and rested her hand on his leg, he laced his fingers through hers. "I don't think we do anything, Gabi. Hope is right. It's not really our business. That's obviously what Mom thinks. Remember how she looked at us, the way she lifted her chin? You know that look as well as I do."

"Proceed at your own risk," his sister grumbled.

"Exactly."

"She's been acting so weird for months. Do you think that maybe she's sick? Maybe she has cancer or some other dreadful disease and that's why she's acting so . . . crazy?"

"Crazy?" Hope repeated. "Again, Gabi, have you looked at Richard Steele lately? He's gorgeous, too."

Lucca shot her a scowl, but his thoughts drifted back to that day at the scenic overlook and Celeste Blessing's advice. "The road of life," he murmured before saying, "I don't think Mom is sick, Gabi. I think she's trying to figure out her way forward. It was her bad luck—and ours—that our paths had to cross while she was doing it."

"I wished I'd stayed on the Riviera. What is happening to our family?"

Lucca leaned his head back against the headrest and closed his eyes. "We're a new constellation and we have to reorient. One of our major stars exploded, but it's refusing to fade away peacefully, and we're left with a nebula that's spewing out massive amounts of gas and radiation."

Gabi shook her head. "You are so weird, Lucca."

"I'm tired. I'm short on sleep."

"Please. I don't want to hear about your sex life," Gabi said. "I'm over my limit."

"Sleep," Hope suggested. "Both of you. I'm a big believer in the healing power of naps. You're not going to solve anything in the next hour of this trip, and you'll feel better if you get some rest. I'll get us home safe and sound."

Gabi balled up her sweater and used it as a pillow. "Good idea. Maybe I'll wake up, and this will all have been a dream."

Without opening his eyes, Lucca brought Hope's hand to his mouth for a kiss. "I'm glad you're with me, Hope."

"So am I."

He didn't speak again for almost ten minutes, and then he asked, "Do you own any black boots?"

THIRTEEN

❧

Monday morning, Hope had to drag herself out of bed. A hangover from Romano family drama, she decided. For once she was glad she didn't have parents and siblings to complicate her life.

Not that she hadn't felt bad for Lucca, Gabi, and Maggie. It wasn't a comfortable situation for any of them, though she did believe that the Romano children would come around once their emotions settled. She just hoped their reactions didn't hurt Maggie too much in the meantime. Maggie was a nice woman who deserved the opportunity to find love again.

A voice inside her whispered, *What about you? Don't you deserve the same? Love, marriage . . . family?*

"No," she said aloud even as the image of Lucca rising naked from her bed flashed through her mind. She'd had family; she'd lost it. She could not—she would not—take that risk again. She wouldn't survive losing it twice.

As usual, a morning spent with kindergarten students revived her. There was nothing like bright minds and inquisitive natures to make her feel like all was right with the world. And it kept her busy enough to shove the memories of caveman sex from her mind.

Then her conference period arrived along with an unexpected visitor. At the sound of a knock, she looked up to see Maggie Romano standing at the threshold of her classroom door wearing jeans, a forest green pullover sweater, and a worried frown. "Maggie? This is a surprise. Come on in."

"Hello, Hope. I'm sorry to bother you at school, and I hate to put you in the middle of a family problem, but I just don't know what else to do. My stubborn, thick-headed children saw me out on a date in an ice cream shop with a nice man, and from the way they've reacted, you'd think they'd caught me robbing a bank."

So much for not being pulled into the middle. Busy with church youth group activities, Hope hadn't seen Lucca or Gabi in more than a day. "What happened?"

"Nothing. Absolutely nothing! Gabi refuses to answer my calls. Lucca has apparently decided to go fishing today rather than come to work. Even Zach has made himself scarce. He and Savannah picked a heck of a time to go to Carolina to visit her nephew. But Richard and I must leave in an hour in order to make our plane, and I want to make one more effort to reach them before I go. You were there Saturday. I'm hoping if you will share what they said it will explain to me exactly why they're acting like five-year-olds. Then I'll know what to say in the messages I leave for them before I go."

Go? Go where? *Please, don't tell me you are going to elope.* Warily, she asked, "Where are you and Richard going, Maggie?"

"Austin. There's an Innkeepers Association meeting." *Oh. Thank goodness.*

Hope had no desire to involve herself in the Romano family drama any more than she already was, but she considered Maggie a friend. Maybe a little communication could help. "Sit down, Maggie."

"Thank you, but I can't. I like to pace when I'm angry and disappointed in my kids." She picked up the apple little Whitney Wilson had brought Hope and absently polished it against the sleeve of her sweater. "Honestly, they freeze me out because they caught me having an ice cream cone with my contractor? Can a woman not have any privacy in this town? Shoot, we went to the *next* town. You'd think I was a teenager looking for some-place to park instead of indulging in a double scoop of rocky road."

Except, it had been more than rocky road, hadn't it?

Hope drew a deep breath and debated how best to answer. She didn't like telling tales, but Maggie proba-bly needed to know the facts to prevent further misun-derstanding. "Actually, it wasn't simply the ice cream that caused the deep freeze, Maggie. Lucca noticed the motorcycle parked in front of the Matterhorn."

Maggie halted midpace. "The motorcycle?"

"In front of the motel. He put two and two together." For the second time in two days, Hope watched the color drain from Maggie Romano's face.

"Oh." The starch drained out of Maggie and she sank into the seat opposite Hope. "Oh. So they know that I . . . that we . . ."

Climbed the Matterhorn? "Yeah."

"I see. Now I understand." Maggie closed her eyes. "No wonder they won't talk to me. That's not what I . . . oh, no. They shouldn't have found out. Not like that."

Seeing her friend's devastation, Hope felt a stirring of frustration with Lucca and Gabi. "I think everyone just needs a little time to process, Maggie. Your children love you, and they'll come around."

"Excuse me. I need to call . . ." Appearing scattered, she fumbled in her purse for her phone, dialed a number, then said, "Richard, I can't go to Austin. I'll call later and explain. You go on without me and please, take good notes at all the workshops."

When she hung up, tears overflowed Maggie's eyes and

trailed slowly down her cheek. If Lucca had been there in that moment, Hope would have balled up her fist and popped his jaw.

"I'm a terrible widow. I don't follow the rules." Maggie lifted her hands to wipe her cheeks.

Hope gave her a sympathetic smile and handed her a tissue from the box she kept in her drawer. "I didn't know there were rules."

"Oh, there are always rules for everything. I broke a big rule when I was fifteen, and it changed my whole life. I told you about Zach. The little boy I named Giovanni. When it comes to rules, I always find out the hard way." She delicately blew her nose into the tissue.

"Oh, Maggie." Hope removed the tissue box from her drawer and set it within Maggie's reach.

"I returned to my hometown after I recovered from the pregnancy and its consequences. Marcello arranged to meet me. I decided then not to tell him about the baby." Maggie reached for another tissue. "On my eighteenth birthday, we married. Eloped."

"Your parents didn't approve?"

"Oh, no. They forbade me from seeing him, but that was another rule I ignored. I was young and in love. Deeply, madly in love. He was so handsome, and I know that he loved me then, too. We were happy. And when the twins came along, our parents came around, and all was right with the world . . . except, of course, we didn't have Giovanni. I almost told Marcello about him when the twins were born, but I knew it would be a mistake. Marcello would have caused trouble. He wouldn't have let it go. He would have found a way to destroy our son's happy adoptive family. I couldn't let that happen. I put our son's happiness first."

"That's what mothers do," Hope said.

Maggie swiped a tissue across the trail of her tears and gave Hope a tremulous smile. "Giving him up was a scar on my heart. I thought our other babies would help it heal, but they didn't."

"I understand, Maggie."

Hope didn't know if the note of sincerity in her own voice tipped Maggie Romano off, or if the woman just had a sixth sense about lost children, but she gave Hope a sudden, sharp look. "Do you? Have you given up a child, Hope?"

Hope's mouth went dry. Up until now, the only person in Eternity Springs with whom she'd shared her story was Lucca. "This conversation isn't about me. Continue with your story, Maggie. I will tell you mine another time."

"All right. I just . . . you *are* a mother?"

Her heart twisted. "I am."

Maggie nodded. "Then maybe you'll understand that as much as I loved my husband, I resented him. I carried the burden all by myself, and even though it was my choice, I held it against him. It was always there, a constant, low-level hum beneath the surface, and it was destructive. So when the twins were eight and I discovered that he was cheating, my bitterness had a foundation."

Hope actually gasped. Lucca's father had cheated on Maggie? Whoa. From everything she'd seen, the Romanos worshipped their father.

"I couldn't leave him. I had four children at home. I believed in my marriage vows . . . for better, for worse—forever. He said he'd ended the affair, swore he'd never do it again. Stupid me, I believed him."

"He didn't end it?"

"He ended that one, but a year or so later, I discovered he had a new mistress. And then another. He wasn't faithful to them, either. He was a faithless husband, a serial philanderer, a cheat. But I loved him. And I despised him."

"I'm so sorry, Maggie. Men can be such jerks."

"That they can. Marcello Frances Romano was such a handsome jerk, so charismatic. His children thought he walked on water. I think he thought so, too."

"Your kids never knew about his infidelities?"

"No. I couldn't do that to them. He was a lousy husband, but he was an excellent father. He certainly didn't want them to know. It would have devastated them. Why destroy their opinion of him? I'd had all the destruction I could handle. Marcello did a number on my self-esteem. My forties were especially hard because he never took a mistress over the age of thirty-five. And by then he'd stopped trying to hide the affairs."

"The bastard."

"I did have some pride. I quit sharing his bed. I was seriously thinking about leaving him when we received word about Lucca's accident. After that, well, it wasn't the right time. Marcello and I actually got along better during those months than we had in years. A crisis with their children can bring a couple together."

Or drive them apart, Hope thought.

"Yet, when he died . . ." Maggie's voice cracked a little, and Hope reached across the desk and took her hand. "Part of me was glad. It shames me to admit that, but it's true. I was happy to be free of him and our sham of a marriage. Yet, I ached for my children, so I did mourn him. I mourned the loss of our family, and the young love we'd shared. But at the same time I felt reborn. Of course, that made me feel guilty as sin."

"We know that life is complicated, Maggie. It's pretty silly to think that death won't be complicated, too."

"That's a good way to put it. It was complicated. My children were suffering, and I was angry. He'd been so disrespectful of me and of the vows we'd made to each other. Disrespectful of our family. And he never had to pay for it. He never had his comeuppance. He died and dodged that bullet, and I was pissed. And, I had to pretend to mourn him."

"Complicated," Hope repeated.

"I was so tired of pretending. They thought I was depressed and maybe I was. More than that, I think I was lost. My sister took me on a cruise, and you know what I did? I had a fling! I had sex with someone other than Marcello Romano for the first time in my life. It was exciting and thrilling and fulfilling—and those wounded pieces of me began to heal. I didn't want to come home."

Oh, wow. TMI, Maggie.

"But I did come home and my kiddos brought me here; they brought me Zach, the missing piece of my heart. It was the greatest gift ever. I started feeling better. Life took on a new vibrancy for me."

"Eternity Springs has a way of doing that for people."

"And I'm so thankful my children loved me so much that they helped me find my way here. I have the best children in the world, and I never wanted to hurt them, but they are adults now, and they have their own lives. And I'm only fifty-four years old. I don't want to live another twenty or thirty or even forty years alone, moving forward but gazing backward." Her expression beseeching, Maggie asked, "Is that so terrible?"

"Of course not."

She closed her eyes. "I shouldn't be dumping all this on you."

"I'm your friend, Maggie. You can talk to me. That's what friends are for."

"You are a dear, Hope Montgomery. I want you to know that I didn't go looking for a man here in Eternity Springs. I came here to concentrate on my family. But one day, there was Richard. He made me realize how much I missed being sexy. How much I missed being teased and openly desired. How much I missed foreplay."

Hope smiled weakly. She really, really didn't want to be discussing foreplay with her lover's mother.

"Richard is good for me," Maggie continued, her gaze pleading for understanding. "I don't know where our relationship is going, if we're looking at something long-term or not. But I don't need to know it yet. What I need—what we need—is to have a little time to figure us out."

She shook her head and sighed. "It's hard to keep anything confidential in Eternity Springs."

Hard, but not impossible, apparently. Hope was now convinced that Maggie didn't know that her relationship with Lucca had gone beyond friendship. No way would she be spilling all these personal beans if she knew that Hope and her son were more than co-basketball coaches.

"Your children love you, Maggie."

"I know that. I know they want me to be happy, too. Just happy by their definition."

"They were caught off guard."

"To put it mildly, I suspect." Fresh tears welled in her eyes. "I knew they wouldn't be thrilled when they first learned that I was dating, so I had planned to introduce the subject slowly and carefully. So much for plans." Maggie rubbed her eyes, wiping away the tears. "What I wouldn't give to be able to go back and change things. What do I do now? I don't know. These are my children, and I don't have a clue what I should do."

"What do you want to do?"

She laughed without amusement. "Run away."

"To Austin?"

"Farther. Gabriella just returned from France. Maybe I should take the hint. Where exactly is Timbuktu?"

"Actually, Maggie, I think a strategic retreat is just what you need right now." When her friend looked at her in surprise, Hope elaborated. "Go to Austin. Give your children some time to digest the change in your circumstances. Then when you come home, they'll be ready to listen."

"I'm not telling them about their father. That would be selfish of me, and it would only hurt them."

"Then skip that part. Speak to them as adults and communicate your feelings."

"But what if they still won't listen? What if they continue to dodge my calls and avoid me?"

"Then pull the mom card. Call a family meeting and demand their presence. If you make attendance compulsory, they'll show. Remember, they do love you."

"Yes. Okay. That sounds like a plan." Having made her decision, Maggie nodded. "I'll go to Austin, and I won't try to contact them. Well, except, maybe I'll send them an email with a date, time, and place for a family meeting and tell them they're expected to attend. If they try to contact me, well, we'll just be taking a break. Give everyone a chance to cool down."

"Sort of like kindergarten time-out."

Maggie laughed. "Yes. Every one of my children has had experience with time-outs. Lucca was the worst."

Hope glanced at her clock. Her conference period was almost over. "You'd better call Richard and tell him plans have changed again. What time is your flight?"

"Four."

Hope winced. "You'll be cutting it close, but I think you can still make it."

Maggie hopped up, full of energy and purpose, and went around the desk to give Hope a big hug. "Thank you. You are such a dear friend. I know you're Gabi's friend, too, and now that I'm thinking clearly again, I realize I've put you in the middle by burdening you with some sensitive information."

"Don't worry about it. I've already forgotten seventy-five percent of what you told me." *Especially the part about foreplay.* "I'm sure the rest will be gone by the time basketball practice begins. Selective dementia, don't you know."

"God bless you, Hope Montgomery. I think you might have saved my family." Maggie pulled her phone from her purse and hit redial.

"No. The Romanos are strong. You're just reorienting your stars."

"What?" But before Hope could explain, Maggie's call connected. She waved good-bye and rushed from the classroom as she brought Richard Steele up to date.

"Well, now," Hope said moments later to her empty classroom. "That was interesting."

When she went to practice that afternoon, she didn't mention Maggie's visit to Lucca. For the next several days, he and Gabi both stayed far away from the subject of their mother.

As the week went on, Hope watched him at practice working with the team. She saw him jogging up Cemetery Road as she drove her bus route. When she delivered her students to school, she imagined a young Lucca Romano in time-out, banished to a chair facing the wall in a corner. She pictured him as a kindergarten student wearing red canvas sneakers and kicking the wall. She envisioned him as a fifth grader condemned to after-school detention, finger-kicking folded notebook-paper footballs toward an imaginary goalpost. She tried not to think about what the middle-school-aged Lucca Romano had done during detention. Probably found a way to flirt with a girl using hand signals or mirrors or even birdcalls.

"Maybe that's why he became a coach," she thought as she dismissed her gym class at the end of school on Friday. "All that experience with time-outs."

Amused at her own joke, Hope indulged her vanity by ducking into the locker room and touching up her makeup.

Basketball practice was scheduled to begin in ten minutes. With their first tournament of the season coming up on the weekend, Lucca had promised to spend some time coaching her about game-time strategy.

A district rule prevented Lucca from actually coaching during the game, so the pressure would be all on Hope. Gabi had come to practice to help, too, and while she worked with the boys, Lucca went over the game plan he'd developed with Hope.

She tried to pay close attention to what he told her, but she kept getting distracted by the scent clinging to his skin. Finally, when he was attempting to explain a new play he wanted to add, her attention wandered a bit too obviously. "Coach Montgomery! You need to pull your head out. What the heck is wrong with you today?"

The players and Gabi glanced in their direction, their expressions ranging from shocked to scandalized to amused. Lucca looked so annoyed with her that she couldn't help but tease him. "Sorry, Coach Romano," she said loudly. Then she leaned forward and dropped the volume of her voice. "Though you know it's your fault, don't you? The scent of your sister-in-law's soap clinging to your skin turns me on. I just want to lay you down and lick it off of you. All over."

Coach Romano's clipboard slipped right out of his hand and clattered against the hardwood floor. Hope smothered a grin.

"What sort of a kindergarten teacher are you?" he murmured after bending to pick up the clipboard. "You'll pay for that remark."

"I certainly hope so."

"My brother Max is visiting from Denver and I promised to meet him and Zach and some of the other guys at Murphy's tonight. How about you come over to my place tomorrow after the game? Bring your whipped cream and chocolate sauce. Plan to stay."

Whipped cream and chocolate sauce? A little shudder worked its way up her spine. Why was it that every time she tried to bait him sexually, Lucca out-baited her?

"Better get some butterscotch, too," he added.

"Enough," she said. "You'll make me . . . oh, wait. Saturday. It's November second. I can't see you on Saturday."

"What's so special about the second?"

"I have a guest coming to visit. My friend Daniel Garrett."

Thinking about Daniel and the upcoming weekend wiped all thoughts of sexy soap and whipping cream from Hope's mind. He'd be arriving sometime that evening and staying at least through Monday. She dreaded the weekend at the same time she looked forward to it. Daniel had done so much for her. Not only did he continue to search for Holly, he'd surely saved Hope's life, making her face her prescription drug addiction and being there for her every step of the way while she dried out. It made her feel good to be able to give him any help at all, but at the same time, these were difficult days for them both.

"In fact," she mused aloud. "I probably should wrap up practice right on time tonight. I have a lot to do before he arrives."

Lucca grunted, and she jerked her gaze up to meet his. He didn't look happy. In fact, he looked a little bit jealous, and that stroked her ego enough that she smiled at him brightly. "So what's next, Coach Romano?"

He set his mouth, then scratched a few more notes on his clipboard. Handing it over, he said, "Here's your game plan. Traditionally, my teams run one final drill at the end of the last practice before a game. It's important for team-building purposes, because for this one preparing-for-war instance, a coach is one with his players. Surrender the 'me' to the 'we.' Any objections, Coach Montgomery?"

She sensed a trap, but she could see no way out. "None whatsoever."

"All right, then. We're running ladders. Coach Montgomery, you run with the post group."

Oh, jeez. Her legs hurt already.

Leaning over the pool table in the game room at Murphy's Pub, Lucca drew back his cue preparing to break. He put all of his anger and frustrations into the stroke. Balls cracked and spread. He sank three in three different pockets, then made two more shots before he missed.

"The man is hot tonight," Max Romano said to his eldest brother, Zach Turner, as he lined up his shot. "Or has he been spending all of his time in Eternity Springs playing billiards?"

Zach frowned at the table when Max sank his ball. "Actually, I'm not sure what he's been doing lately. I just came back from visiting Savannah's nephew last night."

"I've been holding Gabriella's hand," Lucca told his brothers. "She's really upset about Mom."

"What about Maggie?" Zach asked.

Max and Lucca shared a look. "Gabi didn't call you?"

"While we were in South Carolina? Yes, she did. But we were out to dinner with Savannah's family, and she said the conversation could wait. So what's going on? I thought Maggie went to Texas for a B&B conference."

"Have you talked to her?"

"From Austin? No. I got an email from her asking that I attend a family meeting on Monday night. I told her I was scheduled to work, and she told me that I'm the boss so I can change the schedule."

"I got the same spiel," Max said, taking another shot. He missed, muttered a curse, and said, "She's working around Tony's schedule."

"So we're all going to be there? What's the deal? Whatever it is couldn't wait until Thanksgiv—oh." Zach's eyes widened. "She doesn't have cancer, does she? Tell me that's not it. I've already lost one mother to cancer."

"She's not sick," Max said.

"Physically, anyway. I wouldn't put money on her mental health." Lucca strode toward the door separating the game room from the pub and checked to see if anyone was listening before he explained. "Mom is doing her contractor."

Zach carefully lifted his pool cue away from cue ball. "Doing? As in . . . ?"

"Ah, yep." Lucca took a long pull on his beer.

"Richard Steele?"

"Good old Dickie."

In the process of taking a sip of beer, Max spewed. He wiped his mouth with the back of his hand. "You did not just say that."

Lucca shrugged, then gave Zach a quick but thorough summary of the previous Saturday's events. Zach whistled softly. "I didn't have a clue. Every time I've been around them they've acted totally like employer-employee."

"Great," Lucca said. "I didn't think about that. Next thing you know he'll probably charge her with workplace sexual harassment."

Zach rolled his eyes, then asked, "Do I remember that he has kids?"

Lucca nodded. "Two. One is in college, the other married. Steele is divorced."

"I don't get the sense that he's strapped for cash," Zach said.

"He's not," Lucca said. "He sold his business and made a pretty penny on it. Look, I know that Mom is an adult, and she's not married, and she's got the right to do what she wants, and all the other platitudes, too. But, dammit, I can't help but feel like I'm twelve years old. I know it's stupid, but I feel like she's cheating on Dad."

Max gave a snort and Lucca rounded on him. "What? You've been awful quiet. You think it's all fine and dandy that Mom is having an affair?"

"What I think is that I'm surprised it's taken her this long," Max said. "After all, Dad did it first."

Lucca's voice went cold and quiet. "What did you say?"

"Dad did it. He cheated on Mom. Apparently, he did it for years."

Lucca's temper blazed and he snapped, "You shut the hell up."

Max shrugged. "I can do that, but I'm telling the truth. Being silent won't change history."

"That's just bullshit," Lucca fired back, hanging on to denial.

"So says the twelve-year-old." Max set his beer down and picked up a block of chalk. "Take your shot, Zach."

Zach looked from Max to Lucca, then back to Max again. "I think I'll do just that."

As Zach sank the three, then studied the table, Lucca set down his cue and folded his arms. His chin up, he challenged his brother. "Why would you say something like that? Dad loved Mom. He worshipped her."

"He screwed around on her. That's not love."

"How do you know? Proof, Max. What proof do you have?"

Max leaned back against the shuffleboard table and casually picked up a weight. Tossing it from hand to hand, he said, "His current mistress came to the funeral."

"What!" Lucca exclaimed.

"Whoa," Zach said. "That's cold."

"Actually, it was pretty hot. On Aunt Mary Catherine's part, anyway. It was about ten minutes before the mass was due to start. Mom and Aunt Gloria and all of you were inside the church. I'd taken a walk around the block to get my head on straight, and I was across the street from the church waiting for a break in traffic. Aunt Mary Catherine was standing on the church steps greeting the last of the arrivals, and I saw her look at me and then her eyes bugged out. Then I figured out she wasn't looking at me, but past me. I turned and saw a woman I didn't recognize. She was about my age, blonde, wearing black patent stilettos and a skirt that barely reached the top of her thigh. At first I thought Aunt Mary Catherine was freaking out because the woman wore an outfit like that to a funeral mass. I thought the woman was probably one of Tony's groupies."

"But she wasn't," Zach observed.

"No. That would have been way easier."

"So what happened?" Lucca prodded.

"Well, Aunt Mary Catherine came off the steps, and thank God the light had changed and stopped traffic or she'd have probably walked out in front of a car in her rage. She got ten feet away from the woman and started letting her have it. 'How dare she,' 'she wasn't welcome,' 'Jezebel.' Then she hit her. Slapped her right across the chops. Like a movie. I think my jaw hit the sidewalk."

"Aunt Mary Catherine!" Lucca exclaimed again, uncrossing his arms. The woman was four feet ten inches and ninety pounds dripping wet. Hitting someone on a public street? In front of Saint Benedict's, no less?

"Yep. By then my eyes were the ones bugging out. It was an old-fashioned cat-fight slap. There was some back and forth, then the woman said, 'But I loved Marcello.' Aunt Mary Catherine came back with, 'And he just wanted to screw you. You were just the last in a long line of trashy women who couldn't find their own man, so don't think you're anything special.' The woman whirled around and flounced off, and Aunt Mary Catherine turned around and noticed me."

Lucca shoved his hands into his pockets. Zach took another shot and missed. Max set down the shuffle-board weight and picked up his cue. "Her face went from raspberry red to milk white in an instant."

"What did you do?" Zach asked.

"Then? Nothing. I stood there like a statue. I was too shocked to do anything else until the church bells began to toll and we had to get inside, so there wasn't time for me to even ask Aunt Mary Catherine the woman's name. Later at the house, I asked her if Mom knew. She said yes and that she'd tell me the whole ugly story another time. She asked me not to say anything to the rest of you and said it would hurt Mom more if she knew that I knew. So I kept my mouth shut."

"Hell, this is like a soap opera." Zach winced as he rubbed the back of his neck. "Did she ever tell you the whole ugly story?"

"Some of it. I didn't want to hear all of it. I didn't want to know what I knew. Once I started thinking about it, it made some sense. There were clues, though none of us ever picked up on 'em."

"Clues? There weren't any clues." Not any that Lucca wanted to think about, anyway. "I can't believe this. Dad wouldn't hurt—" He broke off abruptly when the sound of Cam Murphy's and Gabe Callahan's voices in the front room of the pub signaled their arrival and pro-pelled Lucca toward the back door. As he shoved it open and stepped into the bitter cold night—without a coat— he heard Max say, "Let him go. He'll cool off quick."

Cooling off took him longer than one would expect with outdoor temperatures hovering in the twenties. For the second time in a week, Lucca had had the founda-tions of his world rocked. He found himself walking away from Murphy's and toward Hope's house, toward sanctuary.

But as he approached, he saw a car pull into her drive. Lucca's steps slowed when a man got out of the car carrying a duffel bag. He stopped completely when Hope's front door flew open, and she ran outside and into the stranger's embrace.

FOURTEEN

The Eternity Springs Grizzlies finished fourth in the tournament on Saturday with Wade Mitchell scoring a personal high forty-five points in the semifinal game. With her concentration on the court, Hope only vaguely noticed that Lucca had taken a seat next to Daniel on the bleachers and that the two men exchanged conversation from time to time.

"So what's the deal with him?" Daniel asked when they returned to her house after the games ended. "For a basketball coach at a basketball tournament, he sure was fishing."

"What do you mean?"

Daniel leaned against her kitchen counter and turned his inquisitive blue eyes her way. "He's very curious about me."

"Oh?" Hope took her wooden recipe box from a cabinet.

"He pumped me for information. He acted . . . territorial."

Really? That should probably bother her, but she felt flattered instead. Lucca's attention didn't totally surprise her. Daniel's tragedy had aged his face but he was still an attractive man, and under other circumstances, they might have tried for more than friendship. Attempting nonchalance, Hope said, "We've been, um, seeing each other."

"I wondered if that might be the case." Daniel eyed the ingredients she pulled from her pantry with interest. "I don't think he liked me."

"You say that with such glee."

"What have you told him about me?"

Her chin came up. "I told him that you are my hero."

Daniel snorted. "I'm sure that went over well."

"Well, you *are* my hero, Daniel. I'd be lost without you. Actually, I'd probably be dead without you. You are my friend. A friend who stood by me when I had no other. You saved me."

"You saved yourself. I just gave you a helping hand. And I think you would have pulled out of it on your own given more time. Your inner core of strength is a force to behold. I just saved you time. Are you going to make ginger cookies?"

"Of course. Don't I always?"

He scooped up her hand and kissed it. "Marry me, Hope."

She laughed. "No. You don't like chocolate. We are simply too different to be compatible long-term. Besides, your friendship means too much to me to risk it for something temporary."

"You break my heart, woman. Not all marriages are temporary, you know."

"True. Just half of them."

He watched her measure out blackstrap molasses, then caught a drip with his fingertip and tasted the sweetness. "Did you tell him why I'm here?"

The very casualness of his tone prompted her to look at him closely, and she spied the pain he tried to hide. "No, Daniel. It's our private business."

"I wouldn't care. I just don't want to talk about it with a stranger. Not this trip."

"I know. Don't worry. Besides, I don't owe anyone an explanation for why I have friends visit." She turned on her mixer, creaming shortening and eggs and effectively putting a period to that topic of conversation.

Daniel put the teakettle on the stove, and by the time her dough was mixed, he'd placed two cups of steaming orange pekoe on the table. As was his habit, he filched a spoonful of dough, tasted it, then sighed. "Marry me, Montgomery."

"Keep your paws out of my cookie dough, Garrett."

He winked at her, then went for another. She slapped his hand. "Drink your tea and talk to me, Daniel. I feel bad that I conked out on you so early last night. I think I need new vitamins. Tell me what's going on in your life."

He licked his fingers. "I took a new case."

"Another infant?"

"Yes. A two-month-old. From 1998. San Antonio. A little boy. Parents both professionals, an architect and a lawyer. The wife's mother was babysitting and someone broke in. Killed the grandmother, stole electronics, jewelry, and the baby. At the time, the cops thought it was robbery that turned into more. I'm not so sure."

"You think the baby was the object of the crime all along?"

"I think that possibility didn't get enough play."

They talked about his case, then he asked her if she'd like to talk about Holly. She rolled a ball of dough in sugar, then set it on the cookie sheet. "You would have called me if you had anything new to report."

"Absolutely."

"And you continue to make your phone calls and distribute flyers and show her picture around immigrant neighborhoods?"

"Every month."

"So, no, then. I don't think I want to talk about Holly."

Surprise shone in Daniel's brown eyes. Frankly, Hope was a little surprised, herself. He was the one person with whom she spoke of Holly freely, and she'd done so ever since she and Mark had hired him to privately investigate their daughter's disappearance four months after the kidnapping. Not talking about Holly illustrated a significant change in her relationship with Daniel. Was it because she'd popped the pressure on that particular cork by talking to Lucca? Possibly. Probably. Was sharing Holly's story with someone other than Daniel a sign that her spirit was healing? Perhaps. Time would tell, she guessed.

She put a sheet filled with dough into her preheated oven, then set the timer. "Shall we talk about tomorrow? I have a couple of ideas about how we can spend the day. We are supposed to have sunshine."

"No skiing. Last time I did that I almost broke my leg."

"Actually, I thought we could either go snowmobiling or horseback riding. The family of one of my students owns a ranch, and he's offered a trail ride. Wade Mitchell. He was my high-point man today."

Daniel looked alarmed. "In the snow?"

"Snowmobiles usually work better in snow."

"I'm talking about the horses. Won't PETA be on your ass for making them go out in the snow?"

"Careful, Daniel. Your Boston upbringing is showing. Horses are quite adapted to cold weather. They have a winter coat, and Storm Mountain Ranch puts them in winter shoes. As long as they don't get wet from rain, snow, or sweat, they are quite comfortable being outside."

"Horses." He looked a little pained.

"Or snowmobiles," she repeated, smiling. "On snowmobiles we'd stay in the valley. Wade said the trail ride would take us high."

Daniel rose and went to peek in the oven. "I've never ridden a horse before. But I like the sound of going high tomorrow."

"Then I'll give Wade a call and take him up on his offer."

The following morning Hope wandered into her kitchen in search of coffee to find Daniel sitting cross-legged on the floor playing with Roxy. When he looked up at her and said good morning, she couldn't miss the bleakness in his eyes.

"Good morning, Daniel," she said lightly. "My dog is in heaven."

"She's a sweetheart. I was just thinking that maybe I could get a dog. Every year I do more and more work from home. I don't travel nearly as much as I used to. I might be able to make it work, but I'd hate to get a dog and then find out I couldn't."

"You could foster for a rescue group and see how it goes until the dog is adopted. If you're gone too much, you'll know without making the commitment to having a pet of your own."

"There's an idea."

"What kind of dog do you think you'd like?"

"Nothing girly like Roxy here. I'd want a big dog. A man's dog." He hesitated a moment before adding, "Justin had a dog. A boxer. He named her Soupy Lou."

Hope's heart twisted. He'd never mentioned a dog before. "Soupy Lou?"

Daniel's lips lifted ever so slightly. "I don't know. Gail said she thought Justin heard it on a cartoon."

"What happened to Soupy Lou?"

Daniel exhaled a long sigh. "I'm not sure. I came home a couple of months after Justin was killed and the dog was gone. Gail wouldn't say where. I looked for her, but . . ."

He shrugged, and Hope crossed the room and wrapped her arms around him in a comforting hug.

Half an hour later, they left her house, driving out to Storm Mountain Ranch in his rental. Daniel was quiet on this, the anniversary of the most horrible day of his life. Hope offered him her silent support, holding his hand for much of the twenty-minute drive to ranch. She directed him to the stables where Wade had instructed them to meet.

Wade came out to meet them, and Hope thought the smiling young man appeared even more at home in this setting than he did on a basketball court. Dressed in jeans, boots, a cowboy hat, and a sheepskin coat, he was the quintessential mountain rancher. Give him five years and women would be swooning all over him. Not that the teens at school weren't doing it already.

At that point, Hope got an unwelcome surprise. Instead of three horses saddled for riding, there were four. Wade wasn't the only person waiting at the stables.

Lucca Romano leaned against the stable door, his arms folded casually, a faintly satisfied grin on his face. Wade said, "Welcome to Storm Mountain, Ms. Montgomery."

"Thank you, Wade." She introduced the boy and Daniel, and while Daniel asked the young man a few questions about riding, she turned to Lucca. "Well, this is . . . unexpected."

"I was at the gym working with Wade when you called. He invited me to tag along."

After you made it impossible for him not to do so, I'm sure.

"I told him you wouldn't care."

Keeping her voice lowered, she said, "You were wrong. You should have asked me, Lucca."

"When? The guy hasn't left your side since he arrived two nights ago. Emphasis on the word 'nights.'"

She folded her arms. "Tell me you don't think I'm sleeping with him."

He opened his mouth, then obviously changed his mind about what he was going to say. "No, I don't. But dammit, Hope, you *are* sleeping with me. I think the least you could do is tell me why another man is spending the night at your house."

Hope was not in the mood for male ego and jealousy, so she snapped. "Because today is the eighth anniversary of his four-year-old son's abduction and murder, and I am his friend."

It stunned him, as she had known it would. The jealous light in his eyes faded to shame, and he glanced over to where Daniel stood talking to Wade about the horses. "I'm so sorry."

"You should be." He'd made a huge assumption and leap of action, and it totally annoyed her. "He has enough to deal with today without you goading him over something that doesn't even exist."

"You're right. I had no idea." He took a step away from her and added, "I'll leave."

"No," Daniel said.

Hope looked around to see that her friend had approached and obviously overheard at least some of her exchange with Lucca. A grin played at his mouth and amusement shone in his eyes. It was such a relief to see something other than bleakness in his gaze that she didn't mind its being at her expense.

"I think it will be nice to have someone else along on our ride," Daniel continued, extending his hand to shake Lucca's. "That way when I fall off the horse and break my leg, Wade will have help hauling my butt down the mountain."

"Would you stop with the broken leg business?" Hope asked, rolling her eyes.

Daniel spoke to Lucca. "Are you an experienced rider?"

"Actually, I am. I did some coaching stints in Texas and the West and learned then."

The conversation was interrupted by the arrival of a Mule—the four-wheeled kind as opposed to the four-legged variety. Wade introduced his father to Hope and the two men. David Mitchell was an older version of his son, tall and broad-shouldered with a weathered face that reflected a lifetime of hard, physical work.

"Welcome to Storm Mountain," he said. "Looks like y'all are going to have a nice day for a ride."

The group exchanged pleasantries for a moment, then David turned to Lucca. "Could we speak privately for a moment, Mr. Romano?"

"Of course."

As the two men walked away, Wade's worried gaze followed them. Family, Hope thought. Sometimes it can be such a burden. Then her gaze fell upon Daniel, who was the closest thing to family that she had. Her brother, in so many ways. The brother whose eyes once again had gone bleak. She crossed to him and gave him a hug. Sometimes, family is all that helps you survive. "If you fall and break your leg, Daniel, I'll make sure the doctor gives you a pretty pink cast."

"You are all heart, Hope."

Then, because Wade looked so miserable and she was, after all, his teacher, she made an effort to take care of him, too, by providing a distraction. "Wade, why don't you tell Daniel the Ute legend about the Storm Mountain hot springs?"

Wade did as she asked, though his gaze continued to dart to his father and his coach. The conversation did look serious, and Hope was as curious as Wade. When the two men finally shook hands and turned to walk back toward them, Lucca caught Wade's gaze and gave him a reassuring wink. Hope relaxed and after a moment, Wade did, too. They climbed onto their horses and started off.

It was a lovely ride. The horses Wade had chosen for them were accustomed to inexperienced riders, having been used for tourist rides the preceding summer. Sunshine and temperatures in the forties cleared the evidence of the previous day's snowfall but for the shaded spots where patches of white would last until spring.

They mostly remained silent while they rode, though Daniel and Lucca did discuss cars and trucks for a time, and the easy way they conversed made Hope glad that Lucca had tagged along.

The man had been jealous. Over her. The tall, dark, and handsome GQ model pro athlete had been green-eyed enough to arrange to be here today. Call her shallow, but nothing had done her ego quite so much good in a very long time.

Wade guided them to a spot that offered a breathtaking view of snow-topped mountains to the west. Someone had fashioned log benches situated perfectly for enjoying the scenery. "Can we stay here for a little while?" Daniel asked.

"Sure. It's a good place to stretch," Wade replied.

Hope sat beside Daniel on the bench while Wade and Lucca took care of the horses. Hope heard the boy ask Lucca about the conversation with his father, but she dismissed her curiosity about that and turned her attention to her friend.

"This was a good idea, Hope," he said. "Though I will admit I was ready to get down from that horse."

"I thought you'd enjoy it."

"A dose of 'peaks' on a day of 'valleys.' You're pretty smart, Hope Montgomery."

She laced her fingers through his. "Do you want to talk about Justin?"

He gave a long pause before saying, "The rage is mostly gone now, which is a good thing. But I walk around with this big, black empty space inside me that I had hoped would go away. Now, I don't think that will ever happen. It's so heavy and dark and cold. Some days it's bigger than others. Some days it's so big that it takes up my whole sky."

"I know," Hope told him, meaning it.

"Gail's sister called me last week. The family is planning a memorial service on the anniversary of her death. They invited me to attend."

"Will you go?" she asked, hoping that this scar, at least, might have begun to heal.

"No. I don't think so." Daniel rose to his feet. "I need to walk a little bit."

She could see the tears flooding his eyes. "Want some company?"

"No, thanks. Just let me . . ."

"Sure, Daniel. Take all the time you need."

When her friend disappeared into the trees, Lucca took his seat beside Hope. "Is he okay?"

"He doesn't like me to see him cry."

Lucca picked a stick up off the ground, tugged a knife from his pocket, and began to whittle. "Tell me about Daniel, Hope."

Her gaze locked on the trees where he had disappeared, she said, "Justin was with his mother at the mall. They were at the food court and a man at the table next to them had a heart attack. Daniel's wife started CPR on him and a group of people surrounded them. In the confusion, Justin got scared and backed away. Someone took him. They found his body four days later. Gail committed suicide seven months after that."

Lucca muttered a curse. "How horrible. How does

anyone come back from something like that? A family completely destroyed."

"It hasn't been easy," Hope continued. "Daniel was a police detective, and after Gail died, he quit the force and went private. He works child abductions, both recent cases and cold ones. We hired him to search for Holly, and he and I became friends. We spend our anniversaries together."

By now, Lucca had sharpened the stick to a pencil point. He flipped it around and began whittling the other end. "He's still looking for Holly?"

"Oh, yes. Holly's is a special case to him. She and Justin shared the same birthday. I think if he could bring Holly home to me, it would help heal his heart almost as much as mine."

"Have there ever been any leads?"

"For Holly?" Hope shook her head. "No. Margarita Santana disappeared into the immigrant community. But that's part of what gives me comfort. I know who stole my daughter. I think she did it because she wanted to mother my girl, as opposed to the perverted murderer who took Daniel's son . . ." Finding it difficult to talk about someone so evil, she hesitated. "To use."

"Did they find the killer?"

"Yes, but not for three years, when he was apprehended for another crime. DNA evidence tied him to Justin's murder. He was a pedophile."

"Dear Lord." Lucca moved his knife with such force that he broke his stick in two. "I cannot imagine anything worse. I'm glad he has you for a friend."

"Me, too." One of the horses let out a loud whinny, and Hope looked over to where Wade stood. "So what did Mr. Mitchell want?"

"An honest assessment of Wade's talent. It sounds like he's trying to come to grips with the idea that Wade might win a college scholarship."

"He didn't ask you to torpedo Wade, did he?"

"No. It's obvious he loves his son. I think David Mitchell is the kind of man who believes in hard work, and if Wade's hard work earns him a collegiate spot, his father won't deny him the opportunity. I don't think he'll like it necessarily, but that might change once he gets used to the idea."

"He's scared of losing his son," Hope said. Then, as Daniel exited the woods a few moments later, his eyes red-rimmed but a gentle smile on his face for Hope, she added, "David Mitchell needs to understand that there is losing, and then there's losing."

"Amen to that," Lucca said. "Amen to that."

"Dear Lord, pray for us," Gabi said as she watched her mother march up the sidewalk toward Aspenglow, where her children waited. "She's on the warpath. Really, she has all the nerve. We're not the ones who were flaunting our illicit love affair in public."

"Illicit love affair?" Max drawled. "Hell, Gabi. You sound like a virgin spinster."

"I may be a spinster, but I'm darn sure not a virgin."

"Aargh!" Zach said. "Please. No more."

One hand on her hip, Gabi dramatically waved the other. "Give me grief if you want, but you weren't there to see it. She all but gave that ice cream cone a blow job."

Max said, "Gabi! Please."

Tony scowled at his brothers. "Leave her alone. She has a point, you know."

Lucca grimaced. Of the five Romano siblings, Gabi and Tony were the only two who didn't know about their father's betrayal. Friday night he and Max and Zach had decided to keep that information to themselves unless it became clear that telling would help the family unit more than keeping silent hurt it.

He hoped they could get through this meeting without

damaging Gabi's and Tony's opinion of their father, but the next few minutes would tell that tale.

Maggie Romano opened the door to her bed-and-breakfast and stepped inside. She unwrapped the yellow scarf from around her neck and hung it on a coat rack before beginning to pull off her gloves, tugging finger after finger while visually taking inventory. "You are all here. Good."

She put her gloves in her coat pocket, then hung her coat on the rack with her scarf. She wore a red skirt and jacket. A power suit. *Okay. This could be trouble. She's not going to go the teary, vulnerable, "please understand" route. She's in "I'm your mother and you will obey me" mode.*

That would work for the boys, but Gabi was a wild card. She could get on her high horse and out-Mom Mom if she so desired. Lucca had seen it happen more than once, and the afternoon in Gunnison had devastated Gabriella.

Nothing I like more than navigating a minefield with two emotional women.

His mother stepped into the remodeled room that would serve as Aspenglow Place's public parlor. Max had built a fire in the hearth, and for a moment, the crackle of burning wood was the only sound to be heard. Then Maggie took a place in front of the fireplace, folded her hands, and said, "Thank you all for coming here tonight. I think it's important that this family continues to communicate. I know you all undoubtedly have things you'd like to say to me. However, I get to go first.

"Due to unfortunate timing, my private business has become family public knowledge. I regret that. It was not my intention to parade my new relationship in your faces. That said, now that the cat's out of the bag, I want you to know that I will demand you be respectful of my choices, just as I am of yours. I want you to know that I will always value your father and honor this family he gave us. I have and will continue to mourn his loss.

"But I am relatively young and I am ready to move forward. Your father would have wanted me to be happy. I would hope that you, my children, would want me to be happy."

Lucca glanced around the room to gauge the temperature of his siblings' reaction. Max and Zach looked cool. Gabi and Tony appeared to be sucking on prunes. He cleared his throat. "We do want you to be happy, Mom. I think everyone was a little shocked at first."

Gabi snorted. Maggie shot her a disapproving scowl.

Max said, "We feel protective of you, Mom. We're afraid that you've gotten too serious with this fellow too soon. After all, how much does anyone know about this Richard guy other than that he's a decent contractor?"

"We don't want you choosing someone just to avoid being alone, Mom," Tony added. "This guy might have substance abuse issues or mental health problems. Is he divorced? Does he have kids? Maybe he's looking for emotional and financial help with his children."

Annoyance flashed in Maggie's eyes. "For heaven's sake, Anthony. Don't you think I have any sense?"

"You haven't dated in thirty years, Mom. There are a lot of losers out there."

"But I'm too stupid to identify them?" She laughed without amusement. "Believe me, son. I have more experience than you know. Look, I'm dating Richard. I'm not engaged to marry him. Right now I care about him, and he makes me happy. Just like I had to grin and bear it when you brought home girls I wasn't certain about, you get to do the same for me. Now, any other comments?"

She folded her arms and looked around the room.

"Gabriella, you look as if you have something you want to say."

"Are you practicing safe sex?"

All four Romano brothers groaned and grimaced and looked anywhere but at their mother, who arched a brow and said, "Gabriella, I learned the consequences of having unprotected sex when I was fifteen years old. It is not a lesson one forgets. And since you brought the topic up, I will add that I trust you all are acting in a sexually responsible manner."

"Can we change the subject please?" Zach asked.

Lucca couldn't have agreed more. Especially since the memory of the recent incident when he hadn't acted sexually responsible suddenly flashed through his brain.

He sat back in his chair. He hadn't thought about it, that first night when Hope had come to him. He hadn't used a condom. He never made that slip, but that night, he hadn't been thinking.

Maybe he should bring it up. Just check and make sure that she's okay and not worried about . . . consequences.

"Do you have any comments or questions, Zach?" his mother asked.

"My situation is different from the others. I didn't know Marcello Romano. I just . . . well . . . you have my phone number. Feel free to call me anytime. And I mean anytime."

His mother smiled at him, then looked at Lucca. "You?"

He winced and rubbed the back of his neck. "I don't have anything against Steele. I do want you to be happy, Mom. It's just going to take some time to get accustomed to you . . . uh . . ." He couldn't come up with a word.

"Living again?" she suggested.

He smiled sheepishly and shrugged.

Maggie Romano turned to her next eldest. "Tony?"

"I don't have anything to say."

The mulish look on his twin's face told Lucca that Tony wasn't going to surrender his anger easily. His mother recognized it, too, but rather than try to coax any more from him, she continued calling roll. "Max?"

Max stretched out his legs and crossed them at the ankles. He glanced from Tony to Gabi, then said, "More than anyone I've ever known, you deserve to be happy, Mom. If Richard Steele makes you happy, then I say have fun. Be careful, but be happy."

Maggie offered up a tremulous smile. "Gabi?"

"I . . . I . . ." Tears swelled in her eyes and overflowed. "Excuse me." She shoved herself from her seat and fled the room.

Lucca pulled his gaze away from his sister and back to his mother to see that now, she'd started crying, too. *Oh, hell.*

Maggie grabbed a tissue from the box on the coffee table and dabbed at her eyes. She cleared her throat, then said, "I expect you all here for Thanksgiving dinner. My kitchen will be complete by then, and it will be my first meal in Aspenglow Place. As is our family custom, you are all welcome to invite friends. I intend to invite Richard. Celeste plans to join us. I ask you to give me a final count on Tuesday before."

Her gaze shifted once more toward the powder room where Gabi had disappeared, then she drew a deep breath, squared her shoulders, and asked, "Anything else?"

The boys shared a look, and their gazes all fell upon Tony. "I'll be bringing two of my players. They don't have family to go home to."

"That's nice." Maggie crossed the room toward the entry hall and the coat rack. "I trust one of you will convey my request to your sister?"

They all answered at once. "Sure." "Will do." "Of course." "Got it covered."

Maggie nodded, then pulled on her coat, her hat, her scarf, and her gloves. "Good night."

The door shut firmly behind her, and one by one, her sons let out a sigh. "That went well," Zach said.

"Oh, yeah," Tony replied, his tone saying the opposite. "Just effing peachy."

Max rose and lifted a fireplace tool from the rack to poke the fire. "It could have been worse."

"Yeah," Lucca said. "She could have brought the steel dick with her."

Max groaned. Tony buried his face in his hands. Zach rose and said, "I'm outta here. I'm working a double shift tomorrow and it starts at five in the morning. I'm going to hit the sack early." Addressing Tony and Max, he said, "So, I guess I'll see you guys at Thanksgiving."

"Yep. Nothing like a family holiday to look forward to," Max said, shaking his brother's hand.

After a short discussion, Tony and Max both decided to leave Eternity Springs and drive partway home to Boulder and Denver, respectively. When they knocked on the bathroom door to tell Gabi they were leaving, she finally exited the room. Soon, just she and Lucca were left. Lucca told her what their mother had said prior to her departure. Gabi rubbed her red-rimmed eyes and said, "I'm a mess. This whole thing has stirred up my grief. It's like we lost Dad last week, not going on two years ago. I'm so sad and so angry, and I know it's wrong of me to be angry. I just can't seem to help it."

Lucca was angry, too, only he was angry with their father, which was wasted energy, considering that Marcello Romano lay in his grave. For a moment, he considered sharing the bombshell that Max had dropped, but he decided against it. While his siblings had all looked up to their father, Gabi's status as the only daughter had always made her relationship with their father a bit different. She had truly been Marcello Romano's princess.

"Mom loves you. You love her. Remember what Nana always used to say? This, too, shall pass."

"But she's having sex with him. He took her to a sleazy motel. I didn't expect her to throw herself onto the funeral pyre, but they were married thirty years. How can she move on in less than thirty months? And why is it that you guys can all smile and be nice about it?"

He chose his words carefully. "We can't know what went on inside their marriage. We have to trust Mom to know her own heart."

Gabi sniffed, then stalked over to the fireplace and held her hands out toward the flames for warmth. "Maybe I should follow your lead and run away to South America."

"Because your mother has a new boyfriend?"

Her rapid blinking began again, and Lucca wished he'd kept his mouth shut. "Because I am in such a bad place right now. I'm adrift. I'm not a cop anymore. I don't have a job. My only constant was my family, and now there's a biker in Mom's bed and a kindergarten teacher in yours. I don't have anyone special, and dammit, I'm lonely."

Oh. That's what this is about. Now it makes sense. "Oh, honey. Come here." He went to her and wrapped his arms around her. "Listen, I'm an expert on bad places. One thing I've come to believe is that it is possible to find your way out of them. You just have to put one foot in front of the other, Gabs, and eventually, the road will lead you to somewhere better."

Gabi drew back and looked up into his eyes. "And your better place? It's with Hope?"

Slowly, he nodded.

"Are you going to hang around that better place for a while?"

"I'm not looking to leave."

"So are we talking something permanent? Say, buying a house in this better place? Putting down stakes? Maybe, with a ring?"

Lucca's heart did a little hitch. Marriage? How had they gone from talking about their mother's sex life to a ring on Hope's finger?

A ring on Hope's finger. Funny, he kind of liked the sound of that.

"Well?"

Lucca was glad to see the spark of interest in his sister's eyes. Anything was better than those great big sad puppy dog eyes. "Can I trust you to keep a secret?"

Interest brightened to sheer delight. "Absolutely!"

"Okay, then. It's too soon to tell, but this is the first time in my life that the m-word hasn't made me shiver in my shoes." He tapped his index finger against her nose. "Now, I know the kitchen here isn't officially open, but since I work here I keep a stash. The coals of this fire are just about perfect for roasting marshmallows. Want to make s'mores?"

"S'mores!" Gabi clutched her hands dramatically against her chest. "Lucca Romano, I love you."

FIFTEEN

For the next two weeks, Gabi managed to avoid working with her mother by returning to the sheriff's department to fill in for one of Zach's deputies who requested family leave to stay home with his newborn baby. Lucca divided his time between Aspenglow and the school's gymnasium, where he worked with the basketball team and with Wade in particular. In the first awkward exchange between Lucca and Richard, the contractor made an "I won't hurt your mother" assertion and Lucca replied with a "Good, because I'll be watching" caution. After that they managed to revert to their prior working relationship.

Hope, meanwhile, continued her dawn-to-dusk schedule, though she found it more difficult to get through the day without running out of steam. Her fatigue bothered her with an unacknowledged concern fluttering at the back of her thoughts like butterfly wings. Three times during the week while grading papers on the sofa in the teacher's lounge during her conference period, she'd ended up taking a nap. With an extra-early start scheduled for the next day—a special preseason tournament had been organized in Serenity Valley to raise funds for a local student in need of a kidney transplant—she regretfully decided that she'd better skip that night's date with Lucca in order to go to bed early.

When he arrived before practice, she took him aside and said, "I'm sorry, Lucca, but I need to cancel our date tonight."

"Okay." Concern creased his brow. "Is something wrong?"

"Not really. It's been a long week and frankly, I'm just exhausted. We need to leave before daylight in the morning, so I'm better off going to sleep early."

He studied her with a frown. "That's the third time I've heard you mention being tired recently. Maybe you should see a doctor."

Those butterfly wings of worry fluttered again, but she quickly swatted them away. "I'm fine, really. I'm still catching up from the sleep I missed when Daniel was here."

His tone droll, he said, "If I weren't a confident man, I might find statements like that worrisome."

"Hey, Coach!" one of the players called as a group of students entered the gym. "Would you settle an argument? My dad says Michael Jordan had a better jumper than Derek Fisher. What do you say?"

Since the question itself proved that the student wasn't talking to her, Hope turned her attention to her practice notes. She was amazed at the progress the team had made since the beginning of the season. Lucca saw the difference in the players, she knew. What she wondered was whether or not he saw the difference in himself.

He enjoyed coaching. She found it endearing that he obviously derived just as much pleasure from the efforts of their benchwarmers as he did from the starters. She wondered if it had always been that way for him, or if the pressure of high-stakes competition had stolen that joy. Well, whatever the answer, she hoped that when he returned to collegiate coaching, he would take the lessons learned in the Grizzlies' gym along with him. *I want you to be happy, Lucca. Wherever you go. Whoever you are with.*

She gave her head a shake, then focused on the business at hand. The boys were full of energy that afternoon and excited about the first away trip of the season. At the end of practice, she called them together to pass out travel information for the players to give their families. "I still need signed permission slips from Billy and Brandon." She made eye contact with the two in question. "I won't let you on the bus without them. Meet in the parking lot at five A.M. We're leaving at ten minutes after. If you're late, you'll have to find your own way to Serenity Valley. Coach Romano, any final words of advice for our team prior to the tournament?"

A shadow crossed his face. "I'll save my pregame remarks for tomorrow."

She looked at him for a beat. "All right, then. In that case, we're done here. See you all in the morning—and go to bed at a decent time tonight!"

As the boys holding basketballs lined up to place them in the rack, Lucca signaled for one to be tossed his way. He held on to the ball, spinning it in his hands, until the last of the students exited the gym. Lucca turned toward Hope. "Where is Serenity Valley?"

"It's southwest of here. About a hundred miles away. Well, actually the short route is a hundred miles, but this time of year we use the longer route to avoid a couple of passes."

"But not Sinner's Prayer Pass."

The direction of his thoughts suddenly clicked for Hope. *Oh, Lucca.* Of course it would be difficult for him. "No, going south it's unavoidable."

Grimly, he asked, "You said you take a bus?"

"Yes, we take my school bus. I drive."

He winced, and his expression grew downright haggard. She placed her hand on his arm. "Lucca, you surely knew the team traveled to away games."

"Yes, of course." He shoved his fingers through his hair. "I knew it, but I never thought about it. The actual transportation part. Easier not to think about it, I guess. Why do you do the driving?"

"Well, because we have only three licensed bus drivers. It's my bus, my team. I get paid extra for driving and, frankly, it's income I need. Daniel doesn't charge me for his time anymore, but I do pay the expenses he incurs in connection with looking for Holly. The driving job helps."

"Basketball season happens in the winter," Lucca said, frustration sharpening his tone. "This is winter in the mountains. Snow happens. Sleet happens."

"And I am very careful. The schools are very careful. This isn't our first winter, Lucca. We pay close attention to road conditions and we reschedule games if the forecast looks dicey."

Lucca bounced the basketball, then took it toward the hoop. Hope stood watching, debating what to say to him. Was there anything she could say that would ease his mind? "Lucca, I've never had an incident with the bus. I've never had a car accident. I've never even been cited for a moving violation of any sort."

He took half a dozen shots. She stood waiting, since it was obvious he was working something out. When he finally turned to her, he asked, "Will it break any rules if I ride along with the team?"

"Lucca, this isn't something you need to put yourself through. Why don't you—"

"Will it break any rules?" he interrupted.

"No."

"Then I'll ride with you. I'll meet you at the bus in the morning. Now, why don't you head on home? I'm going to stay and shoot for a little while longer. Sleep well, Hope."

The man obviously wanted to be alone. Understanding the need to sometimes wrestle with one's demons in private, Hope nodded and left him to it.

She slept well that night and awoke at four-fifteen to the sound of her alarm, feeling better than she had in days. She showered, dressed, and checked the latest weather report while eating a quick breakfast. The slight chance of snow they'd called for the day before had disappeared from the forecast.

"Good," she murmured, closing her laptop. This trip needed to be as smooth and as uneventful as possible for everyone's sake.

She'd made arrangements with a teenager to watch Roxy, so she made sure to leave the front door lock disengaged as she departed. As she glanced next door, her stomach sank in disappointment. It was a quarter to five, and Lucca's house remained dark. Under other circumstances she might have called or knocked to see if he'd overslept, but not today. Recovery came in fits and starts. This particular hill would be a high one for Lucca to climb.

With such thoughts on her mind, Hope was surprised to arrive at the school parking lot to discover Lucca already waiting. "You're here."

"I said I would be," he said, his voice tight with anxiety. "How do you feel this morning? Did you sleep well?"

"I did. I feel great, and I'm so glad to see you."

He tugged her around to the back of the bus away from the glow of the street lamp and gave her a thorough and slightly desperate kiss. "I'm so afraid that I'm going to embarrass myself. Promise me that if I start to wig out, you'll kick me out on the side of the road. Call Zach and he'll come get me."

He sounded so uncertain. Was he ready for this? "You don't have to do this, you know."

"Actually, I do." He lowered his mouth to hers once more and kissed her until the sound of an approaching car had them both pulling away. "I'm hanging on to my man card by a thread as it is."

"Hardly," Hope said, giving her best sniff of disdain. "Darlin', after caveman sex, your man card is made out of platinum."

Calmed, he laughed as they went to meet their team.

For the first leg of the journey, Lucca sat quietly at the back of the bus. All the way at the back. Twice when the kids got loud, he snapped at them to be quiet. When Hope started the climb up Sinner's Prayer Pass, a glance into her rearview mirror showed her that Lucca had a death grip on the grab bar in front of him. His obvious stress affected her, and she was never so glad to reach the flats on the other side of the pass as she was this time. She wondered what her chances would be to convince him to catch a ride home with one of the parents making the trip to Serenity Valley.

They arrived at their destination without incident, and once the students exited the bus, Lucca moved up to the seat behind her. He looked like he'd run a marathon, she thought.

"Welcome to Serenity Valley," she said.

"I made it." He flashed her a relieved grin and added, "Is it too early to start drinking?"

"Yes. So, are you okay?"

"I think I am. It helped that this school bus is such a . . . school bus. I'd forgotten what a lousy ride they are, but it sure helped keep me in the present rather than losing myself in the past. You did a great job behind the wheel, Hope."

"Thank you. Now, let's hope I can do okay with the coach's clipboard."

She did a fine job, with the Grizzlies coming in third place in the tourney, a totally respectable showing. Wade had an excellent outing in the consolation game, and while Lucca treated the victorious team to dinner at a pizza joint, Hope managed to catch a nap on the bus so that she was fresh for the drive home.

The sleet started a quarter mile from the summit of Sinner's Prayer Pass.

The ping of ice pellets sounded like bullets against the bus's exterior, and as Hope's alarm mounted, her grip on the steering wheel tightened. Though she focused her attention on the road, she nevertheless sensed when Lucca moved forward to sit behind her. Tension carved furrows in his brow. "Is there anything I can do to help?"

Hope needed to keep calm for Lucca, for the kids, and for the sake of her own nerves, too. "It's been warm this week. We'll be home before the ice starts sticking to the road."

"That's good to know."

"Talk to me, Coach Romano. I can use the distraction." *So, too, can you, I imagine.*

"All right. What would you like me to talk about?"

She said the first thing that popped into her mind. "Thanksgiving. When I asked your mother what I could bring, she asked me to bring sweet potatoes. So, what sort of sweet potatoes does your family like? Do you go for more simple ones or do you like the whole southern sweet potato pie thing?"

Bless his heart, the man took her cue and offered her his unspoken support. He talked sweet potatoes to her all the way down from Sinner's Prayer Pass, and then broadened to other Romano Thanksgiving fare for the rest of the way into town. By the time Hope pulled into the Eternity Springs Community School parking lot, her hands were shaking with stress and her mouth watered from hunger. "I'll be dreaming about turkey until Thursday," she told him as she shifted into park and cut the engine.

Lucca didn't answer. He was the first off the bus, and he disappeared into the darkness beyond the glow of the streetlight. Exhaustion overwhelmed Hope as she climbed out of the bus and watched to make sure that all her players had rides home. "Where's Coach Romano?" she heard Wade Mitchell ask one of his teammates.

"Guess the pizza didn't agree with him," another player answered. "He's over by the Dumpster puking up his guts."

Oh dear, Hope thought. She saw the last of the boys off, then called, "Lucca? Are you okay?"

"Yeah." He walked out of the shadows, saying, "I'm fine. I'm great. Excellent job, Hope. I don't want to ever ride on a school bus again."

She laughed softly, then said, "I'm beat. Walk me home, Romano?"

"I'll carry you home if you'd like, Montgomery. Thank you."

"For what?"

"For getting us home safely. For letting me on the bus in the first place."

"You're welcome." This had been a victory for him. "So have you put that particular monster to bed, do you think?"

"Partially. I have come to one decision, though. Right after Thanksgiving, I'm going to get professional help."

"You're going to see a counselor?"

"Not that sort of professional help. I have something else in mind. Tell me, Ms. Montgomery: How do you feel about NASCAR?"

After consulting with Gabi, Savannah, and Celeste, Hope made the decision to go with Celeste's southern recipe for sweet potato pie. She figured that any recipe filled with butter, sugar, and nuts had to be a hit. Besides, Gabi had assured her that Maggie always had plenty of fresh vegetables to balance out the fat.

So on Thursday morning with her sweet potatoes still warm from the oven, she knocked on the door of Aspenglow Place. Maggie answered wearing an apron with a turkey on the front and a dish towel thrown over her shoulder. "Hope, welcome. Happy Thanksgiving."

"Happy Thanksgiving. I came early to help. Tell me what I can do."

"Bless you. Come on inside. I'm so glad to have the company. I haven't been this nervous about a Thanksgiving dinner since the first time I cooked for my in-laws."

They walked past the dining room, where a large table was beautifully set. "Your table is gorgeous, Maggie."

"Thanks. This is the first year I've had a room and furniture big enough to seat everybody. No kids' table arguments this year." She gave a nervous laugh and added, "Not that I can count on an argumentless day."

Hope gave her friend a comforting smile. "It's going to be fine. Everyone will behave."

"I know," Maggie replied, leading the way into the kitchen. "I'm just afraid dinner will be awkward and tense. I met Richard's children yesterday. They're just delightful. They seemed so happy that he is seeing me. So different from my brood. Of course, he's the hero rather than the villain in their family drama—his wife was unfaithful and his kids knew it."

She handed Hope an apron, saying, "Would you like to wash and trim the green beans?"

"I'm happy to."

Maggie went back to work forming bread dough into rolls. "I'm excited about having Richard's granddaughter with us today. I've missed having children around at the holidays."

"How old is she?"

"Ten. And she's just a doll. A shy little thing. I made a Jell-O salad that my kids loved when they were children." Maggie looked up from her rolls and studied Hope. "Speaking of children, we haven't had a private time to speak since I visited your classroom. You mentioned that you're a mother, too?"

Caught off guard, Hope snapped a green bean in two. Her heart started to pound. Her mouth went dry. Stupid, really, since she'd suspected the question might come up. She should be able to calmly confide her secret.

Instead, she blurted out. "My little .girl was kidnapped."

In the process of carrying rolls to the oven, Maggie bobbled the baking sheet and almost dropped it. "Oh, my heavens, Hope. Really? What happened?"

After taking the tray from Maggie and slipping it into the oven, Hope relayed her story, managing to share the basic facts without bursting into tears. She considered it a victory. While she spoke, Maggie abandoned all dinner prep efforts and leaned back against the counter with her arms crossed, her gaze reflecting both sympathy and horror. When Hope finally finished her story, Maggie walked over to her and gave her a hug. "I am so, so very sorry, Hope. That's the most horrible story. My heart breaks for you. I know what it is like to give up a child. It created a hole in my heart that didn't heal until we found Zach. But to have a child ripped away from you . . . to not know where she is or if she's safe . . . I cannot imagine the pain. Is that why you haven't talked about it?"

Talking about it stirred up feelings better left ignored. "Mostly, yes. Also, I don't want people to look at me and see a grieving mother. They treat me . . . tenderly . . . and that just makes the whole thing more difficult to bear. It's been easier to be seen as a kindergarten teacher."

"Or a coach?" Maggie suggested. "Rumors are swirling around town that you and my son are bouncing something other than basketballs these days."

Hope felt her cheeks warm. So, Maggie had finally heard. "We have been dating."

Of course, they'd been doing a lot more than that, but she wasn't about to go down that road.

"Well, I'm glad." Maggie beamed at her. "As far as I'm concerned, Lucca couldn't do better. He hasn't had someone special in his life for a very long time."

At the term "someone special," Hope's heart gave a little *ka-thump*. "Thank you for the compliment, Maggie, but I don't want you to think this is more than it is. I don't think Lucca is looking for a long-term relationship, and I'm certainly not. We're friends." Then, because Maggie looked like she was about to launch into a lecture, Hope attempted a distraction. "He is taking me to a high-performance driving school over the weekend."

Maggie gave her a baffled look. "A driving school? On Thanksgiving weekend?"

"Because I drive the basketball team to their away games. You know he went with us to our tournament in Serenity Valley."

"Oh," Maggie said. "I see. Yes, he told Richard that he went. I'm just so thrilled with the progress he's made. But I have to ask: How does high-performance driving school have anything to do with driving a school bus?"

"Apparently, they teach not only how to drive, but how to wreck."

"Ahh. That will make Lucca feel better about the away games. Oh, Hope. To know that he's coaching again, and even riding on a team bus—it makes my heart sing. You've certainly had a positive impact on his life." Giving Hope a speculative glance, she added, "You might think this is a passing fling, my dear, but I do not."

Hope decided to ignore that. "The owner of the school is a friend of Lucca's, a former NASCAR driver. He's arranged private lessons for us on Saturday. I'm looking forward to it. It sounds like fun and"—she gave Maggie a pointed look—"like a carefree, casual date between friends."

"You keep telling yourself that if you need to, Hope," Maggie said. Then she glanced at the clock and changed the subject. "Before everyone else gets here, there's something else I need to say to you. I want to apologize for spilling my guts to you in your classroom that day. I didn't know about you and Lucca at the time. Regardless of how serious it is between you two or not, I put you in the middle of a family drama, and I'm sorry."

"No need for that. I've been your friend longer than I've been Lucca's, and I'm glad you could talk to me."

"If it was awkward for you . . ."

"It hasn't been. To be honest, Lucca hasn't said much about you and Richard since you had your family meeting."

"Really? What about Gabi?"

Hope hesitated. "Gabi is a little more . . ."

"Stubborn?" her mother suggested.

"Expressive."

"I know. She's hurt, and that hurts my heart in turn. But I feel as if I'm at a crossroads here. Even if my involvement with Richard doesn't last, this defines my relationship with my children going forward. Gabi will just have to—"

"Wash dishes after dinner?" the woman herself asked as she breezed into the kitchen carrying a huge bouquet of yellow roses. "It's the twins' year to do it. I keep track." She handed her mother the flowers, and both her tone and her expression grew serious. "I'm sorry, Mom. I acted like a bitch and I feel horrible about it." She laced her fingers as if in prayer and added, "I love you so much, and I want you to be happy. Will you forgive me?"

Maggie transformed in an instant, and in the way of loving mothers, opened her arms. "Oh, baby. Of course I will."

The Romano women embraced, then Gabi pulled back with tears in her eyes. "I don't have to do the dishes, do I?"

Maggie dabbed at her eyes with the corner of her apron. "No, you're right. It is the twins' turn. But you do have to peel potatoes."

Soon easy conversation filled the air along with the appetite-stimulating aromas of roasting turkey. Celeste arrived with pies, and shortly after her, Savannah entered the kitchen carrying cornbread dressing. Maggie added her daughter-in-law's dish to the warming drawer, saying, "We're going downright southern with our feast this year."

"Honey," Celeste said, the sound of her native South Carolina strong in her voice, "wait until you get a taste of my bourbon pecan pie. I do believe it's the one item in my culinary repertoire that could give Sarah Murphy a run for her money. Now, tell us, Maggie. Have you enjoyed your new kitchen today?"

Maggie launched into an enthusiastic endorsement of her new appliances, and she was showing off her dishwasher as her sons arrived. Lucca moved to Hope's side and bent and gave her a casual kiss. "Happy Thanksgiving."

He introduced her to Max and Tony, who made typical ditch-this-guy-and-run-off-with-me brotherly comments that amused her. Just as the conversation turned to the day's football games, Richard and his family knocked on the front door.

"He looks like he's entering the lion's den," Max muttered as the newcomers filed into the inn.

"Can you blame him?" Gabi asked. Then she pasted a big, welcoming smile on her face and swept forward. "Happy Thanksgiving. I'm so glad you could join us for our Thanksgiving meal."

Maggie beamed a smile her daughter's way, then made introductions. Hope shook hands with Richard's son, Andrew, and Andrew's wife, Ellen, then turned to their daughter, Claire. The girl had her father's dark hair and her mother's big green eyes and the cutest little button nose. Hope's hand tightened around Lucca's in a punishing grip. "Hello, Claire. I am very happy to meet you."

Claire smiled shyly. "Thank you for inviting us."

"Hope?" Lucca asked softly. "You okay?"

She looks like Holly. Hope backed away from the crowd congregated in the B&B's entry hall, saying, "Excuse me. I'd better go check on the sweet potatoes."

She retreated toward the kitchen, blinking away sudden tears and embarrassed by her reaction. This was ridiculous. She met ten-year-old girls all the time. Telling Maggie about Holly must have stirred her emotions up. That and the fact that it was Thanksgiving, and holidays were always hard.

Holidays were a time for family. Her family was gone, taken away.

"Hope?" Lucca called after her.

Raw inside, Hope couldn't prevent her tears from overflowing and rolling down her cheeks. Fiercely, she wiped them away with her fingertips as she stepped into the kitchen, Lucca at her heels. "Honey? What's the matter?"

"It's Thanksgiving. My fifth one without her. I should be cooking in my own kitchen with Holly peeling the potatoes like Gabi did for Maggie. I should be teaching her how to make piecrust and watching Santa close out the Macy's parade on TV. I should be continuing our own traditions! But that's not happening. It may never happen. What is she doing today? Is she even having a holiday? Or is she with people who don't celebrate Thanksgiving? Sometimes it's just so hard. I don't know where she is or who she's with. Sometimes . . . oh, Lucca, I hate myself for this but . . . but . . . sometimes I even envy Daniel. Is that not the most horrible thing? It's horrible and unspeakable what happened to Justin, but Daniel knows. I don't know. I may never know."

Lucca reached out to her and tried to take her into his arms, but Hope didn't want to be held; she didn't want to be comforted. "I shouldn't have come here. I thought this year would be okay. I thought that as long as I was with people . . ." Needing something to do, she walked to the range and picked up a spoon to tend to whatever Maggie had cooking in the covered sauté pan. Lifting the lid, she said, "Holidays tear me . . . oh."

The scent of cooking brussels sprouts hit her like a fist. Her stomach turned. Hope dropped the spoon, set down the lid, and clapped a hand over her mouth as bile rose in her throat.

She made it to the bathroom off the kitchen just in time to be wretchedly ill. Afterward, she stood over the bathroom sink and rinsed her mouth, and when she slowly straightened and stared at her pale reflection in the mirror, the knowledge she'd avoided for weeks could no longer be denied.

SIXTEEN

Lucca wanted to put his fist through the wall. He couldn't remember the last time he'd been so angry or felt so helpless. That woman who stole Holly from Hope needed to burn in hell.

The look on Hope's face when his mother had introduced her to Claire Steele broke his heart in two. Her big brown eyes appeared stricken, her smile forced and distraught. Every bit of color had drained from her face before her dash to the bathroom.

She was always so cheery, so positive. Idiot that he was, it hadn't occurred to him that she might be extra sensitive today. He didn't connect Thanksgiving with children, but that was stupid. Here he was surrounded by his big, sprawling family, and he'd never once considered how alone she might feel. When he'd heard Steele was bringing his granddaughter, he'd never thought to ask the girl's age. "You ass," he muttered.

When she'd remained in the bathroom for a good five minutes, his mother came up and asked, "Is she all right?"

When Lucca hesitated, she added, "She told me about her daughter."

Relieved that he need not explain or dodge an explanation, Lucca exhaled a heavy breath. "She said that

Richard's granddaughter looks like her Holly. They'd be the same age. I hurt for her, Mom."

"I know. I do, too."

The *ding, ding, ding* of the oven timer sounded. Maggie squeezed his arm, then went off to the kitchen. He gave her a couple more minutes, then rapped on the door. "Hope? Can I help you?"

She didn't reply, but he heard water running again. A moment later, the door opened. Hope stepped out of the bathroom but didn't meet his eyes. "Well, that was embarrassing."

"Are you okay?"

"I . . . well . . ." She closed her eyes.

When she wove on her feet, Lucca reached out to steady her. "Shall I take you home?"

"No," she was quick to say. "It's Thanksgiving. Stay with your family. I think . . . I just need some fresh air."

"I'll walk with you."

"No, Lucca. I really need to be alone."

"I won't leave you alone, not today."

She brought her hands up and rubbed her eyes. "Okay. Okay. I won't leave. I won't make a scene. I'll stay for dinner. That's what I do, isn't it? I soldier on. I just . . . please . . . I can't be with you right now."

The words, the sentiment, hurt Lucca, and while he digested that reality, she turned and dashed for the back door. He stood staring after her, his hands fisted at his side. He wanted to comfort her, to soothe her. He'd never felt so impotent in his life. Why wouldn't she let him help her?

"Lucca?" Celeste said, coming up beside him. "Is Hope all right?"

"I don't know." He looked down at Celeste and into her kind, peaceful blue eyes. "You're good with people. She doesn't want me around, but maybe you could see if she'd use your shoulder to lean on?"

"Of course. Let me get my jacket."

"Let me give you hers, too."

Lucca watched from the kitchen door as Celeste approached Hope, who had taken a seat on the bench around the stone fire pit he'd built. Hope looked up at her, her expression desperate, but she didn't send Celeste away. Instead, the older woman sat beside Hope and listened as she began to talk. Quite animatedly.

Lucca couldn't stand it. He wanted to know what she was saying. He cared about her. Dammit, he might even be in love with her!

Whoa. Where had that thought come from? Did he really just think that?

Yes, you did. And you do. You know you do. You love her and you've been running from that reality for weeks.

Okay, then. As the man who loves her, I want to know what the hell is going on.

So Lucca went upstairs to the bedroom above the fire pit. Quietly, he slid the window open, leaned forward, and without the slightest bit of shame, eavesdropped.

"My husband was right. I was a terrible mother. I gave my daughter to a stranger. I don't deserve to be a mother."

"Honey," Celeste said sharply. "I don't want to hear you using past tense when it comes to motherhood. Wherever she is, alive or, God forbid, passed on, you are and you will always be Holly's mother. That is reality, and it doesn't change. You can, however, use the past tense when it comes to Mark. He is your ex-husband."

"He was right, though. I didn't deserve her."

"You didn't deserve to have her taken from you."

"What am I going to do? I don't deserve a second chance. I can't do this, Celeste."

Do what? Lucca wondered, unease washing through him.

"Do what?" Celeste asked.

Hope buried her face in her hands. She mumbled something that Lucca couldn't make out. Celeste reached out and enfolded her in her arms, and Hope sagged against the other woman.

What is going on?

The back door opened and Lucca's sister called, "Celeste? Hope? Mom says dinner is on in five minutes."

Lucca held his breath as Celeste murmured something to Hope. She nodded and Celeste called, "We'll be right there."

He didn't step away from the window until the women—both women—rose and entered the house. Then, slowly, his thoughts in turmoil, Lucca descended the staircase, meeting Tony at the bottom. "There you are," his brother said. "You know, bro, I thought you were smarter than this. The time to hide is *after* dinner when dishes need doing."

"Right." Lucca's gaze trailed back toward the kitchen.

Tony gave him a hard look. As was the way of twins, he picked up on Lucca's unease. "Something wrong?"

"I don't know."

Tony waited a beat, then handed Lucca one of the bottles of wine he carried. "Help pour while you figure it out."

Ten minutes later, family and friends gathered around the food-laden table. Lucca sat next to Hope and across from Richard Steele, while his mother sat at the end of the table closest to the kitchen. She'd asked Celeste to take the seat at the head of the table opposite her, in his father's usual spot.

Maggie tapped her spoon against a crystal water glass. "Before we say grace, I want to thank you all for joining me for the first meal here at Aspenglow Place. We are blessed to be surrounded today by dear friends and family. We also remember those loved ones who are not with us today."

Lucca took hold of Hope's hand and gave it a comforting squeeze. She closed her eyes. He couldn't miss the tension in her body.

"My husband had a favorite Thanksgiving quote he invariably repeated as we sat down at the table," his mother continued. "Lucca, would you do the honors?"

He tore his attention away from Hope. "Say the prayer?"

"No. I'll ask Zach to lead us in our blessing. I'd like you to share your father's favorite Thanksgiving saying."

"That's a nice way to remember a loved one at a holiday," Celeste observed.

Yes, Lucca realized. It was. He cleared his throat and quoted not the Bible, nor an ancient philosopher, but the humorist Erma Bombeck. "'Thanksgiving dinners take eighteen hours to prepare. They are consumed in twelve minutes. Halftimes take twelve minutes. This is not coincidence.'"

As one, Tony, Gabi, and Max said reverently, "Amen."

And so, the first Thanksgiving dinner at Aspenglow began with laughter and a prayer.

Lucca kept a close eye on Hope. She took tiny little helpings and picked at those, eating just enough so that his mother wouldn't be insulted or get her feelings hurt. But she engaged in conversation, mostly with Richard and his daughter-in-law, and as the meal went on, he noticed that she did relax. Once that happened, he was able to unwind and enjoy his meal, too.

The food was delicious, as always. Not for the first time, he wondered how it was that the culinary gene had managed to skip his sister entirely. He asked the question aloud, and Gabi threw a roll at him. Little Claire's eyes grew round as saucers. She'd relaxed, too, he realized when he heard her chatting with his mother, and, he was glad to see, with Hope, too.

Well, that's a positive development. Claire was a cute kid. The Steeles were nice people. Richard's kids obviously thought well of him and, upon seeing that, the last of Lucca's reservations about the man melted away.

When he'd eaten his fill, he sat back in his chair and observed the people around him. This truly was a day for Thanksgiving. *I am so blessed. I have such a great family. And Hope . . . I can't give her Holly, but I could give her this. She could be part of it. I could give her a family.*

Would she marry me?

As the question popped into his mind, he reached for his wineglass at the same time Hope picked up her water. That's when Claire Steele asked, "Do you have a daughter, Ms. Montgomery?"

Hope's arm jerked. Lucca's wineglass tipped. Ruby red liquid went flying onto Hope's white shirt and across his mother's peach-colored tablecloth. The crystal glass smashed against the floor.

Hope jumped to her feet. "Oh. Oh. I'm sorry. I'm just so sorry."

"My fault," Lucca said. "Sorry, Mom."

"Don't worry about it," Maggie insisted. "My mother always said that a stained tablecloth was a sign of a good meal."

"I'll get some paper towels." Hope hurried toward the kitchen as his mother said, "Lucca, the broom and dustpan are in the mudroom."

"Yes, ma'am." But the broom wasn't in the mudroom where it belonged, and it took him a few minutes to find it. When he returned to the dining room, Hope wasn't there. "She left," Gabi told him. "She said she wasn't feeling well."

"I'll go check on her," he said as he quickly swept up the broken glass.

Celeste shook her head. "Sit down and have your pie first, Lucca. The girl needs some time to think."

Think about what, he almost asked. Her earlier words echoed in his mind. *What am I going to do? I don't deserve a second chance.* As he tossed the broken glass into the trash bin, he put together the clues. He didn't have to ask. He was pretty sure he knew.

She's pregnant.

He needed to sit down before his knees gave out and he fell down, so it only made sense that he do it at the table. When his mother put thin slices of his three favorite pies on a plate in front of him, it only made sense that he eat them. Then, since it was his and Tony's turn for Thanksgiving kitchen patrol, it only made sense that he show up for duty so that he didn't get his ass kicked by the sibling who'd be called upon to fill in for him.

After all that, considering the task that lay before him, it only made sense to raid his mother's liquor cabinet, pour three fingers of scotch, and sit outside to sip his liquid courage for a bit.

Pregnant. He could be wrong, but he didn't think so. His gut told him otherwise, and as stuffed as he was from Thanksgiving dinner, the message had to be strong to get through.

They hadn't used protection their first time together. She was pregnant. She wasn't happy about being pregnant. Holy hell, this was going to be tricky.

He'd just thought about marriage for the first time today. He hadn't told her he loved her. She certainly hadn't said those words to him. But Lucca was old-fashioned enough that when the woman he loved was carrying his child, he wanted to marry her. Make a family with her.

He recalled her words to Celeste. She didn't deserve to be a mother. She couldn't do this. Hope was scared to death. That was understandable. He was scared spitless himself. And he'd never had a child before, much less one who'd been kidnapped.

What if Hope was too frightened to go through with the pregnancy? He didn't know her views on abortion. They'd never discussed it.

Well, this was a discussion that had to take place immediately. He wanted this baby. He wanted her. He would have them both. Lucca knew how to win, and win he would.

He polished off his scotch, went back inside to make his excuses to his family, then left Aspenglow Place determined to expand the number of Romanos by two.

A short, brisk walk later, he rapped on Hope's front door. She didn't answer. He didn't let that stop him. He tried the knob, expecting to find it unlocked. It was. Roxy met him as he stepped inside, and without thinking about it, Lucca bent and scooped the little dog up into his arms. He scratched her behind her ears as he went looking for Hope.

He found her in her bedroom standing beside her window and gazing out at a snowcapped Murphy Mountain, her eyes red, her cheeks stained with tears. She looked heartbreakingly beautiful, he thought. Then he noticed that she was standing with her hand placed protectively over her lower belly, and in that moment, his worst fears dissipated. This was not the stance of a woman considering aborting her child.

Joy washed through him like a sunshine-warmed stream, filling up spaces inside him that had been dark too long. Strategic thinking cautioned him to keep that to himself for now. Roxy wiggled in his arms, so he set her down. "You ate and ran."

"Yes. It was rude of me, but I had to change my shirt." He dropped his gaze pointedly toward the wine stain on her front, then looked her straight in the eyes. "Is there something you need to tell me, Hope?"

She sank down onto the floor, sitting cross-legged, and pulled Roxy into her lap. The mutt lifted her head and licked Hope's face.

Since his knees weren't all that steady, either, Lucca crossed the room and sat on the floor beside her. "You're upset."

"Almost every day when the weather was nice, I took Holly to play in a park near our condo. She made friends with a group of children whose moms brought them at the same time. One of the little boys came to the park one day wearing a superhero cape, and soon every child on that playground was wearing one. Holly wanted a purple one. Purple was her color. We went to the fabric store and she picked out the fabric herself, then sat beside me while I sewed it."

As her hand repetitively stroked Roxy from head to tail, Hope closed her eyes and leaned her head back against the wall. "When it was finished and I held it up for her to see, she truly beamed. I had never seen her so excited about anything. Not even Christmas morning. Of course, we had to go immediately to the park. Do you know what she did the first thing?"

"What did she do, honey?"

"She climbed up onto a picnic bench, spread her arms, and said, "Look, Mommy. I'm going to fly!" And then she jumped off. It was only a few feet and it certainly wasn't the first time she'd launched herself off into space by any means. But watching her, I could see disaster happening. Another little girl—a toddler—ran right into her path, and I couldn't do anything to stop it. I felt sick." A tear slipped from beneath her lashes to roll silently down her cheek. "I feel the same way now."

Lucca resisted the urge to touch her. "Was Holly hurt?"

"Skinned knees. She broke the toddler's arm."

Lucca winced, then blabbered a platitude that was especially stupid considering that it came from him. "Accidents happen."

"That they do." She set Roxy on the floor. "And sometimes they change lives forever, don't they?"

He thought of bus wrecks and mangled bodies and wanted to weep right along with Hope. But then the image of a beaming Cam and glowing Sarah Murphy as they presented their little Michael for his christening flashed in his mind. "One lesson I've learned from my time here in Eternity Springs—and it's a lesson you've taught me, Hope—is that if we focus on loss, we dishonor living. Life is a gift."

"Some gifts aren't returnable."

For the first time since he arrived, she met his gaze. She looked scared and uncertain, and his heart twisted. "Lucca, I'm pregnant."

Whoa. Even though he'd expected it, hearing it made him flinch. He exhaled a heavy breath. "I thought that might be it, but I needed to hear you say it. I guess it happened our first time?"

"I don't know. Probably. Neither of us was really thinking about . . ."

"No, we weren't. But . . . there's no blame. It just happened. Maybe it happened for a reason."

She rubbed her eyes with her fingertips. "I haven't seen a doctor yet. I haven't even taken a test. But I know. I think I've known for a couple of weeks now, but I couldn't face it. The brussels sprouts clinched it. There were certain smells . . ."

He licked his lips. "Have you thought . . . ah . . ."

Her expression grew fierce. "I won't have an abortion, Lucca."

"I was going to ask about making a doctor's appointment. But . . . I'm glad."

She gave a desperate little laugh. "About the abortion or about the baby?"

"Both."

She sprang to her feet and began to pace the room. "I'm scared to death. I can't do this, Lucca. I can't be a mother again. Look at how it turned out last time. No telling what disaster would befall this child. I'd probably smother her, if not literally then figuratively. She'd grow up smothered and neurotic and unhappy and hating to read."

"Hating to read? That's sort of random, isn't it?" Lucca rose and shoved his trembling hands into his pockets.

"I'm a teacher. Reading is important to me."

He rocked back on his heels. "Maybe if he doesn't like to read, he'll like B horror movies."

She stopped abruptly and buried her face in her hands. Now, he judged, was the time to touch her. Reaching out, he folded her into his arms. "It's okay, honey. Honestly, it's going to be okay. We'll get this figured out. I want you to know that I'm a little scared myself, but I'm not unhappy about this baby. I'm honestly a little excited."

She shook with silent sobs. Lucca pressed a kiss against her hair and murmured, "I won't ask you to marry me right now because these aren't the circumstances such a question deserves. But I want you to know that you can count on me to be there for you and for the baby. Always."

Against his shirt, she said, "Mark asked me to marry him when I told him I was pregnant."

"I'm not Mark Montgomery."

"But I'm still me. I've put the cart before the horse a second time. My mother-in-law said I trap men. Your family is worried about Richard taking advantage of the family. Look at me."

"You're shell-shocked and irrational."

"Lucca . . ." she protested.

"Listen to me, Hope. I am in this for the long haul. I am not Mark Montgomery. I will love this baby. My family will be crazy happy about this pregnancy, and you know that's true. Look, I am not perfect, but I will be the best father I can be for this baby. But when I ask you to marry me, Hope, you will know I'm asking because of you. Not because you are carrying my child, but because you have my heart. I will ask you to marry me because I'm in love with you."

When she started crying harder, Lucca wondered if he'd taken the wrong tack. He was at a loss, speaking from his heart, acting on his instincts. Whether he'd planned it or not, he had his little family right there in his arms. He had to do what was best for it.

"Lucca, I'm so afraid," she said. "I don't deserve a second chance. I don't know if I can do it."

He trailed his hand up and down her back soothingly. "Sure you can. And everyone deserves second chances."

"What are we going to do, Lucca? What do you want to do?"

Marry you. Love you. Love our baby. "I think . . . we don't need to rush. We have time to decide, time to absorb this news. I think you should dry your eyes, change your shirt, and go back to Mom's with me. Have a piece of Celeste's pie. It's amazing. We can watch some football with my brothers and you can pretend you're interested when Mom drags out the photo albums. I don't know why, but she does it every Thanksgiving. Afterward, we can come back here and you can pack for our trip and then we'll go to bed. I want to sleep with you tonight, Hope. I want to make love with you. I want to celebrate."

Her mouth trembled. "Celebrate? Really?"

"Really."

"Oh, Lucca." She looked up at him, a world of hope in her luminous brown eyes as a shaky smile bloomed across her face. "I was so caught up in my reaction, I didn't think about yours."

"I hadn't really thought about it before today, which was stupid of me. I was surprised."

"But a good surprise?"

"Definitely a good surprise."

She sagged a bit in relief. He cared. He had faith in her. He wasn't Mark. "I think I'd like to see your mother's albums. Baby pictures of you . . ."

He groaned. "I have to warn you. It's not just pictures. She has baby porn."

"What!"

"Naked babies in the bathtub. Naked kids running through the water sprinkler. What possesses a parent to take pictures of their naked kids? I swear, if she tried that nonsense today, social services would come knocking on the door. I don't want you to do that to the peanut, Hope. I won't have him being fourteen and having his brothers pull out the photo album as evidence for who has the bigger prick. I'm going to put my foot down about that." He waited a beat, then added, "Of course, I always won."

"Of course," she said seriously. But then she smiled and it made Lucca feel ten inch . . . ten feet tall. "Lucca?"

His gaze had focused on her mouth. "Hmm?"

"Thank you."

Emotion welled up inside him. "Thank you, Hope. I am thankful for you. We'll make this work. I promise. Happy Thanksgiving."

"Happy Thanksgiving."

SEVENTEEN

"Power is nothing without control," Hope said as she walked away from the school bus parked on a track on the wide-open plain of west Texas. "That's a lesson we can apply to many aspects of life."

Lucca nodded. "I'll need to use that one with the Grizzlies."

"I've noticed you often use inspirational quotes with the team."

"They listen to me. I love that about this team. Half the guys at Landry thought they were too good to listen to what I had to say. The more talent a kid has, the more potential, the more likely he is to fall into the believing-his-press camp. They go from being kids who play for the love of the game to egomaniacs."

"How did you avoid that trap with your players?"

"I have a system. The players have to buy into my system. But the young and dumb ones do that, achieve success, then forget the system and think they did it all on their own. It's frustrating. Certainly takes some of the fun out of the job for me."

"I can understand why."

Hope and Lucca had just finished a four-hour private driving lesson with Johnny Tarantino, a former NASCAR driver who now operated a high-performance driving school on a section of his family's ranch in the middle of nowhere, Texas. While school buses weren't ordinarily his ride of choice, Johnny had jumped at the challenge of sharing his expertise with Hope, going so far as to buy a bus for his school. Halfway through the lesson, he'd decided to create a safety course specifically for bus drivers. "It's a great addition to my school," he'd told them. "I'll focus on training trainers. School districts will love it."

She'd had to agree. While she hadn't felt at risk behind the wheel prior to her lesson, the techniques she'd learned did give her a comforting increase in skill.

They climbed into the BMW Lucca had rented at the airport in El Paso and began the drive back to their B&B in Fort Davis. They discussed ranching and reading and rainbows as they drove, having made the decision at the beginning of the trip that the topic of the baby and the future was off-limits for the duration. This time was their breather, their chance to process the change in circumstances. It had proven to be exactly the medicine Hope had needed. Well, she'd needed this breather *and* Lucca's support.

She hadn't taken time to consider his possible reaction to her news before she'd shared it, but he'd convinced her from the first that she could count on him. That his claim didn't surprise her amazed her. Deep down, when she wasn't admitting the pregnancy even to herself, she'd known that she'd be able to count on him. Just exactly what their future held, she didn't know. But her confidence that he stood with her took some of the pressure off of figuring it out right now.

Back at the bed and breakfast, he relaxed in front of a basketball game on TV while she took a nap. After that, she decided to soak in the tub for a bit, thinking she'd relax a little while longer before dressing for dinner.

Then Lucca joined her in the bath and, for the next

half hour, all thought of relaxation went down the drain. His lovemaking was just as erotic and satisfying as ever, but he did it with a tenderness that touched her heart.

Their B&B hostess steered them to a surprisingly good German restaurant—not the sort of cuisine Hope had expected to find in west Texas—and after that, Lucca started on the drive to their second planned destination on their trip, McDonald Observatory. It was the first visit for both of them to the McDonald. Lucca was like a kid at Christmas.

"Orion rising," he said as he parked the car in the observatory visitors' lot. "Orion, the Hunter. It's one of the easiest constellations to find. Look for his belt of three stars pointing almost straight up from the horizon. See the bright orange star to the left and a blue one to the right?"

Hope stepped from the car and gazed up at the starry sky. "I do."

"The stars are Mintaka, Alnilam, and Alnitak. Mintaka is actually a double star. All four are bigger, brighter, and heavier than our sun." Excitement hummed in his tone as he added, "You're going to love this, Hope."

"I'm sure I will." If nothing else, watching him love it would make her evening.

The moonless night was pitch-dark and bitterly cold, and she loved every minute of it. It was a special event night for a membership group Lucca had joined. They participated in a "star party," gazing at the heavens through an awesome pair of telescopes and listening to a guided tour of the night sky. Hope found the guide's program informative, though it lacked the charm and romance of Lucca's backyard lessons.

She told him as much at the end of the evening as they returned to the visitors' center to use the facilities before making the drive back to Fort Davis. "You know what you should do," she suggested. "Once Aspenglow Place is up and running, you could give star tours to your mother's guests. Eternity Springs isn't as dark as it is here, but it's better than most places."

"There's a thought. It'd give me an excuse to score a powerful telescope."

When Hope came out of the restroom, she wandered around a bit before finding Lucca standing mesmerized before a large framed image. She stood beside him. "It looks like twinkling lights on a Christmas tree."

"Newborn stars shining through the wispy clouds of the Orion Nebula. You can see it without a telescope, a smudge of light below Orion's Belt."

"Yes. I remember the guide pointing it out."

"It's a nursery, Hope. A stellar nursery. The nebula has given birth to thousands of stars. Bright, brilliant babies." He took her hand and brought it up to his mouth for a kiss. "Birth is a beautiful thing."

His words and his actions stayed with her as she drifted off to sleep that night, and during their journey home on Sunday. Monday morning, she scheduled a doctor's appointment for mid-December and ordered three books about pregnancy from an online bookseller. Hope was feeling optimistic about the future. She didn't think she could ever have consciously made the choice to have a second child, but now that the proverbial barn door was open, the idea of having another chance seemed like an unacknowledged dream that could possibly come true.

As the days went on, Lucca inquired upon occasion if she was ready to talk about the future. He indicated that he was trying to give her space, though he seemed a little impatient that she had not yet answered yes. But she thought she might be getting closer. On a snowy Saturday afternoon in December with a couple of hours to kill before she needed to be at the gym for a Grizzlies home game, she added a log to the fire Lucca had built before he left to meet his friend James Preston, who had promised to attend the game to watch Wade play. James was a scout, and this was the big chance she'd been wanting for Wade. She said a little prayer that she would be the coach Wade needed and that he'd have a great game. Lifting a fireplace tool, she poked the log, positioning it just right.

"Just right," she murmured, and her thoughts drifted to the previous night. It had been a lovely evening. She and Lucca had stayed in, played Scrabble, and laughed. He'd become a friend to her, and in doing so, made her realize how much she'd missed that component of a relationship. Lucca was her friend and her lover.

She loved him.

It was true. She finally could admit it. She thought she'd probably loved him for some time now. He was a good man. A caring man. A loving man.

Maybe she should tell him that she loved him. Maybe she could finally move forward. Be strong like Maggie. She would always love Holly—always search for her and hope and pray for her safe return. But maybe the time had come to appreciate this second chance she'd been given. With Lucca. With their child.

As Roxy moved from her perch on the third step of the staircase over to her bed in front of the fire, Hope looked toward the manila envelope that had been lying on her desk for more than a week. "Maybe it's time, girl," Hope said aloud.

She opened the envelope, removed one of the pregnancy books, and began to read. Fifteen minutes later, lost in information she'd forgotten over the past ten years, she heard the doorbell ring only because Roxy caught her attention with a yip.

Expecting it to be Lucca she called, "Come in."

The door opened and her welcoming smile died when

a man stepped inside: tall, lithe, blond, and still handsome despite his hard, accusing blue eyes and thin-lipped grim smile. "Mark."

"Hello, Hope."

Shock quickly flared into anger. How dare he. How dare he! She set down her book and rose to her feet as he continued, "You don't mind if I look around a bit, do you?"

"Yes!" she snapped. "I do mind. I've had enough, Mark. This is ridiculous. It has to stop. I want you to leave."

"After I take a look around," he said, moving toward the staircase.

This was wrong. So wrong. After all these years, he still thought she was hiding their child. Like she could hurt Holly that way. Fury roared through Hope, and she moved to block him. "She's not here, Mark. You know that."

He looked at her with Holly's eyes, miserable and filled with despair. *Oh, Mark.* She'd loved him once. How could it have come to this?

Still a big man, he easily shoved her out of the way and barreled his way upstairs. Unable to stop him, she stood at the foot of the staircase and fumed. In the small house, it took him little time at all to search, but it did give her time to think. When he came downstairs, she'd returned to her position in front of the fire. She said, "Mark, this will be the last time. I will not allow you to do this again. The sheriff here is a friend of mine. I am going to take out a restraining order on you. I'll go to the press. I know you have political aspirations. You don't want the press."

His jaw was set, his eyes hard and a little wild. *So angry. After all these years, he's still so angry.* "What, are you spying on me? Do you think I stole Holly and hid her away?"

She closed her eyes for a moment and tempered her own reaction. "You're in the paper a lot. You were my husband. I'm interested."

Once, she had loved this man. Once, he'd been someone she admired, kind and funny and romantic. His chosen career had taken a toll on their marriage. Maybe they wouldn't have made it through the tough times, anyway. Who knows? But Mark Montgomery wasn't a bad man. He'd loved his daughter. He mourned the loss of her, too.

But, according to what I read in the newspaper, he hasn't moved forward. What does it say about me that I have and he hasn't? Does that make him a better father than I am a mother, or is he just not as emotionally healthy?

Well, he does have his mother to contend with. Maybe he needs to move to Eternity Springs, too.

Weariness overcame Hope. She was tired of fighting him. She felt sorry for him. He needed to heal. "Mark, barging in on me this way doesn't do either of us any good. It's not healthy behavior. It's been five years. You know I'm not hiding Holly away from you—that I didn't execute some elaborate plot to destroy our family. You know in your heart that coming here like this is crazy. Why do you do it, Mark?"

"I'm not crazy!" he fired back, his blue eyes flashing. Holly had blue eyes, her father's eyes. She'd had his smile, too. Hope couldn't recall the last time she'd seen Mark genuinely smile. He paced the room, shoving his fingers through his hair. "I'm a father and I don't know where my daughter is!"

"And it's horrible."

"It's horrible for me. I don't know about you. You don't even have her picture out. I need to find her, Hope. I'm her father and I need to find her! That doesn't go away."

The pain, the heartache in his voice reached inside Hope and stirred the embers of the love she'd once felt for him. He was devastated, still, as was she. The wound would never heal. "No, it doesn't. It's horrible," she repeated quietly. "The absolute most horrible thing in the world. I know. I do know, better than anybody."

"I hate you. It's your fault," he said, his voice dead calm with fury.

"I know."

"You did this to me. To us. To *her!* You just couldn't wait for me to . . ." He paused, his speech trembling. "Come home . . . from work. I try to fall asleep at night, and the images . . . The things I hear on the news. All the ugliness in the world that happens to little kids. To know that she's out there, somewhere . . . it's killing me. God only knows what has happened to her. What monster or pervert has touched her, hurt her. All because you left my child with a stranger."

At the horror and devastation in his voice, she swallowed hard. "I know it's my fault, Mark. Believe me, I live with it every day. And I know you hate me for causing you this pain."

He closed his eyes and held his head in his hands. "I don't really hate you, Hope. Oh, and I've tried. It would be a lot easier if I did."

Hearing him say this wounded her more than the words of hate.

"I don't know why. Maybe because you're Holly's mother. Maybe that's why I came here. To see you, because I can't see her. To try and hate you for destroying us. Our family. But I can't . . . I'm in the same limbo as you. I just want to know what happened to her."

And this tore Hope up. Because once upon a time, she had loved him so very much. She attempted to reach him, to show him the compassion she felt. "I do, too. But we have to accept that we may never know. It's been five years. We will never forget her, but maybe it's time to let go, to move on."

"To give up?" He looked at her in shock that quickly transformed to fury again. "I'm not ever going to give up, damn you. I'll search for her until I'm dead. I'm different from you. You and your cozy little life here. I'm never giving up on our daughter!"

"I'm not saying we should give up," she fired back. "I will never stop looking for Holly and praying that we find her, but there's a difference between giving up and moving forward. It's time to move forward, Mark. Whatever the thought processes are that led you to travel from Florida to Colorado in order to spend two minutes searching my home for a child who you know isn't here need to change."

He momentarily closed his eyes, and the hands at his sides fisted. When he looked at her again, the light had gone from angry to stark. "I miss her."

Her heart twisting, Hope took a step toward him. "I know, Mark. But this sort of thing . . . it's not good. I think you need to . . ."

Hope's voice trailed off when she saw him look past her, his eyes widening in shock, his jaw dropping open in surprise. *What in the . . . oh. Oh, no.*

He stared at the book she'd left lying on the table beside her rocker. The title *You're Pregnant, Now What?* all but jumped off the cover. His voice returned to dead calm as he asked, "What the hell is that?"

"Mark—"

"What the hell is that?" he repeated, his complexion pale as he pointed at the book. "Are you pregnant?"

Before she could respond, he accused, "My God, Hope. Are you having another baby?"

Might as well do this. "Yes, I am."

"Who's the father? Are you remarried?"

She straightened her backbone. "We're divorced, Mark. It's not your business."

He looked at her hand. "Guess not, you're not wearing a ring. You're still Ms. Montgomery at the school. I checked." His expression turned malevolent. "Did it again, did you? Got yourself knocked up so some poor sap will have to marry you. Well, well, well . . . always resourceful, weren't you? Mom said you'd do it again once you had the chance. Honestly, I really didn't think you would. I never imagined you'd have the unmitigated nerve to have another child. You certainly don't deserve one."

That stole her breath away, and Hope reached out to grab the back of a chair to steady herself.

Mark picked up the book. "I remember you reading these when you were pregnant with Holly. Funny, you must have missed the chapter about giving your child to strangers." He tossed the book to the floor.

"This man of yours. Does he know what you did? Does he know how irresponsible you are? Does he—" A rap on the door interrupted him, then the door opened and Lucca stepped inside carrying a bag of groceries.

"Hey, beautiful. Guess what they had at the Trading Post this—" Lucca caught sight of Mark and stopped abruptly. "Um, hello."

"So, it's you? You're the guy?" Mark rounded on Lucca, his color high.

"Hope?" Lucca's gaze shifted from Mark to Hope. "Is there a problem here?"

"Oh, yeah. I'd say there's a problem. You're the one with the problem, though. My wife is your child's mother. That's about as big a problem as it gets."

"Wife?" Lucca's expression went blank. "You're Montgomery?"

His voice scathing, Mark said, "Do you know what she did? I bet she hasn't told you, has she? About how careless she is? About how she put her vanity ahead of our family? How she left our child with a criminal so she could go get her roots done?"

"Mark, please," Hope said.

"She'll destroy you, you know. Just like she destroyed me. She trapped me into marriage, and then she stabbed me in the heart. She did it to me, and she'll do it to you. That's what she does." He turned a malice-filled stare upon her. "Is this your replacement for Holly? Is this how you . . . how did you say it? 'Move forward'? You don't deserve a second chance."

"Whoa, that's enough," Lucca said, moving between them, then stepping back to stand beside Hope. "That's quite enough, Montgomery."

"You're damned right it's enough."

Hope's heart bled from the wounds his words caused. "I would never try to replace Holly, Mark."

"Really? Looks like you've made a good start. Looks like you're working at replacing our whole family. Pretty little house with a dog in a pretty little town. Postcard picturesque. Kids don't end up on milk cartons here, do they? Well, until now." He glared at Hope. "Give it time. Hope may need to get her nails done and leave your baby with the stranger next door."

Lucca set down his groceries and walked toward Mark. "You need to leave now."

"I'll go when I'm damned good and ready to go. She's not worth the heartache, you know. You can't believe a word she says. I'll bet she told you that she loved you, right? That this baby means everything. That it's her whole world, right? It's lies. All lies."

Lucca grabbed him by the arm and began to push him toward the door. But even though Lucca was taller, Mark still had an athlete's build. He planted his feet and pulled away. "Don't you get it, man? She's poison. Damaged goods. And I'll be damned if I let her do it to another child. Even if it isn't mine. She has no business being a mother. She doesn't deserve it."

"Shut up, Montgomery," Lucca snapped, his eyes glowing with fury. "I'm sorry about Holly, but you have no right—"

"I have no right? I have no right? Buddy, you don't know the first thing about my rights! I had a right to see my little girl grow up. I had a right to see her at dance recitals and playing softball. I had a right to see her in a cap and gown becoming whatever she wanted to be. I, by God, had a right to walk her down the aisle when she got married!"

"I know, man," Lucca said. "I'm sorry. But—"

"That woman . . . the one you think you're in love with now . . . she took all of that from me. All of it. And now she's got it all back. It's not fair. It's just not right!"

"No," Hope said, having gone as cold as the Colorado winter inside. "It's not fair. It's not right."

Mark appeared depleted as he said to Lucca, "I almost feel sorry for you, hooked up to the likes of her." Turning toward Hope, he added, "You go on and build your new little replacement family, Hope. You just go on and make new babies to replace the one you lost. But think about this. You will never, ever be able to replace my Holly. She was perfect. The only good thing you ever did. I can't believe I'm going to say this, but maybe wherever she is, perhaps it really is better than being with such a sad, sorry excuse for a mother."

His words hung in the air, numbing Hope.

Lucca went at him again, but this time, Mark was finished. He left the house without another word or a look back.

Shaken, Hope sank into her rocker. Nausea roiled in her stomach. She felt as if she'd been hit by a truck, and she started to tremble. Lucca put a hand on her shoulder, offering her support. He looked worried and upset and angry as he asked, "You okay?"

"Sure. Just peachy." Actually, "raw" was probably a better word.

She shook off Lucca's hand. She didn't want him touching her. She didn't want him to be here. She had maybe ten seconds before she started bawling, and she didn't want him around to witness it. Not today. Not when she was shaking and hearing Mark's voice saying "Maybe she's better off where she is."

"I think you'd better leave, too, Lucca."

Leave and stay away, the voice inside her head shouted. *Poison. Damaged goods.*

"No," he told her calmly. "I'm not going to do that."

Hope didn't know why his refusal to leave rubbed her the wrong way, but in an instant, her temper flared hot. She rose to her feet. "Yes, you are. I can't rehash this, Lucca. I can't take any more. I want to be alone. I need to be alone."

"No, you don't need to be alone."

"You don't know what I need, Lucca Romano."

Now his tone sharpened. "Yes, I do. I know you need to not let your ex pull your string."

" 'Pull my string'? Really? You think my heartache is a 'string'? The man I once loved just came into my home and said the most vile things to me. Vile, but true. I did destroy him. Did you see him? Did you see the pain I caused?"

"Still, he shouldn't have said—"

"Why not? It's true!" she exploded. "It's all true. Every single word. I did wreck our family. He was out working hard to put food on the table and what did I do? I decided I had to get my hair done. Now I have to live with that every day for the rest of my life."

"You didn't do anything wrong, Hope. You did what a million other women do. You didn't know. You couldn't have known. He shouldn't blame you, and you can't blame yourself. It wasn't your fault."

"It was, Lucca. At the end of the day, I have no one to blame but myself. I did it. I left her. I was the one who left her. No one else is to blame for that"—she started to sob—"that mistake. Just . . . me."

He reached for her, attempting to touch her. "Calm down, Hope. Don't get overwrought. It's not good for the baby."

It was the absolute worst thing he could have said.

She jerked away from him. "Of course you need to say that. I need to think about taking care of the baby, right? Because I can't think to do it on my own. I'm incapable. I don't have sense enough to know that being an emotional wreck is bad for the baby. But that's what I do. That's what Mark warned you about. I destroy children. My daughter is missing, maybe even dead, and now my overwrought emotions will probably give this baby a birth defect. Mark is right. Children are better off without me."

Lucca's chest lifted as he filled his lungs with air. "Dammit, Hope."

"I asked you to leave, Lucca. This is my house, not yours."

"Fine. I'll go. You're obviously not in the right frame of mind to discuss this rationally."

He turned and headed for the door, wrenching it open. In the threshold he paused and glanced over his shoulder. "Don't forget what you learned at the driving lesson, Hope. You lose control, you cede the power. Don't do that to either one of us."

With that, Lucca walked out.

EIGHTEEN

Christmas lights twinkled in windows along Spruce Street as Lucca drove his friend James and his brother Tony—a surprise visitor to the day's game—to Murphy's Pub to have a beer following the Grizzlies' win. His mood was such that if any movie people were around casting for a remake of *The Grinch*, he'd be a shoo-in for the starring role. "What is the matter with females?"

James and Tony shared an amused look. "Trouble in paradise?" the scout asked. "I sensed a little tension between you and the head coach."

"Tension?" Tony drawled. "It was chillier inside the gym than it is outside. What happened?"

"I don't want to talk about it." Lucca scowled as he pulled into a parking place across the street from the pub. "How can she go from strong and stable to bat-shit crazy in the space of a few minutes?"

"I thought you didn't want to talk about it," Tony said.

"I don't."

"Then why do you keep asking questions?"

"I don't know. Because I'm just as crazy as she is."

"Speaking of crazy," James said. "Who was that woman who stopped you on the way out of the gym? The older one with angel earrings? She sounded like a fortune-teller. What was it she said to you?"

"Celeste Blessing. She is our local . . . well . . . I don't know how to describe her. Our wise woman, maybe. Our angel. She told me she'd had a dream about me and Hope last night, and that when she woke up, she knew she had to tell me to hold on to my patience and listen to my instincts."

"Nothing wrong with that advice," Tony said as they exited the vehicle. "Sounds like something Mom would say. Speaking of, what's the latest in that realm? Is she still with . . . ?"

"Yeah, she is." Despite the completely bizarre topic of his mother's love life, he was glad for the distraction. "I guess it's working. He's a good guy."

"He'd better be."

James shook his head. "I'm having a hard time wrapping my head around Ms. Maggie having a love life. I remember when I skinned my knees on your driveway and she patched me up on the kitchen counter. The whole thing is weird."

"Ya think?" Lucca asked. "Women are weird, period. I'm beginning to think it's something they're born with simply to torture the men around them."

The trio walked into the bar accompanied by the sound of "Silent Night." "I don't recall the last time I heard Christmas carols being played in a bar," James observed. "At least, ones that had the original lyrics."

"This is Eternity Springs," Lucca responded. "I'm surprised they don't play them year-round."

The men took seats at a table near the Christmas tree set up in one corner. Decorated with ornaments made from beer bottle tops and crowned with a star of cardboard coasters, it was quite the sight. They ordered hamburgers and beer from the bartender, and the talk turned, as usual, to basketball.

Lucca slowly nursed his beer as they discussed Tony's team and his expectations for the season. When a waitress delivered their burgers, they broadened the discussion to include a bet on the Final Four teams in March. After that, the conversation finally made its way back to Eternity Springs. James said, "I'm glad you called me. The Mitchell kid is everything you claimed."

Lucca sipped his beer. "I know how to evaluate talent."

"You always have," Tony agreed.

"So, you agree he'll get some Division I interest?" Lucca asked his friend.

"I do. From one of the major programs, too."

"That's excellent news." Lucca smiled his thanks to the bartender when he set a bowl of pretzels on the table. "Knowing the kid, I'll encourage him to look hard at a smaller school. I think he'll be a better fit at a place like Kansas State or Oklahoma State rather than the University of Texas."

"That's good to know."

"I plan on recruiting him," Tony said. "We need to keep talent like his in state."

"I don't know, Tony. Boulder is a great town, but going to school there might be too big a culture shock for Wade, not to mention his parents."

They discussed Wade's dreams and his stats and the film of him that Lucca had sent James. The Christmas music drifting from overhead speakers shifted from religious-themed carols to secular favorites such as "Grandma Got Run Over by a Reindeer" and Robert Earl Keene's "Merry Christmas from the Family." They talked about college basketball, and James asked Lucca when he planned to come back. "I don't know. I don't know if I want to come back." He swirled the beer in his glass as though it were wine. *It's the kind of job that is tough on a family.* "Believe it or not, I like coaching in Eternity Springs."

Tony sat back hard in his chair. "Well, I'll be damned. You're in love with the kindergarten teacher."

He was. Head over heels, no looking back, fist-in-the-face love. "Right now I'm pissed at her."

Tony grinned over the top of his bottle. "But you didn't deny the L-word. Did he, James?"

"Not that I heard," agreed the scout, amusement gleaming in his eyes.

A cold wind swept into the room when the front door opened and a group of newcomers swept inside. As they removed their coats to hang them on the rack beside the door, the bartender asked about the weather. A man replied, "It's started spitting some sleet. Might get bad in a little while."

The newcomers started for a table, then they caught sight of Lucca's group. One of them called, "Coach. Great game today. The Grizzlies are the best I've ever seen."

"Thanks," Lucca returned. "The team chemistry clicks."

"You and Coach Montgomery make a good pair. Those boys like playing for you." He grinned and added, "You inspire them, and they want to show off in front of Hope. Having a pretty female as a high school coach is a secret weapon."

"You're probably right." Lucca had noticed the boys' peacock posturing to Hope on more than one occasion.

"She's a good woman," another man in the group observed. "Sure was nice of her to volunteer to take the Eagles home so they wouldn't be stuck here until their bus gets fixed."

Lucca's spine straightened. "She what?"

"You didn't hear? The visiting team's bus wouldn't start after the game. Ms. Montgomery offered to drive them home. They left about ten minutes ago."

As Lucca processed the news, his hamburger suddenly

felt as heavy as an anvil in his stomach. Today's opponents had come from Creede. That meant driving over Sinner's Prayer Pass. The thought of Hope navigating that challenging stretch of road at night was bad enough. The knowledge that she'd be doing it in a bus with a basketball team on board during a sleet storm played into all of his fears.

Lucca shut his eyes, and when a mental image of Hope's bus sliding off the side of the mountain flashed across his brain, he shuddered.

A sense of urgency swelled inside him. She shouldn't be making this trip by herself. He should go after her, follow along behind her. He needed to see for himself that she made the trip safely.

Because deep in his heart of hearts, he very much feared that she wouldn't.

He wiped his mouth with his napkin, then set it on top of his half-finished meal. "Guys, I'm sorry, but I have to go. Tony, when y'all are through here, if you call Mom, I'm sure she'll swing by and pick you up so you don't have to walk to Aspenglow Place in this weather."

"What? Wait a minute. What are you going to do, Lucca?" his twin asked.

"I know it sounds crazy, but I have a bad feeling about this. I'm going to follow the bus."

Tony nodded. "Okay, I'll come with you."

"Me, too," James added.

"There's no need—"

"Don't argue. Let's pay the tab and go."

They departed Murphy's Pub to the sound of "In the Bleak Midwinter," and Lucca sent up a silent prayer that he was overreacting. However, Celeste's earlier caution now pealed in his head like a clarion call.

Listen to my instincts. He gave his vehicle a little more gas.

Minutes later, he pulled onto the highway headed

south. The tension inside his Range Rover thickened with every mile. Lucca couldn't say why an overpowering sense of gloom had overtaken him, but it was as real as anything he'd ever experienced. "Tony, just in case, keep an eye on the right side of the road. James, you'll watch the left?"

"Sure."

Lucca drove, his hands gripping the steering wheel hard. As they started up Sinner's Prayer Pass, the tension stretched tighter . . . tighter . . . tighter . . . until he expected something to snap. "Talk to me, Tony."

"About what?"

"Anything. Isn't it about time for you to buy a new ride? You trade every two years. What are you thinking about buying?"

"You want a distraction? Now?"

"Please." He wanted to drown out the noise of sleet pinging against the windows. The road wasn't bad yet, but by the time Hope attempted a return trip, who knew what it would be like.

"Okay. I'm thinking about a Ferrari this time around."

Tony's sports car patter provided the background noise that Lucca's nerves needed to settle somewhat. As they reached the summit of the pass, he gripped the steering wheel hard. The ride down would be the most difficult part of the trip under these conditions. "Y'all watch closely. I'm sure she made it fine, but . . ."

Lucca shifted into low gear and took the first switchback. "What color?" he asked his brother.

"I'm thinking white this time."

"Really?" James asked. "Ferraris need to be red."

"I drive red now. I'm looking for a change."

"How about black? Or silver?"

"Perhaps." Tony continued a monologue discussing options and engines and probably making half the stuff up until, finally, they reached level ground. Lucca took his first easy breath. "It's not sleeting on this side of the mountain. We should be good to go. Sorry I dragged you guys along on this wild goose chase. This whole bad-weather-and-basketball-buses thing preys on my psyche."

James said, "Not a problem. I think you needed to pay attention to your angel."

Lucca did, too, which was why he increased his speed, hoping to catch up with the school bus. Honestly, he wouldn't rest easy until he saw Hope step into her house and shut the door.

He intended to have her leave the bus in Creede and ride home with them. His Range Rover handled the road much better than her bus. They could make the return trip over the pass without trouble as long as they attempted it in the next hour or so before the ice began to stick. Tomorrow, someone from Creede could drive the bus back and deal with their own broken one. The weather report called for sunshine and temperatures above freezing. Plus, the plows would be out. That should work.

"I see lights up ahead," Tony said. "Doesn't look like a car. Might be her."

Lucca's foot grew heavier on the gas, and within moments his headlights illuminated the familiar back end of the yellow school bus. "Thank God."

He no sooner exhaled a relieved breath than he saw the lights of an oncoming vehicle and then a shadow cross in front of them. In seconds that seemed to take hours to pass, he watched the oncoming vehicle strike the shadow . . . and veer into the school bus.

It happened in an instant. Hope saw the elk, saw the oncoming truck strike the animal. When the truck headed her way, she knew a collision was coming and recognized it as unavoidable.

Thank God, the district had installed seat belts in this bus. Thank God, she'd made everybody buckle up. Grabbing hold tightly to the wheel, she prepared to put the lessons she'd learned in Texas to use. *Thank God for Lucca.*

Control the crash, she told herself, and she turned the wheel just as the truck collided with her bus.

It seemed to happen in slow motion. She fought the wheel to keep the bus on the road, hearing the echo of Johnny Tarantino's calm instructions all the while. Behind her, boys yelled in fear and panic, but she tuned them out, listing to Johnny talk in her memory. Just when she thought she had won—that she'd managed to keep the bus on the road—the truck that had hit them completed a spin by clipping them again. Momentum carried the school bus onto a bridge.

The front of the bus crashed through the guardrail. Hope felt herself fall forward, and in that instant, for the first time since the initial hit, bone-chilling fear washed through her. She didn't recall this section of the road. This was a bridge over what?

Wham. Crash. Forward movement came to an abrupt stop. Glass flew. Metal crunched. Hope slammed against the steering wheel, her seat belt and shoulder harness restraining her from falling into the broken windshield. When movement stopped, she hung suspended—cut, scraped, and bleeding—but alive.

Her first thought flashed through her mind. *The baby!* Sound that had seemed muffled during the wreck came roaring back. The boys were yelling, cursing, hollering for help. Even as she tried to rouse herself to full awareness of their situation, she heard the most miraculous sound.

Lucca called, "Hope! Hope! Are you okay? Answer me! Hope!"

How in the world? "I'm okay. I'm all right. Boys? Is anyone hurt?"

"We're okay, Coach," one of them called. "We're all okay."

"Thank you, God," she prayed as she became aware of flashlight beams and creaking hinges and men's voices.

She attempted to look behind her and take stock, but she couldn't see anything past her shoulder. All right, then. Think. The bus sloped downward, so it made sense that the back of the bus hadn't left the bridge. She saw no water in front of her. They hadn't landed in a river or creek. Maybe a dry gully only a short drop from the road. Again, she repeated, "Thank God."

"Hold on, Hope," Lucca said. "We're coming. We're going to help you."

"Help the boys first. Get them out of the bus."

"I'm on it," James Preston called. "Don't worry."

Lucca said, "Hope? Are you hurt? Honey? Are you okay?"

She didn't miss the panic in his voice, so she injected calmness into hers. "I'm fine, Lucca."

But, was she fine? The seat belt went across her lap. She'd jerked against it hard. *Is the baby okay?*

Now that the immediacy of the accident was behind her and there were others on the scene to take responsibility for her passengers, Hope was free to focus on what was happening inside her own body. Pain. Soreness. What else? Any cramping? Any fluid between her legs? *Dear God in Heaven, don't let my baby be hurt.*

Then, Lucca was beside her. He tested the handle that opened the door. It worked. She saw him—no, his brother, his twin—standing outside. Lucca said, "You made it down okay. Good. Which way will be easier to get her out?"

"This way," Tony replied. "Hand her to me, bro."

Lucca maneuvered to plant his feet against the console and dash. Then, tenderly, he touched Hope's face. "All right, baby. Let's get you out of here. Ready?"

She saw that fear filled his eyes. "Lucca? Don't let me fall through the windshield."

"I won't let you fall. I'll never let you fall." Lucca released the seat belt catch and she slumped into his arms. "Gotcha. It's good. Now, let's get out of here."

Stepping carefully, he moved toward the door where Tony stood reaching inside. Hope felt Tony Romano's strong arms slip beneath her knees and around her shoulders, and Lucca released her into his brother's care, then scrambled down beside her. "Here. I'll take her."

"I can walk," Hope said. "Set me down."

"Are you sure?"

"I think so."

Carefully, he set her down. "Ankles okay?"

"Yes."

"Good. Let's get you up out of this draw."

It took only a couple of minutes for Hope to climb back onto the road. An ambulance and a sheriff's department's Range Rover arrived at the same time. Hope sighed with relief when she heard James Preston say, "We don't need an ambulance here. The kids are all okay. No cuts or scrapes or anything."

Zach all but flew out of the sheriff's vehicle. "What have we got?"

Lucca carried Hope toward the ambulance, saying, "Hope needs medical attention."

"I could use a hand from someone," Tony called out, and Hope realized he was still in the gully. "Twisted my knee."

"Damn," Lucca muttered as Zach went to help his brother. Standing beside the emergency vehicle, Dr. Rose Anderson gestured for Lucca to place Hope on the stretcher. Speaking softly so that only Rose could hear, he said, "She's pregnant."

Rose stopped a moment, considering this new information. Then she nodded. "Okay," Rose said. "Any pain, Hope?"

She opened her mouth to say no, but she started shaking, trembling like a tree in a gale. Rose called to Zach. "Any other transport needed?"

Zach looked at Tony who shook his head. Following a quick survey of the teens, he said, "We're good, Rose."

"Then let's start back. Lie down, Hope. We'll get a warm blanket around you." The doctor and a tech moved her into the ambulance. Lucca started to climb in with her, but Rose placed her palm against his chest. "There's no room for you back here."

"I'm coming with her, Rose."

"Ride up front, Lucca. I'll take good care of her."

Lucca hesitated a moment, then nodded. Soon, the ambulance began the drive back to Eternity Springs.

Rose put a blanket around her, but Hope continued to shake, her teeth chattering as she answered the physician's questions. When she'd collected the information she required, Rose did a quick external exam and said, "We'll give you a thorough exam when we reach the clinic, Hope, but based on where your bruising is located on your abdomen and in the absence of pain, I am confident that the accident did not hurt your baby. We'll make sure, but I need you to try and relax, okay? I know it's hard, and I know you're scared. I want you to concentrate on deep breathing. You need to get that blood pressure down. Okay?"

Hope's throat went tight and tears flooded her eyes. Rose gave her hand a comforting pat. "Relax. I will take excellent care of you and your baby. I'm a great doctor."

Hope nodded, closed her eyes, and tried to relax. Instead, fears, doubts, and concerns came at her like bullets, tearing into her heart, ripping through her soul, messing with her mind. Echoes of her ex-husband's accusations reverberated through her. As the ambulance began the climb up Sinner's Prayer Pass, seeds of panic found fertile ground and began to sprout an unthinkable idea.

Lucca waited outside the examining room, angry and unhappy. The doctor wouldn't let him in Hope's room during the tests and examination. He wasn't her husband. He had no right to be there. Hope, curse her, hadn't asked Dr. Anderson to let him stay.

In fact, Hope hadn't said anything. She hadn't even looked him in the eyes.

She must be in shock. It was certainly understandable, and he wasn't annoyed with her, just the situation. She was his love; this was his baby. He wanted to share his life with her, both the good times and the bad.

He needed to rethink this whole plenty-of-time business. Maybe once this crisis was behind them, he should put his effort into getting a wedding scheduled ASAP. He paced up and down the hallway in front of Hope's room. Finally, the door opened and Dr. Anderson stepped outside. "Hope gave me permission to speak with you about her condition. She is fine," she told him. "The baby is fine. She's eleven weeks along. Almost through with her first trimester."

"Oh," he breathed, taking the news like a most welcome punch to the gut. "Oh. Good. That's wonderful. That's great news." He fastened his gaze on the door. "Can I go in now?"

"Yes, but don't stay long. She needs to rest. I'm going to keep her overnight just for observation."

"Okay. Thanks, doctor."

She smiled. "You're welcome. And congratulations on the baby."

His smile bloomed slowly and genuinely. This was a first. "Thank you. Um . . . Rose? No one knows. We haven't said anything yet."

"Doctor-patient," she said. "I'm a vault, Lucca."

He waited until she walked away, then he opened the door and stepped inside. Hope lay against white sheets dressed in a blue flower-print hospital gown, her head turned toward the window, where, outdoors, the sleet had turned to snow.

"Hey there," he said, softly.

She didn't look at him. "How is Tony?"

"Tony?"

"His knee. Is his knee okay?"

Oh. Lucca experienced a twinge of guilt. He hadn't thought about Tony. "I don't know. I haven't checked to see if he's come in. I've been worried about you."

She closed her eyes. "Go see your brother. Go see your family."

He crossed to her bed and sat on the foot of it. "I want you to be my family, Hope. I love you."

She shook her head, slowly at first, then faster and faster and faster. "No, I can't. I won't."

"Hope—"

"Stop it," she interrupted, meeting his gaze for the first time, the look in her eyes that of a wounded warrior. "Just stop it. I can't do this, Lucca. I can't. But you can. You are such a good man. Such a smart man. The driving lesson . . . I knew what to do. I thought I knew before the lesson, but I didn't. No telling what would have happened if I hadn't had Johnny Tarantino's voice murmuring in my ear. We weren't hurt because of you, Lucca. You saved the team and me and this baby. You are a wonderful man and you will make a wonderful father."

Okay. Why did he feel like another shoe was about to drop?

Because it was.

"I can't do this. I can't be responsible for destroying another child. I won't do it. I won't be part of this baby's life. I know I must be for the next six months. I will care for him and for myself during the pregnancy, but once he's born, if you want him, he is yours. I will give this baby to you."

Lucca froze. "What? What are you talking about? Hope, don't be ridiculous."

She stared at him with brown eyes that reflected a timeless universe of misery. "I won't be this baby's mother. I won't do that to him."

She'd let her ex get to her. And the accident. These weren't her true feelings. She's overwrought. "You're distraught. Now is not the time for this."

"It's the perfect time for this. I want you to leave, Lucca. Leave now and leave me alone. For your sake. You'll be better off."

"Dammit, Hope. I'm not going anywhere. I love you."

She pressed the nurse's call button, and when a woman answered, said, "I want Mr. Romano to leave my room, and he refuses to go. Will you call security, please?"

Lucca had a thousand pounds of torque in his jaw as he clenched his teeth. He knew she wasn't thinking straight, but this had been a helluva long day for him, too. She was okay. The baby was okay. He needed a drink.

"Fine. I'm out of here. You call me in June when it's time for me to pick up my child."

He whirled around, charged out of her room, and marched down the hall, barreling toward the front door until he almost ran into a woman rushing in. "Lucca?" his mother said, her eyes going wide when she got a good look at his face. She clutched his arm. "What's wrong? Tony? Is he hurt worse than they said?"

Lucca wanted to be ten years old again. He wanted to

climb into her lap and let her hold him and rock him and comfort him.

The dam broke. "She's pregnant, Mom. Hope is pregnant, and she just told me she doesn't want anything to do with our baby. She doesn't want me. She told me she was giving him to me and then walking away. We don't even know if it's a boy. She's not even that far along and she's making all these decisions. I know she has issues because of the kidnapping, but damn. I love her. Why doesn't she want us? Why doesn't she love us?"

Maggie Romano gazed up at her son, her expression filled with compassion and concern. "Oh, Lucca. I'm sure Hope doesn't mean it. Her emotions must be a jumble right now."

He didn't want to hear his mother make excuses for the woman who had just plunged a knife into his heart. Suddenly, he was angry, as angry as he'd been in a very long time. She didn't want him. She didn't want to fight for him. For them. She was letting her past rule her present and her future, and he was tired of coming in second to the lost memories of a life she once had. "You know what? It's okay. I'm done. I have my own demons to battle. If she doesn't want help, doesn't want me, well, fine. I'll be okay without her. The baby and I will be just fine."

"Now, Lucca, don't—"

"No, Mom. It's okay. I'm through fighting this fight. Maybe she's right. Maybe she doesn't have what it takes to be a mother."

"Don't you dare say that to her," Maggie said, her tone and expression fierce. "That's just being stupid."

"No, I was stupid to believe that she'd believe in me. In us. Her ex said she was damaged goods. Hell, maybe he was right."

"Lucca!" Maggie gasped. "You do not mean that and you know it. I will not have you talk like that about the mother of my first grandchild. So stop it. Do you hear me? Stop it right now!"

Lucca was too angry to think. He waved a hand, dismissing her reprimand. He didn't really think Hope was damaged. She was everything he could ever want. She just didn't want him.

"Don't you dare dismiss me!"

Something in his mother's tone brought him up short and cut off his self-pity in an instant. He swallowed, and felt like he was ten years old. "Mom, it's just not that simple."

"Of course it is. You love her."

He did. But what good did that do him? She didn't love him in return. "Where's Tony? Let's go check on him. He hurt his knee again when he climbed down into the draw to help me get Hope out of the bus. I'm responsible."

"Lucca Ryan Romano," Maggie said, more than a little exasperation in her tone. "I know about your brother's injury, and I have a news flash. You are not responsible for everything that happens in this world."

He scowled at the Christmas tree decorated with inflated latex gloves. Did no one in this town have normal tree decorations? "I'm responsible for what's happened here tonight, Mom."

"Oh, sweetheart." She lifted her arms and cupped his face in her palms. She stared deeply into his eyes for a long moment, then gave his cheek a gentle slap. "Now, you *are* going to marry the mother of your baby?"

"Didn't you hear what I just said? She doesn't want us."

"Oh, bull. If you believe that then maybe you don't deserve her. Since when do you give up with time still on the clock?"

"I don't know what to think, Mom. I'm angry. She makes it look like she has her stuff together, but that's all a big act. Maybe she'll never be able to get past what happened to her daughter. I don't know that I want to beat my head against that wall for the rest of my life. Maybe I should say fine, I'll raise the baby myself and Hope can spend her life being lonely and afraid."

"Now, son."

Lucca closed his eyes and rubbed his forehead. "It's been a helluva day."

"Then go on home. A walk in the snow will do you good."

"I think I'll do that." Lucca gave her a hug, then hesitated, "How bad is Tony's knee?"

"I don't know yet. Zach said it was swollen and painful to walk on. Let's hope it's just a sprain and he didn't tear something again."

"I should stay, in case he needs my help getting home."

"Not necessary. Gabi is already here, and Zach is on his way. You go on home."

He ground his molars and cast a glance down the hallway toward Hope's room, then turned and walked away.

The minute he was out of sight, Maggie pumped her fist. *Finally. A grandbaby!*

She decided Tony and his leg could wait. Breezing down the hallway, she paused at the nurse's station and asked for Hope's room. She knocked lightly, then stuck her head inside. "Hope? I saw Lucca as he left the hospital. He told me you were here. Mind a little company?"

"Oh, Maggie." Tears streaming down her face, Hope looked at her and said, "I miss my mother."

"Oh, sweetheart, I know you do." Maggie went to her and gathered her in her arms. "It's a crying shame that you lost her so young, but never forget that a mother's hug lasts a lifetime, long after she lets you go."

Hope rested her head against Maggie's breast. In a little voice, she asked, "Did Lucca tell you?"

"About the baby, you mean? Yes, he told me."

"He's angry."

"He's hurting. But then you are hurting, as well, aren't you?"

"I can't do it, Maggie. I know you'll probably hate me, too, but I simply cannot go through this again."

"I don't hate you. Don't be silly." Maggie stroked Hope's hair gently, offering silent comfort. "I think you have one of the most loving hearts I've ever run across. The change you have brought about in Lucca . . . for that, I will be forever grateful."

"He will be a good father."

"He will be an excellent father." Maggie tilted Hope's chin up so that she could look into her eyes. "And you are an awesome mother."

New tears swelled and overflowed. "How can you say that? I lost one baby and now I'm giving the other away."

Maggie's heartfelt sigh drifted across the hospital room. "I have some experience with this. I don't regret my decision to give up Zach for adoption. It was the best thing I could do for him. That's my advice to you, love. Put your child's needs first and you won't go wrong."

"Are you speaking as Lucca's mother or my friend?"

"It's a fine line I walk, I'll give you that. Luckily, what's best for your child is what's best for mine."

A rap on the door preceded a technician's entry into the room pushing a machine. "I need you to step outside for a few minutes, ma'am," she said to Maggie.

"I need to scoot on, anyway. I need to check on Tony." Maggie rose from the bed, then leaned down and kissed Hope on the forehead. "Sleep well, sweetheart. And don't despair. Things will look better in the morning."

"I won't change my mind, Maggie," Hope warned.

Maggie waved a hand. "I'm not worried. You'll do what's best for my grandbaby. You're a good mother, Hope. Sleep well."

Maggie kept the smile on her face until she exited the room. Once she was alone, her smile faded. After hearing the thread of steel in Hope's voice, she wasn't nearly as confident as she let on.

Lucca might well be in for a bigger fight than she had realized.

NINETEEN

Christmas Eve dawned bright and sunny, but by noon, clouds had moved in, and snow flurried in the crisp winter air. Hope sat on her living room floor surrounded by gift-wrapping paper, ribbon, boxes, and tape. Ordinarily, she enjoyed this particular holiday chore. This year, she wished she'd gone for gift cards.

She wished she'd booked a Christmas trip on a cruise ship or to a beach somewhere, but when she'd accepted Celeste's invitation to a Christmas Eve gathering at Angel's Rest, she had been looking forward to spending the holidays in Eternity Springs. Actually, she'd been looking forward to Christmas in Eternity Springs right up until the accident the week before. Since then, Hope had fantasized at least once a day about running away from home for the holidays.

She hadn't exchanged more than a dozen words with Lucca since she'd thrown him out of her hospital room. At practice and the previous day's game, however, he'd communicated plenty with the angry glares he occasionally shot her way. She had to admit that she'd expected him to argue with her about her decision. The fact that he hadn't fought it convinced her that he agreed that she'd made the right decision. He didn't love her, not really. He'd marry her for no other reason than the baby. Just like Mark. And she'd probably destroy Lucca, too.

Just like Mark.

Hope worked her way through her gifts until she had only one left to wrap—Lucca's. She opened the box and looked at the coach's whistle that Sage Rafferty had designed at Hope's request. She stroked her thumb across the engraving—POWER IS NOTHING WITHOUT CONTROL—then returned it to its box. She'd been so excited to give it to him. Now, it was different. She was different.

You're scared.

"To the bone. So what else is new?" she grumbled, then chose red foil to wrap his package. How could she give it to him, though? How could she go through these holiday motions when what she really wanted to do was run? Why was she going to the gathering at Celeste's, anyway? Why was she putting herself through this?

With the last of her gifts wrapped and ready, she donned a red wool dress, black tights, and boots for the evening. She seldom wore dresses in the winter here, but she'd been raised to wear a dress to church on Christmas, so that's what she did. She loaded her car with her gifts and the appetizers and side dishes that were her contribution to the meal and made the short drive to Cavanaugh House on the grounds of Angel's Rest.

Celeste was a vision in gold and white when she welcomed Hope into her home. "The house is lovely, Celeste," she said. "I haven't been here since you decorated for the holidays."

"Thank you, sugar. I'm just like a little kid when it comes to Christmas and I love, love, love to display my angel collection."

Display she did, Hope discovered as she toured the house. She wondered how many man-hours Celeste had invested in tastefully positioning angels everywhere one looked.

Hope finished placing her gifts beneath a lovely live tree in the parlor as a large group of visitors arrived. The Murphys, the Callahans, and the Raffertys filled the room with excited, chattering preschoolers, bright-eyed toddlers, and infants dressed like elves. "Saint Stephen's added a late afternoon children's service this year," Nic explained. "We're on our way home from there, so the excitement level is really ramped up."

Hope sat on a chair ottoman to speak to the Callahan twins. "What is Santa bringing you tonight?"

"We each get a big present, a little present, and a surprise," Cari Callahan said.

Her twin, Meg, added, "I asked for a sled and a new stuffed puppy."

Cari rolled her eyes. "Daddy said we don't have any room in our bedroom for more stuffed puppies, but Mommy just laughed and told him he was being silly. She tells him that a lot."

"She likes stuffed animals as much as me," Meg added. "When we start school next year and you are our teacher, can I bring a puppy backpack?"

"Absolutely," Hope said. "I love puppy backpacks, and I can't wait to have you two in my class."

As the precocious little girls continued to talk, Hope sensed the attention of a newcomer. Glancing over her shoulder, she saw Lucca standing out in the hallway sipping eggnog from a punch cup and watching her with unreadable eyes.

Her throat tightened, but she turned her attention back to the Callahan twins and enjoyed a story about their father's aging boxer, Clarence. Soon, Jack Davenport wandered into the room, his little Johnny in his arms. Still under a year old, Johnny Davenport sported a darling reindeer outfit, and bright eyes as big as saucers. He pointed toward the Christmas tree and said, "Da Da Da Da."

"He's is such a little doll, Jack," Hope said.

"He's such a little anvil," Jack replied. "I'll be glad when he starts walking. I don't know why his twenty pounds is heavier than twenty pounds of weights."

Hope hesitated. Could she do this? *Of course you can do this. This is what you do. How you cope.* "Let me hold him and give your back a rest, big guy."

"Gladly! I noticed Sarah set out a cookie tray on the dining room table. Mind if I pawn him off on you long enough to score some pinwheels before they're all gone?"

"Not if you promise to bring me one."

"I'll bring you two," Jack promised, handing over his son.

Hope talked softly to the boy, who babbled back, pointing toward decorations on the tree. He smelled like baby powder and Cheerios, and Hope drew in the heavenly scent and tried not to notice that her heart was shattering into little pieces. When she walked Johnny over to the fireplace mantel where an animated angel figurine choir played carol bells, she again caught sight of Lucca standing in the hallway, this time eating the meatball appetizer she'd brought. His gaze remained focused on her.

Cat Davenport found her a few moments later and repossessed Johnny. Hope wandered toward the dining room, thinking she'd try a cup of the hot spiced cider whose aroma drifted on the air. But as she passed the music room, she spied Cam Murphy sitting in a chair and digging in the diaper bag, trying to comfort a fussy Michael at the same time.

"Here, let me help," Hope said, scooping Michael from his father's arms. Was it strength or self-punishment that caused her to interact with these babies? She wasn't certain.

"Thank you," Cam said, lifting the diaper bag into his lap. "I swear, Sarah carries everything but the kitchen sink in here."

Hope rocked the fussing baby and patted his back until Cam pulled a bottle from the bag with a victorious "Yes!"

"Mind if I give him his bottle?" Hope asked.

"I'd love it." Cam shot to his feet, then motioned for her to take a seat. Once she settled in, he handed her the bottle and said, "Can I bring you anything?"

Not hot cider since she was feeding the baby. She smiled up at him. "I'd love a glass of water."

"Be right back."

Hope settled back into the chair and discovered that it was a rocker. She offered the bottle to Michael and smiled tenderly down at him when he latched onto the nipple as if he'd not eaten in a week. She tried not to remember the sensation of Holly at her breast, forcing herself not to picture the same with the baby she carried within her. Cam returned with her water and asked if she needed anything else. When she assured him she was fine, he made excuses to raid the dining table.

After a few minutes, she gently tugged the bottle from Michael's mouth and lifted him to her shoulder. She gently patted his back, listening for the burp. Rewarded, she cradled him again and offered the bottle once more, murmuring sweet encouragement all the while.

Upon feeling Lucca's stare yet again, she looked up, lifted her chin, and challenged him to do something more than stare. "Merry Christmas, Lucca."

"No, I can't say that it is." He turned and walked away.

Hope clutched little Michael Murphy a little tighter and blinked back tears. "I will not cry," she whispered to him. "It's Christmas."

Anger and frustration heated Lucca's blood, so he stepped outside into the winter air in an attempt to cool off and find his Christmas peace and joy. He gripped the wooden porch railing with bare hands and gazed out at the snow-covered grounds of Angel's Rest. His breath fogged as he released a heavy sigh. Hope Montgomery made him crazy.

He heard the door open behind him, and he glanced over his shoulder. He wasn't surprised to see his twin attempting to maneuver through the doorway on his crutches. Tony undoubtedly sensed his turmoil.

"Hold on a minute," Lucca said, moving toward him. "Let me get the door."

After Tony crossed the threshold, he tossed Lucca the jacket he'd draped over one crutch. "Do us both a favor and put this on before Mom sees you."

Lucca's mouth twisted, but he did as his brother asked and then returned to his spot at the railing. Tony hobbled across the porch and stood beside him. "So, do you want to tell me what's wrong?"

"Yeah, but later. Not here."

Tony nodded. "It's obvious that you have a beef of some sort with Hope, so I'm offering a distraction. I have a favor to ask you, bro. A big one."

"Oh?" The prospect of having something to think about other than the situation with Hope pleased him. "Okay, ask it."

"The doctors tell me I'm not gonna heal on my own this time around. I need to have surgery."

Lucca grimaced. "Dammit, Tony. I'm sorry. I feel responsible."

"Good. Because I need your help. My doctor has an opening in his schedule later this week, but our team leaves for New York the day after tomorrow. My head assistant coach is out with the chicken pox, of all things. He caught it from his kindergartener. So . . ." He met Lucca's gaze. "I need you to fill in for me at the Holiday Classic."

Lucca's heart thudded. His mouth went dry. "Coach? You want me to coach?"

"It's an important tournament. You know my system. I need you."

Return to collegiate coaching? Lucca's first reaction was to refuse out of hand, but even as the words formed on his tongue, he hesitated, and his thoughts went to Hope.

How could he argue against her allowing fear to rule her life when he was guilty of the same offense?

He couldn't. He had to do this. For the sake of his child and his child's mother. For the sake of the family he wanted, he needed to defeat this particular fear. He sucked in a deep breath, filling his lungs with freezing air, then exhaled in a rush. "Okay. Yes. I'll do it. I'll coach the Holiday Classic in your place."

Tony's face lit up like a Christmas tree. "Excellent," he said, his smile wide. "I'm so glad. That's the best gift ever."

"So I can take back the one I put under Mom's tree for you?"

"Hell, no."

Lucca laughed, feeling as if a great weight had been released from his shoulders. "Let's go inside. I'm freezing, and, besides, Mom is peering through the curtains at us."

"She's probably ready to go home so she can start cooking our Christmas Eve feast. Did you see the size of that tenderloin roast she bought?"

"You mean the cow that's in the refrigerator?" Lucca joked.

The brothers went inside, and soon the entire family prepared to take their leave. His mood having mellowed, Lucca looked around for Hope, thinking to improve upon his earlier response to her Merry Christmas wish, but Sarah Murphy told him she'd left through the back door while he'd been on the front porch with Tony. Telling himself that he'd catch up with her later, he turned his attention to his family, determined to enjoy the occasion.

The traditional Romano family Christmas meant opening gifts prior to midnight mass on Christmas Eve. This year, following a feast where Zach and Max arm wrestled for the last slice of roast and their mother actually rationed the Italian crème cake, the family congregated downstairs and waited for Maggie to finish a phone call with her sisters. Christmas music played softly in the background, and conversation between the siblings was easy. Richard Steele was in Denver with his family for the Christmas holidays, and Lucca had to admit he was glad. While he and his siblings were growing accustomed to the idea of the new man in their mother's life, he was glad to have another year before they'd need to expand their traditions.

Including a baby would be an easier adjustment. His mother had been preaching about wanting grandchildren for years, and he knew how excited she was at the thought.

"Hey, you," Gabriella said, coming up beside him. "You okay? You've been awfully quiet tonight."

"I have a lot on my mind."

"It's Hope, isn't it? You had a fight? You two hardly spoke to one another at Angel's Rest. Honestly, I expected you to invite her to be here and go to church with us tonight."

"We're having . . . issues."

"What sort of issues?"

He set his mouth and shook his head. "This isn't the time for it. It's Christmas Eve and I haven't even tried to guess your present yet."

He started toward the tree to begin the time-honored tradition of lifting the box marked to him from Gabi to shake, sniff, and study in his effort to figure out its contents. Soon, Gabi's smart-aleck responses to his questions had him laughing, and when his mother entered the room a few minutes later and asked Zach to play Santa and pass out gifts, Lucca was overwhelmed by a warm rush of love for his family.

Max and Tony sat bickering over which songs should be included in a top-ten-rock-songs-in-history list. Savannah teased his mother about one of the gifts Richard had given her before he left that, apparently, his mom honestly loved. *If Dad had given Mom an electric broom, she wouldn't have spoken to him until Easter.* Zach was giving Gabi a hard time about her handwriting on the gift tags, and his sister fired back about chicken scratching on sheriff's department reports.

How incredibly lucky he was.

And how incredibly sad that Hope sat home alone with only Roxy for company.

The last of the anger and hurt that Lucca had nursed for the past week melted away, overwhelmed by a heart filled with love. Celeste had advised him to be patient and to listen to his instincts. Why had he forgotten that?

"Lucca?"

The sound of his name snapped him back to attention. Zach stood in front of him, a stack of gifts in his arms. "Oh, sorry."

As his brother handed over Lucca's gifts, he noticed the medal hanging on a chain around Zach's neck. Savannah wore one like it. He realized he'd seen a similar necklace on a number of people in Eternity Springs.

As Zach returned to the tree to gather another stack of gifts to give out, Lucca turned to his sister-in-law seated beside him. "What's the deal with the necklaces you guys wear? The wings?"

Savannah's hand lifted to touch her pendant. "Celeste gave them to us. She calls it the official Angel's Rest blazon. Sage Rafferty designed it and Celeste awards it to those she deems have embraced healing's grace. Earning it has become a bit of a big deal here in town. She only gives it after a person overcomes a significant emotional wound."

"Really?"

"I'm very proud to wear mine. It reminds me of how far I've come and how blessed I am. On days when I'm a little down or something bothers me, I can touch it and remind myself that I am strong and have the ability to overcome."

"Really?" he repeated.

A ghost of a thought formed on the edges of his consciousness, but before he could wrestle it into form, Zach distracted him by saying, "Okay, I have two gifts left to pass out. One doesn't have a tag at all and the other says . . . to Fig from Nana?"

The unmarked gift was Lucca's for Hope that he'd forgotten to remove from the bag of gifts he'd brought over to his mom's place. The fig . . . well . . . that must be his, too. He knew from his own reading that at eleven weeks, the baby was the size of a fig. He looked at his mother who gave him a sheepish grin. "It's a happy thing. We're all together and I can't keep a secret like this for long."

"I should have expected it, I guess." He shrugged and shared the news with his family. "Hope is pregnant."

They reacted with a loving combination of joy and concern, aware that he had problems with his relationship with Hope. "She's afraid and considering her situation, that's understandable. She needs to be convinced that she's brave enough to tackle motherhood again."

"Again?" Gabi asked.

Lucca hesitated. This wasn't his story to tell, but she'd already shared the facts with his mother and, besides, he wanted to enlist their help. But before he launched into an explanation, the doorbell rang. Maggie answered it and Celeste Blessing stepped inside. "I'm sorry to interrupt, but Maggie, you left your handbag at Angel's Rest, and when I opened it to determine to whom it belonged, I saw you had your church offering envelope inside, so I thought I'd drop it off so you'd have it tonight."

"Thank you, Celeste. I'm so scatterbrained sometimes. I didn't realize I'd walked off without it. Come in and join us, please. Have a cup of cider."

"I don't want to interrupt your family time."

That ghost of thought Lucca had had solidified and he rose to his feet. "Please, Celeste. Do join us. I have something very important to ask you."

"All right." Celeste removed her coat and joined them in the living room. "What can I do to help?"

"You know about Holly, right? Hope told you when you met during her beach vacation?"

"Yes."

He nodded, then turned back to his family and explained about Holly. Shock and compassion filled their expressions. "Poor Hope," Gabi said. "That's the most heartbreaking story ever."

"It is," Lucca agreed. "It broke up her marriage, but it didn't break Hope. Did you see her tonight? Every time I turned around, she had a child in her arms. She doesn't run from kids, she embraces them. She surrounds herself with them. She drives them on a school bus and teaches them to read and coaches them in a sport she hardly knows. She's dedicated her life to children. Is that not the very definition of courage?"

"It's more than I could do, that's for sure," Max said.

"The girl has guts," Tony agreed.

Lucca stared at Celeste intently. "She doesn't see it, and I think she needs a symbol. It's Dorothy and Oz and the Cowardly Lion, only the Yellow Brick Road is a Miracle Road. She's been given a miracle, a second chance to have a family, but she thinks she doesn't have the courage to accept it. Only, she does have the courage. She's proved it by the way she's chosen to live her life since Holly was stolen. Celeste, I think she needs the recognition. She needs the outward symbol."

"You want me to award her an Angel's Rest blazon?"

"I do. I think she's earned it. Don't you?"

Celeste's eyes warmed, and her smile spread wide. "I think that's an exceptional idea, and especially appropriate considering the other purpose behind my visit here tonight."

She reached into her purse and pulled out a small white velvet box wrapped in gold ribbon, which she handed to Lucca. "Word got around that you have agreed to coach Tony's team in a tournament so that he can have surgery on his knee."

"That was fast," Lucca observed, tugging the ribbon.

"The small-town telegraph is a wondrous thing."

Grinning, Lucca opened the box. "A medal for me?"

"Yes. Allow me?" Celeste removed the chain from the box and, after motioning for Lucca to bend down, slipped it over his head. "In recognition of your embrace of love's healing grace as evidenced by your return to collegiate coaching, I award you the official Angel's Rest blazon."

"I'm going to cry," Maggie said.

"Me, too," Gabi added. "I'm jealous. I want one."

"There she goes again," Max said. "Always wanting what everyone else has."

"Oh, hush, or I'll take back your Christmas present."

"Speaking of presents," Tony said. "Can we finally open them? We don't want to be late to church."

"Tear into 'em, kiddos."

Accompanied by the sound of tearing paper, Lucca bent and kissed Celeste on the cheek. "Thank you, Celeste. This means the world to me. And I thank you even more for agreeing to my point about Hope."

"She has a loving soul and a tender heart. You were right to recognize her courage, but I must caution you to remember that her wounds are deeper than most. I spoke to you before about the need for patience."

"You're right. I will remember."

"Oh, cool!" Tony said. "A Nerf Blaster. This is awesome. Thank you, Gabi."

Max laughed. "I got one, too."

Lucca looked at his brothers' gifts from Gabi, then searched for his own present. "Those are solid. You better not have left me out, sis."

Zach shot a dart at Lucca and laughed. Minutes later, the foam was flying as the four grown men reverted to boyhood. Maggie Romano moved to stand beside Celeste. "Gabi always gives her brothers toys for Christmas. It's a Romano family tradition."

"You are blessed with your family, Maggie."

"Don't I know it." Maggie gave Celeste a hug and added, "Blessed with my family. Blessed with my friends. Blessed to have found a home in Eternity Springs."

"Amen," said Celeste. "Merry Christmas."

"Merry Christmas," Hope said as she handed Roxy a big rawhide bone. The dog carried it over to her bed and stretched out to slobber and chew. Hope hummed "Silent Night" as she stoked the fire, intending to chase away the chill that lingered in her bones after the walk home from the midnight church service. Maybe she should have accepted the Davenports' offer of a ride home, but it had been such a gorgeous, starry night, and her heart had been so full and warm from the fellowship of the service that she'd wanted to prolong the moment.

Plus, she hadn't looked forward to going home alone. She glanced over to her Christmas tree, where only the red foil-wrapped gift remained. Had things been different, she might have spent the evening with the Romanos, she knew. She always felt lonely on Christmas, but this year was worse than ever. Walking home from church, seeing lights on in her neighbors' houses, she'd felt a little like Scrooge gazing into Tiny Tim's window.

Better she had attended the daytime service. Nothing felt quite so hollow as standing outside in the dark alone looking inside where people were gathered in a warm, bright place.

"You think you're lonely this year, imagine how you'll feel next," she murmured. Instinctively, she covered her womb with her hand. Could she really give this baby up? Did she honestly believe that her child would be better off without her in his or her life? Or had that been nothing more than panic talking in the wake of the accident?

How in the world would she ever find the strength to walk away from this child? Maggie and Celeste had both said it: *You are always a mother. Always.*

So, was Hope ready to accept that she could take the risk? Did hope spring eternal for Hope in Eternity Springs?

A knock at her back door distracted her from the troublesome thoughts. Her back door? Who would come to her back door on Christmas Eve?

But even as she asked the question, she knew the answer. Maybe he was here to talk. Maybe . . . just maybe . . . her heartbeat sped up. Her mouth went a little dry. On her way to answer the door, she passed in front of a mirror and smoothed her hair.

She opened the door to see Lucca standing bathed in moonlight. He looked solemn and serious. "Hello."

"Come outside, would you? I have something I want you to see."

She hesitated. "It's late, Lucca."

"Give me five minutes. Please?"

"Let me get my coat." She retrieved her long wool coat from the front closet, then spied the gift beneath her tree. She picked it up and stuck it in her pocket, then returned to her back door.

Outside, she looked around but didn't see him. "Lucca?"

"Back here," he called from the deep shadows at the back of the house.

She knew then what his visit must be about. "You got a telescope for Christmas?"

"Not for Christmas," he replied. "I ordered it after our trip to Texas. It's pretty awesome."

"It's huge," she said once her eyes adjusted to the darkness and she was able to pick out the shape.

She realized she had missed her friend. They hadn't talked, laughed, or counted stars in what seemed like ages.

"I didn't ask you out here to look at my telescope. I want you to see a star. Come here and look, Hope. I have it focused on the star I want you to see. Try not to move the scope when you look into the eyepiece."

She wondered if he planned to tell her a Star of Bethlehem story. Looking into the powerful telescope, she spied a whole bunch of stars. "What am I supposed to see?"

"The binary star. See the pair?"

She had to concentrate. It had been awhile since she'd looked at the stars. Without him, searching the night sky had made her sad. "Okay. Yes, I see the pair."

"Now, step away from the telescope. I want to show you how to find it. First, you look for Draco, which is a circumpolar constellation. That means it revolves around the North Pole and it can be seen year-round. You want to find the dragon's head. See these four stars positioned in a trapezoid?"

As he'd done in the past when teaching her the stars, he stepped close enough so that she could smell his aftershave. The memory of lying on his chest assailed her, cutting into her chest like a knife. She mourned the loss of him, and here he was right next to her. "Hope?"

"I . . ." Inhaling deeply, she shook off the feeling and followed the path of his finger as he pointed out the four stars. "Okay. I've got it."

"From the head, the tail slithers through the sky there to there to there," he demonstrated, "ending between the Big and Little Dippers."

She was distracted. She wanted to tell him that she was sorry she'd hurt him. Tell him she was sorry that she was such a mess. Sorry that she couldn't seem to let go of part of her past. That she couldn't see her way forward. "You've lost me."

"Have I?" He studied her, searching her face, his expression troubled. "I can help you find it again."

"Can you?"

"Of course."

She looked back to the stars. "I don't know, Lucca. It's hard."

"It can be. But all you really need to do is trust that once you find a place to start, you can find what you're looking for."

"Trust the trapezoid?"

"Always. It's a center. You just need a center, Hope."

"Okay." With him leaning so close and his coat right there, she seized the opportunity to silently slip his gift from her pocket and into his. *Good. That worked out well. No more worrying about what to do with it. Out of sight, out of mind.*

"From the top right star in the trapezoid, look right and up about forty-five degrees. See the bright star?"

"Yes."

"That's actually two stars, the binary star I showed you in the telescope."

"Okay." She didn't have a clue what they were doing out in the cold looking at stars, but did she care? He was there. With his soft voice and gentle eyes.

"So, you think you could find it again?"

"I may need"—her voice cracked—"help."

"I can help you." He didn't push harder. He didn't touch her. He was there if she wanted him, but he wasn't going to push. "But you can do it, Hope. I know you can."

"The trapezoid is easy to pick out."

"All right, then. That's it. That's all I wanted to show you. I picked it because it's bright, it's always in the sky, and it's easy to locate. No matter where you are, the star is there for you to see. Stars never get lost." He bent down and gave her a quick kiss. "Merry Christmas, Hope."

Then, before she could make sense of what was happening, he disappeared into the deep, dark shadows that separated their houses. "Well," she murmured. "That was different."

She felt raw. He wanted to help. He wanted to make it work. *But dare I try?* "Maybe."

When she turned toward her house to go inside, she didn't feel nearly as lonely as she had before.

She didn't notice the package until she stepped up onto her back porch. She picked it up and carried it inside. Wrapped in a Santa Claus print paper with green yarn for ribbon, the package tag read TO HOPE. FROM LUCCA.

"I guess he was no more anxious to do a gift exchange in person than I was," she said aloud. She set the package on her entry hall table as she hung her coat in the closet. Then she carried it over to the fire, which she stoked to life once again. She held the package for a moment, thinking about the last time a lover had given her a Christmas gift. Mark's gift the Christmas before Holly was taken had been a lovely string of pearls. She still wore them on occasion. They reminded her of one of the most pleasurable holidays she'd ever had. Holly had still believed in Santa, and her joy and excitement when she discovered the Barbie Dreamhouse beneath the tree on Christmas morning had been unsurpassed.

"I wonder what's beneath your tree this year, baby," Hope murmured. She wouldn't believe that her little girl didn't have a Christmas tree. She had to believe that somewhere, a ten-year-old Holly took with her to bed tonight the same happy, excited spirit that the five-year-old had known on Christmas Eve.

Needing a distraction, Hope opened her gift. A Christmas card rested on top of white tissue paper. She opened it and read Lucca's firm handwriting.

Up front, I need to tell you that the scientific community doesn't recognize this gift, but they're not the ones who matter. Merry Christmas, Hope.
All my love, Lucca.

Opening the tissue paper, she spied a framed certificate, the edges of which were trimmed in breathtaking watercolor and ink drawings of planets and stars, novas and—Hope smiled—whimsical angels. She recognized it as the work of Eternity Springs' own famous artist, her friend Sage Anderson Rafferty.

The certificate's words were done in lovely calligraphy and read:

From the night sky of the Northern Hemisphere, a star shines down upon a mother and a daughter, linking them through the geometry of love.

The star at latitude 43:04:33 North, longitude 77:39:53 West
is officially unofficially named
Holly's Star.
Love beams up from the mother
and reflects down upon the daughter wherever she exists.
Love radiates up from the daughter
and shines down upon the mother, in daylight and in darkness.
Starshine,
Loveshine.
Hope and Holly.

Hope released a shaky breath. "Oh, Lucca."

Cradling the frame against her chest, Hope rushed back outside. She ignored the winter's chill and stared up at the sky, searching, until she found Holly's Star.

"Oh, Lucca," she repeated. He loved her. He wanted her. He wanted a family with her. He wasn't just a second chance, a fix to a past she couldn't change. He was the future she could embrace. How could she ever walk away from this man?

I can't.

TWENTY

On December 29, after Lucca had spent almost six months in Eternity Springs, the boisterous noise of midtown Manhattan grated on his nerves like sandpaper as he walked toward the Seventh Avenue entrance to Madison Square Garden. Car horns screeched. A siren blared. Across the street, a jackhammer pounded. He found himself yearning for the peace and quiet of Eternity Springs. "Go figure," he murmured as he walked into the arena.

His phone sounded—Gabi's ringtone—and he reached into his suit coat pocket to answer it. He'd been waiting for this call. "Hey, Gabs. How did it go?"

"Good, I think. It was a bit hard to tell. She seemed pleased, but she cried."

"Good cry or bad cry?"

"Good cry. I think."

"Give me details."

"Okay. Celeste called Hope and asked her to come over to Angel's Rest at ten A.M. to discuss a fund-raising idea for the basketball team. She told the rest of us to be there by nine forty-five."

"Who all came?" He wished he could have been there to see it, but after their last conversation on Christmas morning, he'd decided that the best strategy was to give her space.

"Everyone who has earned one of the medals—except for you—and me and Mom. So, it was Zach and Savannah, Nic and Gabe, Mac and Ali, Sage and Colt, Cam and Sarah, Jack and Cat, and me and Mom. I have to tell you, it's depressing to be paired up as a couple with your mother—especially when she is dating and I'm not."

"What did Celeste say?"

"She stood on the staircase and said she had an announcement to make. She told Hope that after finding out the story behind the Angel necklace, you suggested Hope qualified and that she agreed. She referred to the Wizard of Oz argument you made, and she added that she believed Glenda the Good Witch was actually an angel."

Lucca laughed. That didn't surprise him one bit.

"Then Celeste got serious and told Hope that she's acted courageously and that by wearing her Angel's Rest medal, she will acknowledge her courage and honor her strength. She put the necklace around Hope's neck and told her to let the medal be the talisman that reminds her to live boldly. She said if Hope listened to her heart and intuition as she traveled her life's path, she would recognize the miracles that happen along the road every day. That's when Hope started to cry."

"Did she cry and run off or cry and hug people?"

"Actually, she did a little of both. She did the hugging, but then said she couldn't stay any longer because she had somewhere she needed to be, and she left."

"Where did she go?"

"I don't know. She didn't say."

"Huh." Lucca thought it through and decided to think positively about her reaction. He shouldn't expect to win the race in a hundred-yard dash. This was a marathon. He'd need stamina and patience to win, and win he would. He'd settle for nothing less than victory.

Gabi interrupted his musing. "Now, how about you, Lucca? How are you managing the return to college hoops?"

"It's fine. Really good, in fact. Tony has a good group of talented kids."

"And a talented substitute coach. Mom says when y'all made the semifinals, Tony grumbled that you were bound to take credit for his hard work."

Lucca grinned. "Of course I will. So, Mom told me the surgery went well?"

"Yes. She said she's going to have a hard time keeping him off it for another few days, but then, she's in her glory playing nursemaid."

"True."

"Good luck in the game this afternoon, Lucca."

"Thanks."

"I'm really proud of you. You've given me hope that someday, I'll find my way, too."

"You will, Gabs. I have faith in that."

"I love you, brother."

"Love you, too, Gabriella."

Lucca smiled as he made his way to the locker room where his team awaited. Tomorrow was New Year's Eve and, while he couldn't quite believe it himself, he felt downright positive about the coming year.

Upon entering the locker room, he turned his attention to the matter at hand. "Gather round, gentlemen. We are going to talk for few minutes about the way of the hardwood warrior."

The first half of the semifinal game proved to be a barn burner with their opponents taking a two-point lead into the locker room. Lucca consulted with Tony's assistant coaches and made some adjustments to the game plan, then took them out onto the court for warm-ups early.

He stood at courtside, his arms folded, watching his twin brother's players practice layups and jump shots and enjoying the moment. This was Madison Square Garden, after all, a mecca of the sporting world and the scene of one of his best games as a pro player. He loved the atmosphere, the energy. The sights and the smells. He loved the competition. He loved the game itself.

But he didn't necessarily love it anymore in the Garden than he did in the Eternity Springs gymnasium. Nor did he yearn for the hustle and bustle of big-city living over the slow, laid-back pace of small-town life.

He yearned for Hope and a home with their child and a job helping high school students grow and learn the important life lessons that competing on the hardwood has to teach.

He yearned for Eternity Springs.

"All right, men," he murmured. "Let's win this thing so I can go home where I belong."

Life lessons and basketball. *A man is never too old to learn.*

He watched Tony's star power forward sink a shot from midcourt as a stir in the crowd gradually caught his notice. Then he heard the point guard say, "There's another one. She's older than the usual coeds, though. Hot, too. You might want to consider this one, Coach."

"Excuse me?"

The player pointed up toward the huge scoreboard suspended from the ceiling above midcourt. First, Lucca read the ribbon graphic across the bottom that announced FAN CAM. Then he noticed that the camera had focused a close-up on a sign that read COACH ROMANO, WILL YOU MARRY ME?

He shrugged it off. It wasn't the first marriage proposal sign he'd seen in the stands. It usually happened three or four times a season. College coeds were embarrassingly forward these days. Just as he was about to lower his gaze back to the court, the camera lens zoomed out and Lucca got his first look at the "coed" holding the sign.

He froze. Zoned out. Got swept away by a cyclone to the land not at the foot of the Yellow Brick Road, but smack-dab in the middle of his very own Miracle Road.

Here, caught on the Fan Cam, holding a sign asking him to marry her, stood his Hope.

Joy as fierce as any emotion he'd ever known pulsed through him. Pulling his gaze away from the scoreboard, he frantically looked around. He had to find her. The Garden was a huge arena, packed with people. How could he find her?

Cameras. Look for the cameras. There. Second row behind the home bench.

He took a step toward her, then another, and then Coach Lucca Romano started running. Like the graceful, powerful athlete of old, he hurdled the bench, then grabbed the railing and vaulted over it into the stands. Then, Hope, his wonderful, glorious Hope, was in his arms, and he was kissing her, deeply, thoroughly, and passionately.

Her hands lifted and her fingers laced behind his neck. She melted against him, and Lucca knew he'd found home. He lost track of everything but her. When he finally released her mouth and began pressing kisses across her cheeks, her eyes, her temples, he realized she was repeating those sweet words he'd longed to hear. "I love you, Lucca. I love you, Lucca. I love you, Lucca."

He looked down into her eyes through his own tear-misted gaze. "I love you, too, Hope. Dear Lord above, I love you, too."

Only then did he once again become aware of his surroundings as the sound of catcalls and applause filtered through his brain.

He looked up, saw that the arena cameras were still focused on him and Hope, and he gave the crowd what they wanted.

He flashed a thumbs-up and grinned. "I said yes."

He thought they might have heard the answering roar of the crowd all the way out in Eternity Springs.

January 4th

Daniel Garrett walked into his Boston office with springtime on his mind. News had broken that morning that the Red Sox had traded for a pitcher from Texas who would add depth and a spark to their rotation. The addition excited Daniel. New pitching was a shot in the arm to a ball club that always gave a fan hope. Hope was one of life's great gifts. "Wish there was more of it in my world."

His office phone rang, and with his mind still on the American League, he picked it up.

"Hello."

"May I please speak with Mr. Daniel Garrett?" a hesitant voice said.

Twenty minutes later, he was in a cab on his way to the airport. He figured he should be in time to catch the twelve-fifteen flight to Dallas/Fort Worth. Barring any travel delays, he would make it to the gymnasium before the game ended. "Basketball," he murmured. "Unreal."

While he rode, Daniel worked the phone, calling in favors and collecting on promises. The fact that he was going to a large city in Texas worked in his favor, and by the time he walked into the terminal at Logan, he had the lab and technicians he needed on standby.

When he arrived at the gym at the wellness center of

the suburban Fort Worth church, eight minutes remained in the girls' basketball game.

Daniel's heart pounded. His mouth was dry and his palms were wet. He stepped into the gymnasium and surveyed the players.

He saw her. He knew her. He didn't need fingerprints or DNA, although, of course, he would follow through with them.

"Mr. Garrett?"

He looked around to see a Hispanic woman who appeared to be in her forties. "Yes, I am Daniel Garrett."

The woman's gaze went to the court. "I am Jacinta Guerrero, Amanda's aunt."

"Thank you for calling me, Mrs. Guerrero."

She released a long, heavy sigh. "After Amanda showed this to me, I could do nothing else." She reached into her coat pocket and pulled out a familiar neon pink paper folded into quarters. She opened it, handed it to Daniel, and said, "Look at her. It is obvious. The age progression photograph is amazingly close."

Daniel didn't need to look at the photos on the flyer. He knew them by heart.

Just as he knew that little number six playing guard on the basketball court was Holly Montgomery.

"Here, Gabi, catch." Lucca dropped the empty plastic ornament box through the opening in the attic floor at Aspenglow Place.

"Jeez, Lucca," his sister called. "That almost hit me right on the head."

"Reflexes, sis. Work on 'em."

" 'Work on 'em,' " Gabi repeated, a sneer in her voice. "Come down out of the attic, brother, and I'll show you reflexes."

Hope laughed. "Would you two try to get along, please?"

Lucca descended the attic stairs carrying two more boxes. "That takes all the fun out of it, Hope."

"He's right," Gabi agreed. "Bickering helps us battle through the boredom and physical misery."

Hope arched her eyebrows. " 'Physical misery'? Of taking down the Christmas decorations? Don't you think that's a bit of an exaggeration?"

"Hah!" Gabi looked at her brother. "Obviously, she hasn't experienced the traditional Romano family joy of untrimming a natural tree on Epiphany."

"It's like dancing with a porcupine," Lucca explained. "Pure misery. Every year, Dad tried to convince Mom that this was one tradition we could forgo. Every year, she shut him down."

Hope glanced from Lucca to Gabi, then back to Lucca again. "Okay, I know I'm a little dense, but your mother is in Florida visiting her sisters. She hasn't been here for over a week. If this bothers you, why didn't you take the tree down a week ago?"

"And break tradition?" Gabi scoffed. "We couldn't do that."

Hope sighed. "I can tell already that I'm going to have trouble keeping track of all the Romano family traditions."

"No, you won't," Gabi said. "I've decided to embroider them on a wall hanging to give you for a wedding gift."

Lucca snorted. "Wonderful. You sew as good as you cook, Gabriella."

"Bite me."

"I could. I expect you taste better than your meat loaf."

"Oh stop it," Hope said, grinning at the sibling banter. Of course, she grinned at just about everything these days. She hadn't stopped grinning since she'd left Madison Square Garden engaged to be married.

It had been a whirlwind few days. They'd returned from New York in time for a New Year's Eve party that quickly evolved into an engagement celebration. On New Year's Day, while the Romano men watched football on television, the Romano women got serious about wedding plans. After studying both high school and collegiate basketball schedules and consulting with Hope's principal regarding time off for a honeymoon, Hope and Lucca set the wedding date for February 14. Maggie had assured her that empire waists were making a comeback in wedding gowns this year.

Hope had even been strong enough to reach out to Mark. On New Year's afternoon, with her Angel's Rest pendant held tightly in her grip, she'd placed a call to her ex-husband.

When he didn't answer, she left a voice mail. "Hi Mark. It's Hope. I know your first question would be about Holly, so no, I'm not calling with any news. I'm calling because I wanted to . . . well . . . I want to wish you a Happy New Year. I mean it, Mark. I hope that this new year brings you happiness and, most of all, peace."

Five minutes later, her phone rang. Mark. Her heartbeat thudding, she answered it. "Hello, Mark."

"I got your message. I'm glad you called."

"You are?"

"Yeah." He cleared his throat. "I've thought a lot about my trip to Colorado, about the things I said. I was an ass. I'm sorry."

Hope was shocked. She couldn't remember the last time Mark had apologized for anything, and she didn't know how to respond. Finally, she simply said, "Thank you."

A moment of awkward silence followed, then Mark said, "I saw you on television. I guess congratulations are in order, too."

Her heart twisted. He sounded a little lost and lonely, and compassion filled her. "Remember how Holly woke up excited to meet the day? She taught me what a joyous heart looks like. I'm going to try to live my life with joy. That honors her, I think."

His voice sounded gruff when he replied, "That's nice, Hope."

She licked her lips, then added, "I wish that you could be happy, too, Mark. This may sound silly to you, but I wish you'd spend some time in Eternity Springs. There is something about this town. People come here and find peace."

He released a long sigh. "After I left your house last time, my rental car had engine trouble. I was stalled beside the road waiting for the auto service to arrive, and an older woman riding a motorcycle stopped to offer help."

"Celeste Blessing?"

"Yes. Once she figured out who I was, she said something similar to me about Eternity Springs. Then, she invited me to stay in a little cabin on the Angel's Rest property. I stayed two nights."

"You did! I didn't know that."

"I'm thinking I might come back sometime. That is, if you don't mind. If your basketball coach doesn't mind."

"I think that would be wonderful, Mark."

The doorbell sounded, jerking Hope out of her daydreams. "I'll get it," Lucca said, heading for the front of the house. "You girls get started on the ornaments."

"Make it quick, brother," Gabi warned. Then, once Lucca was out of earshot, she asked, "So, back to your trip to Tiffany's. Did he just say 'Pick out the ring you want,' or what?"

Hope glanced down at the sparkler on her finger. "He was so romantic. He said—"

Lucca interrupted. "Hope? Please come here."

She and Gabi shared a look. "That sounds serious," Hope's sister-to-be observed.

Hope shrugged and walked out of the family room, headed for the front door. Her gaze landed on Lucca, and the stunned expression on his face slowed her steps. "Honey, is something wrong?"

"No, darling. Something is right. Very, very right." He backed away from the door, and Hope caught her first glimpse of the figure standing outside on the porch. "Daniel?"

"Hello, Hope."

"What are you doing here?"

His lips twisted into a crooked smile. "It's the Twelfth Day of Christmas. I understand Romano took care of the golden ring thing and I can't abide drumming drummers, so I figured I'd give you something else. You know what they say about miracles, don't you? Better late than never."

Miracle? Roaring started in her ears. Her stomach dropped. Her heart pounded, and her mouth went dry. "Miracle?"

"I got a phone call yesterday from a woman in Texas named Jacinta Guerrero. Nine months ago, her sister died of pancreatic cancer and left her daughter, Amanda, in her care."

"Amanda." Hope swallowed hard.

"Jacinta hadn't seen her sister Maria in eight years, but she took Amanda in and made her part of the family. They're undocumented, so this didn't go through a system of any kind."

Lucca moved to stand behind Hope, silently offering his support.

Daniel continued, "Jacinta packed away what few possessions her sister left behind, but she gave Amanda Maria's bible. That was her real name. Maria Aguilera.

Around Thanksgiving, Amanda found this while flipping through her bible."

Daniel held out a flyer Hope recognized. She accepted it with trembling fingers.

"Hope, you do know that your proposal to Lucca was the feel-good story of the week, don't you?" Daniel asked. "It was shown repeatedly on ESPN and local sportscasts, made the front page of Yahoo!, and was a trending topic on Twitter."

Hope nodded. "Gabi told me we'd gone viral."

"Best bug you could have hoped for." Daniel's eyes had gone soft with affection. "Amanda saw it—saw you—and she said she got a funny feeling in her tummy. That's when she showed her aunt the flyer."

Hope brought a visibly shaking hand up to cover her mouth. She was afraid to ask, afraid to hope, even though she knew Daniel wouldn't be here talking to her this way if not . . . if it wasn't . . . if Amanda wasn't . . .

Lucca squeezed her elbow reassuringly, giving her strength enough to ask, "She's . . . ?"

"I ran her prints just to be sure, and they match. She doesn't remember the name "Holly," but she does remember that her angel mommy had Bambi eyes. She wants to look into your eyes, Hope."

With that, Daniel stepped aside and another figure was revealed. Strawberry blonde curls. Peaches and cream complexion and a button nose. Her father's blue eyes. Hope gasped, and time stood still.

Memories flashed. The first cry at birth. The moment she learned to crawl, to walk. To ride a bike. To talk. *What's that called, Mommy? Why is the sky blue, Mommy? Can we go to the park today, Mommy?*

Hope steepled her hands in front of her mouth. A prayer.

"I remember you," a little voice said as Holly took a step forward. She wore jeans and a Dallas Mavericks sweatshirt and a shy smile full of permanent teeth, the baby teeth long gone. "I hoped I would. Mr. Daniel said he thought I would. I guess my other mommy made a mistake. She said mean people hurt you, and that you had died and become an angel. So you were my angel mommy, and when I went to bed at night, I'd look out my window to see if I could see you up in heaven."

Weaving on her feet, Hope reached for Lucca to steady her. His hand on her arm was fast and firm, his touch filled with love and compassion.

"Then," Holly continued, her beautiful blue eyes going round with wonder. "I saw you on *SportsCenter.* I really like sports, especially basketball."

"Me, too," Hope replied, choking out the first words she'd spoken to her daughter in five long, horrible years.

Although, not all of that time had been horrible, had it? She'd had a whole progression of little miracles along the way, so much to be thankful for. Making a friend like Daniel, who never gave up—or allowed her to give up. Meeting Celeste, who gave her Eternity Springs. Even adopting Roxy, whose sharp little teeth brought Lucca storming into her life.

Lucca. Her lover, her love.

She lifted a disbelieving look to him. "Am I dreaming?"

His smile was gentle and reassuring. "No, my love. You're awake. Your daughter is really here."

Holly was here. Hope's knees finally failed her, and she sank to the floor. She had a million questions about where Holly had been, why she'd been taken, and what her life had been like for the past five years. But all that could wait. Quaking like aspen leaves in an autumn breeze, tears streaming down her cheeks, she opened her arms. "Holly, can I have a hug?"

Her own warm, precious miracle walked into Hope's embrace.

Holly had finally come home.

Read on for a preview of Emily March's next novel
in her Eternity Springs series:

Dreamweaver Trail

ONE

❦

"I've never seen so many hot men in one room at the same time," Gabriella Romano muttered over her champagne glass. Wasn't it just her luck that they were all either married or related to her?

Earlier today, her brother Lucca had married the love of his life, Hope Montgomery, and now their wedding reception was in full swing at the new event center at Angel's Rest Healing Center and Spa. Gabi was thrilled for her brother and his wife and the new family they'd formed. Hope's daughter, Holly, was a sweetheart, and with a new baby due to arrive this summer, Lucca's world was as bright as sunshine on snow atop Murphy Mountain.

Gabi just wished that Lucca's happiness didn't make her so aware of the gray skies in her own world.

A wave of melancholy rolled over her as the music switched to something low and romantic and guests paired off with their spouses and significant others. Gabi watched her brother Zach give his wife, Savannah, a twirl. She sighed when sexy Jack Davenport nibbled at his Cat's ear, and again when Cam Murphy stroked a finger down the path of his Sarah's spine while they swayed with the music. When Richard Steele let his hand slide south of her mother's hip, Gabi turned away and gazed out at the snow-covered grounds of Angel's Rest, standing silvered in moonlight. *I'm a wallflower.* "Maybe I should draw a big *W* on my forehead."

"*W* for what?" her brother Max asked, his green eyes dancing with amusement as he moved to stand beside her. "Whiner?"

She shot him a glare. "I don't whine."

He arched a cynical brow but wisely remained silent. Gabi's scowl deepened for a long moment before she relented. "*Do* I whine?"

"Not usually. Lately . . ." He shrugged. "You're obviously unhappy, Gabriella."

"Not unhappy," she defended. "I'm . . . drifting."

Since leaving the sheriff's department last fall, she'd helped with her mother's project—turning a dilapidated old house into Aspenglow Place Bed and Breakfast. The B & B had opened for guests two weeks ago, and Maggie Romano had the running of her new business well in hand. "I need a job."

"So you've definitely decided not to work with Mom at Aspenglow?"

"I'm not cut out to be an innkeeper."

Max grabbed two flutes of champagne from a passing waiter and handed one to his sister. "Any chance you'll return to law enforcement?"

"No," she swiftly replied.

Max sipped his champagne and studied her. "You know, honey, there's a reason most departments require an officer to see a counselor after a shooting. I know Zach said his department would pay—"

"No." Gabi cut him off. "I'm not against counseling, and I promise I'd see someone if I thought I needed it. I have no regrets for killing Francine Vaughn. Doing so saved Zach's life, and that's the best thing I've ever done. However, I don't want to carry a weapon anymore. It's as simple as that."

"There are jobs in the field that don't require you to carry."

"Not in Eternity Springs."

"Maybe it's time you come back to Denver."

"Maybe," she said, the word rife with doubt.

Max's expression clouded. "Look, honey, if you're worried about Sobilek, you can give me the green light to have that talk I've been dying to have with the lying, cheating bastard. He won't bother you. I can promise you that."

She couldn't help but smile. Most of the time, big brothers acting like big brothers cramped her style. Upon occasion, however, she basked in their love. "No, Max. Frank Sobilek has nothing to do with this. Maybe I did leave Denver because of him, but I stayed in Eternity Springs because of me. Besides, if I decided I needed to be in Denver, I wouldn't let him stand in my way. I won't give him that power. My broken heart has healed, and it's stronger than ever before."

"Good for you."

Yeah, well, that's what I tell myself, anyway.

She continued, "But I don't think Denver is where I need to be at this point in my life. I don't really want to leave Eternity Springs. I love it here. I love the people here."

Unfortunately, there weren't enough of them. Men, anyway.

Her gaze drifted back to the couples on the dance floor. "You're not with anyone these days, Max. Don't you ever get lonely?"

"Sometimes," Max said, a shadow crossing his face. Just *why* the shadow, Gabi didn't know. Of all her brothers, he was the least sharing about details of his private life. "Not enough to brave the Denver dating scene, though."

At least Denver *had* a dating scene.

Perhaps Max was right. Perhaps it was time for a change of scenery. Gabi had never been one to sit back and wait for life to happen. She believed in being proactive. When she wanted something, she went after it.

"I want passion."

Max winced. "Too much information, little sis."

"Not that kind of passion. Well, okay, maybe that kind of passion, but not only that kind of passion. I want more than a relationship and more than a job. I want a life that I'm passionate about."

"That's a good goal. Though it's a little weird to be thinking about it at our brother's wedding."

"This is the perfect time to be thinking about it," Gabi protested. "Look at Lucca and Hope. Don't they inspire you? They've both gone through so much emotional pain and heartache, but they fought their way through it and triumphed. Now they glow. They're euphoric. They show us what life should be."

Max affectionately thumped the tip of Gabi's nose. "For a tough broad, you are such a starry-eyed girl."

"Bite me, brother. Look, Lucca and Hope and Zach and Samantha and shoot, even Mom and Richard are actively living their lives. Somewhere along the way, I quit living mine. I've been simply marking time. That needs to stop. I need to find my passion."

"If you want it, you'll find it, Gabriella. Of that, I have no doubt. You're as hardheaded as they come."

"You say the nicest things to me, Max," she dryly drawled.

"I'm about to do something nice for you."

"Oh yeah? What?"

"Hold on." He set down his champagne glass on a nearby table, then moved to intercept a waiter. A moment later, he returned with two dessert plates filled with pieces of the Romano family Italian crème cake that had quickly achieved legendary status in Eternity Springs.

He offered one plate to her. Gabi eyed it wistfully. "Mom said we're only supposed to have one piece."

"I thought you wanted to live a little."

"By ignoring Mom's rules? That's a death wish."

Max took a big bite of cake, then tauntingly licked the tines of his fork. "Live dangerously, little sis."

Laughing, she did so. After finishing her cake, she accepted Gary Munroe's invitation to dance and managed to hold her melancholy at bay for the rest of the celebration. But later, as yet another Valentine's Day drew to a lonely close, she crawled into bed with a paperback that couldn't hold her interest because her thoughts kept drifting back to the wedding reception and her big revelation.

It was time to live. Time to search for her passion. How? Where? What did she do to get the ball rolling?

Maybe she should begin with baby steps, get out of town, do something fun and spur-of-the-moment. Unfortunately, the sad state of her bank account limited her options. What she needed was another gig like she'd had last fall for the Thurstons, the über-wealthy owners of a vacation house outside Eternity Springs who had taken her along on their Mediterranean vacation to babysit their beloved dog. A girl could do a lot of thinking while walking a dog along a beautiful beach.

The thought wouldn't leave her alone.

First thing the following morning, she looked up the Thurstons' phone number and made the call. The Thurstons didn't need her, but they had friends who had friends who were desperate for a caretaker for their new puppy.

By the end of the week, and having packed light, Gabi boarded a plane in Gunnison. Eighteen hours of bumpy flights, boring layovers, and a harrowing boat ride later, she arrived at her home-away-from-home for the next four months—a small, sparsely populated Caribbean island—Bella Vita Key.

Liam Seagraves glanced up from the legal document he'd been reading when his lawyer stepped into his office. Matthew Wharton crossed the room and took a seat on the opposite side of the desk. "Margaret asked me to tell you that if you want your morning swim, you should do it now. Since we're leaving this morning, she's decided you need a full breakfast. Can't have you wasting away any longer, you know."

"Not a chance of that. Have you seen all the meals she has put into my freezer?"

"She thinks you need to gain back those fifteen pounds you've lost in the last few months." Matthew frowned and patted his bulging stomach. "And, she wishes *I* could give them to you. She doesn't cook like that for me anymore."

Liam grinned at his friend's glum tone. "Why don't you leave her behind when you go home? I'll take good care of her."

"In your dreams, boss." The lawyer buffed his nails on his shoulder. "She wouldn't leave me for you. If you were a short, pudgy, balding guy, I might worry, but she's not impressed by super-rich pretty boys."

"Just my luck," Liam said as he flipped to the last page of the document.

"Do you have any questions?" Wharton asked, nodding toward the papers.

"No. It's straightforward and clear."

"And unnecessary."

"It's what I need to do." He picked up a pen and signed the paper and then another stack of documents that Wharton had brought him. When he was done, he returned them to a file folder and handed it over to his attorney. "I need a new start, Matthew. I know it's symbolic, but symbolism matters."

"So do patents. You are walking away from so much."

"I walked," he corrected, gesturing toward the file folder. "Past tense. It's official now, right?"

"I have to file the paperwork, but yes."

"Liam Brogan," he said, testing his new name aloud. "My mother's father would be proud that I've taken his name."

"Your mother's father would kick your daddy's ass for his actions these past few months. But back to those patents . . ."

"No longer my property. It's okay, Matthew. This is the way I wanted it. Don't worry so much."

"After the past two years, it's a habit." His attorney and friend shook his head. "You do know that selling your company and changing your name won't keep the vultures away. They'll track you down."

"I expect they will, but living on the island won't make it easy on them. Plus, I'm determined to be boring. They'll lose interest, and pretty soon I'll be old news."

"I swear, the worship of celebrity in this world is a disease."

"Look on the bright side," Liam advised. "If not for my celebrity status, you wouldn't have an open invitation to visit my island paradise any time you like. Now, I'd better hit the pool so I have a big enough appetite to do Margaret's efforts justice. Want to join me?"

"Are you kidding?" Matthew looked appalled. "If I exercised I might lose my pudginess, and my bride might take a second look at you."

"Damn. You saw through me." Liam pushed away from his desk and stood. "Do I have half an hour?"

"Forty-five minutes, I'd say. She's going all out."

"In that case I'll swim an extra couple of laps."

He took the stairs two at a time to reach the master suite, sparing the spectacular ocean view out the west-facing window only a glance. Despite all the banter with his friend, today's actions weighed upon him. A man didn't turn his back on his very identity without it leaving a bruise or two.

He changed into his swim trunks, looking forward to the distraction of a good hard swim, a hearty breakfast, then a day on the water as he ferried his attorney and his wife up to Nassau so they could catch a plane back to the States. He exited the suite by way of the spiral iron staircase that led down from his bedroom verandah. A dozen varieties of tropical flowers perfumed the air, and thick green grass provided a soft path for his bare feet as he crossed the lawn toward the pool. There he discovered a couple of trespassers—two large lizards swimming in the water along with leaves and flower petals that had blown in during last night's storm. He retrieved the skimmer pole from the storage shed and set about cleaning his pool.

His thoughts returned to the stack of documents and contracts he'd handed to his attorney this morning, and with his focus on paperwork, he didn't immediately notice the noise.

The movement caught his attention.

A fluffy white dog dashed through the evergreen hedge at the far side of the yard just as Liam scooped a lizard into his net. The dog—a puppy—spied Liam and altered his course, heading directly toward him, yapping all the way. Liam started to grin at the puppy when another figure fought through the hedge. Liam instantly went on guard.

The woman was beautiful. Supermodel tall, tanned, and nicely curved, she wore a yellow bikini top, shorts, and flip-flops adorned with sunflowers. She'd pulled her dark hair through the back of a Colorado Rockies baseball cap into a ponytail. She did not have a camera in her hands or hanging around her neck, but experience had taught Liam that that didn't mean a damned thing.

"Bismarck! Get back here!" the woman called as she plucked leaves from her ponytail. "You can't just . . . Oh." Her gaze meeting Liam's, she flashed an apologetic smile. "I'm so sorry. Bismarck and I are still establishing who the alpha is in our little pack."

The dog dashed up to Liam, then plopped down at his feet. The woman scowled down at the dog, who studiously ignored her. "It's only been two days. It's bound to get better." Then she extended a hand toward Liam. "I'm Gabriella Romano. Gabi. I'll be pet sitting next door for the next few months while the Fontanas are on an extended vacation."

His neighbors were named Fontana, although he had yet to meet them. Maybe she wasn't a paparazza after all. Maybe.

"I'm Liam." He shook her hand, then spoke his new name publicly for the first time. "Liam Brogan."

Sounds good, he decided. Not weird at all. An underlying tension about his name-changing decision that he hadn't previously recognized evaporated. He had done the right thing.

"Nice to meet you, Liam. Do you service next door, too?"

He blinked. "Excuse me?"

She closed her eyes and her cheeks stained pink. "Oh, jeez. That didn't come out the way I intended. Pool service. Are you the pool guy for next door, too? The Fontanas didn't leave me that info amid all the other numbers. If you are, there is something growing in the water. I was really bummed because I wanted to swim this morning, but once I got a good look at the pool . . . it's nasty. I've never owned a pool, so I'm not sure what it needs."

She thinks I'm the pool boy. If Liam was 100 percent

certain that this wasn't a setup, he'd enjoy this exchange a lot more. "I'm afraid I don't clean the Fontana's pool."

"Oh. Well. I'll figure it out. I'm resourceful." Then she stared down at the dog and sighed. "Except when it comes to a certain Samoyed puppy, I guess."

"He's a Samoyed? I think of Sammys as cold-weather dogs."

"Yes. Well." Her lips formed a rueful smile. "Don't get me started. He sheds everywhere. He jumps on everything. He barks constantly and chases and nips at everything that moves. He's as stubborn as my brother Max, and believe me, that's saying a lot."

"Love your job, do you?"

"I sound awful, don't I? I do love animals, dogs in particular, and he's a sweet little guy . . . honestly . . . for about five minutes every hour. We're in an adjustment period. He's a puppy being a puppy. I'm sure it will get better."

She reached beneath the lounge chair for the dog, but before she could grab hold of him, he scooted out the other side. With that, he was off. She darted after him. "Bismarck!"

Liam should have set down the pool skimmer and attempted to help, but two things prevented him. First, while he tended to think otherwise, the dog-sitter thing could be a ploy. Second, and of more immediate concern, he couldn't drag his gaze away from the lovely sight of a scantily dressed, long-legged beauty racing across his lawn.

The dog ran back through the hedge, and before she dashed after him, Gabriella Romano paused and waved. "Nice to meet you, Liam. I'll be seeing you around."

Liam watched her disappear into the hedge, her voice bellowing out "Bismarck!" He set down the pool skimmer and prepared to dive into his pool, a hint of a smile playing on his lips.

Gabriella Romano. Dog sitter or snoop? It served his best interests to find out.

Of course, he could surely find out everything he needed to know in five minutes on the Internet, followed up by a couple of phone calls. But where was the challenge in that? Liam was a sucker for puzzles, and one had just blasted through his hedgerow. Maybe he'd play the game a little first, rather than skipping ahead to the finish line.

With that, Liam executed a sleek racing dive into the deep end of the pool, and before he'd completed his first lap, he had a germ of an idea for how to conduct his investigation. By the time he finished his swim, he had a full-blown plan.

Liam showered and changed in the pool house, then strode inside wearing gym shorts, a T-shirt, and a smile.

This was going to be fun.